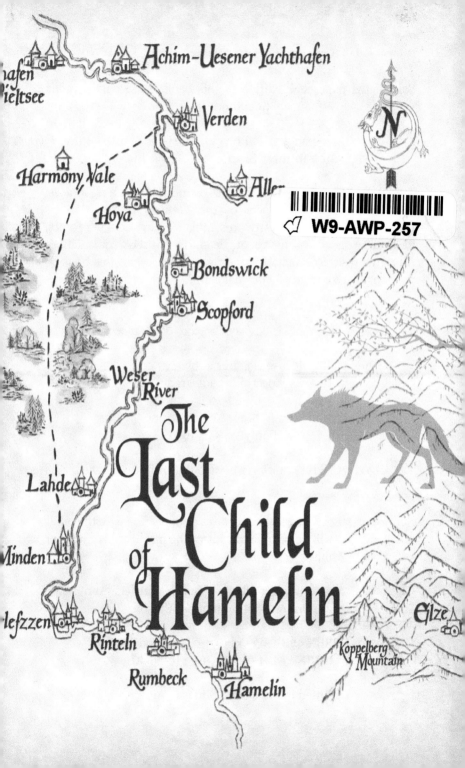

Spencer Hill Press Middle Grade
An Imprint of Spencer Hill Press, LLC

Contact:
Spencer Hill Press, PO Box 247, Contoocook, NH 03229, USA

Please visit our website at
www.spencerhillmiddlegrade.com

First Edition: August 2014
Ballantyne, Ray, 1944

The Last Child of Hamelin : a novel by Ray Ballantyne - 1st ed.
p. cm.

Summary: A boy's musical gift creates a connection with the piper of legend, but will he be able to control the magic of his music or will it control him?

Cover design and interior illustrations by Patricia Ann Lewis
Interior layout by Jennifer Carson

ISBN 978-1-937053-55-0 (paperback)
ISBN 978-1-937053-61-1 (e-book)

Printed in the United States of America

The Last Child of Hamelin

The Holme Grade Kids,

Do you hear it?

[signature]

Ray Ballantyne

SPENCER HILL
MIDDLE GRADE

To Louise, the magic and music of my life

I bid the chords sweet music make,
And all must follow in my wake.
           —Johann Wolfgang von Goethe

For he led us, he said, to a joyous land,
Joining the town and just at hand,
Where waters gushed and fruit-trees grew,
And flowers put forth a fairer hue,
And everything was strange and new;
The sparrows were brighter than peacocks here,
And their dogs outran our fallow deer,
And honey-bees had lost their stings,
And horses were born with eagles' wings.
        —Robert Browning, *The Pied Piper of Hamelin*

Prologue

Oskar dreaded the rats. But he steered his wagon for Hamelin nonetheless.

He hunched forward on the wooden seat, urging his weary horse up the hill. The old yellow wagon groaned; pots rattled, wheels creaked.

"Hah! Get up, Rosie, old girl. Almost to Hamelin," he encouraged.

The aged mare plodded on.

The old peddler ran a hand through his grey hair. He had not plied this route for over a year. But business had been dreadful in Elze, so he decided to cross the mountains to fair Hamelin, tucked in beside the Weser River.

Fair, but overrun with rats. Last visit, even his favorite inn, The Tong and Anvil, had vermin scurrying under the tables and darting through the kitchen. And the smell had made the air all but unbreathable.

Gunther Braun had apologized over and over. "Those foul rats are everywhere, Oskar. There's no ridding Hamelin of this pestilence. They've even bitten babes in their cradles."

Ah, well, thought Oskar, shifting his weight on the seat. Maybe they would buy some of his powders and potions to kill the filthy creatures, although he doubted they'd do much good. And despite the rats, Gunther would surely have a bit of mutton or a nice stew ready.

"And some oats for you, girl," he called. "A bit of rest after your long pull. A bit of rest for us both."

He squinted ahead. The sun had started its descent, sending a harsh light into his eyes. It shaded the edges of the clouds with red and gold. The evening air smelled fresh, bracing. "Almost, old girl." He pulled his hat lower on his forehead.

The road changed pitch under the wagon and they crested the pass. "Yes! There it be. We made it!"

Rosie snorted, a new eagerness in her step.

But long before they reached the town gates, Oskar grew uneasy. No one traveled the road—not a herd boy bringing in the cows, not a wagon laden with hay, not a single traveler to be seen.

The banners on the ramparts hung limp in the still air. And all of them were black.

He passed through the gates and entered the silent town, the street bordered by closed doors and shuttered windows. He saw no sign of an attack. He caught no odor of the plague. Nay, it smelled of stale fires and neglected refuse.

Not even a rat lurked in the shadows. The silence sent a shudder up his spine.

He guided Rosie over the grimy cobblestones toward The Tong and Anvil. He could usually barter a room for whatever pots or spoons or tools Gunther needed.

The inn stood locked and dark. No scent of mutton turning over the fire or bread baking. Not even a wisp of grey smoke drifting from the chimney.

What had happened to Hamelin?

A scraping noise beyond the inn caught his ears. A young boy limped around the corner.

"Child," called Oskar. "Come here."

The boy froze, his eyes wide with fear. His clothes hung on him, filthy rags that had seen much wear.

"Lad, where is everyone?"

The boy swallowed, huge brown eyes darting back and forth. "In...inside," he stammered.

"It's not yet sundown. What are they doing?"

The boy's gaze fastened on the wagon. "Do you...have food?"

"Yes, of course," said Oskar gently. "Come, share a bit of bread."

The boy edged toward him. His sunken eyes spoke of hunger and fear at once. He dragged a twisted leg behind him.

At last, he snatched the bread Oskar offered and sat on the ground, leaning against the large yellow wagon wheel. He tore off chunks with his teeth and swallowed with little chewing.

Oskar settled beside him. He knew it would hurt to get back up, but he needed to know what this boy could tell him. "What's your name, lad?"

"Simon," he mumbled through a mouthful of bread.

"I'm Oskar. A tinker. Maybe you've seen me come through Hamelin before."

Simon nodded. "I like your yellow wagon."

"As do I. So, tell me," said Oskar, "what is everyone doing?"

Simon stopped chewing, staring down at the dust. "Most of them are crying."

"Crying? Why?"

Simon's chin trembled. "The rats—they were terrible. Everywhere, they were. But—" He squeezed his eyes shut.

"Aye. I well remember the rats. Go on."

"Then the man came."

"What man was that?"

"Wore yellow and red, he did. Played a pipe. Piped all the rats away. Right into the river."

Oskar had heard such tales before, although he had doubted the truth of them.

Simon continued to stare at the ground, his bread forgotten.

"There's more, isn't there?" said Oskar softly.

Simon peered up at him through moist eyes. "I'm the last one."

Oskar frowned. "The last what, child?"

"All the others...he took them. Just like the rats." Simon ground his fists into his red eyes. "I'm the last child of Hamelin."

Chapter 1

Sixty Years Later

A baby wailed in the darkness.

Pieter sat up, wide awake. Below his sleeping loft, Agnes gasped in air as she gathered herself for another cry.

A deep voice thundered through the house. "Quiet that brat! Right *now*!"

Pieter threw off his blanket, just as the baby howled. He crawled toward the ladder, his heart pummeling his ribs. The cooking fire had burned out, shrouding the room below in deep black.

"Martha!" growled Father. "Get out of bed and do something before *I* do."

Pieter knew what his father would do—spank Agnes or shake her or even hit her.

He heard the creak of the ropes of his parents' bed. Alarm shot through him. Pieter found the ladder and swung his feet over the edge of the loft. He scrambled down so fast he lost his purchase on the rungs and slid to the bottom. He hit the dirt floor on his hands and knees, sprang up, and dashed toward the cradle.

Before he could get there, he heard a thump. Something crashed. Agnes screamed. He tried to cry out to her, but the words caught in his tight throat. Somehow Mother managed to light a candle. The meager light showed the cradle on its side, with Agnes sprawled on the floor. Father hovered over her, one huge hand raised.

Pieter dove past him and threw himself facedown over the baby. Father's blow caught him in the side of the head.

His head snapped to one side. Pain shot down his neck. He rolled on the floor in agony.

"Karl!" Mother cried. "Leave them alone. The baby's sick, that's all."

Father turned slowly, still in a crouch. He started toward Agnes, glaring and snarling. He hadn't had time to sleep off his drunkenness, and his anger burned the hottest when he was awakened.

Pieter raised himself to his knees, scarcely able to breathe. He scooped up the baby. He bolted for the ladder, clutching her to his chest. With one hand he clambered his way into the loft.

Agnes's cries resounded through the house. "Get back down here!" yelled Father.

Pieter scooted into the back corner of the loft, until he smacked his head on the sloped ceiling. The loft shook, and Pieter knew his father was coming up the ladder.

Pieter held Agnes tight, a warm bundle against his chest. Too warm. Her entire body radiated heat. Sweat and tears dampened his shift.

Nails shrieked as they pulled from wood. The ladder held for a moment, then tipped backwards. He heard his father crash onto the floor. Pieter crept forward and saw the man seize the ladder in both hands and throw it across the room. It hit a chair, which burst into kindling.

Pieter retreated to his corner. He tried to keep his body from shaking, but it wasn't possible. When Father's rage reached this point, he needed to do more than throw things—he needed to hit someone.

Since he couldn't reach him and Agnes, Pieter knew Mother would be his target.

Indeed, he heard the sound of a slap. And then Mother screamed. The candlelight vanished. After a pause, the front door smashed closed so hard the floor of the loft shook.

Then the only sounds were the soft sobbing of his mother and Agnes crying in his arms.

Without leaving his spot, Pieter called out, "Mother?"

"Do you have Agnes?"

"Aye. But—"

"Keep her up there with you," Mother said. "Is she injured? Are you?"

"We're fine. Did Father hurt you?"

Pieter was certain he had, but she said, "All is well. Just keep her the rest of the night."

"Of course. But Mother, she's so hot."

"I'll toss up a wet cloth."

As soon as he had the cloth, he laid it on the baby's brow. As he settled on his mattress, the reeds inside crackled, a familiar, comforting sound.

He pulled the blanket off Agnes. It was a warm night and she was making plenty of her own heat. Already his shift was soaked where she lay against it. Her crying had dropped to a hiccupping sob.

Agnes even smelled sick, a sultry, cloying odor that drove fear through Pieter's chest.

The wet cloth warmed quickly. He didn't want to leave her to get another, and he had no ladder anyhow. He almost called for Mother, but held himself, knowing that she was no doubt in pain.

Agnes seemed to grow heavier, and Pieter hoped that meant she was falling asleep. Would Mother be able to sleep as well?

He sat staring into the darkness, thinking about what had happened. What would Father do when he returned? He didn't have to be drunk to be in a mean temper. Pieter carried fear like a rock in his gut. He could not remember a time it hadn't been there.

Compared to his brawny father, Pieter was a scrawny boy, with thin sticks for arms and legs. But he was fast, faster even than other twelve-year-olds. He could get away from his father if he had to, but that left Mother and Agnes to face his anger.

Still, once his father was at work, Pieter would escape Hamelin for a while. That, of course, would also anger Father, but then everything seemed to. As soon as he had a chance, he would slip away toward the mountains.

Half the morning passed before Pieter had a chance to leave. Mother, quite good with tools when she needed to be, had repaired two broken rungs in the ladder and set it against the edge of the loft.

Agnes still had a fever. She lay listlessly in his lap, by the fire. He watched her when Mother left for the market. Pieter didn't mind, although he was eager to be gone before his father came home.

Father hadn't returned during the night. He'd probably found more ale and ended up passed out in a ditch somewhere. Pieter had seen his jugs stashed behind a trunk in the blacksmith's shop.

When Mother returned with a long loaf of bread and a head of cabbage in her basket, Pieter laid Agnes in the cradle and slipped out the back door.

His mother never stopped him, as though she understood how much he needed his escapes. He slipped out the back door, leaped the low stone wall, and threaded his way through the alleys and back ways of Hamelin.

When he reached the east side of town, he heard voices raised in anger. He darted behind a sprawling laurel hedge. Ahead, on the north side of the road, stood a cottage. A strange old man had lived there forever. What was his name? Simon?

He knew who the boys were—Hans and his pack of ruffians. They had harassed Pieter many a time, although they had yet to catch him.

He peered from behind the hedge. Rocks flew through the air, peppering the walls and roof of the cottage.

"Hey, you old geezer!" one of them shouted. "No one wants you here."

Aye, that was Hans, no doubt. Pieter scowled. Why were they bothering a harmless old man?

"We don't want your curses in Hamelin!" yelled another. "Take your black magic somewhere else."

Curses? How strange. Pieter shrank back and began a wide circle around the cottage and the boys. *I should help the old man. But what could I do against Hans and his gang?* Hans was the same age as Pieter, but probably twice as big.

So often he had been the target of Hans's malice. Pieter had no idea what sparked the boy's hostility. Perhaps he merely wanted to show the younger boys that flocked around him how very tough he was.

And of course, Pieter, being small and wiry, was the perfect prey.

Once one of them had caught Pieter humming. The bruises on his face had taken weeks to heal. Father had glared in disgust each time he saw those purple and green welts—proof of his son's weakness.

For a moment Pieter considered how he could help Simon, but of course there was nothing he could do. Nothing that wouldn't result in another beating at least.

His father's thrashings were enough.

Chapter 2

Within an hour Pieter reached the foothills, then hiked into a grassy dell to the south of the trail. The little valley was far enough from both Hamelin and the road that no one would see him. Or more importantly, no one could hear him. For he had come to this vale to sing.

Pieter had never actually heard a song nor any sort of music. He had no idea why, but music bubbled out from a place deep inside. Widow Bonney and his father, among others, had taught him not to sing anywhere in Hamelin. Father with his fists, and Widow Bonney with her sharp tongue.

So he only sang in his loft, and then almost in a whisper, when Agnes needed a lullaby and he was sure his father was deep in sleep or gone.

But now he had his dell, his secret vale of music. Someday he would bring Agnes to this place. But no one else. Not ever.

He sat cross-legged in the grass. At first, his throat clogged with worry, too dry to sing. But what was he worried about? No one had ever come near this secret place. He walked to a tiny stream and drank deep. With a quick glance back the way he had come, he took in the sweet-smelling air, rich with the scent of new leaves, fresh grass, and spring. His breathing slowed. Some of the tightness in his neck and shoulders eased.

A melody poured out at last, a song he had sung in this dell many times.

The first time he had found the words to a song, it had been that lullaby for Agnes. Today the song was inspired by the birds.

Tiny brown birds flitted from branch to branch in nearby shrubs. Crows bickered and screeched in the oaks, while high above a bird of prey, probably a small eagle, drifted on the thermals. The chirping and trilling of countless birds filled the air of the glade.

Pieter smiled. The contrasting songs wove a spell. And soon they created a harmony. A song floated from his mind to his mouth to the air of the grassy dell.

Birds in the blue sky,
Birds in the tree.
Singing pure joy,
Singing for me.

Great eagle gliding,
Suspended on air,
Screaming his power,
Diving to his lair.

Darting specks of sparrows,
Flitting branch to twig,
Delicate wee bodies,
But songs that peal so big.

How would you be knowing,
All these different songs?
How do you remember,
To whom each tune belongs?

For a long time Pieter let the echo of the music drift about the dell. He breathed deep, ready to begin a new song, when he heard a noise behind him.

Not a bird or small animal. No, something large and low in the grass. In fact, the birds had left their roosts and were spinning and crying into the sky. At the same time a confusing whirl of thoughts tumbled through his mind.

At first he could not move. Then he slowly turned his head toward the sound.

A growl—wild and untamed.

A dog from the village perhaps?

No. A wolf.

From the foliage a white muzzle pointed toward him. White with a black nose and a smudge of black on its chin. The wolf crept forward, revealing a black and grey head. And startling eyes. *Blue* eyes.

Pieter leaped to his feet and faced the creature. He stood rigid, scarcely breathing.

The wolf stepped out and regarded him with those strange blue eyes. Her left front leg was so white it almost glittered. The rest of her legs were black, with a body of grey and white with streaks of black woven in.

An odd calm came over him. Pieter was astonished by his own lack of fear. He rubbed his forehead, his mind muddled by a tangle of images in his head. Nothing would come clear, save this—the animal was not a danger. In fact, he had the sense that the wolf had been *drawn* to him. How he knew this, he couldn't say, but he was sure.

The wolf's nose wrinkled as she sniffed the air. Then in a flash, the wolf spun and disappeared into the trees, making not a sound.

Long after it vanished, Pieter stared at the spot where the animal had stood. Such a magnificent creature. A sense of loss filled him. He stood, unable to move, waiting, hoping that the wolf would return.

At last he shook it off. Such a strange episode. It could not be explained, but he felt the seed of another song growing in his breast.

Not now, while the wonder of being face to face with such an animal remained. But soon.

He hadn't realized how quiet the dell had become until the birds once again took up their keen melodies. He threw off the spell of the wolf and glanced at the sky with a frown.

It was time to leave. He needed to finish his chores before Father came home. Most likely Father would head for The Tong and Anvil after he finished his work, but Pieter couldn't risk it.

As he walked, he ran through his bird song once again, until he was satisfied that every word, every note was etched in his mind. Someday he would sing it for Agnes, right here in his dell, with the birds as his chorus.

The wolf song took shape as well, the first notes, the beginning of a tune celebrating the beautiful animal. Would he ever see her again? Already he longed for it.

He smiled to himself. Her? Aye, she was female. He was surprised to be so sure, but there was not the least doubt in his mind.

Just before he reached the road, he caught the sound of someone walking along. Nay, more like stomping. His pulse quickened. He ducked behind a rock. There was no real reason to hide, but he wanted no one to know he spent so much time in the hills.

The tread was odd—uneven, with a hard thump after each stride. Pieter peered around the rock and saw an old man heading away from him, back towards Hamelin.

Simon.

No one else his age lived in Hamelin. No one else shuffled along, dragging a twisted leg. Or carried a carved walking stick that he drove into the earth in what seemed to be great anger.

Pieter watched until the old man was out of sight. He knew that Simon had been spared the fate of all the other children of Hamelin. That his crippled leg had prevented him from keeping up and had left him as the Last Child.

Pieter found himself wanting to know more about the old man. More about the Pied Piper. More about why, sixty years later, Hamelin remained a town without music.

And why Pieter wanted—nay, *needed* to sing.

Chapter 3

"You'll be working at the blacksmith shop today," Father said a few days later. He stuffed a piece of bread into his mouth.

Pieter's brow tightened. The blacksmith shop? That was the *last* thing he wanted to do. Still, it was safer to agree. "Yes, Father."

"Otto closed the back forge last night. Got to get it cleaned out today. Tomorrow it's gotta be back in service."

"Very well."

Father sat forward, looming over the table, his massive head thrust toward Pieter. "And you'll do good work, ya hear? Don't try to get by with a botched job." His foul breath, still ripe with the stench of ale, all but choked Pieter.

He leaned back. "I won't."

"Hmph," grunted Father. "We'll see about that. Come on." He pushed away from the table.

Pieter hadn't finished eating, but he slid off the chair. Mother sat in the rocker with Agnes in her lap. Pieter leaned over and planted a kiss on the baby's head, relieved that the fever had abated. Agnes giggled and reached for him, but he hurried after his father.

They walked in silence. Pieter had to trot to keep up with his father's long, heavy stride. The man swayed his wide, heavily muscled shoulders. Anyone would have taken him for the blacksmith he was.

At the shop, Pieter rolled the wheelbarrow over to the back forge and began shoveling out the ash and clinkers.

Those lumps of unburned coal were easy, but every shovelful sent more black soot into the suffocating air. He didn't mind working, but he hated the grimy smell. Dust filled his nostrils and clogged his throat.

The shop did not belong to Father, a point of resentment and anger. Otto was the blacksmith of Hamelin, and Father was condemned to always be his assistant. Pieter wasn't surprised that Otto had not come in. The blacksmith preferred The Tong and Anvil to the shop, so Father ended up doing most of the work, and that at journeyman's wages.

A huge hand clapped him on the shoulder. "You dolt! Work faster!" Father growled, squeezing Pieter's arm. "That furnace is gonna be ready tomorrow, even if you gotta work all night."

Pieter knew he should simply agree, but his annoyance slipped out. "I *am* working fast."

He was sent sprawling to the floor with a flick of his father's wrist. "I said *faster*." He whirled and stomped away, mumbling, "Lazy boy. And weak as a baby buzzard."

Pieter climbed to his feet, glaring at his father's back. He brushed the coal dust off his clothes. It didn't really matter how hard he worked, or how fast he was, or how good a job he did. His father would never be satisfied.

No one would ever mistake Pieter for a blacksmith, with his scrawny arms and spindly legs. He shrugged. There were worse things than being pushed to the floor. At least he hadn't had to endure a beating.

By the time Father began closing up shop, Pieter's clothes were caked with coal dust. Black grime had collected in every crease of his hands. His arms were thick with gritty powder. He knew that no amount of scrubbing would clean his fingernails of the filth.

Father locked the large doors. "You get home and take care of the wood." He clomped away in the other direction, without a doubt heading for the tavern.

When he arrived home, Mother had a tub of water for him, from the rain barrel outside the door. When Pieter finished cleaning up, the water was black, with congealed dust floating on the surface, and his skin still felt rough and gritty.

He headed inside to play with Agnes. She sat on the floor, contentedly chewing on an old piece of leather. A rope, tied around her ankle, was anchored to the central support post of the house. Pieter had spent many years tethered in the same spot, where the hard dirt floor had been worn into a shallow bowl by the generations of babies who had played there.

Agnes looked up, her eyes bright.

"Sorry, little one," he said. "I'd best do the wood first." Whenever Father finally came home, he would be drunk. Pieter didn't want to do anything that would anger him.

As he worked, he began to hum the bird song he had created in the dell. He wondered idly if Simon had heard him singing. The Last Child, as he was called by the people of Hamelin. No matter how old the man became, it seemed he would always be known as the Last Child.

Pieter slammed the axe into a new chunk of wood. The tale of the Pied Piper was all nonsense, anyway. It had to be.

Still, Simon was the only elderly person in the village. Widow Bonney was maybe ten years younger, but there was no one else Simon's age.

True or not, the story of the Piper haunted Hamelin.

The town with no music.

The town without old folk.

And once, the town without children.

Chapter 4

Pieter watched the old man through the green, glossy leaves of a laurel bush. Simon hobbled out his back door, a threadbare grey cloak hanging from his thin shoulders. He started toward the nearby hills. With each awkward stride he stabbed the ground with his old walking stick.

Still, his steps were brisk for such an old man.

Pieter slipped from behind the bush and crept after him, stealing from oak tree to bristly shrub to pine.

At twelve, Pieter was no more stealthy than most boys. No matter how carefully he followed, sticks snapped under his tread and rocks skittered noisily away. Yet Simon never seemed to hear.

In an odd way, Pieter wanted Simon to notice him, although the thought was also frightening. But Simon never turned or changed his steady pace.

Pieter knew these hills well. For years, at least since he had been six or seven, he had slipped away into the nearby dell where he sang. Perhaps he would meet the wolf again. In truth, he desperately needed to see her, although he couldn't think why it was so urgent.

In a strange way, he was certain she was nearby. Odd images flitted in and out of his thoughts—rocks and rhododendrons and waving grass. Not things Pieter could see. The view was too low, more like—like an animal. Like the wolf he had seen?

The trail ran directly east, straight for the mountains. Straight for Koppelberg. Why, of all places, was the old man returning to that mountain?

Simon continued through the rich green hills, then up the slopes of Koppelberg Hill. He reached a sheer grey cliff, sat on a wide rock, and stared at the side of the mountain without moving.

As though he were waiting.

But for what?

On this spring day, with breezes stirring the new leaves and the hills glowing verdant in a sea of fresh grass, Pieter wondered if the old man would find what he awaited. Perhaps he would learn the old man's secret.

Pieter darted out of sight behind a scraggly pine. The old man settled himself and began his strange vigil.

Pieter sat cross-legged on the fallen needles, breathing in the sharp scent of pine and the crisp mountain air. Like Simon, Pieter was waiting, although he could not have said for what.

After a time, he grew restless. He had work to do at home, and his father was always angry about some task that was not accomplished.

He climbed to his feet, but something held him. For a fleeting moment, a sound had reached his ears. He turned his head back, listening hard.

No, it was nothing, he told himself. But somehow he knew it was much more. A sound floating on the breeze. Like music.

He hurried away, leaving Old Simon alone to stare at the cliff.

When Pieter turned onto his street in Hamelin, the familiar odors of wood smoke, simmering stews, and, yes, emptied chamber pots welcomed him. The sun had dropped behind the buildings.

He broke into a run, for he had done none of his work for the day. He flung open the door, relieved to see that his mother was not in the room. Agnes sat in her usual spot, tied to the center post.

Mother entered from the back, potatoes in her upraised apron. "Pieter. There you are. Best chop more wood before your father gets home." Mother emptied her apron into a basket.

"Yes, Mother."

If his father returned from the blacksmith shop before Pieter had done his work, there would be a beating for sure. Mother should not have to do his tasks. He scooped up the split wood. With a quick glance at the darkening sky, he headed for the door. It opened with a bang and his father's massive presence filled the frame.

The man's scowl deepened. When angry, the scars and pocks on his wide face turned livid red. "That's all?" he rumbled. "The wood box should be filled by now."

"I'll have it done in—"

His father's thick hand struck Pieter's cheek, sending him sprawling. Wood clattered across the hard, bare ground.

"No supper till the wood's in," said his father. With a grunt of disgust, he disappeared into the house.

Pieter clambered to his feet. His check burned and his stomach roiled. He gathered the wood back up. He had to wonder how his burly father had ended up with a scrawny son like him. He suspected Father wondered the same thing.

Pieter delivered the load as fast as he could and hurried back to the woodpile.

By the time he finished, his father was gone—to The Tong and Anvil, most likely, or off to his drinking place in the woods. If Pieter was lucky, his father would fall drunk into bed and be asleep before he thought to beat his son.

Mother sat with her needle, repairing a pair of large tan breeches. She did not look up. Agnes dozed on the floor, her round rump in the air.

Pieter helped himself to the thin stew in the pot. No meat, but some good cabbage and a few leeks. He took a slab of bread and sat, absently chewing.

Immediately, a tune flowed through his thoughts. A song about the Piper. He came near to bringing it up with his mother, but held himself. She was not open to any talk about the Pied Piper.

The tale of the Pied Piper? Something in Pieter knew it was not over. Simon lived it every day. They all did. And the very air of Hamelin wafted with the despair the Piper had wrought.

Chapter 5

or the next two days, Pieter had no chance to seek out Simon. His father once again dragged him to the blacksmith shop. That meant cleaning and scraping and hauling burnt clinkers away until black dust seeped into every pore. Or, worst of all, hours on the bellows until his arms ached. Then doing all the rest of his chores in the evening before he ate.

But the next morning, Pieter found that his father had left without him. He hurried through his chores. The axe flew in his hands, and he filled the woodbin faster than ever. He scrubbed out the cooking pot, watching his mother with a stealthy eye. As soon as she disappeared into the back, Pieter gave Agnes a quick tickle and slipped out.

If Old Simon had trekked up to Koppelberg today, Pieter could catch up. He approached the cottage from the back, relieved to see Simon's wooden walking stick leaning outside the door. He settled down to wait.

It wasn't long. Simon burst out, snatched up the walking stick, and hobbled away as though chased by demons, his old grey cloak streaming behind him.

Pieter waited a moment, then started after him.

When Simon reached the cliffside, Pieter dropped behind an outcropping of rock, one hand on its smooth, cool face.

"Why are you here?" barked a voice.

Pieter jumped, whacking his elbow against the rock.

Without turning his head, Simon spoke again. "This is not your place. It is mine. Leave this mountain."

Pieter backed up two steps. He wanted to say something, but no words came. He had longed to speak with the old man, but now that would never happen.

Simon stood, turned, and glared. Pieter leaped away down the slope. Before he had gone ten strides, he froze. Off in the distance, he heard a noise.

No, not noise. *Music.* He turned his head. The faint but clear notes...the sound of a pipe.

He stood frowning for a moment, unable to force his feet to move. The notes hung in his mind, lingering like the fading echo of a bell. He shuddered, as though casting off a spell, and fled down the mountain.

$$\text{\textbraceleft}$$

Pieter was back at the blacksmith shop the next day, working the bellows until he could scarcely lift his arms. The day ended without a clash with Father. Pieter had decided long before the workday ended that somehow he would slip away to the mountains the next morning.

When Pieter climbed the ladder to his bed in the loft, his father was not yet home. When he woke the next morning, the house stank of ale, so he was able to leave while his father slept off the night's binge. Instead of going to Simon's cottage, he headed straight toward the clearing that lay before the cliff. Somehow, he would speak to the old man. Simon's words of anger no longer stung. At least the man had spoken to him.

When he reached the cliff, he turned a slow circle, straining to catch some distant note, some slight breath of music.

But all he heard was silence. Deep and expectant. Sweat dampened his tunic. Should he be here at all?

Nevertheless, he sat on Simon's stone and waited.

Little by little, faint sounds emerged from the silence. The whisper of the breeze. The scurrying of some small animal in the rocks. The cry of a distant eagle, a speck against the pale blue of the sky.

He strained, hoping to catch the growl of the wolf, but he heard nothing.

Not even the music. He listened so hard he forgot to breathe.

Old Simon dropped beside him so unexpectedly that Pieter cried out.

"You'll hear nothing that way, foolish boy."

Pieter leaned away, his eyes wide. Simon sat, feet apart, walking stick upright between his legs, gnarled hands tight on the carved wood. He did not look at Pieter.

Pieter stared at the wrinkled face. He had never been this close, never noticed the old man's eyes. A brown edging toward copper. They were the saddest eyes he had ever seen.

Simon twirled the walking stick on its point and took a new grip. "You can't force it, no matter how hard you screw up your face. Let go. Then listen."

Pieter nodded. But the more he tried to relax, the harder it was to hear anything.

"Come on, lad," barked Simon. "Think of something you care about deeply."

Agnes, of course. Lying on the dirt floor, kicking her chubby white legs, her tiny fingers reaching for him.

The air in the dell stirred. Pieter's eyes widened. There it was. That faint light note. Then more notes...a melody.

He snatched at it. The sounds vanished, like a shadow at the edge of a dream.

Simon snorted and shook his head.

Pieter took a long, slow breath.

There it was again! The song! It floated through his mind.

Old Simon nodded. "Aye, now you hear it. I feared as much."

"You hear it as well, don't you?"

"Aye, child. All my miserable life. Since that day long ago."

That day. Pieter did not have to be told what day that was. He stared at the smooth grey cliff. "This is the place, isn't it? He brought the children here."

"Aye."

"But the trail ends. There is nowhere to go."

"That day there was. A great gap in the face of the cliff, filled with a glowing yellow light, like the brightest summer day you've ever seen. Into that opening they all did go, following the man with the pipe."

Except Simon. "And because of your leg—"

The old man turned on him, sudden anger in his eyes. "It is not as you imagine." The walking stick trembled in his grasp. He lurched to his feet and pounded the stick into the dirt.

Almost! Simon had been on the verge of telling his story—a tale Pieter longed to hear. And now he had angered the old man. He wanted to plead with him to stay, but no sound came.

Simon stormed away, throwing his last words over his shoulder. "You know nothing, *nothing* about what happened."

Chapter 6

An orange light from the dying fire flickered below. Agnes cried out, then gurgled back into her infant slumber.

Pieter fingered the edge of his rough wool blanket, thinking not of his father's blow, but of Koppelberg. The music—the piping he had heard—was silent in Hamelin Town, but it remained in his mind. Every note, every trill, vivid and clear and constant.

The song was so beautiful, but more than that, it was haunting, compelling him to return to the mountain.

The cost of his trek into the mountains had been a beating. But his father had been drunk and his blows had not found purchase. Save one on his mouth. Pieter fingered the cracked corner. It would be swollen for a few days. All in all, it was a small price to pay.

Agnes cried out again. Pieter threw off his blanket and lowered himself down the shaky ladder. A few coals winked orange in the fire pit. The smell of ashes and smoke mingled with the scent of last night's soup. The dirt floor was smooth and cool under his bare feet.

He scooped Agnes out of her cradle. Holding her tight with one hand, he scrambled back into the loft.

He wrapped her close in his blanket. Agnes wasn't ill; she simply wanted something their mother could not provide. Or would not. She just wanted to be held, to have someone coo soft words into her ear, cuddle her, sing to her.

Pieter did not doubt that his mother loved him, but she had not been able to give him those things, either. Had it been different when she was young and strong? Before she had endured years of her husband's angry words and thrashings?

Agnes had played all day on a dirt floor, but she smelled earthy and sweet regardless. Pieter began humming a little ditty he knew Agnes liked, something he could do only while the rest of the family slept. The tune had come to him one night while rocking his sister.

But this night the melody would not hold. Try as he might, it kept changing itself into the song he had heard on Koppelberg. Agnes did not seem to mind. Soon her head lolled against his chest and her breathing became deep and regular.

His swollen lip still throbbed, but he knew that in the morning he would earn another blow. He had to talk to Simon again. And he could not ignore the music, for he was sure that it was the Piper's call.

Pieter crept across the dirt floor. He had dressed in the dark, then climbed down carefully to return Agnes to her cradle.

He reached for the latch on the back door, scarcely breathing. His trembling fingers hesitated above the iron. His ears searched for any sound in the early morning stillness. Nothing. Once he was in the yard, he would climb the woodpile, leap over the wall and be gone. He lifted the latch and a huge hand clapped onto his shoulder. He was jerked back into the room.

"What I gotta do to keep you home?" his father rumbled. "Break your legs?" With a flick of his massive arm, he tossed Pieter to the floor.

A candle flickered to life from the far corner, revealing his mother. "Karl, no!"

Father whirled and glared at her. She backed away, clutching her shift. Agnes woke with a yowl.

Pieter scrambled to his feet and burst toward the door. He wrenched it open, but his father was on him, lifting him by the back of his tunic. He tossed him with both hands. Pieter crashed into a chair, sending pieces of wood flying. He struggled to his feet and stared at his father's shadowed face and saw something frightening flash in his eyes. Something that had not been there before.

Not the swaggering bully. Not the red bleary look of a drunken temper. His father was stone sober. The rage that blazed in those eyes came from deep inside.

Fear burned in Pieter's gut and stung his throat. "Father, I was just going to—"

The big man lunged at him.

Pieter rose and backed away. Something metal snicked from his father's belt. A knife appeared in his beefy hand, glittering in the yellow candlelight. "No more of yer smart mouth. I've had enough," he growled, holding the blade high.

"No, Father—"

The man feigned a knife thrust. "Shut your mouth. I'm done with you." He hovered over him.

Sweat ran in rivulets down Pieter's back. He knew to the bone that this was no bluff, that his father meant to use the knife.

He was distantly aware of his mother's screams, of the wails of baby Agnes.

His father crashed toward him. Pieter leaped to the side and hurtled toward the back door. His father sprang after him with a roar. As Pieter bolted through, something snagged the back of his tunic. He wrenched free and dashed through the small yard. Hitting the woodpile at a dead run, he vaulted over the stone wall. He raced down the narrow alleyway and into the maze of pathways between the buildings.

On and on he fled until all strength left him. He collapsed behind a wagon, gasping for breath, the yellow morning sun in his eyes.

Agony lanced through his shoulder. Bright red blood welled up through a gash in his tunic. He'd been *stabbed*. The last thrust of the knife had struck home.

How had he not felt it before? He tried to steady himself, but the world spun around him. He squinted against the sun's glare in his eyes. East. He had run east. He stared at the craggy crest of Koppelberg Mountain, black against the sunrise. He had fled directly toward it.

Able to breathe once again, he clambered to his feet and started along the path. But in a few strides, he stumbled against a rock, slid, and dropped to the rough ground behind it.

He had to *think*. Now that the raw terror of the attack had faded, he had to *do* something. But what?

Go home? Never! The knife would be waiting for him, and he sensed that wasn't going to change.

He must leave Hamelin.

Sudden sorrow welled up in his chest. Not for his home, although he could not imagine living anywhere else, but for his mother, who surely loved him in spite of her coolness. And for wee Agnes. Who would go to her in the night? Who would tuck her yellowed blanket around her? Who would hold her and tickle her feet?

Would he ever see her again?

There was a village east, past the mountains, called Elze. Surely a strong boy of twelve could find work there. It couldn't be more than fifteen miles away.

He gripped the rock and tried to pull himself up. Instead he screamed and clutched his shoulder. The morning light whirled in grey specks before his eyes and he fell again.

Groaning, he rolled slowly to his knees, trying not to move his back muscles. It was impossible. Little by little he struggled to his feet and stood, swaying.

He staggered, knowing only hot pain and the next halting step, then the next. One foot in front of the other.

How long he reeled down the road he did not know, but when he looked up, he found himself in front of Simon's stone cottage.

He stumbled toward it, then collapsed against the wall to catch his breath. One shuffling step at a time, he managed to work himself around the house to the back door.

Before he could muster the strength to knock, the door opened and Pieter collapsed into the old man's arms.

Chapter 7

Pieter opened his eyes and looked around the barren room. One thick-planked table, a couple of sturdy chairs. A trunk. The bed he lay on. Little else.

The room smelled of split logs, spices, and a sharp, earthy odor like crumbled leaves. The blanket tucked around him seemed much softer than the ones he was used to. An actual pillow, smooth and plump, was under his head.

The ash from the fireplace had been swept to an even ridge across the front. Not a spider web or forgotten bit of dirt marred the stark cleanliness of the room.

Simon's house.

Pieter threw off the blanket and tried to sit up. He cried out in pain and flopped back, clutching his shoulder.

The back door flew open and Simon rushed in. "Lie still, foolish boy," he ordered. "Don't try to move without me."

He rolled Pieter gently onto his side and lifted the poultice.

That was the sharp smell.

Simon studied his wound. "At least no stitches pulled. Looks mighty red and swollen, though. Now stay where you are."

Pieter didn't need to be told again. His shoulder throbbed. He raised his head to accept a drink of water from a brown clay mug, but even that small movement sent pain down his back.

"So," said Simon, easing Pieter's head onto the pillow, "I stitched you up. And put some salve on it." He regarded

Pieter with clear brown eyes. "It's a nice clean cut. Too clean. Like a cut from a knife."

Pieter nodded. "My father, he was awful angry. It's all my fault."

"Horse crap, boy. It's not your fault at all, you hear me? I know Karl well enough. Still—" He ran a hand through his grey hair. "That leaves you with a bit of a problem, doesn't it?"

Pieter nodded. But Simon was wrong. It *was* his fault. He should have backed down from his father. He should have done what he was told.

Simon sat silent, his arms folded across his old brown tunic, waiting. Finally, Pieter said, "I thought I'd head for Elze."

"And do what?"

Pieter shrugged, wincing as he did. "Ask around. Find a job. I'm stronger than I look."

Simon shook his head. "You're not going anywhere until that wound is healed. What you need is time to rest and recuperate." He rubbed more salve into the wound, and the smell of crushed leaves filled the cottage. "We'll talk more later."

Pieter found he could scarcely keep his eyes open. Soon, Simon's thin face dimmed and Pieter dropped into a restless sleep.

When next he opened his eyes, Simon sat at the table, a huge piece of parchment spread out with a rock at each corner. Two white candles burned. The windows were squares of black. Pieter's fingers stroked the supple fabric of his blanket.

The old man looked up. "Hungry?"

"Are you *reading*?" Pieter blurted.

Simon gave him a hard look. "One of my many talents."

"How?"

"I taught myself, as far as I can remember. It seemed to just come to me." He pushed himself up from the chair and brought over a tin plate, which he set on a stool next to the bed.

"Now," said Simon, "I'm going to scoot you up so you can eat. Ready?"

Pieter tensed, his jaw tight. Simon grasped him under the shoulders and lifted. It hurt, but not as much as he expected.

Simon stuffed another blanket behind him, then set the plate on his lap—sliced apples, a small wedge of white cheese, and a bit of dark bread.

The cheese proved to be soft and flavorful, quite different from the occasional dried-out chunks his mother served. He bolted it down, followed by the warm, tender bread. How was the old man able to buy such food?

Simon was back at the table, bent over the parchment. His gray head nodded as he moved a finger.

"What is it you're reading?" No one had taught Pieter his letters, for there was no need. Unless he entered a monastery or became a scribe, he would have scant reason to use the skill.

Simon sat back and rubbed both eyes. "It's from the archives at Town Hall."

"Archives?"

"Aye. Records from a while back."

"How far back?" he asked, sure he knew.

Simon glared at him. "Lots of questions, boy."

"How long—"

"Sixty years," barked Simon. "Sixty *long* years. Does that satisfy you?"

Nay. It only stoked his curiosity. He licked his lips and leaned forward, holding his breath. Perhaps the old man would answer some of his questions at last.

Chapter 8

"**H**ow did you get that parchment?" asked Pieter.

"Angus. He cleans and repairs things around the Hall. He slips me things from time to time. He found this song many years ago and brought it to me." His brown eyes held Pieter for a moment. "It's about the Pied Piper."

Pieter longed to hear more of the story. So why the sudden knot in his gut? Why the sweat collecting under his arms?

Simon regarded him, then shifted in his chair. "I call it the Piper's Song. It is not the one he played for the children. Nay, it was sung for the Town Council. A monk, Brother Lawrence by name, recorded the actions of the council in those days. He had an amazing memory, it seems. He recorded every sentence, every word, every syllable."

Simon moved the rocks, one at a time, until the parchment rolled of its own accord. He picked it up and hobbled over, dropping onto the stool. "He preserved the Pied Piper's exact words. This scroll is from the day when the Piper returned for his money. Before demanding the payment, he sang a song to them. They were puzzled, but they were thinking about the money, so they dismissed its importance. But the old monk wrote it down, word for word.

"When the Council refused to pay him what they had promised, the Pied Piper stormed out. You know the rest."

"I never knew the Piper sang a song."

Simon unrolled the parchment in his lap. "After what happened next, no one paid much attention to it. But this is the song he sang:

A child shall surely hear,
Though 'tis silent to the rest,
A song that needs shall send him,
Upon a shadow quest.

Follow yon Pied Piper,
Though you know not why.
For music is magic,
And the lost be nigh.

Aye, hear yon Piper's music,
That lingers in the air,
Arcane and veiled riddles,
Shall lead the Piper's heir.

"A strange song. What does it mean?" asked Pieter. "It makes no sense."

Simon's face hardened. "If you will listen for a moment, it will."

Pieter shrugged, but in truth the song unnerved him. He had been curious about the Pied Piper, yes. But for some reason he disliked the words on the old man's parchment.

His shrug had clearly annoyed Simon. "Pieter," he said, his voice soft but forceful, "you *must* listen."

Pieter stared, his throat dry. Ire glittered in the old man's eyes.

"Very well," said Pieter.

Simon released a shuddering breath. "I have waited a very long time for this. You have many questions about the Pied Piper, do you not?"

"Aye."

"This song is part of the answering. I will try to explain it more clearly." Simon thought a moment, then said, "You understand, do you not, that the song is about a journey? Remember, it is a quest."

Alarm stirred in Pieter again. "What do you mean, quest?"

"A journey that leads toward some definite purpose or goal."

Pieter could make no sense of that, but he nodded and forced himself to attend to Simon's words.

"The second part," continued the old man, "consists of the riddles mentioned in the first. In truth, the riddles are clues to the places on the journey."

"The journey to where?"

"Ah, that is indeed the question. The riddles are most difficult. I have not yet solved them, although the first clue seems to refer to the north, where the Weser River meets the Aller."

"And why do you travel to this unknown place?"

"That is the purpose I mentioned. We go to find the Pied Piper's heir."

Pieter frowned. "I don't understand what this has to do with me."

Simon shook his head. "You mean you don't *want* to understand."

"Nay, I just—"

"Pieter," he snapped. Then his face softened and he said, "I know but one thing for sure—I *must* follow the call of the song."

*E*xhaustion flooded Pieter's body. *If Simon leaves Hamelin, what will become of me? Surely the old man will not be leaving straightaway.* He had to wonder why Simon had not left on the "quest" long ago. After all, he had possessed the Piper's Song for many years already.

While Pieter did not understand this business about the Piper and all those foolish clues, the notion of being left behind frightened him. He had dealt with his father before; he could again, should he return home. And Agnes needed him, as well as Mother.

No. He remembered his father's eyes. The anger, the hatred. He could not face that again.

He tried to sit up, but his muscles failed him.

"Relax," said Simon. "You don't want to tear out my beautiful stitches, do you?" He adjusted the parchment, holding it so Pieter could see the letters, and pointed. "Here's where the riddles begin."

In spite of his unease, Pieter found himself curious about the riddles in the rest of the Piper's Song. And Simon clearly wanted to share them.

"So," said Simon, "here's the first."

Toward the bridge o'er the Aller,
On your left the rising sun,
Your path must needs run hither,
Your journey thus begun.

"Where's the Aller River?" Pieter interrupted. Hamelin lay on the Weser, and that was the only river Pieter knew.

"The Weser and the Aller come together northwest of Verden. The town is on the Aller. So that is our first destination."

Pieter caught the word "our" but decided to ignore it. "What about the rest of the riddles?"

"Sad to say, I am baffled by them all."

That gladdened Pieter's heart. If Simon couldn't solve the other clues, surely he wouldn't be leaving any time soon.

"Here's the next one," said Simon.

Black rock be cleft by unknown hand,
Mid branch and vine and creeper.
A vale of flower and harmony,
Where dwells the faithful Keeper.

"A vale?" said Pieter. "That's a little valley, isn't it?" He had always thought of the place where he sang as a vale.

"Aye," said Simon. "But there are many, many vales and dells in this countryside." He sighed. "And the last two clues are even more vexing, I fear."

Beyond the bridge town's streets,
Grey stones be sanctified,
And singing fills the evening.
The cloth shall be your guide.

Where candle flickers feeble,
Where bitter bond be made,
Hidden midst the stones,
Where it can never fade.

A cross shall point to barrels,
That rose on ancient stone,
Now lost in verdant cover,
This be your guide alone.

"Then, the chorus repeats."

Follow yon Pied Piper,
Though you know not why.
For music is magic,
And the lost be nigh.

Pieter found himself turning the riddles over and over in his mind. So strange and unknowable, yet compelling all the same.

Simon sighed. "There is much to think about. For example, did you notice the line *that leads the Piper's heir?*"

Sudden fear coursed through Pieter. His jaw tightened. At first he had been filled with curiosity. But suddenly he wanted nothing more to do with it. Indeed, he wanted to forget the whole thing. "This is mad. What does this old song have to do with anything?"

Simon took a shuddering breath. "Listen to your heart, lad. Then you will know."

Pieter glared at the old man. "This has nothing to do with me. *Nothing!*"

He turned his face to the wall.

Chapter 9

The day passed in a brittle silence, as though if either of them spoke, their words would lead back to the Pied Piper.

Pieter didn't know if he was "listening to his heart" or not. He certainly could not stop thinking about the full story of the Pied Piper, but now that Simon suggested it had something to do with him, it sent a cold chill down his spine.

Two lines in the Piper's Song kept coming to the surface:

*A child shall surely hear
Though 'tis silent to the rest.*

For a long time he stared at the rough wooden beams over his head. Then he drifted into a shallow slumber, with the Piper's Song still echoing in his mind.

A noise jerked Pieter from his nap. He struggled a moment to get his bearings. The sound came again—something striking the side of the house?

"Simon!" he called. "What is it?"

"Bunch of boys," growled Simon. "Pelting rocks again. Don't let it worry you."

Pieter sat up on one elbow. He had seen them bother Simon before. "It must be Hans and his bunch. Why do they treat you like this?"

"Because I'm an old man. Because they think I'm mad. Don't worry. I keep the shutters closed. They'll leave before long."

"Hey, devil man," came a voice from outside. "We want you out of Hamelin."

That's Hans for sure, Pieter thought. Even some of the adults in town feared him.

Simon grunted. "They show up every once in a while. Throw a few stones, get bored, and leave."

"We know what you did, Mad Simon," shouted Hans. "You killed Karl's boy. We found his blood. Give us the body and we won't have to kill you."

"What the..." muttered Simon, and Pieter caught a touch of fear in his voice. The old man hobbled to the front door. "He's not dead, you young fools," he called without opening it. "He's right here."

"Lies! Lies, devil man. Pieter's father saw you stab him. Now come out."

"Simon's telling the truth," yelled Pieter. He struggled to sit up on the edge of the bed. "I'm here, and I'm definitely not dead."

No response.

The sudden quiet outside sent a shudder up Pieter's spine. He wobbled toward the door. "Hans, listen to me. I'm here with Simon." He steadied himself with a hand on Simon's shoulder.

Something thumped on the roof. Simon's eyes shot to the spot. "Lord have mercy," he murmured.

Then Pieter smelled it.

"Out the back," barked Simon, grabbing Pieter's elbow.

The first whiffs of smoke drifted down from the thatch. More thumps, which meant more torches.

They hobbled out, arm in arm. Luckily, the boys had run after tossing the torches. Pieter and Simon lurched together up the trail. The pain in Pieter's shoulder spiked with every step.

The two of them crested a rise and dropped to the ground. They peered over the hill and Pieter's mouth dropped. The entire roof blazed hot and orange. Already the thatch buckled and sagged, leaving smoky holes. The air stank of foul smoke and ash.

Simon dropped his head onto the ground, as though he could no longer bear to watch.

They lay side by side on the grass as long minutes passed. Pieter found it impossible to look away from the inferno. When the roof collapsed with a rumble, Simon sighed and raised himself up. "Come on, son," he whispered. "Time to go."

"Where? Where can we go?" asked Pieter, following Simon up the slope. "Wait, Simon. I have to know. Where are we going?" The old man waved him into silence.

When they had topped the next rise, they both turned. A rancid plume of black smoke rose high into the air. "Away. Away from this cursed town."

Chapter 10

How long they staggered through the hills, Pieter could not tell. He knew only the agony of his shoulder and Simon's solid presence beside him. The odor of burning had been replaced by the deep green aroma of the woods.

Over and over Pieter glanced back, expecting to see someone in pursuit. Hans, with another torch in his hand. Or Pieter's own father, still holding the bloody knife.

The old man began to pull ahead of him. Pieter grabbed a tree branch to steady himself. The trees around him began to waver in his sight.

"Simon..." he gasped.

The old man whirled and hurried back to him. He grasped Pieter under the arm. "I know it hurts, son, but we must continue."

"Why? We're far from— Oh!" He caught a sound. Faint but real. Something picking its way through the bracken. Something following them.

"We're in danger," said Simon. "In the woods—" He pointed off into the trees.

Pieter tried to tamp down the terror rising in his chest. Odd images rushed through his mind. Low views of tangled brush. An image of a warm, dark space—dirt and roots and the smells of rich loam—a place of safety and comfort. A den! Then he knew. "Simon, it's a wolf."

"Aye. They are rare in this area. We must hurry."

"No," said Pieter, squeezing Simon's arm. "I've met this wolf before. She won't harm us."

Simon shook his head, clearly thinking Pieter was addled by a fever.

With Simon's help, Pieter staggered on.

Should I tell him about the wolf? But pain flamed through his shoulder, and he was conscious of nothing else.

By the time the sun disappeared behind the hills, Pieter guessed they had traveled a good three or four miles. The trees thickened as they moved farther into the forest.

His legs ached; his breathing tore at his lungs. Worst of all, he knew the cut on his back had broken open. His shirt clung, warm and wet, to his skin. One moment he trudged along, the next he was on his knees. Again, Simon lifted him to his feet.

"Rest," said Pieter, his voice hoarse. "Just want...to lie down."

"No," barked Simon.

Despite the pain and weakness, an unexpected calm flowed through his chest. "The... wolf... "

He had a shadowy memory of being lifted into Simon's arms, of night closing in, of slow lurching movement, but he had no idea how much time had passed when Simon pounded on something wooden. The sound was so loud Pieter trembled.

A wedge of warm yellow light cut through the night. Pieter stared. A door had opened. A man's scraggly face peered out.

"Simon!" the man said. "Mercy. What are you doing out here this time of night?"

"Fleeing," said Simon.

"Then get inside, for the love of the saints."

Simon shifted Pieter and carried him into the rough cabin. A fire roared in a massive stone fireplace. The smell of the room—smoke and leather and something akin to ale— gave Pieter an unexpected sense of safety.

Simon carried him across the room and laid him on a narrow bed with coverings of rough wool.

"Pieter," said Simon as he slipped a folded blanket under his head, "this is my friend, Tracker."

Pieter nodded. The man was at least as old as Simon, which meant he was not from Hamelin. His hair and beard stuck out like a brush around his head.

Pieter said, "I didn't know anyone lived up here."

Tracker grinned through his bristling mustache. "Just the way I like it. Only Simon comes up this way."

Pieter lifted his head to look around the cabin. The room spun. He dropped back on the pillow, gripping the edges of the mattress.

"Now," said Tracker, "fleeing what, pray tell?"

"I need to tend to the boy first," said Simon. "Can you sit him up and hold him?"

Tracker put an arm under Pieter's neck and lifted him. He sat on the bed and held him so Simon could reach his back.

Pieter leaned his forehead into Tracker's chest. The man smelled of cows and goats, of the forest, and the sweat of hard labor.

Simon peeled the tunic away, little by little. It made a tearing sound as the bloody fabric separated from the slash. Pieter clung to Tracker's arm as Simon's touch sent pain stabbing through his torso. He squeezed his eyes shut, clutching Tracker with all his strength.

"Mother Mary!" exclaimed Tracker. "That's a knife wound. Not too deep, but it's awful red, ain't it?"

Simon nodded. "He's pulled his stitches. Pieter, I'm going to have to clean it. It's going to hurt. Are you ready?"

Pieter thought he was, and he nodded, but he cried out when the cloth touched his skin. He clamped his teeth until his jaw muscles ached.

"Tracker," said Simon, "I'll need a needle and some catgut."

Tracker hurried to a small rustic chest sitting near the fireplace. He lifted the plain plank lid and rummaged inside.

He held up a large needle. "Got this one I use to stitch leather. That's all."

"It will have to do," said Simon. "Put the whole thing in the flame a minute."

Holding it with a pair of tongs, Tracker thrust the needle into the fire. When it cooled, Simon took it, along with the length of catgut.

Oddly, the needle hurt less than the cleaning had.

When Simon finished, he sat back and said, "Pretty rough. You're going to have quite a scar, my friend. Tracker, do you have any ointment?"

Tracker returned to the chest and came back with a brown clay jar.

Pieter braced for it to sting, like the foul green ointment his mother used. But to his relief it did not. "Sure stinks," he said. Like a mixture of ash and old urine.

"It's better to stink than get worse," said Simon, rubbing it over Pieter's shoulder.

When he finished, Simon wrapped a linen cloth around Pieter's torso and up over his shoulder.

"Pain...not as bad," murmured Pieter. He remembered his eyes closing, and hearing a distant gruff voice. For a fleeting moment he sensed a blanket being laid over him.

And not too far away, an animal presence. Waiting. Watchful.

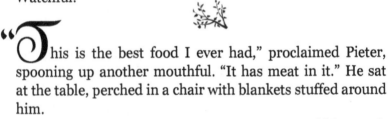

"This is the best food I ever had," proclaimed Pieter, spooning up another mouthful. "It has meat in it." He sat at the table, perched in a chair with blankets stuffed around him.

"Tracker is a fine cook," said Simon. He wiped his mouth with the back of his hand. "Fine, indeed."

Pieter scraped the last bit of broth from the bowl and licked both sides of the wooden spoon. "How long did I sleep?"

"Let's see," said Tracker, "we just had lunch, so, I'd say 'bout eighteen hours."

"Eighteen hours? That can't be right," said Pieter. "No one can sleep that long."

"It was good for you," said Simon. "The more you rest, the faster you heal."

"You must've had some pretty wild dreams," said Tracker, collecting the bowls and spoons and dumping them into a large pot of water.

"How do you know?"

"Well," he said, pulling at his thick brown beard, "for one thing, you talked in your sleep."

"More like yelling, actually," said Simon.

"I see such strange things in my head sometimes," said Pieter.

"So it would appear," said Tracker. "A couple of times you were practically howling. Now that was peculiar, I have to say."

Simon's face looked grave, and Pieter wondered if he was remembering the wolf that had followed them. While lost in pain and confusion during the escape from Hamelin, Pieter had sensed the wolf. He knew it was the very one he had met in the hills above Hamelin.

Tracker shook his head. "But the singing was even stranger. I never heard nobody sing in their sleep before."

"Sing? I wasn't singing," Pieter protested.

Simon smiled. "Oh, but you were. And quite well, I might add."

"But I'm not allowed to sing."

Tracker grinned. "Looks like someone forgot to tell your heart that rule, lad."

Pieter ran a hand through his hair. "That's how I found Simon. I started going up into the hills so I could sing. One day, I saw him and followed."

"Aye," said Simon. "And I've listened to that singing many times. You were so intent on your music, you had no idea I was there."

"Don't tell my father," Pieter blurted out. "He's angry enough already."

Tracker's grin vanished. He sat forward and said softly, "Angry enough to take the knife to you?"

Pieter studied the tabletop, tracing the grain with one finger. "He must have guessed where I'd run, Simon. And now your house is burned down and it's my fault. I should have—"

"Pieter!" said Simon, his eyes flashing. "It is not your fault. Do not say that again. It was those ignorant boys who threw the torches."

"Simon," said Tracker, putting a thick hand on his friend's arm. "I think you'd better tell me the whole story."

Simon carried Pieter to a huge chair near the fire. He draped a warm but scratchy blanket over him. Tracker added a huge oak log that sent hot orange sparks up to the smoke hole. He sat down to listen. Simon pulled a bench over and began.

Pieter said not a word as Simon spun the tale. He relaxed when the old man made no mention of the Pied Piper or the Piper's Song on the parchment. Still, it left the tale somehow lacking.

Fear crawled through Pieter's belly. Not of his father or Hans or anything in Hamelin, but fear of what Simon meant to do next. His chest ached thinking about it.

When the old man finished, he leaned back and crossed his arms. "I'm not going back to Hamelin. Neither is Pieter."

Tracker nodded. "Then you're welcome here; you know that. Not much room, but we can make do." He gave Simon a deep scowl. "Just don't you try tidying up the place, you hear?"

"Don't worry. We're not staying here either."

"Of course you are. Where else you gonna go, old man?"

"I may have a few years behind me, but I'm not too old to travel."

Tracker's face deepened into a glower. "Where are you going, Simon?" he asked, suspicion in his voice.

"Along the Weser. Then north. Maybe Verden."

Tracker's voice exploded. "So that's it. You old fool! Don't think I don't know what you're up to."

Chapter 11

"Aye," said Simon. "A fool I am; I do not doubt it. But, Tracker, I have waited a long time, and now Pieter has found me."

Pieter gaped at the two men, his throat dry. What did Simon have in mind?

"This is that Pied Piper crap, isn't it? That song you got from Angus?"

"Aye. That's why we must go."

Pieter scowled. "We? What do you mean, we?"

Simon scowled back at him. "I read the Piper's Song to you, didn't I?"

"Yes, and I told *you* that it has nothing to do with me. I just want to get away from my father."

"Aye," said Simon, his eyes glittering. "But there's more, isn't there, lad?"

"Do you mean I'm supposed to listen to my heart again?"

"That would be a good start."

Pieter shook his head, even though it hurt his shoulder. "The Pied Piper came a long time ago. I wasn't even born."

Simon nodded. "Sixty years. In all that time, I'm the only one who ever heard the sound of the pipe on Koppelberg. Until you, Pieter."

"I still—"

"No one else in Hamelin hums a song wherever he goes. No one else seeks out a mountain dell so he can make music. And in all the years I have gone to Koppelberg, no one else ever followed me to that cliff."

"What? You yelled at me up there. You told me I had no business on your mountain."

"He yells at everyone," said Tracker.

"Why?" Pieter asked Simon.

"To see if you were determined enough to return. Which you were."

"This is crazy." Pieter scooted to the edge of his chair. "I'm going out to... " He had no idea what was outside Tracker's house. All he wanted to do was find the wolf. Instead, he swayed and nearly fell off the chair. Simon caught his arm and guided him back down.

"Sit still," said Simon. "Listen again to the song."

"No," cried Pieter. "Put that parchment away." Somewhere outside, the wolf howled. Pieter held his head. "I am the son of a blacksmith. Nothing more."

He looked at the two men, frozen, staring toward the wall with wide eyes. The howling had alarmed them.

Simon's gaze returned to the table. "Very well. You need not listen. But I believe I shall read it to Tracker." Simon unrolled the parchment on the rough table. "Right here, old friend," he said pointing.

A child shall surely hear,
Though 'tis silent to the rest,
A song that needs shall send him,
Upon a shadow quest.

Simon crossed his arms and leaned back. "Tracker, I have found that child."

Chapter 12

The next day, Pieter was able to walk to the table to break his fast. But he had slept poorly, disturbed as he was. The old man seemed determined to wrench him into the Pied Piper story.

After Tracker served up breakfast, a pottage of oats and pieces of apple, he joined them at the table. As he ate, Pieter eyed the two men. Simon's brow was pulled down over his eyes and he glowered at his food. Tracker concentrated on his eating, spooning it in with a determined motion.

When he finished eating, Pieter pushed his bowl away and leaned back, his arms crossed. *Simon's not done with this Pied Piper nonsense.* His jaw tightened as he waited for what Simon was going to say.

Simon cleared his throat. "Pieter, we need to make some plans. Are you going back to Hamelin?"

He shook his head. "I don't see how I can." He put his head in his hands.

"Then you have no home."

"Tracker would take me," he said, hoping it was true.

"I would, indeed," growled Tracker.

Simon waved the idea away. "Of course you would, old friend. But, Pieter, you're asking him to support you and raise you. He has little money. He owns nothing but this cabin and a bit of land. And like me, he is no longer young."

Pieter glared at him. "And you have money, I suppose?"

"Actually, I do."

Pieter scowled. "But you live like a pauper."

"Aye."

"But why?"

"I was waiting. Biding my time until a certain person showed up."

Pieter ignored that. "How did you get money?"

Even as he asked, Pieter realized he knew little about Simon's life. When the Pied Piper came, Simon had been the Last Child, the one who had been left behind. As an old man, he lived in a run-down cottage east of Hamelin.

In between? Pieter knew nothing.

"When the Pied Piper came," said Simon, "I was a child of the streets, as bad as the rats. I lived in dark corners, traveled through the sewers. I lived off what little I could beg or steal. Gunther, Sam's father, ran the Tong & Anvil in those days, was kind to me, let me do odd jobs around the inn. With a withered leg, most people considered me useless."

"And after the Piper?" asked Pieter.

Tracker sat in the corner, scowling at Simon.

Pieter sat forward. For the moment, curiosity was stronger than the kernel of fear in his chest.

Simon went on. "A tinker came into town, Oskar by name. Two days after the Pied Piper stole the children. He took me on. I traveled with him for years. Little by little, we turned a tinker's wagon into a thriving merchant business.

"We settled in Jesteburg, not far from Buchholz. He was already getting on in years when we met, so I was soon running the business."

"Why did you come back?"

The old man shrugged. "Oskar got old, and one sad day he died. I felt drawn back to Hamelin. Gunther's son, Sam, ran The Tong and Anvil by then. He had become a friend over the years. Besides, you weren't likely to find me in Jesteburg, were you?"

"*Find* you?" He could think of no words to push Simon off this irritating Pied Piper track.

Simon studied his face. "Pieter, Pieter. Why do you fight against it?"

Pieter laid his head on the rough table. The grain pressed into his forehead. A journey led by an old song? How could it be?

Still, he couldn't go home. That murderous look he'd seen in his father's face... No, the man meant to kill him, one way or another.

And Simon was right. He couldn't force himself on Tracker. He raised his head and locked eyes with Simon. "Very well."

"You'll join me in the quest?"

"Nay," he said, his voice sharp. "It's your quest, not mine. But I will travel with you."

"That will do," said Simon, relief in his face.

"I don't seem to have much choice, do I?" Despite the hours he had slept, a deep weariness swept over him.

"Rest," said Simon. "It will be some time before you have your strength back."

Pieter nodded. At least that would end this exhausting quest talk. He staggered to the bed and crumpled onto the blankets.

Chapter 13

That evening, the tension between Pieter and Simon choked the little cabin. Tracker fussed with one task and then another, not looking either of them in the eye. Simon busied himself creating designs on a new walking stick, a strong, straight branch of ash, almost white with a light-brown grain. He carved a series of rings in the center, then smoothed out a grip at the top.

With a grunt, he set it aside and moved to the table. He unrolled the parchment and turned it over. He fumbled in his pouch until he came out with a quill and ink bottle. "Lad, would you like to learn to read?"

Pieter's head came up. "Now?"

"It will take a day or two to get ready for our trip."

"Why?"

"Oh, I need to pack a few things and, uh, run an errand or two. So you might as well learn your letters. It might be a good use of our time."

Pieter moved to the table, eagerly if a bit gingerly.

It was amazing. By the end of the first lesson, Simon's scribbles had transformed into letters, and then, to Pieter's shock, into some words. Bending together over the parchment, much of the uneasiness between them melted away.

Tracker, whittling by the fire, looked relieved.

So the days drifted by, and Pieter was totally content living with the two old men, as long as they avoided talk about old songs and pipers and quests.

Simon worked his way through a pile of gear, cleaning, packing, tying bundles together. Much of it was purchased from Tracker, after a heated conversation about whether to pay or not.

Each night, he and Simon worked on his letters. Pieter loved those times, loved the scent of the ink and the parchment, loved being close to the old man. Although Simon didn't say much, Pieter knew he was doing well. The number of words he knew increased every evening.

On the third night, when he rolled up the parchment, Simon said, "Tracker and I have some business. We'll have to leave you alone tonight."

Pieter shook his head. "I'm healing fast. I can go with you."

"Nay, lad," said Simon. "You need to rest. The sooner you heal, the sooner we're off to Verden."

Pieter swallowed hard. "How late will you be?"

"We'll be back before dawn. You go to bed when you get tired. We'll be along."

"Should I do something with the animals?"

"They're fine," said Tracker, throwing a dark cloak over his shoulders. "All fed and down for the night."

Pieter felt safe in Tracker's cabin, but alone at night? Why did that conjure pictures of Hans creeping up with a hot orange torch?

Simon patted a piece of parchment. "I wrote some words on here. You can practice your letters until you're sleepy."

Pieter nodded and glanced toward the window, sorry to see that it was already dark. Tracker bolted the back door and closed the wooden shutters on all three windows, blocking out the black night but not the sense of dread in Pieter's stomach.

After the men left, Pieter latched and locked the front door. He stood for a moment, listening to the night. Or, rather, the haunting silence of the night. The stillness shattered with the howl of a wolf. Pieter smiled to himself, wondering whether Tracker and Simon had heard. The creature was not far off.

He turned to the parchment on the table. It took Pieter but a few minutes to read over the words Simon had written. He copied them out in his fast-improving hand. None of them were hard. So far, learning his letters didn't seem that difficult.

Again, Pieter became aware of the images floating in his mind. The wolf. But the impressions were sharper, clearer than before. Did that mean she was closer? Before long, he caught a picture of the cabin itself—*from the outside*. The wolf waited just beyond the walls of the cabin.

He crept to the door, unlocked it, pulled it open a crack and stared into the blackness. After a time, the scene resolved into shadows and shades of black. Then he saw the eyes.

Beautiful blue eyes, but wild and fierce. The eyes drew closer. A sound—something between a growl and a whine. Again, strange images flooded his mind. He couldn't sort them out, but together they sent a message. *The wolf will be there for me. She will keep me safe.*

They regarded each other for a long time, boy and wolf. Pieter wanted to rush to her, longed to touch her, but he could not make himself do it. But in that moment he knew her name. Nay, she *told* him her name. *You are Silverfoot*, he thought, and he was sure she understood.

Even in the dark, her white paw seemed to glow. The azure eyes gazed at him for a moment, then disappeared and Pieter knew she was gone.

He shut and locked the door. Immediately, the wolf—Silverfoot—began to howl. He smiled to himself. *I'm here*, the wolf was saying. *I shall always stay nearby.*

He wandered back to the table. *Why would she do that? How do I deserve such a companion?*

On the other end of the table lay a larger scroll, still held down by stones on its corners.

The Piper's Song.

He leaned forward and studied it. To his own surprise, he could make out many of the words. In fact, after two or three tries, he could read most of them.

That's odd. He scanned a verse. *I don't remember Simon reading this part.*

Seek fauna on your journey,
Fierce ally clad in grey,
Lest you miss the very being,
Who will aid you in the fray.

He had no idea what "fauna" meant. And someone who wore grey would help them? Well, it wasn't Tracker. He wore mostly brown.

Pieter sat up and rubbed his back, giving no more thought to the verse. As he read on, a melody formed unbidden in his mind. And like any melody, it longed for release.

Tracker said he had sung in his sleep. And he had done it in secret for years. It awoke a spark of fear in his chest. But he was no longer in Hamelin. So, why not sing if he wanted to?

So he took a deep breath and began.

The song came forth fully formed and somehow exactly right for the words on the parchment.

But even as he sang, a sense of alarm took purchase in a deep corner of his heart. Not of the night, nor the wolf. Not of the music itself. Oh, no, there was naught to fear from that. Perhaps it was the fact that the Piper had used the music for evil. He had stolen the children from their parents. He had torn the heart out of Hamelin with music.

And the town bled still.

Was this the kind of person Pieter would become? Should he become a piper, as Simon seemed to hope, would Pieter, too, use his gift for petty revenge?

The words swam on the page. His head nodded and his eyes closed.

noise.

Pieter's head jerked up from the table. Someone banged on the door. "What?" He staggered to his feet. "Who is it?"

"Me! Tracker! With Simon. Open up."

Pieter padded to the door and released the lock. Simon and Tracker trudged in, each carrying a brown leather bag.

"Still up, boy?" said Tracker, frowning at him. "You were supposed to rest. Nearly morning. Still, we would have had to wake you to get in, eh?"

Pieter rubbed at his stiff neck. "I guess I fell asleep."

A howl in the night. Tracker growled, "Blasted wolf. Never heard one in these parts before. Driving me crazy."

Simon nodded. "We heard howling all the way from Hamelin." They dropped their sacks on the table.

Pieter swallowed hard, his gaze on the sacks. "Are you two thieves?"

Tracker threw back his shaggy head and laughed from deep in his belly. "Thieves? That's a good one. The Tracker Gang, is that it?"

Simon grunted. "We were simply getting back what's mine."

Tracker dumped out his sack. A blackened pot. An odd-colored knife. A scattering of woodworking tools.

From the other, Simon pulled out a second knife, this one cased in leather. Then a smaller bag that landed on the table with a clinking sound.

"The townsfolk pretty much made off with everything that didn't burn," said Simon. He picked up the bag and shook it. "It's a good thing I had a few hiding places."

"Pull out the right stone in the fireplace," said Tracker with a grin, "and, behold, a treasure."

"Not a treasure," grunted Simon. "But at least a few coins to get us on our way."

Pieter shook his head. "I still don't understand why you lived like a pauper."

Tracker laughed again.

"If you look poor," said Simon, "nobody bothers trying to rob you. Let's take a look at your shoulder." The old man's fingers pressed Pieter's back. "It's closing well. Today, we finish our preparations. Tomorrow morning, we're off."

Fear nestled again in Pieter's chest. Hamelin was his past. He was not going home. When would he ever see his mother or hold little Agnes again? And who knew what lay at the end of Simon's strange journey? Why couldn't they stay here with Tracker? He and Simon and Tracker—they could make a life, couldn't they? Why did they need to leave?

He could work. Tracker could use the help. The man's cows and his grey donkey needed care. Pieter could fetch and chop wood, even cook. Once he learned how, he could hunt. That would work, wouldn't it?

The answer came, but it was not the one he wanted—the haunting melody of the Piper's Song, now etched into his mind.

How he hated it!

But oh, how he loved it.

Chapter 14

Early on their departure day, Pieter and Simon peered out of Tracker's barn into a downpour. Pieter had listened to it hammering the roof most of the night.

"Shall we leave tomorrow, then?" Pieter asked hopefully.

"Nay," Simon answered. "Oskar used to tell me that a task delayed is seldom done. It is time to leave."

After a quick farewell, they splashed away through oozing muck, Simon leading Tracker's loaded grey donkey.

Pieter pulled his hood tighter as he tromped along next to the pack animal. His feet and legs were soaked before they had gone a hundred yards. He shivered so hard, he had to gasp for air. What were they doing, leaving that snug cabin and trekking off in the rain?

Simon hobbled in front of him, stabbing his new walking stick into the mud with each stride.

As the morning passed, the remainder of Pieter's good spirits were washed away by the relentless deluge. Simon trudged ahead with his ungainly gait. One gnarled hand clutched the walking stick, the other the donkey's lead.

He should have stayed with Tracker. But in truth, it was Simon he needed to be with. And that meant putting up with his Pied Piper nonsense. And this rain! The road had become a churned mass of mud and puddles, resembling a brown creek more than a road.

"Simon!" Pieter called. "We need to get out of this weather."

Simon didn't turn. "No, we don't."

"This downpour is terrible," Pieter whined.

"Try singing," said Simon, glancing over his shoulder.

Singing? He was too miserable for music. Besides, here in the open, someone might hear him. And yet it was better than fixating about this wretched weather.

To his surprise, a song came to him straightaway, about—what else?—the unending rain.

Rain-o, rain-o,
Cover up in vain-o.
Rain-o, rain-o,
Will this downpour wane-o?
Rain-o, rain-o,
Has leaked into my brain-o.
Rain-o, rain-o,
I shall go insane-o.

The words traveled but a short way in the water-laden air. But they did indeed lighten Pieter's mood.

"Well," growled Simon, "that certainly cheers me up. My brain might be better off watered down a bit."

The donkey seemed content in spite of her load and the wretched weather. "How will Tracker get his donkey back?" called Pieter above the roar of rain.

Simon shook his head. "I bought her, remember?"

Pieter did. Again, Tracker had wanted to just give them the animal, but in the end Simon had forced some silver on him.

"What's her name?" asked Pieter.

"I know not," said Simon without looking back.

Pieter double-stepped to catch up. "Didn't Tracker tell you? She has to have a name."

"It's just a donkey."

"What about calling her Rosie?"

Simon's head snapped around. "Rosie?" he barked. He shook his head. "You can't name a donkey after a flower."

"Sure you can."

A faint smile appeared on the old man's face. "Very well. Rosie will do. She's a bit up in years, but a tough old girl."

Pieter dropped back and laid one arm over the little beast's head. "Rosie?"

The donkey cocked her head, which placed Pieter's hand directly behind her ear.

"Aha," said Pieter, giving her a good scratch through her wet, plastered hair. "So that's the spot you like."

The spry little beast stepped higher, sending great globs of mud into the air. Pieter found a tune running through his head. Before they had traveled half a mile, he had the words as well.

Sweet little donkey,
Clip-clops through town,
Big eyes a-gazing,
Deep and glowing brown,

Prancing through the meadow,
Never seems to tire,
Clopping down the roadway,
Trekking through the shire.

Maybe it was just being away from dreary Hamelin. Or perhaps it was simply the open road or even the cleansing rain. More likely, it was the simple freedom to sing, but whatever it was, Pieter belted out the song. They were traveling away from Hamelin. Away from the fear of music. He had created two songs already, and it was only the first day of their journey.

After a long day of slogging through the mud, Simon found a dry spot under a cedar where the branches bowed to the ground. It formed a green-shaded shelter, with a dry bed of sharp-smelling needles on the ground. Pieter was amazed there was a place in all Brunswick that was not wet.

So large was the interior that even Rosie could enter. She stood steaming, adding the pungent smell of wet hair and donkey breath to the shelter.

"No fire tonight," said Simon. He pulled off his soaked tunic. "Still, best shed those wet clothes. Let me help you with that tunic."

Simon grabbed the bottom edge and gingerly pulled it up and over Pieter's head. The pain in his shoulder shot down his arm. "Wouldn't a small fire be okay? These needles should burn."

"Aye. Too well," said Simon. "This whole tree might go up, in spite of the rain."

Pieter dug around in his bag and found his spare cloak—in truth, one of Tracker's old garments. When he managed to get out of the rest of his wet clothes, Tracker's cloak enveloped him like a tent. But it was dry and warm, and that was all Pieter wanted.

Rosie settled onto the ground and Pieter curled up next to her with his supper—some dried beef and black bread. He had stopped shivering, but he couldn't imagine their clothes would be dry by morning.

Simon jumped at the sound of a wolf's howl. A piece of meat dropped from his mouth. "That creature is a menace." He stormed to his feet and snatched his walking stick. "I'm going after it."

Another howl. Rosie brayed and surged to her feet, sending Pieter sprawling. He stumbled to his feet, tripping on the edge of his cloak. With a cry, he lunged for Simon and managed to grasp the man's cloak. "No! You can't!"

Chapter 15

Simon, please," said Pieter. "You can't hurt the wolf."

The old man shook his head. "A wolf means danger. I need to protect us."

"With a stick? Listen to me. We are not in danger," said Pieter.

Simon gave him a sharp look. "You can't know that."

"In a way, I know this wolf," Pieter said.

"In what way?"

"She...Silverfoot came to the vale where I used to sing. I think she was drawn by my music."

Simon stared in the direction of the howl, unmoving. Pieter shifted uncomfortably. Unable to stand the silence, he said, "Simon, I—"

"Son, I do not doubt you have seen this creature. I have witnessed how the birds respond as you sing. I have watched an unspoken connection between you and Rosie." He leaned closer. "But this is a *wolf*. It is a hunter by nature. It must kill to eat."

"She will not hunt us. Nor Rosie."

Another howl echoed into the night.

Simon's head jerked up. "That sound doesn't frighten you?"

"No," Pieter said. "She is singing."

Another long silence filled the space between them. Then Simon swept off his cap and scratched his head. "Pieter, know this. I *will* defend us if she attacks."

"Aye," said Pieter. "She knows that."

Simon gave him a long look, then spread out his bedroll.

Pieter soon lay in the dark, breathing air saturated with the perfume of cedar. Rosie had yet to settle, fearful still. In a soft voice, Pieter began to sing.

Sweet donkey Rosie,
Faithful to the end,
Working, pulling, hauling,
Helping like a friend.

The donkey folded onto the ground. She snuffled at the needles, then dropped onto her side. She laid her head down on the thick needles. Her brown eyes regarded Pieter as though to say that she had calmed, but she wasn't happy.

Rosie, grey Rosie,
She'll never go astray.
Rosie, strong Rosie,
Friend in stippled grey.

The soft stirring of the donkey and the cries of the wolf eased his heart and lulled Pieter to sleep.

Pieter sat up in the darkness, the image of his father's face in the dream still vivid. A face quivering with anger, eyes a molten blue-black. What had Pieter ever done to kindle such wrath? At the worst, he had skipped some chores and run off to the mountain a few times. Nay—many, many times. Still...why would that drive his father to want to kill him?

He went cold, in spite of the pile of blankets. That knife, glittering in his father's hand. So many beatings over the years, but this time it had been a *knife*.

It was more than his father's temper. More than the ale. It had to be.

And now Pieter was on a journey to who-knew-where.

"Simon? Are you awake?"

"Aye, lad."

"Why Verden?"

"It's in the song."

"I know. But it only says 'toward the bridge.' Maybe Verden isn't first. The meaning is all tangled up."

Simon snorted. "Aye. It's meant to be hard. It was not written for just anybody."

"What if you're wrong about Verden?"

Simon chuckled. "Then I shall enjoy a fine meal at my favorite tavern in Verden ere we depart. At the moment, however, we'd best prepare for the day."

The rain had stopped, but the grey sky threatened a new deluge at any moment. In some places, they were able to travel along the grassy shoulder to avoid the mud. They plodded along in silence. Simon seemed to have used up all his words the day before.

As Pieter had feared, his clothes remained damp. He wondered when he would ever be warm again.

The road narrowed. Puddles of rainwater were marbled with tan and brown swirls. Pieter sang through his two new songs, enjoying the fact that he had created them.

Simon looked back. "Maybe you need a lute."

"What's that?"

"A wooden instrument. You pluck the strings. That way, you can sing and play at the same time."

Pieter nodded with excitement. "That would be perfect!"

"I'll look around in Verden. A lot of minstrels use them." He resumed his awkward stride, the mire clutching at his boots.

"Minstrels? What are they?"

Simon shook his head in sorrow. "Oh, lad, I forgot. Growing up in Hamelin, you have never heard one. Minstrels travel from town to town, making music. You know, at inns and taverns and such, but also in castles and the houses of rich people."

"People do that?" said Pieter, excitement bubbling in his words. "Travel around and just make music? Why?"

Simon smiled. "Because they have a heart like yours, young Pieter. And they earn a living at it—if they are good."

Pieter could only gape. Money? For making music? No one could ask for a better life than that.

By late afternoon, the road straightened as they came into a countryside of orderly farms and groomed fields bursting with new growth. Low stone walls, green with moss, framed the fields. The smell of freshly plowed soil and something minty filled his nostrils.

"Where will we stop next?" asked Pieter.

"Minden, hopefully. Small town tucked along the Weser. But no inns. Camping is safer."

The trek to Minden took the entire day, for Simon swung them out and around a huge bend in the Weser. He explained that it would keep them away from most other travelers, who moved along a road that shadowed the river.

After camping near Minden, they left the Weser and traveled for a day north along a narrow country road.

Pieter wondered how Silverfoot would fare in this open country. What if he could not hear her tonight? It didn't seem likely in lands this settled.

As dusk approached, Pieter began wondering where they would sleep. Even though the rain had stopped, he was quite weary of camping. "When—" he started.

"In a mile or two," said Simon. "There's a monastery just this side of Hoya. They'll give us shelter for the night."

That sounded better. Warmth and good food, mayhap. He hurried his pace.

Ahead, a flock of sheep spilled across the roadway. A boy in a ragged grey tunic and a floppy hat walked behind, waving a crook in the air.

They caught up quickly to the shepherd, but the boy did not look back at them.

Rosie shook her head and brayed her irritation at the delay. The sheep bleated and cried in panic. The boy yelled and waved his crook, but the terrified animals scattered. Some leaped the low stone wall along the road. Others broke into a run. Despite the boy's efforts, the sheep churned in a maelstrom of wool and fear.

Rosie brayed again. The boy whirled so fast his cap flew off. "Quiet that idiotic animal."

Pieter stared at the reddish-brown hair that had fallen to his—no, *her* shoulders.

"My apologies, my lady," said Simon gallantly. "Pieter and I will help you round up your sheep." He pulled Rosie to the side of the road and tied her to a bush. She munched the tall grass, seemingly unconcerned about the ruckus around her.

It took a good long time before the sheep were in some semblance of a flock. Their help had not mollified the shepherd girl. "Now I'm late," she complained, jerking a thumb at the sun dropping behind the dark hills.

"Pieter will help you get them home."

"Me?" said Pieter. "I know nothing of sheep."

"You've been chasing them around for the last hour," said the old man. "That's a start."

"Offer accepted," huffed the girl.

"Rosie and I will go on ahead. I'll meet you at the monastery, Pieter. It's just another mile, up on the hill to the north. You'll see it up where the road bends to the east."

As Simon and the grey donkey disappeared around a bend, Pieter found himself plodding behind the flock, next to the girl and unable to think of a single thing to say. This many sheep certainly had a strong odor—not totally unpleasant, but rather pungent. He would never mention it, but the girl smelled much the same.

"Move, Silkie," called the girl. "Yup, yup. Get on, Marta."

Pieter noticed she waved the crook over their heads but never actually touched the animals. The flock moved as one now, so there was really nothing for him to help with. He risked a sidelong glance. "So, what's your name?"

"Gretchen. And you're Pieter. You thought I was a boy, didn't you?"

"Oh, no," he answered, too quickly.

To his surprise, she laughed, her auburn hair swinging. "That's fine with me. Who wants to chase sheep in a dress, eh? Besides, people on the road are more likely to leave me alone. Stocker! Yup! Move your wooly rear, you lazy creature!"

"Where do you live?" Pieter asked.

"Around the bend. These stupid sheep ate our pasture down to the nubs. Now I have to drive them into the hills every day. Then bring 'em back again."

"Don't you have help?"

Her face turned stony. "I don't need any help."

They rounded a curve and came upon a weathered gate set in a stone wall. A narrow path ran along a field toward a small cottage. Little grew in the field, save ragged clumps of grass and scattered weeds. Simon and Rosie stood waiting just past the entry path.

Gretchen pushed the gate open and the sheep moved on their own down the lane, toward the cottage.

She regarded Simon with squinted eyes. "I thought you were headed for the monastery."

"Aye," said Simon. "But I thought this might be your place. It crossed my mind your father might have some chores we could do. You know, because we disturbed your sheep."

Panic flickered in Gretchen's green eyes. "No, thanks. My father...he, uh, doesn't like strangers."

Simon gazed down the path toward the rundown croft. "I see."

Gretchen shut the gate behind her, leaving Simon and Pieter on the road. "So you can be on your way. No hard feelings."

Simon put a foot on the lower gate board and leaned over the top. "I have food on the donkey. I could conjure up a bit of stew for supper."

Gretchen hesitated. It was only then that Pieter noticed how thin her face was. Her eyes were set in dark hollows, although they glittered an intense green. A scattering of freckles stood out starkly against her pale skin.

"No thanks," she said. "I have to get the sheep into the pasture." In a quick move, she started down the path.

"How long has your father been gone, lass?" asked Simon.

Chapter 16

Gretchen eyed Simon for a long while. Her gaze flicked to Pieter, then back to Simon. She let out a long breath. "My father left six months ago."

"Does anyone in Hoya know?" asked Simon.

Gretchen lifted her chin. "It's none of their concern. It's not yours either, come to think of it."

Simon nodded. "True enough. But it seems to me you and your mother could use—"

"I said, it's not your concern." She stalked away down the overgrown lane.

The sheep were milling around the cottage. Pieter watched as she drove them into the pasture and shut the gate. He saw the little farm through fresh eyes. A collapsed shed. A sunken area of blackened thatch near to caving in. The lack of smoke from the hole in the roof. "Simon, I'm wondering if there's a mother there."

"Aye."

"I wonder what she's going to do."

Simon rubbed the back of his neck. "Well, I'm thinking she's wrong."

"About what?"

"About it being none of our concern."

Pieter frowned. "She seems quite sure it isn't."

"Perhaps," said Simon. "But we know she's in trouble. So that makes it our concern, whether she likes it or not. Come on."

They started down the path. Pieter wasn't sure he wanted any more to do with the sharp-tongued lass. But the closer they came to the cottage, the worse the whole place looked. If not for the sheep, it seemed abandoned.

The door opened, hanging askew on its leather hinges. Gretchen stepped out, a mixture of fear and anger in her face. "What are you doing here? I told you I don't need help."

Simon shrugged. "Too bad. I make a fine stew."

"Simon," said Pieter, "she's—"

Simon waved him quiet with a gnarled hand.

Pieter watched the struggle in Gretchen's face. He had no idea if she would let them stay or not.

She blew out an angry lungful of air. "Oh, very well."

That evening, they sat together in the decrepit cottage, perched on low wooden benches, eating Simon's stew. The food warmed Pieter like the meager fire could not. No fire had burned in the hearth for a long time, and it would take a few days to reheat the stones of the pit. The grey smoke drifted about, seemingly unable to find the vent in the roof.

The smell of the smoke mingled with the odor of dampness and decay. The cottage's condition was worse than it looked from the outside. It was near to falling apart.

An image came from Silverfoot. She lay on a grassy hillside, her mind peaceful. To his surprise, she urged his thoughts in another direction. Toward the sheep. Now he sensed a hazy merging of many dim minds, but the overall impression was of serenity. He smiled. The wolf's message was clear—she would be causing no distress in the flock this night.

Simon crossed his arms and regarded Gretchen a moment. "Tell me about your mother, child."

Gretchen studied the floor, then looked up with moist eyes. "Fever got her. About ten days ago."

Pieter's eyes widened. "She died?"

Gretchen glared through her tears. "I did everything I could. But she just grew weaker and weaker."

Simon shook his head. "I am so sorry. There's little that can be done for some, I fear."

Her head dropped. "I tried to bury her, but I couldn't dig deep enough. So...so I wrapped her in a blanket. And covered her with some stones. It's not enough, but it was all I could do."

"No one would help?" asked Pieter. "Why?"

Gretchen snorted. "Because I'm nobody. My father was a peasant who never owned an inch of land. We couldn't leave, because we owed the master so much money."

"I don't understand."

Simon leaned forward. "Her father was bound to the land. Once he was in debt to the owner, he was a slave for all intents and purposes."

Pieter had lived in a town his whole life. He hadn't thought much about the farmers and workers in the countryside. He certainly had never thought of them as *slaves*.

"Gretchen, what about other family?" asked Simon.

"No one close. Maybe in Achim-Uesen, but I'm not sure."

"That's a start," said Simon. "Whose sheep are those?"

"Master Camber, in Hoya."

"And the land?"

"His, too. We take care of the sheep and he gives us a share, but..." Her voice trailed off.

"But he hasn't, has he? I'd bet not for a very long time," said Simon.

She nodded. "If he knew Father was gone and Mother had died, I don't know what he'd do."

Simon sat back. "So, no one knows your father is gone. Except us."

Gretchen gave a quick nod.

"You've taken care of the sheep by yourself? For months?"

"Aye."

A long silence filled the cottage. Pieter's mind raced, but he could think of no way to help the girl. Perhaps they could leave her some food or bring in a load of wood. Do some repairs before they left.

"Tell you what," said Simon. "Let Pieter and me borrow a bit of floor to sleep on. In the morning, we'll bury your mother proper."

"Would you? That would be..." She wrapped her arms tight. Her chin trembled, but she seemed determined not to weep. "Thank you."

The next morning, Pieter found a shovel and an old pick in the rubble of the collapsed shed. The ground behind the house had dried so hard, the recent rains had just rolled off. They found the spot where Gretchen had started to dig. A sickening smell oozed from the cairn of rocks next to it.

They took turns loosening the hard-packed soil and hauling away the light-brown clods. Pieter's hands throbbed, and a nasty blister rose on his left palm. After many hours, a crude grave began to appear beside the cairn of stones. It was near to evening before the hole was deep enough.

"The boy and I can move your mother," said Simon, pressing a hand on the girl's shoulder. "You needn't help."

She nodded curtly and disappeared inside the house.

One by one they rolled the rocks off the makeshift grave. A horrible stench escaped from the partly rotted wool blanket. *It's a person*, Pieter reminded himself, struggling to control his stomach. *It's Gretchen's mother.*

The rancid blanket held, and he and Simon laid her gently into the new grave. Moving the body had released a wretched odor of death and decay. They shoveled in enough dirt to cover the corpse.

When Gretchen reappeared, they stood silently around the grave. Something needed to be said. This woman had to be honored.

To his own surprise, a melody came, utterly different from the foolish ditties he'd been singing on their journey up to now.

The sadness of it shook Pieter, but he knew it was right. Even without words, it seemed the song captured the grief, the pain—Gretchen's, but also his own. Before he knew it, he had the lyrics as well. With a shaky breath, Pieter sang.

No more shall yon lady,
Grace this meek home.
No more shall this mother,
Sing in the gloam.

How shall we bear it,
In sorrow to dwell?
How shall I grieve her,
As teardrops do swell?

Alas, she hath left us,
Bereft and alone.
The twilight consumes us,
And joy hath flown.

All color and brightness,
Hath faded to grey,
And naught can restore us,
Nor tears can allay.

When he finished, he found Gretchen staring at him through watery green eyes.

"Amen," said Simon, taking the shovel. "Pieter and I can finish up."

"No," she said, her eyes still on Pieter. "I need to help." A muffled sob broke, emotion she'd been holding in.

"But, Pieter. That song," she said, her voice breaking. "The things you sang about...the grief and the sorrow. How did you know?"

Chapter 17

By that evening, the chill had eased its grip on Gretchen's cottage. Pieter felt warm for the first time since they had left Tracker's. Simon had put together a meal of dried fish, dark bread, and cheese.

No one spoke as they ate. They sat around the fire pit in silence. Pieter squirmed in discomfort. He gazed through the flames at Gretchen, then Simon, then Gretchen once more. He saw the same question in both faces.

What now?

Gretchen tightened her arms across her chest. "The pasture was fine for one day, but in the morning, I need to take the sheep back up to the hills."

Simon took a sip of some ale he had found in the back of a cupboard. "What then, lass?"

Gretchen shrugged without looking at anyone. "At dusk, I bring them back."

"That's not what I'm asking."

She studied her clenched hands. "I know."

He scratched at his beard. "Here's what I'm thinking..."

"No." She glowered into the flames, then threw a dark glance at Pieter.

It took a moment before he understood. Was Simon actually thinking about bringing her along? *She isn't a part of this. This concerns Simon and me and no one else.*

"Listen a moment, lass," said Simon. "We are going at least as far as Verden. Perhaps we'll find news of your family there. Or we can help you get to Achim."

She shook her head. "I can't. I have to take care of the sheep."

Simon worked himself to the edge of the chair, then pushed himself up. "Tell you what. You two take the sheep to pasture tomorrow. I'll go into Hoya and have a chat with Master Camber."

Her voice rose in alarm. "About what?"

"About how he needs to find a new shepherd. Right away."

Pieter broke in. "Simon, she said she doesn't want to go." He knew his voice was too sharp. "Why do you keep harping on it?"

Simon gave him a cold look, then turned back to Gretchen. "What do you say?"

She opened her mouth as though to object. Instead, she shrugged.

he next morning, Pieter followed Gretchen back along the road he had been traveling. It was drying out from the recent rains and turning a rutted, dusty tan. Not a word passed between them.

Pieter did not want to spend the day watching a bunch of dirty sheep. Nor was he interested in spending time with this girl. It was time to load Rosie, time for him and Simon to be on their way.

They left the road and trekked up into the hills. "This is the place," said Gretchen.

The sheep fell to grazing. Thick, verdant grass covered the hill, sprinkled with flowers of yellow and white. Pieter sat on a rock, watching Gretchen make a circuit, checking behind the grey boulders and in the tangled green thickets.

She returned and perched next to him. The long silence was beginning to stretch Pieter's nerves. Finally, Gretchen turned to him. "You and your grandfather, why do you travel to Verden?"

"He's not my grandfather," said Pieter. "Just a friend."

"I see." She scanned the flock with a quick eye. The question of Verden hung between them.

"Where are you from?" Gretchen said at last.

"Hamelin."

Her head turned. She regarded him for a moment. *Is she thinking about the Piper? Does the name Hamelin bring nothing else to mind?*

A deep breath escaped from her mouth. "Pieter, that song you sang for my mother. It was quite amazing. Where did you get it?"

Pieter's face warmed. "It just came to me."

"When?"

"Right then. After we laid your mother in the grave."

Gretchen's mouth dropped. "You are gifted, Pieter of Hamelin."

He shrugged. How could he take credit for music that just appeared in his mind?

"You could be a minstrel," she said.

"Maybe," Pieter answered. "But Simon thinks there's something I need to find first."

"In Verden?"

"For a start. Or mayhap beyond that."

"What does he think you need to find?" she asked.

Pieter gazed at the flock of satisfied sheep, their heads down, consumed with the task of eating. He tried to relax his jaw, but it remained tight. "Simon feels we need to find out more about, well, about some music." He did not wish to open up the subject of the Pied Piper.

"Music? But why?"

"To find out who I am, I suppose. But I'm not sure. Simon may be wrong."

Gretchen flicked a stone that landed near a wandering sheep. "Get back, Satin. Back, back." The ewe meandered back into the flock.

"Where's Rascal?" Gretchen sprang to her feet on the rock. "That stupid lamb." She leaped off and stalked over the hill.

Pieter scrambled to follow when he heard Gretchen let out a scream of rage, followed by a nearby growl. As he crested the hill, he saw her staff humming in an arc in front of her. It caught a wolf in the head.

Was it his? His chest tightened so tight it ached. His pulse raced. It couldn't be *his* wolf.

No, this wolf had a black and brown mottled coat and was smaller than Silverfoot. It squealed and crouched. Another swing of the staff and it slunk away into the brush.

On the ground lay a young sheep, its head cocked at a dreadful angle, blood oozing from its neck.

"Ah, Rascal," said Gretchen, flinging her staff away and dropping to her knees. "You brainless creature. You just wouldn't stay with the flock, would you? Always running off." She stroked its head. "Always running off."

She exploded to her feet, sending Pieter backing away. She scooped up her staff and charged in the direction the killer had escaped. "Come on, you mangy cur."

Her fury startled him. Such wrath! Yet he thought he understood. He had listened as she talked to her sheep. He had seen how she stroked the dead lamb. To lose one must be shattering.

Her staff whipped through the grass, then shattered a tangled shrub on the return stroke. "I'll get you, you flea-bitten son of the devil."

Chapter 18

When a number of plants had succumbed to her rage, Gretchen abruptly sagged to the ground, her anger spent.

After a moment, she held the staff out. "Take this," she grunted. Heedless of the mess, she hoisted the lamb and heaved it over her shoulder. Bright blood dripped down her tunic.

"That was a wolf, wasn't it?" he said, relieved it wasn't *his* wolf.

"Nay. Just a stupid dog." She trudged back toward the flock.

Pieter trotted to keep up. "A dog will kill a sheep?"

"Some will," she said. "Watchdogs or hunting dogs that get away or are let loose. They return to their wild nature. They're worse than a wolf any day."

"Why?"

"Because they're desperate." She dumped the sheep onto the ground and scanned the flock. "All the rest are here. Damn, that's the second sheep I've ever lost."

The hillside no longer seemed as idyllic now that death had visited. The singing of the birds had changed in an instant to a deathly silence. The thick bushes suddenly seemed perfect cover for predators. A chill swept down his back.

Gretchen leaped onto the rock again. She stood rigid, scanning the flock over and over. "Come on, you cur. Come back so I can get you," she muttered.

Pieter couldn't imagine the dog would return. Gretchen was much stronger than she looked. She had wielded that staff with enough power to break a bone, he was sure. And she had thrown the dead sheep onto her shoulders as though it weighed nothing.

How could someone my own age be so brave? I could never have gone after an attacking dog like that. He could see how she had survived alone. But as strong as she was, how could she continue on like this?

It's not my problem, he tried to tell himself. *I hardly know her.*

The sheep began to mill around. Frantic bleats cut through the air. "The dogs are still near," muttered Gretchen as she laid the dead sheep on the ground. "Might be a pack. Go lower down the hill and keep the sheep from running toward the road." She snatched the staff from Pieter's hand so quickly it stung his hand.

He stumbled downhill through the grass, sweat breaking out on his neck and forehead. Now he heard the growls. More than one dog indeed. He turned around and waved his hands. "Back! Back!"

But the panicked sheep were not to be contained. Some surged past him. The rest scattered in other directions. "No, no," he cried.

Up the hill, he heard Gretchen's shouts, heard the whir of her stick, the low growls of the dogs.

He stood helpless in the center of a surging mass of wool. A flurry of fearful images swept through his mind. The panic of the flock was so real, it was though *he* was the one who was terrified.

And then, for reasons he didn't understand, he began to sing.

It was just his silly donkey song, but the sheep held in their flight. Slowly the heads turned toward him; dozens of black eyes met his. They began to surge in his direction.

For a moment, Pieter all but panicked as they flooded toward him. He lost the song, and in that moment, terror returned to the flock.

"'Donkey,'" he bellowed, "'*she was my pretty donkey.*'" And he began to stride up the hill.

The sheep followed. The ones ahead of him stood waiting until he passed, then joined the flock. Every one of them trailed along. The sounds of the dogs faded. Pieter walked and sang until they had almost reached the top of the hill. The terror that had flooded his mind stilled.

At that point, Gretchen caught up. She held only the broken end of her staff, and it was bloodied. She ran to him and grabbed his arm. "They followed you."

Pieter grinned. "I'm surprised they like a song about a donkey."

Gretchen shook him. "No, listen to me. They followed you. They followed your music."

A cold wave rippled down his spine. "Lord save me," he whispered. "They did. They *followed* me."

At the top of the hill, they found two of the dogs. Their stomachs had been ripped open and their entrails coiled in the dirt.

"Now that looks like the work of a wolf," said Gretchen.

Pieter stared at the disgusting mass of guts. He knew who had done this. "Yes, it was a wolf." Silverfoot had protected them.

Gretchen gave him a strange look but said no more. Pieter suspected the creature was as much on her mind as it was on his.

When they returned that evening, they found Simon waiting in front of the cottage. Gretchen dropped the dead sheep in front of him. "Ever done any butchering?"

Simon squinted at the limp body. "I have indeed. Shall we have a bit of mutton for dinner?"

"Aye. What happened with Master Camber?"

"As of tomorrow, you're a shepherd no more. I'll fill you in over dinner."

Gretchen regarded him for a moment, gave a quick nod, and disappeared around the corner of the house.

Simon bent over the sheep. "Hold the front legs, Pieter."

Pieter didn't move.

Simon looked up and squinted at him. "Something the matter, lad?"

Pieter shook his head. In truth, he couldn't forget the sight of those sheep following him. And the images—he must have perceived them from the sheep. He gingerly grasped the black hooves. Before he was ready, a knife appeared in Simon's hand. In one motion, he sliced the sheep from throat to tail.

Pieter dropped the legs and stepped back. After the disemboweled dogs, this proved too much. Nausea built in the back of his throat. A pile of pale green and grayish organs spilled from the incision.

Pieter stumbled away. "What are you doing?"

"Town folk," grumbled Simon. "Get away before you spoil the meat by puking on it."

Pieter did so gladly. He slipped into the cottage and plopped on a chair, holding his stomach. Slaughter was certainly a messy business. It probably looked worse when Silverfoot ate, but Pieter had never had to watch that.

Gretchen wasn't in the cottage, so he built up the fire and put water in the kettle. When the water was hot, he poured it into a clay bowl and scrubbed his hands over and over. *Those sheep. It was just music. It was just the song that had attracted them, that's all. I'm not like the Pied Piper.*

Simon soon had a shank of meat spitted and roasting over the fire. The cottage brimmed with delicious aromas. Pieter didn't ask where Gretchen had been.

"There's no time to smoke or salt any of it," said Simon as he turned the spit. "I hate to waste good meat. But what else can we do?"

While the mutton sizzled, Pieter settled on a bench with his leather bag. He pulled out the parchment and unfolded it in his lap. Each time he read the words, they seemed more vivid.

Gretchen peered over his shoulder. "What are you doing?"

"I'm learning to read," said Pieter. "Simon's teaching me."

She watched for some time. "It makes little sense to me."

"Aye. But you could learn if you wanted to. Simon could explain it."

Gretchen shrugged as though it were unimportant. She wandered toward her bed, perched on the edge, and pulled out a tunic to mend. Nevertheless, Pieter suspected she would very much like to learn to read.

Later, the three of them sat around the fire pit, enjoying the meal. Never in Pieter's life had he been able to eat all the meat he wanted. The little his mother bought always went into pottage or pie.

Mother.

A vivid memory of her appeared in his mind. Bent over the fire, preparing a meager meal with grain and a bit of cabbage, Agnes nearby tethered to the center post... A sob lodged in his throat, so unexpected that he choked.

Sweet little Agnes.

Chapter 19

The thought of Agnes, all alone in that loveless house—such sorrow swept through him he could scarcely breathe. Tethered and forgotten on the hard dirt floor, there was no one to give her what she really needed.

He dropped the bite of meat back onto his trencher; it was suddenly tasteless. He leaned back, one hand over his eyes. Agnes needed him, and he was traveling farther and farther away from her. *When will I return? Or will I ever be back in Hamelin?* He had little need to see that town again, but he ached when he thought of his little sister.

Gretchen regarded him for a moment, then turned her attention to Simon. "So, did you like Master Camber?"

Simon grunted. "Not much. That's why we won't tell him about *this* sheep."

"What's he going to do with the flock?" she asked.

"That's his problem."

"But my parents—well, they worked for him."

"Aye," said Simon. "But you do not."

She frowned. "How's that?"

"I bought your freedom." He shook his head in disgust. "He's a vain and stingy man, but he had no use for a young girl without parents. We came to an agreement."

"He must be angry."

Simon shrugged. "It doesn't matter to me, and it shouldn't matter to you. Now, lass, gather up whatever you think we should take, considering we have only our backs and one donkey."

Pieter sat up straighter. When had all this been decided? All of a sudden, it was definite that the girl was coming with them?

Pieter stood. "Simon, may I speak to you outside?"

Simon turned to Gretchen. "Excuse us."

They stepped out. Pieter pulled the door closed behind them.

Before Pieter could say a word, Simon barked, "Pieter. You are being most ill-mannered."

"I am not. When did—"

"She knows very well why you wanted to talk."

"Simon, we cannot take her."

The old man crossed his arms, his eyes flashing. "And, pray tell, why not?"

"Because she's not part of this. There's nothing in the song about her."

"Oh, so you now have faith in the Piper's Song? I thought it had naught to do with you."

Pieter shook his head. "That's not it."

"No, I didn't really think it was. I know very well what this is about."

"Simon, I—"

"Listen, you little ass. She's coming if she wishes to. She has no one else. You, of all people, should understand that." He stomped back toward the cottage, disappeared inside, and shut the door behind him.

Pieter stood in the dark for some time. He had never heard Simon so angry. *What's the matter with me? Why am I am being so unkind?* But Gretchen was so fearless. Having her along changed everything. *Will it change our quest? Will Simon prefer a strong girl over a scrawny boy like me?* At last he pushed through the cottage door.

Gretchen sat on a bench, her face tight. "Never fear, Pieter. There is no need to take me along. I'll be just fine."

"Nonsense, Gretchen," said Simon. "It's decided. You will travel with us. Right, Pieter?"

Pieter stared at the floor. Blood rushed to his face. Truth be told, he *was* being an ass. But dammit, Simon belonged to *him*.

He looked up and met Gretchen's eyes. "Yes. Please join us." He knew his voice was hard, but it was the best he could do.

Her eyes softened. "Thank you," she whispered. She twisted a lock of hair around a finger. "Do you think there's room for a lute?"

"You play the lute?" asked Pieter.

"A little."

"Why didn't you tell me?"

She cocked her head and regarded him with a direct gaze. "Why would I?"

Simon clapped his hands together. "Well, well. We meet a shepherd girl on the road, and she turns out to be a musician. Pieter, my lad, it makes me believe we've taken the road we were meant to. We've found the place in our story where she belongs, it seems."

That nonsense again about what they were meant to do. If Simon caught the frown on Pieter's face, he didn't acknowledge it. The old man turned to Gretchen. "Play for us, lass."

"Oh, I only play for myself. It helps pass the time watching the sheep."

"Nevertheless, honor us with a bit of music," said Simon. "If you will."

She nodded and pulled a rolled red blanket from under her bed. Tenderly she unwrapped the instrument. It was plain and unadorned, fashioned from some sort of dark wood. It looked homemade, but she handled it as though it were a treasure.

She tucked her auburn hair behind her ears and positioned the lute. The first few notes sprang from the strings.

Pieter's breath caught. From that simple instrument flowed clear, rich notes that shimmered in the air. He glanced at Simon, who stared at the girl with his mouth hanging open. The room fell away, until all Pieter could see were Gretchen's dancing fingers, and all he could hear was her music.

A faraway expression filled her face, as though she had floated off to another place, a place without missing fathers and dead mothers.

A place with hope.

Pieter did not know when he started to hum. It was as though he had always known this melody, as though he had long waited to sing this very song.

Gretchen's music changed. It slowed. Sadness crept in, and Pieter's humming changed with it. She played, and he sang a wordless tune, and it was a song of loss. His loss. Gretchen's loss. And yes, Simon's as well.

As the song reached its quiet, wrenching end, Pieter eyed Simon.

The Last Child of Hamelin wept.

Chapter 20

$\mathcal{P}$ieter trudged along next to Rosie. They had hurried through Hoya early enough that no one had noticed them. None of them wanted a confrontation with Master Camber.

With Hoya far behind, the farms became more scattered, until by noon they trekked through forest once again. Pieter glanced back at Gretchen. He had fought the notion that she should come. But the way she played the lute—it had changed things. Something now connected them. Still, he remained uncomfortable. Her sharp tongue and abrupt ways annoyed him. How he was going to put up with her day after day he didn't know, but the music would help.

He discovered he was shy about singing on the road with her there, but the Piper's Song ran through his mind, over and over until he thought he'd go mad. He finally stopped fighting it, and began to puzzle about the words and their meaning. According to Simon, the first clue clearly referenced Verden.

But even though that was the first clue, Pieter sensed that it pointed to a direction, not to a destination. "Toward the bridge." Pieter thought the next cue was more important. If they missed the "black rock", they might miss everything.

The yellow morning sun spread over the fields and lit the treetops. Pieter searched Gretchen's face. He could read no emotion, but she walked with a resolute stride, as though determined to ignore him.

Again, the lyrics pulsed through his head.

Black rock be cleft by unknown hand,
Mid branch and vine and creeper,
A vale of flower and harmony,
Where dwells the faithful Keeper.

He looked up and saw that the others were pulling away from him. He hurried along until he caught up with Simon and said, "I am worried about the song. I think we need to talk about the riddles."

Simon halted Rosie, who cast a look at Pieter as though she thought this a foolish place to stop.

"Very well," said Simon with a hint of impatience.

"The riddle about the black rock. I think it comes first."

"Then why does it come second in the song?"

Pieter wasn't sure how to explain it. "The first merely points us north. 'Toward the bridge,' not necessarily *to* it."

"I see," said Simon, crossing his arms. "Suppose you explain why."

He glared down at the rutted road. "I cannot."

"As I thought. On to Verden, then." He turned and gave Rosie's halter a light tug.

Rosie took one step before Pieter shouted, "No!"

The old man turned back, glaring. Pieter lifted his hands hopelessly. "I'm sorry I yelled. But I feel we are about to miss something. Something that will assure our quest. Or destroy it."

Simon regarded him for a moment. "Verden draws me on. I have a yearning for a bit of ale in an inn I know of. Nevertheless, I am willing to listen if you have another thought."

"Let me look at the parchment again. Perhaps I have the words wrong."

Gretchen stood watching them warily. Simon untied a bag on Rosie's back. He pulled out the scroll and unrolled it on the flat surface of a nearby rock.

Pieter found the lines and read them out loud.

"Black rock be cleft by unknown hand,
Mid branch and vine and creeper,
A vale of flower and harmony,
Where dwells the faithful Keeper."

He let out a disappointed huff of air. He had remembered the lines perfectly. "Alas, I see no more than I ever did."

"Nor I," said Simon. "Shall we sit by the side of the road until inspiration strikes?"

Pieter's jaw tightened. "If we have to. What's the use of traveling on if we ruin the entire quest by missing the black rock?"

"I'm waiting, then. Bless me with your wisdom."

Gretchen put a hand between them. "Hold on, you two."

"This doesn't concern you, Gretchen," Pieter snapped.

Her eyes blazed. "If you think that, you are a fool."

Pieter rounded on her. "What did you call me?"

"Listen to what I have to say."

It was Simon's turn to intervene. "Pieter, stay your anger. Let's hear her out."

Pieter glowered at them both but said nothing. His face warmed, and he knew it was red with anger.

"Go on, Gretchen," said Simon.

"I have an idea what those words mean."

"You?" snapped Pieter.

"Stop talking and listen," said Gretchen, her voice hard.

Pieter crossed his arms.

"Look," she said, "I don't know much, but I do know the country around here." She waved her hand in an arc. "I've been here before. Summer before last, we had a heat wave. Our pastures dried up. Even the nearby hills were parched. My father—" She swallowed hard. "We brought the sheep to this area looking for pasture."

"And?" said Pieter, beginning to listen.

"The locals warned us of a giant living nearby. 'Don't take your sheep into his valley,' they told us." She paused. "The giant was called Keeper."

"Keeper?" Pieter asked. "That's in the song."

"They thought it meant he'd take our sheep, or maybe capture *us* if he was in the mood."

Simon frowned. "It could be anything. A keeper of chickens, for heaven's sake. A shopkeeper."

"No," said Gretchen. "That was the giant's name. Keeper."

The old man leaned closer. "So what does he keep, lass?"

"That I do not know."

Pieter squinted at the parchment. "So does 'black rock be cleft' mean anything to you?"

"Aye," said Gretchen. "There's a path that starts in such a cleft. It leads to Harriminy Vale."

"Harriminy?" said Pieter slowly. "The song has the word 'harmony' in it. Could it be the same place?"

Simon glanced from the parchment to Gretchen, then back to the words. "Well, lass, how long do we stand here? Lead on."

Gretchen grinned. She whirled and started down the road, almost skipping. Pieter waited impatiently as Simon rolled the parchment and returned it to the bag. Unable to stand it, he scurried around the bend after the girl.

There stood Gretchen, in front of a black boulder that towered a good forty feet above her head.

And the rock was split, as though a giant had broken it apart.

Pieter stared. "A little further on the path we were on and we would have missed it."

Simon and Rosie approached. "Well, now, that was a near thing," said the old man, hobbling up to them. "In spite of my stubbornness, it seems we were meant to find it."

The cleft was wide, giving even Rosie plenty of room. However, a tangle of brush had grown up, almost closing the trail.

"The locals avoid Harriminy Vale," Gretchen said.

That tightened Pieter's throat. Half to himself, he said, "I still wonder what he keeps."

"Stray children, I hear," said Gretchen, with glee in her eyes.

"Gretchen!"

"When he's tired of keeping them," she leaned close, "he eats them."

Pieter swallowed hard. "Seriously?"

She grinned and shrugged. "I already told you. I have no idea."

He glared at her, his face warming. Was she mocking him?

They struggled through the brambles. The flora cast off the odor of broken branches and crushed leaves, an almost-sweet smell, touched with some sort of mint.

The overgrown trail came out of the rock cleft and traveled through a grassy knoll. They crested it and Pieter looked down on a verdant little valley. "Harmony," said Pieter, his voice hushed.

A bright blue stream ran along the vale's floor. A multitude of trees grew on each side. From a distance, they appeared to be fruit trees, as though this valley was tended, not wild.

Vivid spots of color, reds, bright yellows, and lush oranges, suggested clusters of flowers.

"What is it that crosses the valley?" asked Gretchen. "A wall?"

"Nay," said Pieter. "I think it's some sort of hedge. Aren't those flowers on it?"

The hedge spanned the valley, from cliff wall to cliff wall. The stream flowed under it near the center.

Gretchen let out a soft sigh. "What a peaceful place."

Simon nodded. "It does not make one think of a ravaging evil giant, now, does it?"

Pieter had to agree, but his heart thumped nonetheless. What if danger lay hidden in all this beauty? He frowned. "Why would the Piper send us here?"

Gretchen shrugged. "It feels right, doesn't it?"

"Aye, that it does," said Simon.

But Pieter was not so sure. Harmony Vale, if that's what this was, had knotted his stomach with dread.

Chapter 21

"Look!" cried Gretchen, pointing. "Smoke! Beyond the hedge. It must be a house of some sort."

The home of a giant? Pieter wondered, running a hand through his hair. Sometimes tales contained some truth.

As they dropped into the valley, the hedge became more visible. The leaves seemed more purple than green. Although the brambles looked thick and impenetrable, thousands of white flowers, like stars against the night sky, spangled the foliage.

The trail that descended into the valley proved even rougher and more overgrown. By the time they reached the valley floor, Pieter had scratches and red welts on his arms from whipping branches and clawing stickers.

He reached out and snapped off an offending twig. A buzzing sting swept up his arm. He stared. It was a vine maple. It felt more like he'd touched a nettle.

With a frown, he moved a few steps down the trail until he came to a rhododendron, laden with pink blossoms. Pieter grasped the base of a flower as though to pick it. Again, a sting swept up his arm.

"I think we're not to touch the plants," said Pieter, rubbing his hand on his tunic. "Nor pick or break anything growing in this place."

Simon nodded, but Gretchen gave him a look that seemed to say that anyone should know that.

At last, the trail opened onto the floor of the dell. The trees were indeed fruit trees. Shiny purple apples, dark red cherries, lustrous peaches. Even some produce that Pieter didn't recognize.

They all bore fruit, and yet blossoms opened to the sun on the same branches. Between the trees grew thick grass, spotted by flowers in colors so bright and vivid they almost hurt the eyes.

When they reached the hedge, they walked back and forth, failing to find an opening.

"I suppose we could cut our way through," said Gretchen. Her tone suggested she knew that might prove to be an ill choice.

Pieter stood on the bank of the stream where it disappeared into the hedge. "Maybe we could swim in?"

Simon peered over his shoulder. "You, perhaps. Not this old man."

Shadows had begun to fill the little valley, turning the greens to a dusky grey. Evening came early to this place enclosed by high cliffs.

"I think we'd best tackle this in the morning," said Simon. He pulled the bags off Rosie and they began to set up camp.

Pieter peered long at the hedge. "I wish I knew who dwells on the other side."

"A *giant*," declared Gretchen with a grin.

Pieter didn't believe that, and yet—

They built no fire. The notion of burning any of the valley's plants seemed totally wrong. They gathered close to share a cold meal of cheese and dried fruit.

Pieter found it hard to relax, not knowing what lay ahead. Of course, he didn't really believe Gretchen's nonsense about children being eaten. But still, they knew nothing of this "Keeper." In spite of the beauty of this place, there might be good reasons that the locals avoided it.

In truth, the ember of fear tucked in his heart threatened to flare into a wildfire. He wished he had a better sense of Silverfoot, but the wolf was far away. Pieter was sure she had not followed them into Harmony Vale. He glanced up at the top of the cliff, its jagged edge a black silhouette against the night sky. *Are you there, Great Hunter? Don't leave me.*

The response was faint, just a touch. But enough for Pieter to know she was near.

Their meal finished, they wrapped in blankets and sat in a circle, as though gathered around a cheerful fire. No one seemed ready for sleep, but no one had anything to say either. An almost-full moon floated white in the center of the ribbon of stars above them.

At last Gretchen spoke. "This song, the one with the riddles. What is it all about?"

Pieter's jaw tightened. Would she just laugh when she heard the story?

Simon took a long breath. "Do you know the tale of the Pied Piper?"

"Aye," said Gretchen. "I have heard a bit."

So Simon told the tale, and through his words Pieter lived it once again. The rats. The day the Piper had come. The children.

"Hamelin has never been the same," said the old man. "In fact, few children were born over the next few years. And always, hovering over everything, was the fear that it would happen again. That the Piper might return."

Pieter frowned. "There are children in Hamelin now."

"Aye. At last, the town returned to more normal times. People tend to get back to their lives sooner or later. And yet, the shadow lingers."

Gretchen shook her head. "Lingers enough that no music is allowed? After all these years?"

Simon nodded. "Hamelin is a town that is fading. Each year, fewer people stay, more people leave."

Gretchen is right, Pieter thought. *It was so long ago. How could the Piper's action still be the bane of Hamelin?*

Gretchen's brow furrowed in concentration. "There's one part I don't understand. How does this involve you, Simon?" A hand went to her mouth. "Oh, my. I believe I know."

Simon scowled, his eyes dark. "Aye. The one left behind, the one who did not pass into the mountain. I am that boy."

Pieter searched the old man's face. Until she asked, he had left himself out of the tale. But everything in the story turned on the Last Child.

"So, now you know that this old man is a part of the tale," said Simon.

It had grown dark in the valley. The moon crept beyond the rim of the canyon, leaving only the meager glow of the stars. Pieter pulled the blanket tighter. He knew the next part of the story, and he dreaded it.

Simon ran a spotted hand through his white hair. "And Pieter is in this story as well. For a number of reasons," he said, "I am convinced that Pieter is the child foretold in the Piper's Song."

"That makes sense," said Gretchen. "After all, the sheep did follow you on the hillside."

Already she was taking Simon's side. He didn't need both of them goading him about the Pied Piper. Pieter scowled at her. "That doesn't make me a piper."

She shrugged. "Yet, here you are, following Simon on his quest."

"I had nowhere else to go."

"Is that it?" she said.

"Stop this," snapped Pieter. "Don't you join Simon with this Pied Piper nonsense. It's only an old song."

"Is it?" She gestured to the vale. "It has brought us to all this. Tell me this valley is nonsense."

Pieter leaned closer to her, until they were face to face. "I told you that none of this makes me a piper." He paused and swallowed hard. "And no, this valley is not nonsense. It is full of something quite strange and potent, yes. But whether for good or ill, we know not."

She grunted. "You may not know, but I do. This valley is a magical place. I think you just choose not to accept it."

Pieter wanted to grab her and give her a shake. He clenched his fists in his lap. "I'll tell you what I *choose*, shepherd girl. I choose to escape Hamelin. That's all."

"And it appears you are still trying to escape—escape who you are."

"I have escaped my father and his knife. I suppose I chose that as well?"

Gretchen waved a tired hand in his direction. "Of course not. Let's leave this. I grow weary."

Weary of me? Is that it? Pieter held his tongue. What was happening? Not only did Simon favor her over him, but now he had two people believing that he was the child in the Piper's song.

Why had Simon remained quiet during their argument? His silence made Pieter feel quite alone. He wished Silverfoot were closer, near enough that she could curl next to him as he slept, although it was a rather shocking notion. A wolf sleeping next to a boy? Impossible.

The night pulsed with questions and uncertainty. The wool blanket around his shoulders itched his neck. The coarse fibers thrust Pieter's memories back to Hamelin. How often he had wrapped Agnes in such a blanket and sat holding her, humming and singing.

A wave of sorrow swept through him and made the little spat with Gretchen seem rather trifling. How he wished he could rock Agnes now. How much better it would have been if he'd left Hamelin with her and their mother.

Thinking of Agnes brought to mind the little lullabies he had sung to her. He caught himself starting to hum, then stopped abruptly.

I don't have to stop, he reminded himself. *This isn't Hamelin. I can hum and sing all I want.* But would music forever be wrapped up in fear?

He pushed that notion away and thought again of his sister. It had been, what, two weeks? How big was she by now? Babies grew so fast. Was she crawling? He hummed a soft lullaby. The humming changed to singing—lyrics of love that brought him closer to her though separated by so many miles.

Oh, sweet little bairn,
Tucked safe in my arms,
With eyes of deep wonder,
And laughter that charms.

Oh, come, my sweet Agnes,
The sun's going down,
Soft shadows your bunting,
Warm darkness your gown.

Now sleep, little Agnes,
Just close your wee eyes.
Soft slumber enfold you,
'Til soon the sun rise.

So sleep, precious Agnes,
So warm in my arm,
I'll always watch over,
And keep out all harm.

"Lovely," said Simon softly. "The wee bairn must miss you terribly."

"Perhaps." Pieter's eyes misted. "I broke my promise to her."

A rustling noise in the dark startled them. Pieter peered into the blackness until his eyes ached, but he could see nothing. It wasn't Silverfoot; she was a creature of the wild, and this place was a garden. She no doubt waited somewhere along the rim.

Simon shrugged and stretched out on the grass, wrapped in his blanket. Despite their fight, Gretchen gave Pieter a nod and a small smile before she followed suit.

Pieter stared into the sky. The rustling did not return; the only sound in the vale was a symphony of crickets and the occasional call of an owl. And yes, the far-off howl of a wolf. *My wolf.*

In this strange, lovely valley, Pieter slipped into a deep and restful sleep, in spite of all his fears. When he awoke, it was still dark. He sensed, however, that it was near to dawn. In fact, as he gazed into the blackness, he realized there was enough grey light to make the trees and flowers visible.

He turned on his side and stared in the direction of the hedge. Little by little the purple bramble emerged as dim light spread in the valley.

With a cry, he scrambled to his feet.

A path had opened up in the night.

Chapter 22

Pieter's cry brought Simon and Gretchen stumbling to their feet.

"It opened!" said Gretchen, her face full of joy.

With a happy squeal, Rosie moved closer, as though eager to move through the portal.

"How could this be?" Pieter said. He stood torn between his desire to rush down the path and the fear that roiled in his belly.

Gretchen took two long strides in, then looked back. "Come! This opened for us."

"Are you sure?" said Pieter. *She keeps rushing into things. I can hardly keep up.* His jaw tightened. *Why can't I be brash like that?*

But Rosie gave a great cry of joy and plunged through, past Gretchen. Pieter shrugged. Without bothering to pack their things, the trio followed the excited donkey.

The path ran straight, with the tangle of foliage forming a dark arch over their heads. Dim morning light filtered through the purple leaves and lit their way.

Rosie had been more than happy to race ahead, but Pieter had to force himself to take each step. Simon and Gretchen followed, as though this was something Pieter had to lead.

His back went cold as a deep shiver ran down his spine. Why was he so frightened? It wasn't because of childish stories about a giant. No, it was more like some terrible truth lay at the end of this tunnel, something that would somehow bind him.

After about a hundred paces, they emerged into a clearing, where Rosie munched on lush grass. A log house stood against the cliff, huge and sturdy. On the front porch waited an enormous man.

Not a giant perhaps, but certainly taller than any man Pieter had ever seen. And wide! His massive shoulders and thick muscular arms ended in enormous hands. One could have covered Rosie's head. Once Pieter took in how big he was, his eyes were drawn to the man's face, a face that was somehow...not right.

A slack mouth hung under a wide nose that looked to have been broken in the past. His thick black hair stuck out in clumps and tufts, as though it had never been washed or combed. But it was his eyes that discomforted the most. Squinty grey eyes that angled toward his nose, with crinkled skin at the outside corners. Eyes that gazed at nothing for more than a moment. And he was rocking, his fingers fluttering, his eyes shifting, shifting, shifting. Rocking, rocking, a mindless, eternal rhythm.

"Here they are," he crooned in a high squeaky voice. "Here...here they are...the Last Child comes...at last, at last, at last."

He had not yet looked directly at any of them.

"Yes...yes, yes...the Last Child comes." Rocking, fluttering fingers, shifting eyes.

"He's addled," said Gretchen in a loud whisper.

And yet, he had called Simon the Last Child. How could he possibly know that?

"Addled..." said the man. "Oh, yes...addled. Keeper is wonderfully addled." Rocking, fingers fluttering. Pieter noticed black stains on the tips of the fingers and thumb of his left hand.

The man swung his massive head toward Pieter, who backed away. "And the Piper!" said the man. "The Piper is here...the Piper at last."

Pieter gaped at the huge man, whose grey eyes held him for a moment, then slid away. He could scarcely grasp what the man had said. "Wh—what did you call me?"

"Piper...of course. At last, at last."

"I'm *not* a piper," said Pieter, his fear now mixed with anger. "I have no pipe."

"No, no...not yet. Someday...follow the song...someday."

"Never!" cried Pieter. "I am a singer." After fighting about this with Simon and Gretchen, having this strange man broach the subject of the Piper—it was almost enough to make him want to turn and flee.

"Yes...yes," said the huge man. "That you are. Your song... your lullaby...it opened the hedge... Opened, opened it up."

Keeper took a long stride from the porch, so suddenly they all took a step back. Pieter guessed he towered well over seven feet. But still he rocked, and his fingers continued their odd patterns in the air. A sleeveless brown tunic covered his massive torso and fell to his knees. Thick black hair curled on his arms and legs, but his face was as smooth as a baby's.

He looked directly at Gretchen. His rocking stopped. "A gift!" he cried. "A surprise...a gift! We...are blessed!" He danced about, waving his hands in the air.

Gretchen? A gift? Pieter snorted. He pulled on Simon's sleeve. "Let's leave now," he whispered. "He's going to hurt someone."

"Nonsense," said Gretchen, with a big grin. "He's part of this. Besides, look." She pointed behind them. The path through the brambles had closed.

Rosie let out an enthusiastic bray that echoed off the canyon walls. Keeper squealed in delight and rushed toward her, crying, "Horsie! You brought a horsie!"

He bent over and engulfed Rosie's head and neck in a crushing hug that the old grey donkey clearly loved.

Simon walked up to the man and introduced himself. "I'm Simon."

"Of course you are. You came. The Last Child is here... at last." He released his grip on Rosie and gave Simon an embrace only slightly less massive. "And I'm Keeper. That's all. Just Keeper."

"But what is it you keep?" asked Gretchen.

"I thought you knew. Don't you know?" He put one hand beside his mouth and in a hushed voice said, "Songs."

"What songs?" asked Pieter, his voice matching Keeper's secretive whisper.

Keeper scowled, as though losing patience with their dim-witted questions. He waved his arms and fluttered his thick fingers in the air. "All of them, of course."

Chapter 23

Keeper grinned at Pieter. "I keep your songs, too...have them all. 'Cept last night's lullaby. No time yet, but soon... soon I write it down."

"I've never met you. How could you know any of my songs?"

Keeper looked away, fingertips tapping under his chin. "I just...I just hear them." He shrugged. "Don't know how...I just do. Hear them and keep them, keep them and hear them. That's why I'm Keeper... That's what I do."

"How?" said Pieter, full of doubt.

"In here," he said, pointing to his temple. "Then here," and he pantomimed writing. That explained the ink-stained fingers.

"Could you show us?" Gretchen asked.

"Yes! Yes!" he cried, jumping up and down like a toddler. "But first...we're hungry! Time for breakfast!" He rubbed his belly and trotted toward the house.

They all looked at each other, uncertain whether to follow. Before they could decide, he reappeared with a tray laden with fresh fruit and small loaves of bread. "Ready all night...hedge opened but they didn't come."

They sat on the grass and enjoyed fat green grapes, sliced apples with purple skin, and some sort of orange melon Pieter had never tasted before. And the bread! Not black and hard, but light and tender and moist. His concerns about Keeper had not vanished, but Pieter found himself relaxing his guard in spite of himself.

Given the man's size, one would have expected Keeper to eat voraciously, but he only nibbled on a slice of apple.

"Done?" he said at last. "Done? Come in!" He sprang to his feet surprisingly quickly for such a large man. "Come, Last Child. Come, Piper. And you, sweet Gift...come into my house."

Pieter stepped onto the enormous porch, then froze. Keeper led Simon and Gretchen through a door high and wide enough for a horse to enter.

Gretchen turned back and frowned. "Are you coming?"

Something near to panic gripped him. This was worse than walking through the hedge, but akin to it, as if with one step into Keeper's house, many paths would be closed to him.

Nay! he told himself. *I am walking into a house, nothing more. This changes nothing.* With three quick steps he was through the doorway.

Pieter expected to see a cabin much like Tracker's—tools, plain sturdy furniture, central fire pit. But once his eyes adjusted to the dim interior, the first thing he noticed was that the entire room was crammed full of parchments. Tall piles on the floor. Scrolls thrust onto shelves at odd angles. So many that the only way to move about was on paths between stacks of parchment. The house smelled of musty paper, ink, and firewood, mingled with the aroma of fresh-baked bread.

One path led back to a little kitchen area, the only place free of piles that Pieter could see. Another led to a high table on one side that held a brass pot of ink and an assortment of quills, some black, others white, and one a bright red.

The third path wound to an open space that Pieter could not see into but suspected was Keeper's bed. Near the fireplace in the kitchen sat an enormous chair made of dark ebony wood, and still more parchments tottered on the seat.

Keeper pointed to a bench at the side of the doorway. "Sit! Sit!" He shuffled down the trail to the chair and snatched the top few parchments. "Here! Here!" he cried, rushing back. He held them out to Pieter. "Look!"

When Pieter saw the top parchment, he gasped. The title, inked in clear, well-formed script, was "Elegy for a Lost Mother." It was word for word the song he had sung the day they buried Gretchen's mother.

"This song is mine," he said, looking up. "Gretchen, I sang this for your mother. No one has heard it but the three of us."

Pieter looked through the pile. "And my donkey song! And here's the one about the rain."

Gretchen peered over his shoulder. "It's true." She looked up at Keeper, her brow furrowed.

The man grinned back, delight shining in his tilted grey eyes.

"And all these others?" asked Simon, waving his hand toward the piles. "They're all songs?"

"Songs! Yes...oh, yes."

Simon pursed his lips. "I recall one I heard in Hannover once—'The Ballad of the Ninth Star?'"

Keeper nodded eagerly and worked his way down the path that led toward the kitchen. He paused at a stack, reached partway down, and snatched out a parchment.

He proceeded farther along and removed another from near the bottom. The stack wobbled, but Keeper shifted it a bit and returned to Simon.

"Version by Theodus of Portishead," he said, holding up the first one, sticking out a broad, fissured tongue. He shook his head vigorously, sending spittle flying. "Bad." He dropped the parchment on the thick-planked floor and held out the second. "This one older...but better. Look at this one."

Simon took it and Pieter peered over his shoulder. Below each line of words ran a series of small marks, some placed higher on the parchment, others lower. He squinted a moment, then said, "See these squares? I think they show the melody. They are placed higher and lower as you go along. That matches the tune."

Simon examined it. "I believe you're right. That's brilliant."

"Yes," agreed Pieter. "Anyone who knows the code can sing the tune. Keeper, did you think of this?"

Keeper squinted. "Think of it? No, not think of it. Just know."

Pieter hummed under his breath, running a finger along the line of squares. He broke into song. Before he knew it, he had sung the entire ballad.

"Oh, my," exclaimed Keeper, clapping and dancing in a circle. "The Piper sings! The singer pipes!"

Pieter started to correct him, but decided it would do no good.

"Next," exclaimed Keeper. "One for the girl...from the Lady."

Before they could ask him to explain, he returned with another parchment. It was entitled "The Lady of the Lays." Pieter read over the lyrics, a lovely ballad about an old woman who sang and lived in a strange tower. But why was this one for Gretchen?

By late afternoon, Pieter had read and sung dozens of songs. No one had given lunch a thought.

Finding the portal open again, Gretchen took Rosie back and returned with their packs and baggage. She brought her lute into the house. "I think I can match the squares with the strings on my lute. At least, I'm going to try."

When not fetching more manuscripts, Keeper rattled around in the kitchen. To everyone's delight, he produced a delicious supper of more fresh bread and a red pottage, thick with carrots, turnips and onions. They continued their music throughout the evening until the fire died low and Pieter's voice began to wear.

"I think that's enough for my fingers," said Gretchen, shaking her hands. She had figured out the pattern of notes on the parchments and how they connected to the strings of her instrument.

"Oh, no! Sleep!" cried Keeper. "Where? Where to sleep?" He looked around, worry creasing his round face. "Ah, girl gets my bed. Come! Come!" He led her down an aisle away from the fireplace.

Gretchen crept over and glanced down. Pieter followed and saw a tangle of worn blankets knotted on the floor.

Keeper dropped to his knees, yanking at the blankets. "Just tidy up a bit. There we go."

"Uh, that's kind of you, but I think I'd like to sleep under the stars," said Gretchen. "I have a bedroll."

"And the night is warm," added Simon quickly. "It will be most pleasant out there in front of your house."

Long after they had spread their bedrolls on the lawn and retired for the night, Pieter lay on his back, staring again at the crooked band of stars scattered from black cliff top to black cliff top.

An urgent voice pressed into his mind. At the same moment, a howl echoed over the vale. But the howl wasn't in anger or fear. It was as though she were calling to a friend, eager to keep contact.

Easy, friend Silverfoot, thought Pieter. *We are safe here.* He gazed toward the line of the cliff. For an instant, he thought he saw her silhouette against the night sky. He squinted, but the shadow had vanished. *Stay nearby. For now, I must remain here and sing.*

The howl came again, not urgent, but louder than all the rest, as though she were assuring him that she understood. It brought Simon's head up. He gazed around, then fell back to sleep. Gretchen stirred and rolled over.

Pieter lay for some time enjoying the wolf's song, as it grew softer and more distant.

Keeper had so many songs. As many as the stars, it seemed. He had pulled out tune after tune, and each time it had been perfect for Pieter's voice. And he had loved every one.

He smiled. If anyone tidied up or organized all that parchment, Keeper would probably never find anything again.

Pieter ran over some lyrics in his mind. To his surprise, he remembered all the words. His mind jumped from song to song. It was true of them all. With that one session, he somehow had learned the words and the melody to each one.

It had been a perfect evening. Except for the fact that Keeper insisted on calling him the same irksome thing.

Piper.

Chapter 24

The days in Harmony Vale flew by, full of music and sunshine and good food. Pieter and Gretchen learned scores of songs—rollicking folk songs, merry jigs, somber lays. He continued to find that, once he sang a tune, he had it tucked away in his memory. His repertoire grew by the hour.

And Gretchen seemed just as skilled at retaining the lute notes. Like him, she was immersed in the music. They got along much better when they were creating music. At meals and other quiet times, he found himself still resenting her presence, but, in truth, it was hard to carry any ill will while in Harmony Vale.

When Keeper wasn't fetching a parchment, he sat writing at his enormous oak table. For hours at a time, his quill scratched across the paper with no sign of fatigue, the white feather dancing across the page. When the thick black ink had dried, he took it to a stack somewhere in the house and laid it tenderly on top.

On the fifth day, Simon appeared rather subdued. "Keeper," he said, pushing his porridge bowl away. "There's a song I need."

The giant's face sagged. "Yes...yes...Keeper has it. Knew...knew you would ask."

Pieter and Gretchen exchanged puzzled glances.

Simon let out a long breath, as though he dreaded what he might discover. "Some sixty years ago..."

"Keeper knows..." His chin trembled. "Keeper knows. The Pied Piper...he came here...often came here."

"He came here?" exclaimed Pieter. "He's been to Harmony Vale?"

Keeper ran a shaking hand through his tangle of black hair. "But he is lost now...no more songs from the Pied Piper."

"I see," said Simon. "Before he dealt with the rats in Hamelin, the Pied Piper sang a—"

Keeper cut him off with a wave of his hand. He shuffled to a shelf and pulled out a scroll without looking. "I wrote it down...long time ago... Knew...knew you'd come... Someday... Hoped you wouldn't ask, though." He shrugged, handing it to Simon. "Don't know why."

Pieter realized which song Simon had asked for. How old *was* Keeper? The Piper had sung it sixty years ago. So Keeper was...older than Simon, it seemed, although one would never guess by looking at him.

Fingers fluttering, Keeper stood and rocked back and forth on his heels. Simon cleared a space on the table and unrolled the scroll. Next to it he spread the parchment they had carried from Hamelin.

No one talked as Simon compared the two manuscripts, line by line, word by word. Finally, he leaned back. "Brother Lawrence did very well. He recorded it without a single error."

Pieter peered over his shoulder. "Look! I had the melody right. Exactly the same as the squares."

Simon looked up. "Of course." He sighed again. "Keeper, my friend. It is time for us to leave."

Tears filled Keeper's eyes. "Keeper knows... Ask for the Piper's Riddle Song, then you go. Can't be helped...can't."

Dread filled Pieter's chest. His idyllic time in Harmony Vale was at an end. At that moment, he cared little about the Pied Piper's song. He simply wanted to make music. He didn't want to leave Keeper, even with his piper talk. All he wanted was to stay with him.

"Tomorrow, then," said Simon, and he turned away.

As they climbed out of Harmony Vale the next morning, a light rain began to fall. Keeper's final words had been, "Piper...Keeper will see you again. Later...later...I will see you once more."

Yes, I shall return, thought Pieter, trudging up the steep trail. He took a last breath of the clean air of Harmony Vale, the scent of eternal spring.

But it will be Pieter *who returns. Pieter the* Singer, *not the Piper.*

Chapter 25

The weather turned nasty again, but aside from the rain and wind, the trip to Verden proved uneventful. Gretchen fussed about her lute, even though Keeper had scrounged around and found a piece of oiled leather to wrap it in. "For the Gifted One...a gift," he had said.

The only one who seemed glad for them to be leaving was Silverfoot. She scampered along, out of sight but closer than she'd ever been before.

Now that they had left Harmony Vale, Pieter found his irritation with Gretchen growing again. He knew it made no sense. They had created music together with no difficulty. So why was he angry with her? Nothing had happened to cause these feelings. It was just that...that he felt like a milksop alongside her.

Sting it, she was so strong. She had protected her sheep and killed the wild dog without hesitation. She kept dashing ahead when he held back. And he...well, acted like such a weakling in comparison.

The donkey frisked along, sending dirty water and globs of oozing brown mud flying with every step. She threw back her head and let out a joyous bray. "Rosie!" cried Pieter, as though his irritation were her fault. "Will you stop that splashing?"

Gretchen laughed. "That donkey is like a toddler playing in the mud."

Yes, thought Pieter. *Agnes would delight in this muddy mess.* But she would never have a chance to do it. Mother would never allow it. Once, when he was little, he had played with boats in a gutter. In fairness, it hadn't been Mother his play had angered. Father had wrenched him up by one arm, but he had no notion why he cared whether Pieter was dirty or not. His cheek tingled at the memory. He had been no more than three, but he recalled the slap clearly.

Now Pieter had abandoned little Agnes. What was happening with her? Who was shielding her from Father? *I never should have left her.* His jaw tightened. *Despite Father, I will return. I don't know how, but I swear I will protect her once again.*

Pieter moved closer to take Rosie's halter. Her playfulness spent, she fell into her usual plodding pace. Silverfoot continued to lope along, and her presence in his mind heartened him. He didn't know how she traveled through an area with farms and stone walls and villages filled with people. *Be stealthy. Don't be seen,* he thought to her.

Always, came the answer.

They began to see more travelers on the road, most also heading toward Verden. A farmer passed them, his wagon piled high with turnips. A family traveled ahead of them, the father pushing a grey wooden barrow loaded with chairs and benches. A baby was perched on top, wrapped in thin leather against the rain.

As Pieter walked past them, he gazed at the baby as long as he could. She was about the same age as Agnes. He glanced at the mother, hunched on the bench. Did she sing to the baby? Did she hold her when she was upset?

Oh, Agnes. I'm so sorry that I left you behind. I had to. I didn't want to, but I had to. He longed to wrap her in a blanket, snug in his loft. He wondered if that would ever happen again.

Later in the afternoon, a tinker overtook them, his wagon painted red and blue, with yellow wheels. Simon looked at it fondly. "Oskar's was all yellow," he told them. "But the brightest, sunniest yellow you ever saw. I repainted it many a time. I wanted to use some new colors, but he insisted on yellow."

"That must have looked quite merry," said Gretchen.

"Aye. It was mostly to get people's attention. 'People watch for the yellow wagon,' Oskar had said. 'And they know it's Oskar.' After that many paintings, I'm surprised I don't *still* have yellow paint in my hair."

In the afternoon they approached a narrow stone bridge. "Here we cross the Weser," said Simon. "We're drawing near to Verden at last."

The Weser flowed thick and brown under the span. The floor of the bridge was laid with flat stones that gave good traction, even when wet. It seemed as though the moment they crossed, the rain worsened. The muddy road ran straight to the northeast.

Late in the afternoon, Pieter pointed through the grey curtain of the downpour. "Look! I see buildings."

"Aye, that would be Verden," said Simon.

"Where's the other river?" asked Gretchen. "The Aller, is it?"

"The Aller runs right through the center of town. We won't cross it today."

"Why not?"

"Because we're stopping at an inn just inside the gates."

An inn! The Tong and Anvil had a few rooms to let, but no one thought of it as an actual inn. The rain dripped off Pieter's hood onto his face. Mayhap a bed tonight? And a meal, hot and tasty, with *meat*?

"It's a good inn," said Simon. "I've stopped there often over the years. Besides, I think it's time to unveil the musical team of Pieter and Gretchen."

"What?" asked Pieter. "What are you talking about?"

"I think he means you and I should perform together," said Gretchen.

"You mean...sing?" asked Pieter, his voice rising. "In front of people?"

"Well," said Simon with a smile, "it wouldn't hurt to have a bit of extra coin, now would it?"

Gretchen snorted. "No one's going to part with their money to hear two younglings make music."

"You don't know until you try," said Simon, wiping rainwater from his forehead.

Pieter glanced over at Gretchen, who frowned. She shrugged. "We might as well. It can't be worse than gutting a sheep."

Pieter wasn't so sure. He had hoped she would give him an excuse to back out. But if the shepherd girl was brave enough to do it, he couldn't very well refuse.

"Besides," said Gretchen, wringing water from her hair, "it might even be dry in there."

"To be sure," said Simon. "The Square Pig is as fine an inn as you could find."

"The Square Pig?" asked Gretchen.

"Aye, I have no idea where it comes from, but it's an easy name to remember."

The buildings of Verden, a streaked grey through the pouring rain, rose higher than any in Hamelin. As they entered, they came to a street that had been churned into brown muck by hooves and boots, creating the stench of manure mixed with mud and refuse. As in Hamelin, it seemed the town of Verden emptied their chamber pots right into the street.

Everything about Verden was big—the three—and even four—story houses, the wide streets which had changed to cobblestone. Through the rainfall, he caught a glimpse of the white spire of a cathedral. As they trudged their way down the ruined street, Pieter stopped, catching a strange sound. It was an off-key song warbled by a woman behind the closed green shutters of a house.

Pieter found himself smiling. In Verden a goodwife could *sing* as she did her work, with no fear at all. Perhaps this town was a place that would suit him, after all.

Chapter 25

As they neared the center of town, Rosie seemed to love the cobblestones, making the loudest possible *clip-clop* she could muster.

Like everything else in the town, The Square Pig proved larger and more imposing than The Tong and Anvil back in Hamelin. The rain battered a large sign that showed a huge pink pig that was, indeed, square. The red letters showed even through the rain.

"Around the back," said Simon, gesturing. "Rosie comes first."

As Simon led the donkey into the stable, she jerked on the reins, pulling toward a tub of drinking water. "Right, old girl," said the old man, leading her over. "Water first, eh? Don't blame you."

By the time Rosie was settled in the spacious barn, dark shadows filled the yard. They hurried back to the front door and stumbled in out of the downpour.

The main room could have held Hamelin's inn twice. The air smelled of roasting meats and fresh reeds on the floor, as well as ale and unwashed men. Huge fireplaces anchored each end of the room, both roaring with yellow and orange flames.

Pieter stared. "It's not The Tong and Anvil, is it?"

"Sam does his best," said Simon, "but The Tong and Anvil tends to be like the rest of Hamelin. Dreary and dying."

Near the north fire sat a man dressed in a green velvet tunic. Across the table sat another man in a flowing black cloak. Nearby, a soldier in a red-and-white uniform peered out from a dark corner. The only other customer was a rotund monk, sitting with his back to them.

Behind the polished bar stood a dark, robust woman wearing a low-cut frilly blue dress, white apron, and cap. A warm smiled glowed in her ruddy face. "Well, here's a strange company come to our humble inn. Do you need a room, my friends?"

"Might be," said Simon. "Is Big Baldric about?"

She turned and bellowed, "Big Baldric! Ragged old man to see you!"

A short man, not even as tall as Pieter, appeared from the back. He looked almost skeletal, with thin arms and a narrow frame. *And this was Big Baldric?* His wrinkled face was topped with a shock of grey hair. He wore all white, except for the stains on his apron. He peered at Simon. "Old man?" he squeaked. "I'm older than he is."

He reached the bar, and his height rose about a foot as he stepped up on a box or a rail. He grinned at Simon, displaying an impressive set of crooked yellow teeth. "So, young fellow, how are things in Hamelin?"

"Dull as King Edward's wit," said Simon. "I had to come to Verden for some excitement. And, of course, for some music."

"You're in luck, old friend," said Baldric, leaning forward, his elbows on the bar. "We have a minstrel tonight from Portishead. Have you heard Theodus?"

Pieter had heard that name somewhere, but he couldn't remember where.

Simon grunted. "Too many times. Is that all you have?"

"All? The man—"

"The man doesn't know a melody from a pig fart." Simon crossed his arms. "Lucky for you, I'm here to save your business."

Big Baldric scowled. "What are you talking about?"

"I'm talking about the Minden Twins here." He waved toward Pieter and Gretchen.

"But we're not—" Pieter began.

Gretchen elbowed him and broke in. "—not busy tonight."

The innkeeper studied them, his eyes shifting back and forth. "They sure don't look like twins, Simon."

"I take after our mother," said Gretchen. "Sadly, Pieter here looks more like our Uncle Jack from Ufflington, who didn't look that great even before he got hit in the face with a shield fighting the Danes."

"Watch your tongue, uh, sister," Pieter growled.

Baldric grunted. "I don't much care if they're twins or not. But I got no need for any youngsters squeaking out songs. If I wanted bad music, I could sing myself. Now take a seat by the fireplace and warm yourselves. You look like you need a bite to eat. Mary Helen?"

The woman waved and disappeared into the back.

Simon found them a table against the wall, not far from the fireplace at the near end.

"Well, do you have any other ideas for the 'Minden Twins?'" asked Gretchen, scorn in her voice.

"Do you like the name? We passed through Minden, so Minden was the first name that occurred to me. Do not worry yourself, lass," said Simon. "Big Baldric is quite curious just now. You'll be making music before the night's over."

The food arrived in bread trenchers, something Pieter had never seen. Mary Helen also set down tankards for all three of them.

Pieter leaned forward and sniffed. "Cider?"

"Aye, but fresh," said Mary Helen, her voice filling the room. "Can't have you snookered when you're singing, eh?" She winked and scurried away.

Well, *she* seemed to think they would perform tonight. As they ate, Pieter again noticed the monk, who they now faced. It was difficult to guess his age—maybe late thirties, but his brown robes had seen plenty of wear. Dirt and grease spotted his ample belly. The reddish fringe of hair around his pate, badly in need of trimming, had been plastered down and shone with oil.

His soft, round face and multiple chins suggested that any vows of poverty did not include food. In fact, the monk stuffed a huge slice of meat into his mouth, even as he eyed Pieter with dancing blue eyes.

Pieter looked away, uncomfortable under the monk's gaze. He continued his meal, but he couldn't keep from glancing at the man. Each time, the monk was regarding him.

Big Baldric came by and leaned over Simon's shoulder. "Maybe one song," he said before he moved on. Simon nodded with a satisfied smile.

The Square Pig had begun to fill. Men bristling with weapons, but also craftsmen and farmers. Pieter started when a thick-chested man in a leather apron entered, no doubt a Verden blacksmith. Pieter couldn't stop himself from shuddering; the man looked too much like his father.

Unlike in Hamelin, many richly dressed villagers, in their velvets and brocades, also joined the crowd. The congenial noise of conversation and laughter took over the room. Pieter's thoughts turned to what was coming—he was going to *sing* in front of all these people. The very thought clogged his windpipe with phlegm. He found himself continually clearing his throat and swallowing, despite a dry mouth.

Why had Gretchen forced him into this? Why did she agree without even asking him? He could see no way out and wished he hadn't eaten so much, for the meal sat heavy in his stomach.

Chapter 26

A noise at the door drew Pieter's attention. A couple of boys carried in fancy wooden boxes, but all eyes were on the flamboyant man in a red brocade cape who entered after them. Slender, with long fingers and a narrow face, it had to be the minstrel.

Perhaps in his thirties, his black, oiled beard came to a perfect point over his thin chest. He paraded to the front, moving as though he expected accolades to come his way. Indeed, an odd hush fell on the room, one full of anticipation.

"Theodus of Portishead himself," whispered Simon. "This should be interesting."

Pieter understood Simon's antagonism. There was something about the man's manner and the way the two boys scurried that stuck in Pieter's craw. The assistants spread a blue rug on the floor and over one of the boxes. An ornate stool made of dark polished wood appeared. One boy reverently lifted a green velvet wrap from a box.

Had Keeper mentioned this Theodus?

With a flourish, Theodus removed his outer cloak, revealing a purple velvet tunic stitched with intricate designs in gold thread. Then slowly, with drama in his every movement, the minstrel unfolded the velvet and held up an instrument.

A harp! Pieter had never seen one, but it had to be a harp. The rich brown wood was intricately carved with flowers and vines, with the head of a maiden at the top, all inlaid in gold. Pieter hadn't known an instrument could be so beautiful.

Pieter leaned toward Simon. "How can we—"

"Shhhh," Gretchen hissed. "I want to hear this."

He gave her a hard look, then settled back to listen.

The minstrel enthroned himself on the stool, then placed the harp just so on his lap. With a regal smile, he held his fingers poised next to the strings. There was not a sound in the room; even the kitchen was quiet. Pieter realized he was holding his breath.

The man's slender fingers moved at last, and the strings hummed.

Pieter winced. Something was wrong. The tones were not true, although Pieter could not say why. Gretchen shook her head and snorted under her breath. "His harp's not right," she said in a loud whisper. "He didn't tune it before he started."

Simon nodded, a small smile on his face.

The minstrel looked about and his glare landed directly on Pieter. Or was it Simon? Simon crossed his arms and returned the glower.

"Tonight," said Theodus, "I shall present much fine music. Those who have no appreciation of such should leave right now."

Pieter's face grew warm, but one glance at Simon and Gretchen and he knew nothing would persuade them to leave.

"Not bloody likely," said Simon under his breath.

The minstrel shrugged, as though to say, "What can you do about such fools?"

Simon and Theodus know each other, thought Pieter. *And they are not friends.*

Apparently satisfied that he had made his point, Theodus turned his gaze to the audience. He began a ballad, in a voice at least more pleasant than the harp.

He sang well enough, but there was no...no what? Pieter couldn't think of the word. All he knew was that he cared little for what he heard. It was so different from listening to Gretchen play the lute.

The song was not one that he had learned in Harmony Vale. The story in the ballad intrigued him, but he knew he would sing it differently. The patrons of The Square Pig gave the minstrel an enthusiastic ovation. Pieter watched Theodus—the way his smile flashed, how he bowed as though he expected a rousing response. As though he had gifted these mere peasants with his very presence.

He sang two more ballads, each worse than the first. Pieter's mind worked on two levels at once, absorbing the story and the tune in the ballad, and at the same time critiquing the performance.

Then Theodus spoke, his voice rich and commanding. "I have created a new ballad," he announced. "The fine folk of Verden will be the very first to hear it performed." He paused to allow the crowd to murmur their amazement.

Pieter leaned forward in expectation, and in that moment he caught the gaze of the monk. To his surprise, the man gave him a fat wink.

"This ballad," said Theodus—another pause and he looked directly at Simon, "is the Tale of the Pied Piper."

Simon stiffened in his chair. "Son of the devil."

Pieter went cold. The Pied Piper?

He peered at Simon's face, watched his eyes harden. *I was right. Simon abhors this man,* Pieter thought. *And Theodus of Portishead knows his story.*

Theodus strummed the harp and began. The melody meandered from one pitch to another. The words scarcely fit the tune, when there *was* a tune. But, however poorly rendered, the words pricked like a needle.

Two lines of his song burned into Pieter's mind:

Eyes pale and sharp as shards of ice,
The Piper demanded they pay the price.

The image of those eyes sent a cold shudder down Pieter's spine. Oddly, the description fit the eyes of the minstrel just as well.

When the minstrel finished, the patrons applauded, but the room seemed ill at ease. The song had troubled them, and Pieter could see why. It made the folk of Hamelin look like idiots. The Pied Piper was portrayed as evil, as always. In a strange way, the ballad suggested that music itself was wicked. But worst of all, it made out the last child of the story to be a coward. He didn't venture a look at Simon, but he could sense the tautness in the man's body.

The minstrel sang another song, but Pieter scarcely listened. The man's Piper story buzzed in his head. It wasn't right. Of course, the story had become folklore, so Theodus could add what he wished and leave out whatever he fancied. But there was one thing Pieter knew beyond a doubt. The true story of the Pied Piper had yet to be told.

Chapter 27

Pieter was startled from his thoughts by Big Baldric stepping to the dais. Theodus had finished and his assistants were rolling up the rug. Seeing Baldric, Pieter remembered in a rush what was coming next. Sweat trickled down his neck as Baldric addressed the restless crowd. "And now, from, uh, from a distant town, The Square Pig introduces the Minden Twins!"

To his horror, Pieter realized he and Gretchen had planned nothing, had not even discussed what song to do.

Simon pulled them close, one on each side. "Forget all these people. Make music for yourselves. And for one old man."

Gretchen grinned at that. Picking up her lute, she strode onto the stage and placed herself on a rustic stool that had replaced the minstrel's fine one.

As Pieter followed, she bent over the instrument, turning the pegs and listening intently to the pitch of each string. She looked up and nodded at Pieter.

The many faces seemed but a blur. By then the sweat had spread down his back and into his small clothes. His throat was as dry as his back was wet. He could not think of a single note. Not a word nor melody came to mind.

The patrons of The Square Pig sat stone-faced. Then one face came into focus—Theodus, who stood in the back against the wall, a mocking smile on his gaunt face. How could Pieter sing with that man leering at him? He was on the verge of dashing from the room.

Make music for yourselves. And one old man.

Gretchen struck the first chord on her lute. She began a lay they had learned at Keeper's. Her playing laved away most of his fear and, little by little, replaced it with the song he wanted to sing.

The crowd had vanished. The minstrel's face had disappeared. There was only the song, only the music.

For a while longer, Pieter floated on Gretchen's chords, recognizing the ballad from their time at Keeper's. Then the perfect measure came and he began to sing.

The song burst forth with such force he could not have kept it in if he had wanted to. The lute and his voice became one, and even though it was about some ancient battle, it came from his heart.

When it ended, the crowd exploded into cheers and shouts. Some banged the tabletops. Others stood, applauding vigorously. Again an urgent need to flee overwhelmed Pieter, but a single note plucked on the lute held him. The room stilled in an instant.

When she played the second and third notes, establishing a minor key, Pieter knew it was "Farewell to the Light," a song he and Gretchen had created one night in Harmony Vale. On the fifth note, he entered.

I search for what I fear to find.
I search for what I know will bind.

The song ended with the room in silence. Pieter gazed at the faces, seeing no response. Had it been so terrible? He stumbled off the dais and threw himself into the chair next to Simon. His head dropped on the old man's shoulder.

A gentle hand touched his head. "Lad," said Simon softly. "You misunderstand. Lift your head and look about."

With effort Pieter obeyed. He saw in the people's faces not coldness, but something between awe and sorrow. Was it possible? Had they lost themselves in the music, just as he and Gretchen had? He hadn't known that could happen.

If so, this was why you gave yourself to music. To bring others with you on the journey.

Of all the faces, the monk's stood out. His face glistened, his eyes almost puffed closed. Damp trails ran over his round cheeks.

Gretchen sat next to Pieter, clutching his arm. "They... they didn't clap or anything. What happened?"

Simon smiled. "Why, I do believe you have won your audience."

At that, timid applause began, then built little by little into a tumultuous ovation.

Big Baldric rushed to the table, a huge smile splitting his thin face. "Oh, my. By the Saints, your music was angelic." He dragged a chair to the table and sat across from them. "I can offer three marks a night for, shall we say, a week's trial?"

Simon folded his arms across his chest. "For angels? I think three for each of them per night—"

"Agreed."

"—plus a room and meals."

"Done!" cried Baldric, bobbing with excitement. "Mary Helen! Prepare the Blue Room for our guests."

After he scurried away, Pieter said, "Simon, what just happened?"

"The Minden Twins," he said with satisfaction, "have just been hired to sing at The Square Pig for a week."

"Three marks a night?" cried Gretchen. "That's twenty-one a week!"

Simon nodded. "For each of you. Plus a fine place to stay. A good start for this musical pairing, I have to say."

More food arrived, but Pieter could eat little. His stomach remained knotted, but this time with excitement.

Chapter 28

$\mathcal{L}$ater, after a meal and a time relaxing by the fire, Mary Helen led them up the stairs and down a long hallway. Ornate sconces held white candles that sent yellow flickers across the painted walls.

"Sweetie," Mary Helen said to Gretchen, "your fingers on that lute, they simply danced. Danced, I say. And you, young man"—she punched him in the arm—"a voice from heaven itself. Here we are." She opened the door and stood aside. "The Blue Room."

The first thing Pieter noticed was the floor. He had never seen a room with a *carpet*. Shades of blue and green and brown created an intricate floral pattern so beautiful he wasn't sure he should walk on it.

"Go on in," said Mary Helen with a wide smile. "It's yours."

Pieter stood just inside the door, unable to move. It was a room fit for a duke, a nobleman. Cloth hung on the wall, drawn back to reveal a floor-to-ceiling window divided into dozens of panes with real glass.

A fire crackled in a fireplace built right into the wall, like Tracker's, but larger and fashioned with stones of white and grey and black. The tapestries that covered the walls showed battles and hunting scenes and great banquets.

And the furniture! A wide bed in an alcove, a curtain tied back on each side. A large desk with an inkpot. A long padded chair that Pieter thought was called a couch.

Gretchen turned back to Mary Helen. "Are you sure this is the right room?"

"Quite sure, sweetie." She patted Gretchen on the head, then left, closing the door behind her.

Simon pushed his hand gingerly into the blue blanket on the bed and grunted. "Way too soft. Lass, you'd better take it. Pieter, you can have the couch."

"Where will you sleep?" asked Pieter.

"The floor will be fine. All I need is a blanket and—"

A loud knock sounded on the door.

Simon scowled. When he pulled the door open, Theodus of Portishead stood in the hall, a strained smile on his thin, pale face. "Simon of Hamelin. It has been too long. How nice to see you again."

"What do you want?" said Simon in a hard voice.

The minstrel entered the room, pushing past Simon, his green velvet cloak swirling around him. He ensconced himself on the couch, crossed his legs and smiled again, but with no warmth in his sharp blue eyes.

Gretchen gave Pieter a puzzled look.

Simon stood by the door, his arms tight over his chest. "We wish to rest. State your business."

"To the point and direct," said Theodus. "That's what I like about you, Simon of Hamelin."

Pieter didn't miss the slight mockery as the man emphasized the town's name.

"In a word," said Theodus, bringing his fingertips together, "these two children have a certain, uh...potential." He sounded as though he was lecturing a slightly dim child. "Their talent is rough, of course, but with some guidance they might become quite good."

Simon growled, "They are already quite good."

Theodus nodded. "Yes, but what they need, of course, is to be apprenticed to a master musician."

"Indeed?" said Simon. "And who might that be?"

"At the moment, I myself have room for them among my students."

Gretchen snorted, then covered her mouth.

Simon's arms tightened. "How fortunate."

"Yes, isn't it? I'm willing to offer most generous terms. By performing with me, they will be able to earn almost all the apprentice fees over, shall we say, the next ten years?"

Pieter could only stare. Apprenticed to this man? The minstrel was a performer, perhaps, but not a musician. He had no music in his heart. Pieter looked in panic at Simon and was relieved to see the coldness in the old man's eyes.

"I have a better offer," Simon said, stepping closer.

"Only seven years, then?"

"I think not."

The minstrel opened his slender hands, stark white against the deep purple of his tunic. "I'm listening."

"I'm thinking we should apprentice you to *them*."

"I beg your pardon?"

Simon smiled. "I'm sure Gretchen could improve your fingering in no time. Though it might take Pieter a bit longer to help that warbling you call a singing voice."

Theodus's lips went white. "Be careful with your humor, old man." He sat taller and fastened his eyes on Simon. "Besides, by what right do you speak for these, uh, twins?"

Simon shrugged. "They leave it to me to deal with all the rogues and fakes we come across."

Theodus of Portishead turned scarlet. He surged to his feet. "You have no standing here. You are not their grandfather, are you? Are they your wards? I daresay not. Why should you make decisions for them?"

He turned to Pieter, straining to create a smile. "What do you say, young man? This old hermit cannot decide for you." He stepped closer. "I work all the best inns in the regions of Brunswick and Brandenburg, even in Hamburg itself. I have wintered with nobles throughout the land. We would do well together, you and I."

Pieter wanted to back away, but the wall already pressed his back. "Simon speaks for me." He wanted his words to sound firm, but they came out in squeaks.

The man's lips tightened into a bloodless white line, stark against the anger in his face. "I strongly advise you to think on this. Sooner than you imagine, your singing voice will begin to crack and break. You will need someone to guide you to maturity."

"I'll manage," said Pieter.

The minstrel whirled to face Gretchen. She grinned at him. "Save your breath, Theodus of *Wart*ishead. Your singing almost snapped the strings on my lute."

The man's eyes darkened. "Very well. I have made a fair offer. Beware, my little peasants. I am first among minstrels in the valley lands and beyond. All I need do is put the word forth, and you two will never work in Brunswick again."

Simon cleared his throat. "It would appear this conversation is over."

Theodus glared at him. "For the moment. I do hope you enjoyed my little Pied Piper number."

He turned for the door.

Gretchen called out, "Mind your harp, *Wart*ishead. It's horribly out of tune."

The minstrel whirled in the doorway. His mouth worked, but before he could get the words out, Simon slammed the door.

Chapter 29

The next few days were a blur of practicing, performing at The Square Pig, resting, and practicing again. They refined two or three of Keeper's ballads each day. The inn was packed every night, until they were forced to perform twice each evening, then thrice.

If Theodus had made good on his threats, Pieter could see no sign of it at The Square Pig. Nor did the minstrel reappear. Still, Pieter worried that their troubles with him were not over.

It would have been a perfect week, had he been able to think only of the music. But the shadow of the Piper darkened everything.

Strangely, no one had spoken of the Pied Piper or his song since they had arrived in Verden. Nor had Simon mentioned the minstrel's barbed ballad about that fateful day in Hamelin. They had been so certain that Verden, "bridge town" in the song, was the correct place, that they had not even discussed it. But that was only the first line of the clue. Sooner or later, they would need to ponder the rest of the verse:

Beyond the bridge town's streets,
Grey stones be sanctified,
And singing fills the evening.
The cloth shall be your guide.

Pieter thought perhaps "singing fills the evening" meant The Square Pig, but he doubted it. The trek did not end here. Even though he wished it did.

On the fourth day, they returned to their rooms after supper in the common room. Pieter halted in the dim hallway. The door to the Blue Room stood open.

Simon pushed by but paused in the entry, his eyes dark. Pieter peered around him. Their belongings had been tossed about the room. Almost every bag and satchel had been dumped out.

Pieter rushed to the saddlebags on the floor. They remained buckled, so perhaps the thieves had missed them. His fingers would scarcely work as he attempted to unfasten it. His breath burst out in relief. The parchment with the Piper's Song remained tucked in the side. He knew he had it memorized, but what if someone else found it? What could someone like Theodus do with the song? The name caught in his throat.

"Sting it *all*!" cried Gretchen.

Pieter turned. Behind the door, the floor was littered with jagged pieces of wood, some still attached to the strings—all that remained of her lute.

"Who? Who would *do* this?" she cried.

Pieter knew exactly who. A quick glance at Simon told him that he knew as well.

"*Sting* it!" Gretchen kicked at the smashed lute. She whirled and plunged from the room. Her footsteps pounded along the hallway and down the stairs.

Gretchen returned that evening, wrath still flashing from her eyes. Pieter wondered where she had gone and how many things she had torn apart before she came back.

As they ate, the fat monk approached them for the first time. "Minden Twins," he said in a high, breathy voice, "my name is Brother Rufus." He looked at Gretchen. "I understand your precious lute has fallen on hard times."

Gretchen eyed him coldly. "And how do you happen to know about *that*?"

Pieter feared she was about to attack him, although the monk surely had nothing to do with it.

He smiled. "There is much talk around the town. A number of people believe they know the culprit."

"As do we," said Simon. "The man will answer for this."

"Ah," said the monk, "it's a pity he's gone. On to Achim-Uesen from what I hear."

"We'll find him," said Simon with a growl.

"In the meantime," Brother Rufus said, turning back to Gretchen, "I discovered the monastery has a number of unused instruments. Including, I'm glad to say, a lute. Would you like to try it?"

Before she could say a word, he held out something wrapped in a blue cloth.

Gretchen stammered, "I...I can't take something from you."

"Perhaps a trade?"

"I have nothing to trade."

Rufus nodded. "I understand. What if you sing a song of my choosing at the next five performances? Then we shall call it even."

Gretchen unwrapped the lute and stared at it. Her broken one had been rather crude, but this one looked worse. The wood was dull and the shape odd, the body almost a circle rather than the usual oval.

She extended a hand and plucked a string. To Pieter's surprise, it sounded better than her old lute—a rich brown tone that pulsed through the room. Heads turned to find the sound.

"Oh, my," she said, picking it up. She quickly checked the strings, then fingered a melody. She looked up. "It sounds... lovely."

Brother Rufus grinned. "So, do we have a deal?"

She nodded, even as a melody sprang from the lute and danced throughout the room.

*hat's too slow," insisted Gretchen. "The pace is absolutely *plodding*."

Pieter grew so weary of fighting her about every song. They argued about tempo, key, pitch, everything.

Pieter glared at her. "It fits the mood of the song."

Gretchen shook her head. "This is not a funeral dirge."

He huffed out a breath. This was near to unbearable. Was there nothing the two of them could agree on? "Very well. We'll try it faster."

The worst part was that she was right. It *was* better at a quicker pace. Fortunately, none of this seemed to carry over into their performances. By the time they took the dais at The Square Pig, they were in accord. Which was amazing, considering their tense practice sessions.

He missed Silverfoot. He couldn't feel the slightest hint of her mind. Had she given up? This time, had she left him? He pushed his mind until sweat broke out on his forehead, but no contact came.

Each evening after performing, Pieter worked on his letters. Big Baldric had brought him some parchments with stories that Pieter read and loved.

But after five days, Pieter could stand it no longer. It wasn't the constant arguing with Gretchen. It wasn't the silence from Silverfoot, although that gnawed at him. Nay, something else hung over him, darkening the days. "Simon," he said during a midday meal, "I've been thinking about—"

"Aye. As have I."

Gretchen's eyes flashed at each of them. "Back to the Pied Piper, is it?"

"Aye," said Simon. "We have tarried here long enough."

She frowned. "I wondered how long this would last."

"Our time in Verden has been lovely," the old man said. "But it is time to move on."

Pieter leaned forward. "On to where?"

"That is the question, indeed. Do you remember the next lines of the song?" asked Simon.

"Remember them?" said Pieter. "They haunt me."

Beyond the bridge town's streets
Grey stones be sanctified,
And singing fills the evening,
The cloth shall be your guide.

"That makes little sense to me," said Gretchen, her knee bouncing in impatience.

"A sweet mystery," said Simon. He pushed his trencher away. "However, while you two have been practicing, I have not been idle."

"You understand the clue?" said Pieter. "Why didn't you say so?"

"Nay, lad. We won't solve it quite so easily. However, I have discovered a few things."

Pieter sat up straighter.

Simon's voice dropped. "First of all, I was rather curious about the monk who loaned us the lute. This Brother Rufus has come to each and every performance."

Gretchen scowled. "If we leave, I'll have to return the lute."

"Aye," said Simon, "but you two have earned a tidy sum this week. I found no lute to buy in this town, but we will keep looking. Perhaps if we travel on to Achim."

"The man seems to come just to eat," said Pieter.

"So I suspected at first," said Simon. "But I've been watching him. In truth, he does love his food. But he nurses one tankard of ale and makes it last all evening."

"And the songs he has picked out have been excellent," said Pieter. "But on the first night, when he first caught my eye, do you know what he did? He winked at me, of all things."

Simon leaned on his elbows. "He lives, of course, at the Saint Ignatius Monastery, south of town, between the two rivers. It seems our Brother Rufus is considered a rather poor example of a devout monk." Simon smiled. "My favorite kind."

Pieter sat in thought, idly scratching the back of his neck. There *was* something odd about him. No, not odd— *different*. The fact that he was not a good monk made Pieter want to find out more. The man certainly seemed to love their music. Besides, he had offered Gretchen a lute. He seemed to want to be a friend.

A line in the Piper's Song burst into his head. "In the song! 'The cloth shall be your guide.' A man of the cloth, perhaps?"

Simon nodded. "You may have something there. 'Sanctified' means made holy."

The table grew quiet as they pondered what it might mean. Put together, it certainly appeared that the clue referred to a monk. And who could that be but Brother Rufus?

Pieter spoke first. "I think we should pay a visit to Saint Ignatius."

He could tell from Gretchen's face that she agreed, although she was staying rather quiet.

"Aye," said Simon, pushing back his chair. "And right now would be an ideal time, don't you think?"

Chapter 30

he path to the monastery twisted back and forth through a thick stand of towering firs and pines, then zigzagged up a slope. They climbed on a carpet of needles, which cast off a pungent odor as they walked.

From time to time, Gretchen's head tilted up, as though she had caught a sound. Pieter heard it, too. Sheep, almost certainly.

A grey wall appeared, plain rough stone, without turrets or crenellations. *Grey stones be sanctified.* Pieter felt more and more certain that this was where the clue was sending them. The wall guided them to a wide oak door with iron hinges, closed fast. Simon pounded on it with his walking stick.

The monk who answered was the complete opposite of Brother Rufus. Tall and thin, he leaned toward them with a spectral gaze. His bulging eyes reminded Pieter of a buzzard about to pounce. He wore the same brown robe as Rufus, albeit his was much cleaner.

"Be welcome to Saint Ignatius," he said in a nasal voice that did not sound welcoming at all. "How may I serve you?"

"We seek Brother Rufus," said Simon.

If possible, the man's face became even less welcoming. "I see. And who is it that asks for him?"

"I am Simon of Hamelin. This young man is Pieter, a minstrel in training."

The man's face tightened. "I see."

Simon gestured. "And this young lady, Gretchen by name, is the finest lute player in Brunswick."

"Indeed. I fear Brother Rufus is not available. He is doing penance. Come back in three days."

Gretchen said, "He gave me a most wonderful boon, and I need to thank him."

Pieter stepped forward. "It would only take a few minutes. It's important that we see him."

"There is little about Brother Rufus that is important," the monk said, his mouth twisting. "He may not leave the monastery. Good day."

Before Pieter could take a breath to respond, the door closed.

"Well," said Simon. "Not an admirer of our Brother Rufus, it would seem."

"I think Rufus will get to The Square Pig tonight, one way or another," said Gretchen.

"Aye," said Pieter. "He hasn't missed a day yet. We can talk to him then."

They started back down the path. The moment the trail flattened out under the trees, a voice called out, "Wait! Wait!"

Brother Rufus burst into view, red-faced and sweating. "Oh, my. A moment..." He bent over, breathing in ragged gasps.

"I thought you were confined to the monastery," said Gretchen.

"Ah, yes...so I am. But then..." He managed to stand erect, hands on his wide hips. "I happen to know...a number of ways out."

"Won't you get into trouble?" asked Pieter.

The monk laughed, which sent his chin to jiggling. "I am *eternally* in trouble, lad. But I've been at Saint Ignatius so long, they don't know how to rid themselves of me."

Simon said, "We urgently need to speak with you."

"Aye," answered Rufus. "I've been hoping you'd come."

"You have?" said Pieter.

"This way," said the monk, pointing into the woods. "There's a place nearby where we can talk without being seen."

He led them away from the trail, into the densest part of the forest, where the deep green firs gave way to a pine grove. There a cliff appeared, covered with vines. Rufus pulled aside the trailing plants to reveal a small cave. Cool, sweet air wafted around them. The scent of lush leaves and water filled the space.

It was furnished with a couple of trunks, a comfortable-looking chair, and a rough plank table. A large barrel sat in the back. Light streamed in from a cleft in the roof.

"My little hideaway," said Rufus, wiping his forehead with his sleeve. "Please. Have a seat."

They found places on the trunks as the monk seized four ceramic mugs from the table. He dipped them into the barrel and served them. "Ignatius spring water. Quenches your thirst like nothing else." He proceeded to down his mug without taking a breath, even though water dripped down the front of his brown robe.

"Ah," he said, making use of his sleeve again. He held up his mug. "Enjoy!"

Gretchen took a deep quaff. "I heard sheep. Smelled them, too."

"Aye. One of the sources of coin for the monastery. We sell wool at the spring fair. Do you know sheep?"

"I tended sheep, before..." Her voice trailed off.

The monk leaned back. "Yes, before. I am sorry, lass. I do not know what you have endured, but I see the grief in your eyes." He cleared his throat. "How is the lute?"

She gave him a small smile. "It's a lovely instrument. It plays much better than it looks. Better than my old one."

"Excellent," he said. "And your original lute's music was quite lovely."

"Thank you."

The monk nodded with a smile. His gaze turned to Simon. "I believe you have visited Verden in the past."

Simon regarded him without answering.

"Now," said the monk, folding his hands across his belly, "perhaps you should tell me why you seek this renegade monk, Brother Rufus."

Pieter glanced over at Simon. Now that they were here, he wasn't sure what he wanted to say or ask. Simon also looked uncertain.

Finally, Brother Rufus spoke. "Well, then." He folded his hands over his stomach. "I believe I can get the conversation started with three words—the Pied Piper."

Chapter 31

Pieter almost dropped his mug. "The Pied Piper? Why would you say that?"

Simon merely nodded. "Just as I thought. You knew him, didn't you?"

"Aye," said Rufus. "When I was but a lad. An old, sad man, he was. Sad indeed."

Gretchen glared at him. "I think you'd better tell us about it."

Rufus regarded her with a smile. "You, my dear child, are an unexpected gift."

Pieter's mouth dropped. That was what Keeper had called her—a gift. She didn't feel like much of a gift to *him*. Except, perhaps, when they were performing.

"Someone like Pieter here, I anticipated. And I've always hoped the Last Child would come, although I didn't know your name."

Simon nodded.

The monk's face grew serious. "It would seem someone is upset with you people. I wonder who it could be?"

Simon grunted. "We all know who it is, as we told you before."

"The *story*," demanded Pieter. "Tell us of the Piper."

"Aye, the story." He stared off into the trees for a moment. "Verden is my hometown. Before I was born, they say the Pied Piper came to The Square Pig often. My father heard him many times."

Gretchen said, "Your father? Who was he?"

"A simple tailor," said Rufus. "But a lover of music, all the same. He sewed much of the Pied Piper's performing attire. Most importantly, he created the Piper's yellow-and-red pied cloak, which the minstrel wore from then on."

That cloak is in all the stories, thought Pieter. Perhaps it had begun as the Pied Piper's sigil. Now it was an emblem of loss and evil.

The monk took a long breath and went on. "He called himself a minstrel, but according to my father, he was much more than that." He shook his head. "His music was compelling, they say. But so much so, it made some people, including my father, wonder about the source of that power. It was as though he could induce you to do anything just by making music."

Pieter stared at the monk's face, amazed at the depth of feeling in his features.

Rufus cleared his throat. "As later events would prove, the power of his music was tragically real."

"Then he was evil," said Pieter in a hushed voice.

"Evil? No more than any of us. At least, not in those years. But he had power, more than he himself understood."

All at once, Rufus jumped to his feet, water sloshing from his mug. His eyes grew wide.

In the next heartbeat, Pieter knew what had startled him—a sound he had been hearing for some time without grasping what it was. A howl. It was odd for her to howl in the daytime. Perhaps she was responding to his anxiety. Nay, not anxiety, but some sort of wonder mixed with worry. They had been out of touch for so many days that it was a relief to hear her.

Simon edged in front of Brother Rufus, his walking stick held ready, his face ashen. A knife appeared in Gretchen's hands. As though a stick and a knife could protect them from Silverfoot.

Pieter hated to see the fear in their faces. If only they could grasp that they didn't need protection from Silverfoot, but Pieter despaired about how to help them understand.

The sound changed to a distant rumble that Pieter knew came from deep in Silverfoot's throat. A sound of uncertainty and concern. *Fear not.* Pieter sent an image to the wolf, an impression of a small cave, a den that she would understand as safe.

Silverfoot howled once more, a mixture of recognition and caution.

Pieter cut in front of Simon and Gretchen. "I swear to you," he said, one hand on Simon's stick, "this wolf will not hurt us or anyone else."

"A wolf this close to Verden?" said the monk. "During the day? What about our sheep?"

"She will not harm them, either." Pieter said.

Brother Rufus crinkled his brow. "And how, pray tell, would you know that?"

"I know it from the wolf herself. She is my companion, and in a way, she can tell me things."

The monk gave Pieter a long, probing look. "I see. I suppose, when you think about it, it stands to reason."

Simon said, "Why, Pieter? Why would this wild animal attach herself to you?"

"I know not," he said. "But she has. In truth, I don't believe Silverfoot knows why, either."

The old man turned to Rufus. "We have heard the creature many times, although Gretchen and I do not find it as comforting as Pieter does."

"Aye." He pulled out a cloth and patted his damp forehead. "I can understand that."

Silverfoot's noises faded away. The cave became still. Outside the opening, it seemed even the birds in the pines had hushed.

"Well, now," said Rufus, refilling his mug. "When I can breathe normally again, I shall go on with the tale." He took one last look in the direction of the howls. "Before my birth, when the Pied Piper was young, my father said that at first he did well as a minstrel. But within fifteen years he was near to starving."

"Starving?" exclaimed Gretchen.

Pieter sat forward. This story had taken an unexpected turn.

"Aye," said the monk. "His music was enthralling, do not doubt. But at the same time, there was something almost... frightening about it."

The notes Pieter had heard on Koppelberg were like that. Enthralling and yet laced with fear.

"The Square Pig was the last inn that would hire him," said Rufus, leaning back in his chair. "Big Baldric's father held on, but the inn's business languished. At last he, too, would no longer engage the man. And the Pied Piper had not yet seen his fortieth birthday."

"What did he do?" asked Gretchen.

"They say he traveled. Took his music to places that hadn't heard of him. Sold the magic of his playing to various people."

"Sold?" asked Pieter.

"Aye. Tasks like leading a pack of wild dogs into the wilderness. Helping calm horses when they panicked. Ridding a town of flies and pestilence. Always with animals, for he had discovered that beasts of all sorts responded to his music just as people did."

Pieter cast a worried look at Gretchen, remembering how the sheep had followed him on the hillside. To say nothing of the wolf that trailed them on their journey.

Brother Rufus sighed deeply. "When the Pied Piper was about fifty, he evidently heard about Hamelin."

"We know that part of the tale," said Simon. "Spare us, please."

"Aye. So I shall. But after Hamelin, he disappeared yet again. No one seems to know where he was all that time. Then, when I was about ten, he returned to Verden.

"Few would hire him, but he played here and there, mostly outdoors at fairs and markets. When I heard him, he was quite old, but his music was still forceful."

Rufus gazed out of the cave mouth for a long moment. Then, with a shake of his head, he went on. "It wasn't just his pipe. He could still sing like the hosts above. And his harp? Oh, I believe it rivaled King David himself, even though his fingers were beginning to stiffen with age."

He hefted himself to his feet and refilled his mug. After a long quaff, he sat and continued. "As with many gifts, the Piper's had two sides. Like a stone on the bank of a stream—a clean side and a muddy side. The man was light and dark. At once."

He sat in silence so long, Pieter wondered if the tale was at an end. He rubbed at his neck, feeling a vein pulsing, waiting for the man to finish.

Simon spoke. "Is that all?"

Rufus shook his head. "When he left Verden, no one thought they would ever see him again. Then, when I was a young novice at Saint Ignatius, he returned to Verden one last time. He no longer performed, and most people did not even realize who he was. He asked for sanctuary at Saint Ignatius, and there I befriended him, but he was a bitter, broken man.

"One day, he told me of the song he had sung for the council in Hamelin. Someday, he said, the Last Child and his heir would come, following the clues in that song."

Simon nodded.

"How he knew his heir would come from Hamelin, I cannot guess. He remained at the monastery for a short time. Then he vanished once more, never to be seen again. But I remembered the song, and I have watched and hoped."

And to Simon he said, "And you, my friend. You are indeed the Last Child."

Pieter watched the old man's chin tremble. "Aye," Simon said, his voice a whisper.

The monk shook his head sadly. "The fortunate child who resisted his song."

Simon sprang to his feet, his face a sudden red. "Nay," he cried. "It wasn't like that. I *longed* to go with the rest. Yea, I *still* yearn to follow."

"But your leg—" began Rufus.

"It was *not* my damn *leg*." He threw the mug across the cave. He stood trembling for a moment, then dropped back into the chair. He covered his face with his hands. "I could have gone. I could have kept up."

Silence.

Then, in a broken voice he said, "Don't you understand? I was too afraid to follow."

Chapter 32

A brittle silence filled the cave. No one moved, not even Simon, frozen with his gnarled hands over his face.

The monk's voice startled Pieter. "The Scriptures tell us that the truth will set us free."

Simon shook his head in anger. "How can that be, when the truth tears your heart in two?"

Rufus squeezed Simon's shoulder. "Especially then, my friend. Especially then."

Pieter recalled the day on Koppelberg Mountain when Simon had blurted out this part of the story. And hearing it again, just knowing Simon's anguish, had only deepened his love for the old man.

"The song says, 'The cloth shall be your guide,'" said Pieter.

Brother Rufus closed his eyes. "And that is what I would hope to be, if you are willing."

"Of course," said Pieter.

"Which brings us to the next question. Where does this tale take you next?"

Simon looked up with a hopeless shrug. "If only we knew."

"Brother Rufus," said Pieter, "we have long studied it. We have come this far, but the next step eludes us. We hoped you would know."

Rufus shook his head. "Nay. I do not know the words of the Piper's Song. But here you are, so it seems you have done well."

"Gretchen has done well," said Pieter. "Without her we would have missed Harmony Vale."

Gretchen cast a surprised look his way.

Pieter gave Brother Rufus a hard stare. "But do not be so sure I am the one you await, Brother Rufus. I may not be the Piper at all."

The monk smiled. "Have I not listened to your singing night after night? Have I not heard you lay bare your heart in song after song? Oh, lad, you are indeed the one."

Pieter's breath quickened. His damp tunic clung to his back. "I don't *want* to be the one," he whispered.

"You do not want to be *like* the Pied Piper," Rufus said, laying a hand on Pieter's shoulder. "And for that I am grateful. And that is one reason only you can be his heir."

Pieter stared at the monk, alarm coursing through his chest. This man was deadly serious. "I do not want anything more to do with the Pied Piper. Simon, let's go back."

"Back where?"

"To Hamelin. No, to Tracker's."

"We could," said Simon, fresh sorrow in his eyes. "But you would someday regret it. You would end up like me, full of bitterness and anger and—"

"An end to this!" cried Gretchen.

Pieter stared at the girl, his mouth agape.

She grabbed the old man's arm. "It's not too late, you fool. There is redemption for us all. Isn't that what this journey is about? All we need is the courage to find it."

A silence, so full of colliding emotions that Pieter could scarcely sit still, filled the cave.

At last Simon raised his head and smiled at her. "Truth, child. You speak the truth."

Brother Rufus chuckled. "'*And a child shall lead them.*' One of my favorite thoughts in Scripture."

Gretchen scowled. "Then let's solve this onerous riddle."

Chapter 33

It was late afternoon when they left Brother Rufus. The monk had agreed to meet them after the evening's performance to address the Piper's Song once more.

As they traipsed down the cobblestones and came within sight of The Square Pig, Pieter spied a large man guarding the front doors. He wore a long sword belted at his waist. His torn and stained tunic matched his dirty, glowering face. A scraggly brown beard failed to hide the deep scar on his cheek.

As they approached, he moved in front of the door. "Tavern's closed," he growled, pulling his sword. He looked the sort that would enjoy using it.

"Nonsense," said Simon. "This inn hasn't been closed in a hundred years."

"'Tis now," he growled, lifting the sword. The stench of ale and filth wafted from him.

"But we have lodgings here," said Simon.

"Not anymore, you don't. Duke's orders."

"You can't do that," snapped Gretchen.

Pieter was amazed she could talk. His own throat was clogged with fear.

The man pointed his sword at her chest. "This piece of steel says I can. So be off." He spat on the ground, almost at Simon's feet.

"Very well," said Simon. "Good day to you, sir." He led them away, then turned up the next lane.

Gretchen grabbed his elbow. "What are you doing? Are you going to let some bully run us off?"

"Ever heard of back doors, lass?"

Another turn brought them to an alley that led behind the barn and to the rear of The Square Pig. The back door stood unguarded.

Pieter ran ahead and burst into the inn's kitchen.

Big Baldric and Mary Helen, sitting at the small table, both jumped in alarm. Baldric held a kitchen knife in his hand.

Mary Helen bellowed, "What are you doing? Trying to scare us to death?"

Gretchen arrived, followed by a hobbling Simon. "Baldric," said the old man. "What happened?"

"I've been closed down. By order of Duke Dahlenberg."

"But why?" asked Pieter.

"The sheriff says I'm behind in my taxes, but that's not true." He covered his face. "How could this happen?"

"I have a strong notion of how," said Simon. "This smells of that black-hearted minstrel. I'd wager every coin I have that this is the work of Theodus of Portishead."

Chapter 34

*M*ary Helen and Baldric prepared a quiet meal of cheese and bread, since the kitchen fires had died. Gone were the familiar odors of baking bread, roasting mutton, and burning oak, leaving a chill, damp scent in the air.

They huddled together around the table, eating solemnly and without conversation.

At last Gretchen slapped a hand on the table. "Are we going to let that emaciated harp-tinkler keep us from performing?"

Big Baldric shook his head. "That guard out front is not emaciated, and neither is his sword."

The door burst open. Pieter choked on his bread, sure it was the soldier. Instead, Brother Rufus barreled in. "That man in front was quite rude," he complained. "What is this all about?"

"We've been closed down," said Baldric. "They say I owe taxes."

"Nonsense," said Rufus, hands on his hips. "You're the most responsible merchant in Verden."

"Simon thinks Theodus is behind it," said Pieter.

The monk joined them at the table. "Theodus, you say? Why would—ah." Understanding showed in his face. "Jealousy, of course."

"It's a bit more than that," said Pieter. "We didn't mention it before, but he came to talk to us that first night. He wanted Gretchen and me to join him as his apprentices."

Gretchen nodded. "When we refused, he became rather annoyed. I believe his exact words were 'You two will never work in Brunswick again.'"

Big Baldric grimaced. "I should have told you. After he left your room that night, he threatened me as well, warned me not to let the Minden Twins sing again. I told him where he could put his pointy head, I did. His response was not very, uh, musical."

"What do you think, Rufus?" asked Simon quietly.

"That guard," said the monk, shaking his head. "I know his type. He'd lop off his mother's hand for an extra mark or two."

"Perhaps it's time to move on," said Simon. "At least we've added to our travel money."

"But we still don't know which way we should go." Pieter was beginning to wonder if they would ever unravel all the mysteries of the Piper's Song.

"And I say again," cried Gretchen. "Are we to be run out of town by that scarecrow?"

"You're right, Gretchen," said Pieter, sitting taller. "Who says we have to perform at The Square Pig? Sorry, Baldric, but there are other inns in town."

Baldric's brow furrowed. "I suppose that would work. Although I'd hate to put anyone else in danger."

"Then we won't use an inn," said Pieter. "It's summer. We can perform outside."

"The town square?" ventured Baldric.

"Nay," said Rufus. "Those thugs would find you too easily. They'd come up with some reason to run you off."

"Rufus," said Pieter. "Why not the monastery?"

"Oh, lad," said the monk with a huge grin. "You've hit upon it for sure."

Simon smiled. "Perfect!"

Pieter looked at Brother Rufus. "Do you think the other monks would mind? When we went there looking for you, the man who answered the door didn't seem very friendly."

"Oh, that's just Brother Darius. Never mind him. We just won't tell him what we're planning."

Pieter caught the look on Baldric's face. Theodus had harmed his livelihood as well. "Is there some way The Square Pig could sell food and drink?"

Brother Rufus scratched his head. "Well, we've never done that before, but why not? Let's do it! Baldric, can you provide the food?"

"Absolutely," he said, his wide grin exposing his crooked set of teeth.

"Excellent," said the monk. "You might very well make a good profit."

"There's not enough time to get it ready for today." said Simon. "Let's plan for tomorrow evening. Will that be enough time for you, Baldric?"

"Mary Helen and I can do it."

Mary Helen nodded. "Meanwhile, I can spread the word. I've got three brothers and five sisters, and all but one's got kids. They'll all help if I ask them to."

"What should I do?" asked Pieter, excitement building.

"You and Gretchen practice," said Simon. "Leave everything else to the rest of us."

"Where?" asked Gretchen.

"Go to my cave," said Rufus. "No one will hear you there."

The gloom evaporated from the room. Mary Helen served some food to Brother Rufus, and they spent the rest of the evening in excited chatter.

Chapter 35

The next morning, Pieter found Mary Helen bustling about the kitchen. The others soon arrived and they gathered around the table. They had been as quiet as possible during the night and used no light, and it appeared the guards had not known they were in The Square Pig.

Mary Helen had prepared a fine breakfast, in spite of the lack of fire. Cold slices of chicken, cheese, and the last of the inn's wrinkled apples. She also served some two-day-old dark bread, hard but satisfying.

Pieter had little interest in food. An odd restlessness twitched his legs. During the night they had settled on one thing—they needed to leave Verden, and soon. After this concert, it was time to move on.

Simon peered at him, his brow wrinkled. "Uh, lad—"

"I'm fine," Pieter said with a wave of his hand.

"On that point, I must disagree," said Simon. "You are thinking about our next destination, I would guess."

Pieter nodded. "Aye. Today, Gretchen and I must practice. Tonight, we make music. Tomorrow, we travel on. But to where?"

Gretchen gave them both a quick look and swallowed a bite of bread. "For now, let's just think about our performance."

Pieter covered his face. "A part of me wants to flee back to Tracker's cabin and hide. Or stay right here in Verden and make music for the rest of my life." He dropped his hands and looked first at Simon, then Gretchen. "But it seems

I cannot do either one, because my heart tells me I must follow the Piper's Song."

Gretchen grinned.

A mix of weariness and relief filled Simon's face, but he nodded. "Aye, lad. Of course you must."

Thanks to Mary Helen, hardly a person in Verden and the surrounding valley had failed to hear about the concert. Even better, they all knew why The Square Pig was closed and who was behind it.

The monks opened wide the gates to the monastery after the midday meal. People began gathering on the green, although it was hours before the music was to begin.

Baldric and Mary Helen had a serving table set up just inside the gates, with barrels of ale waiting behind them and a pig roasting over a nearby fire.

Pieter had chosen a spot near the outer wall, and a crude but sturdy dais had been put together by a group of monks. Pennants and flags had been displayed, and a large tapestry hung on the stone wall behind the dais, depicting a great white stag leaping a fallen log. The green had acquired a festive air.

Pieter sat on the steps to the chapel, staring at the gathering crowd. Families spread blankets. Mothers unloaded hampers of food. The squeals and shouts of playing children resounded happily off the buildings and walls. Mary Helen had already rushed back to the inn for more mugs and trenchers.

Brother Rufus appeared and perched next to him. He wore a fresh brown robe, his pate shone, and his fringe of reddish hair had been plastered down with oil. "'T'will be a grand event, eh, lad?"

"So many people already," said Pieter, his voice hushed.

Rufus stroked his chin. "Listen, I was wondering what you would say to having another musician or two join you."

"Now? Without practicing?"

"I assure you they'll keep up with no trouble."

"I don't know," Pieter said slowly. "What do they play?"

"Brother Matthew plays a drum he brought with him from Ireland," said Rufus. "It is decorated with all sorts of green and red standards. Quite lovely. And Brother Henry is rather good on the viol."

"Viol? I'm not familiar with that."

"It has strings like Gretchen's lute, but it's played differently. You'll see."

"Very well. I'm sure we'll make a fine ensemble," said Pieter.

Later, after a light supper in the monastery's refectory, Pieter and Gretchen met their new musicians. Brother Matthew was older than Rufus, perhaps as much as fifty, but he had a quick smile and laughing green eyes. It took both his arms to carry the drum.

Brother Henry looked broad and strong. About the same age as Brother Rufus, his wide face carried a scar across his cheek to one corner of his mouth. He looked more like a warrior than a monk. Despite that, his blue eyes were kind. His smile, crooked because of the scarring, seemed warm and friendly. "A chance to perform," he boomed in a deep bass. "This will be great fun!"

He held the stringed instrument that Rufus had called a viol. In his other hand was a stick that appeared to be fashioned with stretched strands of hair, perhaps from a horse's tail.

"Shall we find a place to practice?" suggested Pieter.

"Practice?" cried Brother Matthew. "That would ruin my rhythm. I never practice."

"Word has it," added Brother Henry, his blue eyes glittering, "that the Minden Twins are masters of improvisation." He held up his viol. "As am I."

Gretchen frowned at his instrument. Nearly three feet long, it was made of a bright, almost orange wood. "It has but three strings."

"Indeed," said Brother Henry. "You play it with this." He held up the stick. "It's called a bow." He stood the viol on the floor. With a flourish, he drew the bow across a string, drawing forth a deep, velvet sound.

"That tone," said Gretchen, her eyes wide. "It's quite lovely."

Brother Rufus surveyed the gathering audience. "No chance to practice even if you wanted to. It will soon be time to begin."

Pieter glanced at the sun through the branches of an oak. It was later than he had thought. As they made their way toward the stage, the crowd quieted.

As soon as the monks were seated, Gretchen began a wild riff on her lute. Brother Matthew's drum immediately caught both the rhythm and the spirit.

The party began.

Pieter sang "The Fox and the Hen" first, a folk song most of the people would know. Many sang along or clapped to the rhythm of Matthew's drum. Children scampered and danced about, so Pieter whispered to Gretchen, "Let's do 'The Donkey Song.'"

As he sang, Pieter was delighted to see the youngsters frolicking to the tune. Especially since it was his own song. In front of the stage, two little girls of three or four years danced clumsily but joyfully. Even a baby, scarcely walking, bobbed and laughed.

Pieter's breath caught and the song faltered. Would Agnes ever caper like that to a song? Would she know the joy of music? An ache gripped his stomach. But Gretchen continued playing, and in a moment he was swept back up in the music once again.

After that the numbers came one after another, some that Pieter had created, others that he had learned at Keeper's. And the two monks matched every rhythm, every mood. The drum added wonderful rhythms, and the viol's long tones created a rich counterpoint to the melodies Pieter sang.

Little by little, Pieter became aware of another voice— beyond the walls of the monastery, and yet as close as his mind. Silverfoot was not howling or making a noise anyone might hear. And yet she was responding to the music. And she was expectant and watchful. But for what?

As they acknowledged the applause for Pieter's rain song, he caught sight of a group of men trudging through the gate. Not soldiers exactly, but certainly guards or mercenaries. He went cold. They reminded him of the man at the door of The Square Pig, and they did not look friendly. And strolling in behind them was Theodus of Portishead.

Chapter 36

Theodus wore a wide black hat with a red feather. A rich blue cape hung from his shoulders. He sauntered into the courtyard, a leering smile on his face.

Pieter's throat tightened. He doubted he could produce a single note. Even the lyrics had vanished.

Gretchen nudged him in the ribs. "Are you ready?"

He did not move, except to close his mouth.

"Pieter," she whispered, "Forget that scarecrow. I'm starting the next song."

She did, but when she reached the entry, nothing came. Sweat dampened his shirt.

All at once, Gretchen began to sing. Pieter whirled and gaped at her. She was *singing?* Not only had she stepped in where he had failed, but her singing was quite good.

He took a step back and let her take center stage.

Pieter turned his attention back to the gate. An older monk with a white beard stood eye to eye with Theodus. Something in the monk's manner suggested he had authority, though his robe did not differ from that of Brother Rufus.

Their talk was not pleasing the minstrel, judging from his gyrating arms. Theodus thrust a piece of parchment into the man's face. The monk knocked it on the ground. His finger stabbed Theodus in the chest so hard, the minstrel took a step back.

Gretchen finished her song, and bowed to wild applause.

Pieter was still caught up in the confrontation at the gate. At last, Gretchen shrugged and said in a loud voice, "Our next song is 'Bar the Door.'"

She began plucking notes as soon as she returned to her stool. This time, Pieter found his voice. In this number, Gretchen took the Goodwife's part, speaking the lines rather than singing. Soon the entire crowd joined in each refrain with a hearty, "Get up and bar the door!" Brother Henry boomed it out the loudest.

But even as he sang, Pieter kept an eye on the gate. To his relief, the armed men filed out. Theodus was nowhere to be seen. Gretchen continued to choose the songs, each one something the crowd would be familiar with, but also building to a memorable closing.

Gretchen choose "The Rose of the East" for the last number, a joyous finale that brought the evening to an ideal end. The response of the people swelled Pieter's heart. He had never known a more satisfying moment. Before the cheering ended, Simon rushed to the platform. "Into the monastery," he barked. "Now!"

They scurried after him, following Brother Matthew and Brother Henry, who led them down a dim stone hallway, lit by an occasional sputtering lamp. The air smelled musty, spiced with the scent of wax and aging parchment.

Brother Rufus appeared from a side hall, his face flushed. He fell into step with them, his arms flailing in anger. "That Theodus brought soldiers inside. Into a holy place! Weapons on the grounds of Saint Ignatius!"

"What was he trying to do?" asked Pieter.

"Ah, there you are," came a deep voice. Pieter turned. It was the white-bearded monk he had seen confronting Theodus.

Brother Rufus gestured toward the monk. "This is the leader of our order here at Saint Ignatius, Abbot Elisha."

The abbot nodded his head. "That sinful minstrel will never set foot on this holy ground again," he said. "Not if he cares a fig for his immortal soul."

Brother Rufus shook with anger. "What I wouldn't like to do to that scoundrel."

"Aye," said Abbot Elisha. "The Lord forgive me, but I was about to do more than simply poke him."

"But why was he here at all?" asked Brother Matthew, still clutching his drum.

"The soldiers came to arrest Pieter. Simon and the girl as well, I'm afraid."

Chapter 37

Arrest us? Sweat ran down Pieter's spine. He knew Theodus was angry, but to have them arrested?

Simon sputtered with rage, his face a vivid red. "That son of the Devil. For what possible reason?"

"Stealing a sheep, is what he told me," said the abbot.

"A sheep? Oh, my," said Simon thoughtfully. "Our minstrel friend has a long reach, does he not? Apparently that includes Master Camber in Hoya."

"He owed me that sheep!" cried Gretchen, her green eyes blazing.

"I understand," said the abbot. "But he nevertheless has a valid arrest warrant for all three of you."

"Then what shall we do?" said Pieter.

"For now, you have sanctuary here, of course. After that, I know not," said Abbot Elisha.

"Explain it to the sheriff," said Gretchen. "He must know what a weasel Theodus is."

"Aye," said Pieter. "And, Simon, you had an agreement with Camber."

"I did, but nothing in writing, I fear. Nothing we can prove."

"This is stupid," cried Gretchen. "They can't arrest children."

Rufus put a hand on her shoulder. "I'm afraid they can. Especially an orphan. Oh, they'll say they're finding you a new home or assigning you as an apprentice somewhere, but it will be much worse than that."

Simon blew out a long breath. "It seems surrendering is out of the question."

"Can't we stay here?" asked Pieter.

"As long as you wish," said Abbot Elisha. "But at some point, you will no doubt wish to leave."

Simon growled in his throat. "And Theodus is not going to forget about this. Did you see his face? The Minden Twins have shamed him with their music."

Brother Rufus nodded. "The lot of the mediocre, it seems."

"What about Baldric and Mary Helen?" asked Pieter, with sudden fear.

"The soldiers had no interest in them," said the Abbot. He shook his head, sending his beard quivering. "Soldiers! In Saint Ignatius!" He shook his head. "Unbelievable. Well, for now I shall leave you in the care of Brother Rufus. He will show you a place to sleep for tonight." He put a slender hand on Pieter's shoulder and on Gretchen's. "Thank you both for your music. It was a wonderful concert. May the Lord bless you and keep you."

As he walked away, Rufus led them the other direction, down the hall, and into a small, barren room with walls of whitewashed plaster. The floor consisted of aged, uneven boards. A plain but solid table and chairs sat in the middle, where a lamp burned.

"There's a sleeping cell for each of you," he said, gesturing toward the three doors that exited the room. "But first, sit down, please. Supper has been prepared."

They settled at the table. A young monk appeared with a tray of food. For a few minutes, they ate in silence.

Finally, Simon looked at Gretchen. "Well now, our minstrel friend was not the only surprise."

"Aye," said Brother Rufus. "It seems our young shepherd girl can not only play the lute, she can sing."

It was the first time Pieter had seen her blush. Her freckles stood out against the red. She shrugged. "I tried, at least."

Simon smiled. "You did more than just try. You were wonderful."

Pieter's gut tightened. What was all this acclaim about? *He* was the singer. Of course, she had done well, but no matter what she did, she was praised and adored. He kept his eyes on his plate and nibbled on a slice of apple.

Gretchen glanced at Pieter. He sensed she wanted to say something, but she remained quiet. Brother Rufus cleared his throat. "Back to our present difficulties. There are ways out of Saint Ignatius that few know of. What direction are you planning to travel?"

"I wish we knew," said Simon. "Hopefully, we'll be able to tell you in the morning."

"That will do. Good night to all of you." He stood and left.

Pieter wasn't at all sure they'd have the clue solved by morning, but weariness flooded him. They all took to their beds with no more talk.

When Pieter stumbled out of his cell the next morning, Simon already sat at the table, chewing on a chunk of bread, a parchment spread out in front of him.

Stacked near the door were their packs and bags from The Square Pig.

"Simon! How—"

"A friend of Baldric's. I'm no longer nimble enough to sneak into an inn, but he knows people who are. We could have replaced anything but this." He pointed at the parchment.

Pieter couldn't believe he hadn't thought of that himself. He'd been too worried about escaping those soldiers. He was confident he had the song memorized, but they couldn't chance it. More importantly, they could not let it fall into the hands of someone like Theodus. For a panicked moment, he wondered if the man had read the song and then returned it to the saddlebag. No, it didn't seem likely. They had thrown everything else around the room.

Gretchen came in dressed, with her traveling cloak over her arm. Pieter glanced at a window high in the wall. Full daylight flooded in. He had slept much too long.

"So," he said, sitting down opposite Simon. "We have the same problem as always. Where does the song take us next?"

Gretchen sat down next to Simon, glancing from him to Pieter, as though eager to be on the road.

"Aye, lad. That is the question at hand." His brow wrinkled. "I have read and reread it. It means nothing to me."

With a quick knock at the door, Brother Rufus hastened in. "Good morning. How goes..." He glanced at each of them. "Ah, well." He sat down without another word.

Gretchen bent over the manuscript. "Read it out loud, Pieter. Sometimes that helps."

Pieter recited the words, almost singing them.

Where candle flickers feeble,
Where bitter bond be made,
Hidden midst the stones,
Where it can never fade.

A cross shall point to barrels,
That rose on ancient stone,
Now lost in verdant cover,
This be your guide alone.

Simon leaned forward, studying the words. "What am I missing?" he murmured. "Gretchen? Any thoughts?"

Pieter gave Simon a hard look. Why had he asked her first? It was his riddle song.

"Not yet," she said.

Pieter frowned. "We could go on to Achim. The song has taken us north the whole way."

Simon sighed. "I don't know if we dare take the risk."

Gretchen leaned forward and studied the manuscript. "Our Piper likes wordplay. I think I see something."

"What's that?" asked Pieter.

"That phrase 'candle flickers feeble.' What does that suggest to you?"

"A flame?" suggested Pieter. "A lantern, perhaps?"

"Or..." said Gretchen. "Maybe the wick. Lots of towns have wick in their name."

"Aye," said Rufus. "This whole area is called Brunswick."

"There's Hasselwick, about a hundred miles north," said Simon.

"And Wickburg, near Githorn," added Rufus.

"Don't forget the rest of the clue," said Gretchen. "'Binding.'"

"A bond!" cried the monk. "Bondswick! It's a town about twenty miles from here."

"North?" asked Pieter.

"Nay, south."

Simon growled, "But that would swing us back toward Hamelin."

Back? How could that be? He was *fleeing* Hamelin.

"Does it matter?" asked Gretchen. "We go where the song takes us, right?"

Pieter watched Simon's face tighten. The old man shook his head. "I am not going back to that miserable town. I am *not*."

Pieter agreed with the man, yet if that was truly where the song led, what else could they do? Still, they were many long miles from Hamelin.

Simon glared at each of them in turn, as though daring someone to contradict him. All at once, he swept the parchment off the table. An unlit candlestick clattered to the floor.

Before anyone could respond, another knock came at the door. Brother Rufus rose and opened it. He talked briefly with someone in the hall, then closed the door behind him.

"We must leave within the hour," he said. "The sheriff has an entire squad of soldiers coming from Hannover."

Chapter 38

"I thought they couldn't arrest us in a monastery," cried Pieter.

"They can't," said Brother Rufus. "But they can surround the walls and keep us from leaving."

"Over a sheep?" said Gretchen, her voice rising.

"Rather feeble, isn't it?" said Simon. "Theodus poked around until he found something, that's all. He probably paid off the sheriff *and* the good Master Camber."

"Well, I hope this bankrupts the hypocrite," said Gretchen.

Rufus gestured impatiently. "Messengers say the soldiers are about three hours away."

"We're ready to go," said Simon, retrieving the parchment from the floor and rolling it up.

"Yes, but to where do you travel?" asked the monk.

"Bondswick," said Pieter, trying to sound more sure than he felt.

Rufus frowned. "Bondswick, eh? I should tell you—it's not much of a town."

"Pieter's right," growled Simon. "Bondswick it is." He pushed the parchment into one of the leather bags on the floor. "Thanks to this fair lass, we have solved the riddle. So no matter what sort of town it is, that's where we are going."

Pieter glared at the "fair lass," but she didn't seem to notice.

"Then gather your things and follow me," said the monk.

he torch in Brother Rufus's hand cast dancing yellow light on the rough tunnel walls. Pieter pulled his cloak tighter against the cool air.

They moved along a paved passage, with the sharp odor of dirt and damp stone. Water puddled on the floor in low places. Once in a while a door appeared in the tunnel walls, but Brother Rufus led them straight on.

Simon's hard tread showed his anger had not abated. Pieter's feelings were about the same. Except for his mother and sister, he had no reason in the world to return to Hamelin.

"In what direction are we going now?" asked Simon.

"Southeast, along the Aller. We will swing back, toward the Weser River later," said Rufus, glancing back. "Then we'll hit the Bondswick road."

"We?" asked Gretchen.

"Oh," said the monk. "I thought I'd travel with you for a ways."

"That's wonderful," said Pieter. To his surprise, Simon's face darkened. Was he afraid the heavy man would be unable to keep up? He was no doubt too big to ride on Rosie.

"Rosie!" he cried. "She's still at the inn!"

Rufus chuckled. "Nay, lad. She's tethered where the tunnel ends, along with my traveling bag. We Saint Ignatius monks have seen to every detail."

"Why are you coming?" asked Gretchen, just a hint of irritation in her voice. "I don't see what help you can be past the tunnels."

"Gretchen!" said Pieter.

"No, no. A fair question," said the monk. "For one thing, I know the country around here. And remember *aided by the cloth*." Rufus face went serious. "The truth is, I may or may not be any help, lass. But I *must* know what awaits at the end of the Piper's Song."

He stopped and looked directly at Simon. "I've been waiting, too. Not as long as you have, Simon, but many years."

Simon nodded brusquely, but Gretchen still looked doubtful. Pieter, however, welcomed the man's companionship.

They had entered the tunnel from the monastery's deepest cellar, so they had to be far underground. However, they had walked for some time, so Pieter guessed they were beyond the walls by now. He hoped so. The air grew cooler with every step, and the dampness had reached his skin. The rough walls were laced with narrow veins of white that flaked off and gathered at the edges of the path.

Discomfort nibbled at the edge of Pieter's mind. He stopped suddenly, his eyes at the roof of the passage. Silverfoot. Where was his wolf? He reached out, but he could sense nothing but a faint niggling.

But it was enough. That light touch told him what he needed to know. Silverfoot shadowed them, somewhere far above.

"Why was this tunnel built?" asked Gretchen.

"Even the Church has enemies. The Danes, for example, have attacked and slaughtered men of God for hundreds of years."

They trudged along in silence for what seemed to be hours, although Pieter's heart had been lifted, knowing Rufus would be with them.

All at once, the tunnel ended at a massive oak door reinforced with iron bands. Brother Rufus handed the torch to Simon. With a struggle, he lifted a heavy oak crossbeam and set it against the tunnel wall. He pushed on the door. It shuddered, sending dust into the air. A white spider scurried away into the darkness. But the door did not open.

"We haven't used this door for a while," he said. He took a deep breath and put his shoulder into the oak. The door groaned, then gave way, but opened less than a yard. Warmer air wafted through the gap.

Brother Rufus stood panting. "That's enough. If I can get through, that is."

He squeezed into the opening, heaving his mass with a groan. All at once, he popped through. He reached back in for the torch. Gretchen slipped through after him.

When Pieter followed, he found himself in a small cave. The torch illuminated dark rock walls streaked with even more lines of white spidering in every direction. Unlike the tunnel, the air was musty, but dry and much warmer. He smelled decaying grass and the ash from an old fire.

When Simon arrived, he asked Rufus, "Do we close the door?"

"Aye. Brother Henry will be along shortly to bar it." Once again he put his shoulder against the heavy wood. It shut with a heavy thud.

Daylight filtered through leaves and vines that covered the entrance to the cave. It reminded Pieter of the monk's hidden place at the monastery.

Rufus turned to Gretchen. "My child, we need a scout. Go through and look about. If you see *anyone*, we'll have to wait for nightfall. Listen intently, too. For horses, voices, anything."

Pieter started to object, but Gretchen nodded and slipped out.

Irritation enveloped Pieter and quickened his breathing. *He* should have been the one to spy out the land. Instead of insisting on going, he had just stood there and let Gretchen take the lead. Again.

Chapter 39

I should have gone, Pieter thought. It's not her quest. Now everyone would be nattering about how brave she was. Just when Pieter had resolved to push through the green vines after her, she shoved back through. "One guard," she said, fighting for breath. "Think...he saw me."

Simon turned to Brother Rufus. "Is there another way out?"

"Many," said the monk. "But it would take most of the day to reach any of them. And they may be more heavily guarded than this one."

Panic swept Pieter. All this way, just to be caught now?

"Did the guard leave to spread the alarm?" asked Rufus.

"Nay. He came after me." She stood up straighter. "He looked like a boy dressed as a soldier. We can handle him."

Simon shook his head. "We have no weapons but my knife."

"And my meager eating blade," said the monk.

"We have another," said Gretchen. "May I borrow that fine staff of yours?"

Without a word, the old man handed it to her.

"I'm coming, too," said Pieter.

She nodded. "You can distract him."

Pieter could think of no retort, so he pushed through the vines after her. They crept up a small hill. Gretchen stretched out on her stomach and Pieter lay down beside her. They peered over the crest. There was the guard, wandering about as though puzzled about where Gretchen had gone.

Gretchen put her mouth to Pieter's ear. "Move off to the left. When I signal, we'll rush him."

"Wait. I think—"

"Just do as I say," she hissed. With that, she began crawling away.

He felt his face burning, but he did as she ordered.

The guard called out, "I know you're there. You won't get away."

When Pieter had crawled about twenty yards, he stopped and watched Gretchen. She was crouched, ready to charge, but she held out an upraised hand to hold him in place.

"Listen!" cried the guard. "You'd best come out now." His voice cracked, but the sword Pieter had seen in his hand looked lethal enough, notched and stained as it was.

Gretchen called out, "I'm just a shepherd girl. I'm looking for some lambs that wandered away."

"Really?" said the boy with a sneer. "And I'm King Edward himself."

Pieter's body tensed, waiting for Gretchen's signal to rush the boy.

Instead she called out, "Have you seen any sheep around here?"

All at once Pieter heard the boy running toward the sound of Gretchen's voice. Pieter sprang to his feet and showed himself at the crest of the hill. "I'm the other shepherd," he called.

The guard froze, unsure which way to go. He waved the sword toward Pieter. "You're no shepherd. You're that sissy singer I'm s'pposed to arrest. I saw you at The Square Pig."

Pieter shrugged, being careful not to glance over at Gretchen. From the corner of his eye, he saw her advancing, holding the staff with both hands. "If I am, it looks like you'll have to come and get me."

"Aye," he said, closing in on Pieter. "Whatcha gonna do? You gonna sing me to death, you milksop?"

The thought sent a stab of fear through Pieter. He feared he could if he tried. The boy advanced on him. The tip of the sword wobbled as he attempted to hold it ready.

Pieter backed away. All he had to do was draw him off a little farther.

The guard laughed. "Where you goin', sissy boy? Think you can outrun me? Wanna try?"

Pieter suspected he could indeed outrun the boy, encumbered as he was with ill-fitting chainmail and too-large helmet, to say nothing of a sword he could scarcely hold up.

"Listen," said Pieter, taking another step back. "We're not here to make any trouble."

"That right? Well, I am."

The boy was nearly close enough to use his sword. Pieter's bravado was fading.

His heel struck an outcropping of stone behind him. Before he could catch himself, he sprawled backward, hitting the turf hard enough to force the air from his lungs.

The guard grinned and cocked the sword over his shoulder.

Chapter 40

Pieter scrambled backwards, one arm held up over his face.

The sword began its forward motion, shaking in the guard's hands. But even a feeble stroke might prove deadly.

With a burst of courage, Pieter rolled to the side. The sword sank into the turf. As the guard tried to wrench it free, Gretchen charged from the side, Simon's staff whirling in front of her. It hit the boy's wrist. Pieter heard the snap of the bone.

The guard screamed, but grabbed the sword with his other hand. He took a wild swing at Gretchen that only missed by inches.

The staff blurred and struck again, slamming into the guard's ribs. The sword flew from his hand.

He grunted, staggered for a moment, then, with a cry, he charged. He drove his shoulder into Gretchen's chest, knocking her to the ground. The staff clattered against a stone.

The boy towered over her, his wrist clutched against his belly. "You broke my arm, you brat. You're gonna pay." Before Gretchen could move, he knelt and clutched her throat with his good hand.

Gretchen grabbed his arm, pulling until she trembled. Little by little, she forced the guard's arm away. Pieter leaped up and wrapped his arm around the boy's throat, wrenching him off Gretchen. They thrashed about until the guard found his feet. He dove for his sword before Pieter could reach it. Pieter struggled to stand, but the guard held the sword at his throat before he could find his feet. The boy pushed it against Pieter's skin.

Gretchen had recovered her staff, but she stood, wavering. The guard's pale face hovered above him. Pieter could see the pain and fear in his eyes.

In a high voice, the guard said, "Listen, girlie. All I gotta do is lean a bit, and this milksop is dead."

Gretchen nodded.

"Drop the stick."

She did.

A deep snarl broke through the air.

The guard flinched at the sound. In that instant, Gretchen launched herself off the ground and kicked his broken wrist. Pieter rolled to the side.

The boy screamed and collapsed to his knees. "You're dead, pretty girl," he hissed between his teeth. He staggered to his feet and raised his sword.

Pieter rose and stumbled toward the guard's back. He clutched the boy around the midriff and twisted to throw him down. The guard elbowed him in the ribs. Pieter doubled over from the pain shooting up his side, falling to one knee.

The guard turned back toward Gretchen, who had recovered the staff. The two stood facing each other. His sword wavered in his grip as he advanced on her. He drew the weapon back. "You gonna kill me with a stick?" he snarled.

She grinned. "How's your wrist, little man?"

He screamed and charged at her. But the sword wobbled, and Gretchen sidestepped easily. She glanced at Pieter as the boy stumbled by.

Pieter struggled to regain his feet, but he was too slow. "Gretchen! Look out!"

The guard had spun and his sword was arcing in a strong backswing. Gretchen tried to turn, but her feet caught and she went down. With a cry of triumph, the guard rushed for Gretchen, the sword swinging forward, hissed through the air.

At that moment, a growl, deep and full of menace, came from the grass. A huge grey blur flew toward the guard. He stayed his swing and looked to the side, his eyes wide. Before he could change the course of his blade, the creature's teeth had sunk into his throat.

A confusion of images flashed through Pieter's head. Anger, tenacity, bloodlust. A savage blur of sensation that left Pieter woozy.

Silverfoot shook her massive head. With a snap, the boy's neck broke.

Then, she turned toward them, fire in her eyes. Blood dripped from her muzzle. Her piercing blue gaze locked on Pieter. After a long moment, she turned and disappeared over the rise.

Pieter stared at the crumpled guard, bile burning in his throat. He was *dead*. A moment ago he had been a living boy. Now...he was not. It had happened in an instant.

Simon and Brother Rufus rushed toward him. "Are you injured?" Brother Rufus cried.

"I didn't..." Pieter stammered. "I didn't want to see him *killed*."

Brother Rufus laid a hand on his shoulder. "Death is a great sorrow, even for a poor wretch like this."

"Just a boy, in truth," said Gretchen.

"Aye," said Pieter. "Only a few years older than me."

Simon shook his head. "So very young. Alas, when you choose to wear a sword, you must be prepared to face death itself." He shrugged, then knelt by the body, his fingers finding the puncture wounds on the guard's neck. "This is an animal bite."

"A wolf," said Gretchen, glancing at Pieter.

"It was Silverfoot," Pieter said. "The wolf who has shadowed us from the beginning." He was reluctant to say more, to reveal the fact that strange images flowed through his mind when the wolf was near. That he knew her by the name the other wolves called her.

They all stood staring at Pieter. Words had not convinced them that Silverfoot was a friend, but surely this did.

He regarded the two men. "Simon, Rufus, I don't think we could have overcome the guard by ourselves."

Simon gazed another moment at the dead guard, then at the hills around them. "Then she saved your lives."

"Aye," said Gretchen.

"Whatever else she does," said the old man, "I am thankful for that."

"We must leave," said Brother Rufus. "We have been too long in the open."

"What about the soldier?" asked Pieter.

Simon shook his head. "We can do nothing for him now. And we dare not tarry."

"There is one thing I can do," said the monk. He knelt next to the body. In a soft voice, he chanted a string of words in another language. "Now we can go," he said.

Gretchen said, "With that wolf about, I hope Rosie is not injured."

"She will not harm the donkey," said Pieter.

Gretchen gave him an odd look but said nothing more.

They followed the monk past a grove of pine trees and over the crest of a hill. There Rosie waited, unhurt and tethered to a scraggly oak. Her welcoming brays sent panic through Pieter.

Simon hurried over and clamped both hands over her muzzle. "Shhhh, sweet girl." Rosie twisted her head, but when Simon moved one hand to scratch her muzzle, she calmed down.

Pieter had hoped to transfer some of his load to the donkey. But two large leather bags had been left for them on the ground. As soon as Rosie was loaded, they set off toward the east, a heavy bag dangling still from Pieter's shoulders.

The fight had left him exhausted. His ribs throbbed and every breath hurt. It was an effort to force one foot in front of the other. He glanced over at Gretchen, striding as though she hadn't been fighting for her life scant minutes before. How was she so strong?

Rufus led them in a wide arc through the green countryside. Broken-down walls showed where crofts had once stood, but no one seemed to live there now. Pieter caught glimpses of the Aller River, but Rufus did not take them near it.

By midmorning, their path had turned southwest. Soon they reached what Brother Rufus called the Bondswick road, although it proved to be little more than a rough path.

As they rounded a bend, Simon stopped and knelt. He studied the ground for a moment. "No recent horses. It looks safe for now." He struggled to his feet, putting most of his weight on his walking stick.

They strung out along the trail with Rufus in the lead. Despite his bulk, he set a brisk pace. Pieter glanced back at Simon. It looked as though his bad leg was bothering him, but he was keeping up.

The country was peaceful, but Pieter could not shake the memory of the guard, his throat torn apart, his head cocked at such a terrible angle. He could not forget how Silverfoot had looked when she'd charged—teeth bared, rage in her eyes, that deep growl in her gullet, a sound that stopped Pieter's heart. In that moment, she had been the savage creature that the others feared.

Nonetheless, he longed to feel her touch. In his mind, yes, but he also yearned to touch her with his hand, to dig his fingers into her thick fur. Someday it would happen.

He had to admit that Gretchen had been courageous. She had attacked the boy without hesitation. *She fought for me.*

I ought to thank her. To tell her that she was brave. But he could not bring himself to do it.

Someone had died for this quest. *Died!* This was no longer a song-filled romp. It was serious enough to cost a life.

*xcept for a quick midday meal, they traveled without pause or rest, through rugged country with only a few small pines and ash. Everyone seemed lost in their own thoughts. Shadows were growing long as the sun settled toward the west.

"It's getting late," said Brother Rufus, peering up.

"Aye," said Simon. "We'll soon need to make camp."

"I wish we could get through these mountains before dark, but we won't make it," said Rufus.

"Mountains?" scoffed Simon. "This is what passes for mountains around here?" They did appear rather meager compared to those east of Hamelin.

Gretchen asked, "How much farther to Bondswick?"

"We'll arrive before dark tomorrow. Assuming the road is clear."

"Clear of what?" asked Pieter.

"Mudslides, fallen rocks," Rufus answered. "Or, uh, other things."

Pieter was sure the monk was worried about something more than rocks. "You mean more of those guards?"

Rufus gave a quick nod and trudged away.

Pieter wondered if they knew that Silverfoot guarded their flank. He decided not to mention it. If the wolf's attack on the guard had unsettled him, he could imagine how it had affected the rest of them.

As they traveled through the desolate country, Pieter had no desire to sing. In fact, every noise in the fields and hills they passed through played on his nerves.

A good song would have eased the tension, but nothing came to mind, except a dirge for the dead soldier. This, however, was not the time for that.

They drew closer to the "mountains." The foothills of Koppelberg would have towered over all of them. Nevertheless, the road began to rise, twisting gently among the hills.

At dusk, Rufus said, "There's a common camping spot about a mile ahead. Travelers use it regularly."

"I don't know," said Simon with a frown. "That sounds too exposed and well-known."

The monk gave him an odd look. "It's perfectly safe. We've left the monastery far behind."

Pieter saw Simon's face change. "Let me make something clear. We are grateful for your help, but this is not your quest."

Chapter 41

Simon and the monk locked eyes. Pieter held his breath until dizziness swept him. He thought the two men would never stop glowering at each other.

At last Brother Rufus bowed his head. "My apologies, Simon. This is not seemly. As the song suggests, I am only along to help in any way I can."

Simon gave a curt nod. He soon found a suitable spot behind an outcropping of dark grey rock, far from the road. As they huddled over a cold meal, Pieter shivered. Even in summer, evenings proved cool in the mountains. How he wished he were back in Verden, singing at The Square Pig, anticipating a good meal and a snug room. Perhaps they'd find such a place in Bondswick.

The next day, they were well into the hills by midmorning. The road became a narrow path of ruts and potholes, some still holding brown puddles. Pieter wasn't sure he could have followed the path without Brother Rufus. And though Simon never slowed his pace, he gripped his walking stick with white-knuckled fingers.

Brother Rufus and Simon had not said a single word to each other since they had argued about where to camp. It looked as though Rufus was staying back and letting Simon lead. His face suggested he understood the old man better than most.

Pieter glanced at Gretchen. She looked more irritated than worried at the tension between the two men.

The day warmed, then grew hot. Pieter pulled at the sticky neck of his rough tunic. The monk's face had turned an alarming shade of red, but he slackened his pace not a whit. He sucked in great gasps of air on one step, and blew them out through his mouth on the next.

Pieter had only a lingering sense of Silverfoot. Perhaps she was hunting. Something pricked at the edge of Pieter's hearing. He stopped and cocked his head. The ground under his feet trembled. "Behind us," he hissed. "Riders."

Without losing a step, Simon led them off the road. Some ten yards away stood a craggy grey boulder. They dodged behind it and clustered together, Rosie in the midst of them.

"Pieter," whispered Simon. "We must keep that donkey quiet. Scratch her like your life depends on it."

With trembling fingers, Pieter obeyed.

The sound of shod hooves echoed among the rocks. Simon clamped his hands over Rosie's grizzled muzzle again while Pieter gave her the scratching of her life.

Even to Pieter's ears, the horses did not sound like the mounts of ordinary travelers. The heavy report of their hooves brought to mind large mounts, perhaps warhorses.

Without warning, the riders halted, so close Pieter could hear the blows and snorts of their horses. His legs wobbled with fear. Sweat streamed down his forehead and into his eyes, but he did not wipe it away.

He hoped Silverfoot was far off. If these were armed soldiers, they might prove too much even for a wolf.

A green fly buzzed and settled on Rosie's rump. Gretchen swatted it away. One of the horses on the trail whinnied. The still air smelled of sweat and donkey, with the scent of fear pervading all. Pieter forced himself to breathe lest he end up gasping.

A surprisingly cultured voice rang through the trees. "I don't see how they could be ahead of us."

"Aye," growled someone in answer. "Musta gone another way."

"He thought they'd head for Achim, anyway. No reason for them to go south."

"There's tracks, but they's all mixed up. Maybe a donkey, I don't know."

"How much we getting paid?"

"Not enough to take us any farther," said the first voice. "Unless that scarecrow comes up with more coin."

"Aye," said the other. "And we've earned a tankard or two for all this extra running around. Let's find a tavern."

Pieter had not the slightest doubt which scarecrow's coin they had taken. How deep did the minstrel's malice run? He heard the horses turning.

Soon, the sound of the hooves faded to the north.

Rufus held a finger to his mouth. They remained silent. Time crawled.

Simon crept around the rock, then quickly returned. "They're gone."

"Praise the Lord," said Rufus. "It sounded to me like they rode back up the road. I think they're heading to Verden."

Pieter leaned limply against Rosie. "Good girl," he said, flexing his aching fingers.

"Those men," said Gretchen. "They rode warhorses, didn't they?"

"Aye," said Rufus. "Mercenaries, I'd warrant. Without more pay, I doubt they'll be back."

Pieter pulled his damp tunic away from his skin. "Isn't Theodus going to run out of money?"

"Sooner or later. Sooner, I hope," growled Simon. "Let's move on. I don't like these hills."

By midafternoon, they crested a low pass. Below them, a river curled its way through the valley.

"Is that the Weser?" asked Pieter.

The monk nodded. "Indeed it is. You have a good head for geography, lad."

So here he was. Back to the Weser, the river Pieter had known all his life. His jaw tightened. He agreed with Simon—

he did not like traveling toward Hamelin. "The song can't be taking us *back*," he said in a tight voice.

"It is not what I want, either," said Simon. "But perhaps after Bondswick, we will be sent in the opposite direction."

"Only one way to find out," said Gretchen. "Let's get on with this."

As they started down, Pieter's heart grew heavy. He couldn't bear the thought of returning to Hamelin, except for one thing—to see his mother and Agnes and to get them out of that place.

They crested a rise, and for the first time Pieter viewed Bondswick. "What is this?" he said with a groan. Smaller even than Rumbeck near Hamelin, it consisted of one dirt street bordered by weathered shacks and decrepit cottages. Stables and sheds leaned toward imminent collapse.

Stay away, Silverfoot. You will only frighten the townspeople.

Hunting. Return soon.

None of the land was being farmed. No livestock grazed nearby. A few stone ruins at the river suggested Bondswick had once been a river crossing and had perhaps been more prosperous.

One faint path intersected the road near the water, but it quickly disappeared in each direction. A wooded island sat not far from the riverbank.

"We've made a mistake," said Simon, surveying the dismal town. "There can be nothing here that will help us."

Chapter 42

"Bondswick has to be the place," said Gretchen, her chin raised. "The clues were clear."

"Perhaps," said Simon. "But this place doesn't appear promising to me."

"And I don't see a church," Pieter said, thinking of the cross in the song.

Gretchen scowled. "I have to wonder what we will find, at the end of all this," she said, her voice sharp. "What now?"

Pieter shrugged. "I know not. But I've decided one thing. We must go on. It's like being...pulled. No...drawn. Like when Rosie smells water."

"Perhaps," said Brother Rufus, gazing toward the distant mountains, "this journey is not about what we will find, but about who we will become."

"I admit," said Gretchen, "that I too have sensed the lure of the Piper's Song. I just wish I knew what awaits at the end." She waved toward Bondswick. "Well? What are we waiting for? Let's get down there and search for that clue."

"Aye," said Simon. "Ruin or not, this seems to be the place we have been led to."

Gretchen nodded. "There ought to be a barrel down there someplace. Come on."

Pieter smiled, remembering the clue about a barrel in the Piper's Song. "And surely a cross, as well."

Standing in the middle of the barren road, Bondswick looked even more dismal. And it reeked of garbage, rot, and human waste. The first cottage in the village was fashioned of simple straw and mud. The thatch had grown grey and black. Moss on the walls gave the house a sickly green shade. A bony brown dog growled but did not approach them.

The door opened and a thin woman looked out, her face shrunken, her eyes protruding. A grey dress, worn and soiled, hung on her skeletal frame.

"My child," began Brother Rufus in his best pastoral voice, "is there—"

"Go away," she rasped. A dirty-faced toddler with sores around his mouth peered around her legs.

Pieter swallowed hard. The child was about the same age as Agnes. Pieter's throat burned as he watched the naked boy, shrunken except for a protruding belly.

"We will bring no harm to fair Bondswick," said the monk.

The woman snorted. "Fair? This town's nothin' but a heap of stinkin' refuse. You'd best be off."

Brother Rufus folded his hands across his stomach. "What is it that frightens you, my child?"

"Nothin' you can help with."

A child inside began wailing. The woman did not turn around.

Rufus seemed to understand what the cry meant. "I would like to talk with you. Perhaps while we eat. Would you and your children care to have some of the food we have brought?"

She laughed, showing rotting teeth. "You wouldn't offer if you knowed how many brats I got." She scowled a moment, then said, "All right. But not inside. I'll get the children."

Soon they were sitting in the dirt. The rough ground poked Pieter no matter how he shifted. He counted seven young ones, the oldest about nine or ten. The odor of filth and befouled rags came off them in waves. The haunted look he'd seen in the toddler at the doorway was starvation. All the younger children had distended stomachs and spindly legs. How long had it been since they'd had a meal?

Rufus broke a loaf of bread into pieces. "Not too much at first, my children. We'll leave plenty for later."

The woman watched her children closely. Satisfied they all had enough, she took a small piece of bread for herself. She ran a finger along the crust, as though she held a precious object. Without eating, she looked up. "So, you got some questions?"

"Aye," said Rufus. "We are on a pilgrimage, sent by the Lord to find a holy place, a shrine near here."

Pieter frowned and looked over at Simon, who looked puzzled, too.

"Ain't no shrines 'round here," said the woman.

"Oh, it's been long forgotten. The abbot of Saint Ignatius has given us the mission of finding it. He wants to restore it as a place of worship."

She shrugged, taking another bite of bread. "Never heard of nothin' like that."

"What a shame. We had hoped Bondswick would be the place. The shrine was in honor of Saint Theodus."

Gretchen snorted. Pieter covered his mouth to hide his grin.

Brother Rufus went on smoothly. "Saint Theodus was a barrel maker before he became a man of God."

"That right? Used to be a cooper out on the island."

The monk frowned. "Why would a cooper have his workshop on an island?"

The oldest boy spoke up. "Didn't used to be. Used to be part of the shore. Right, Ma?"

His mother nodded. "Remember all that flooding 'bout ten years ago? The Weser changed course. Cut off part of town, so it's an island now. We call it Cooper's Island."

Pieter looked over at Gretchen, who was grinning in triumph. An abandoned cooper's workshop—it had to be connected with the barrel in the song.

Brother Rufus raised both hands. "Praise the Lord. The island must be the place. Hallelujah! The Shrine of Saint Theodus is on Cooper's Island."

"Maybe," said the woman. "But I wouldn't—"

"Hey!" yelled a man. "What's this, then?" He stomped toward them. "Strangers!" He spit the word like it was poison. The man had a haggard face and wore a ragged brown tunic, but also carried a large knife on his belt. Pieter didn't believe it was possible, but he stank worse than the children.

Pieter's throat tightened. He doubted Rufus could cajole *him* with his nonsense about a shrine.

The woman just glared at the scruffy man. "Strangers what brought us food, Caleb. Speak kindly; we got a man of the cloth here."

Caleb's eyes widened as he saw the monk's robes. His hands trembled. "Oh, please forgive me, Father."

"Brother," corrected Rufus. "Brother Rufus of Saint Ignatius monastery."

"I ain't been doing no sins, Father. Don't listen to what this woman tells you. And I prays all the time."

Again Pieter had to hide a smile.

Brother Rufus smiled benignly. "I'm sure you do, my friend. The Lord bless you."

"Oh, he does, for sure and certain. Look at all these dear children he done give me." He forced a smile, revealing blackened teeth. "What brings you to Bondswick, Father... uh..."

"Brother. Rufus." The monk spun his story about the shrine again. "The Church is thinking of building here, perhaps a chapel in honor of Saint Theodus. It would bring many pilgrims to your excellent village."

The man's eyes glittered as though he was already counting the coins. "Oh, this be a fine place for a chapel."

"I agree," said Rufus. "We're planning on looking around. There are no doubt remnants of the old shrine. Perhaps out on the island."

The man's eyes narrowed. "Cooper's Island? Oh, no, Father. Not there."

"Brother," said Rufus without a hint of a smile. "Why ever not?"

The woman chuckled. "It's being used for something else."

"Quiet, woman," Caleb said sharply. She shrank back.

Rufus nodded. "I'm sure you're right. The old shrine is probably not on the island. Do you mind if we look around here in this part of Bondswick?"

Caleb shrugged. "Don't matter to me. Just stay off... I mean, don't go to the island. Uh, if you please...your graceness."

"Very well," said Brother Rufus. He placed a hand on the man's greasy hair. "May the Lord bless you and keep you. And may He take mercy upon you. And forgive *all* your trespasses."

Panic filled Caleb's eyes. "Oh, He will, won't He? I tries to be a good man. I don't want to go to...ah, you know where. It ain't proper to say in front of the little ones." He backed away, turned and ran off.

"Well, my good woman," said Rufus, wiping his oily hand on his robe. "I have to wonder how your husband earns a living."

"He ain't my... I mean, uh, he's what you might call...a man of commerce, he is."

"Is that right?" Rufus set the bag of food in front of her. "This is for you and the children. I'm sure Caleb has his own somewhere."

She nodded, not taking her eyes off the bag. Her hands snatched it off the ground. Within seconds, she and all the children had disappeared inside the tumbledown cottage.

"Saints preserve us," said Simon. "That was quite a tale you spun."

Brother Rufus grinned. "Yes, I thought it was rather good." He looked toward the sky. "And may the Lord forgive all my prevarications."

Pieter cocked his head. "All your *what*?"

"Enormous and flagrant lies." Simon laughed.

"But Saint *Theodus*?" asked Pieter.

"Ah, yes. The rich pleasures of irony." Brother Rufus smiled.

They walked along the dirt street, past more cottages, most in worse shape than the first one.

"A 'man of commerce?'" asked Gretchen with a snort.

Simon nodded. "Yes, unless I miss my guess, our friend Caleb is a scum-of-the-earth thief."

"No gardens, no livestock," said the monk. "You are quite correct, Simon. Fortunately, our friend Caleb is also quite worried about his immortal soul."

"I'd bet he has good reason to worry," said Gretchen. "Did you see the size of that knife on his belt?"

Simon grunted. "And I'm guessing there's a whole nest of scorpions out on Cooper's Island."

They sat together under a large oak, about fifty yards from the river. Pieter looked from Rufus to Simon. "How are we going to find the barrel?"

Simon shook his head. "Like Gretchen said, the Piper likes to play with words. Things don't always mean what you think at first."

"True," said Pieter.

Gretchen nodded. "So 'barrel' might not be an actual barrel."

"It might refer to the place they were made," said Pieter. "Cooper's Island."

"I think so, too," said Gretchen.

"And 'cross' might not be a thing, but something you do. Like crossing the river."

"Nay," said Simon. "Cooper's Island wasn't yet an island when the Pied Piper wrote this."

"Then it could be crossing the road," said Gretchen. "Crossing a field. Anything."

"It's the island," said Pieter. "I'm sure of it."

Rufus sighed. "Which takes us to a place swarming with thieves."

"Who at night are off, uh, working," said Simon. "So that's when we shall visit."

Chapter 43

It was only midafternoon, so Pieter had plenty of time to worry about their coming adventure. That island out in the river was the last place he wanted to go. And yet, they had to.

He saw no way Silverfoot could help with this, and although it would have been reassuring to have her at his side, he wasn't going to ask her to stop hunting. The only image he received was of great concentration and a raging hunger. He did not doubt she would relieve her hunger soon.

Pieter did wonder, however, how long it would take her to reach him if he needed her.

In spite of poking along the reed-filled shoreline for hours, they found not a single boat, which seemed rather strange for a town set along a river.

When he mentioned the oddity, Rufus laughed. "You'd almost think someone doesn't want anyone near that island."

"Where's Simon?" asked Gretchen.

"Checking upstream," said Rufus. "He slipped away some time ago."

Late in the afternoon, Simon returned, poling a raft of sorts. The logs were weathered grey and splitting along the grains. Pieter couldn't imagine how it held together, but it floated.

"I found a torch, too," said Simon.

They huddled together in a cluster of thorny shrubs and river grass, waiting for dark. Pieter wished they had saved some of the food, although that woman and her younglings had certainly needed it more than he did. The moss and grass near the water smelled of rot, and a scattering of dead fish added to the stench. To make it worse, people had clearly been dumping their night soil along the shore. He drifted into sleep, only to jerk awake. How late was it? "Is it time?" he whispered to Simon.

The old man took another look at the stars. "Aye. Close to midnight. Let's be off."

They left their supplies hidden in the brush, with Rosie tethered nearby. She seemed uninterested in their furtive activities, concentrating instead on a meal of fresh grass. They had created a stack of greens they hoped would last her the rest of the night.

Pieter and Gretchen stepped onto the raft first. Cold water sloshed over their feet. They scooted to the far edge. Simon boarded and settled himself in the middle. The raft rocked gently beneath them.

Rufus put one foot on the boards. "I find myself feeling somewhat dubious about this craft." He shifted his weight forward. The raft tipped, sending Pieter and Gretchen sliding into Simon.

A huge splash, then someone spitting water. "Bloody stupid—" gasped Rufus. The raft shunted away from the shore.

"Rufus?" called Pieter in a loud whisper. "Rufus! Are you all right?"

The monk reared up from the water, sending waves sloshing in all directions. "The Lord be praised," he said with a growl. "I'm wet and muddy but not drowned."

"Move back to the edge," said Simon to the children. "We need to get this thing balanced."

Brother Rufus sloshed back to shore. "Damn, but that's cold... How can a river be this cold?"

"I still have the pole," said Simon. "We're coming back." When the raft hit the bank again, Pieter could hear Rufus squeezing the water out of his robes.

"Are you ready?" asked Simon.

"With the strength of the Lord, I can—"

"Slowly this time," interrupted Simon.

Rufus took his time. At last he situated himself in the center of the wobbly craft. Simon balanced Pieter and Gretchen on the opposite side before he began poling.

"Thank you, Lord," said the monk. "And forgive my language."

Pieter scarcely breathed during the crossing. Such a stark black night—he could not even see the island ahead of them. A cloud cover blocked the stars, adding to the gloom. At least the air was now clear of the terrible stench of the riverbank.

He could hear Simon's soft grunts as he heaved on the pole. At long last, sand scraped beneath the logs. How had Simon been able to locate it on this starless night?

They disembarked without another crisis and gathered on the shore. Pieter crossed his arms and shivered in the cool air.

"Now what?" whispered Gretchen.

It was a good question, for the interior of the island was a mound of blackness.

"Hmmm," muttered Rufus. "A bit darker than I expected."

"The torch is still dry," said Simon softly. "I had it wrapped in oilcloth. Who has—?"

From somewhere in the dark came the sound of running feet. Before Pieter could take a breath, he was grabbed by arms as strong as pincers. He screamed, but a rough hand clapped over his mouth and a thick forearm pressed again his neck.

Pieter twisted and thrashed. He struggled to get air.

Gretchen cried out. Something—someone?—landed in the sand. A man grunted.

His captor flung Pieter over his shoulder, which at least freed Pieter's windpipe. He wheezed, trying to scream, but found no breath to do it. He sensed he was being carried deep into the island's woods.

Soon light and shadows from a fire danced on the trees and ground. The next thing he knew, he was thrown to the ground, landing hard on his back. The air burst from his aching lungs.

When he found his breath, he pushed himself up on his elbows. The thick forest had drawn a curtain around the bonfire. They had failed to see it from the shore.

Another man approached carrying a wildcat over one shoulder—Gretchen. Her fists pounded the man's back. She managed a couple of stiff-legged kicks to his chest, despite his efforts to hold her legs. With a quick twist, she wrenched herself over. She clamped her teeth on his ear.

"Get this hellion off me," he roared.

Someone by the fire laughed uproariously. He picked up a rope and tossed it over. "You take care of it, Elias. I ain't getting near that one."

The man started to put her down, but Gretchen squirmed around and scraped her nails across his face. With a scream, he threw her to the ground. Blood streamed from his ear. It looked like Gretchen had taken a sizeable chunk of it with her.

Pieter's face grew hot. Gretchen had fought them every step, while Pieter had just let himself be carried along. *If I get a chance, I'm going to make them pay.*

"She bit my ear!" the man cried. "She tore up my face! I'm bleeding! Bleeding, I tell you."

"Don't worry," said the man at the fire. "You couldn't get much uglier than you already was."

That's Caleb's voice, thought Pieter. *He must have figured we would come to the island. We walked into a trap.*

The bleeding man grabbed the rope with one hand and held off Gretchen with the other.

Stung by how Gretchen had fought her attackers, Pieter watched for his chance. *Now!* He launched himself toward the back of the man's knees. His captor collapsed with an angry cry, just missing landing in the fire.

Someone jerked Pieter to his feet and wrenched his arms behind him. "You'll be sorry for that one, laddie." The man's foul breath almost choked him.

The man he had knocked to the ground staggered to his feet and slammed a fist into Pieter's stomach. He doubled over, struggling for air. A rough rope soon bound his wrists. He was shoved to the ground. Tears pooled in his eyes, but he blinked them away, hoping Gretchen hadn't noticed.

"His ankles, too," said Caleb.

The man wrapped the thick rope around him and pulled it so tight, Pieter cried out. The coarse fibers bit into his skin. His gut ached and the night swirled with grey specks.

Before he could orient himself, Gretchen landed beside him, wrapped tight in a corset of rope. In the firelight, Pieter could see blood on her face. He wasn't sure if it was hers or the man she'd scratched.

"Gretchen?" he whispered. "Are you hurt?"

"Not as much as that bully over there. I got in one last kick. He's going to be bending over for a while."

A fourth man arrived, pushing Simon in front of him. The old man was soon tied and lying beside them.

Caleb sauntered over, holding out his knife. He loomed over them a moment, looking as if he'd enjoy a chance to use it. To Pieter's shame, the shiny blade sent terror through his body. The scar on his back throbbed.

"Won't be long," Caleb sneered. "Boss'll be here by morning. Then the real fun begins." He chuckled and returned to the fire.

"Where's Rufus?" hissed Gretchen.

Simon only shrugged.

Pieter's wrists and ankles pulsed, but at least he could breathe. He could smell his own sweat, and it reeked of fear. Was Silverfoot near? Could she swim out to the island? Hunting had probably taken her far afield. He reached for her anyhow, but caught only a faint touch of her presence. Too far away, but he called for her nonetheless.

The men settled around the fire—four of them, in tattered tunics and cloaks of brown and grey. Firelight flickered in their faces, making them look like vile, brutal specters.

A root dug into Pieter's back. The ropes chafed his skin, and he suspected his wrists were bleeding. Was this where the quest ended? On a remote island by a putrid little town?

As much as he wished it, he feared Silverfoot could not arrive in time to help them. Her hunting images were weak and hazy, far away, although it was hard to know for sure.

"What happened to the priest?" asked Caleb, slipping his knife back in its sheath.

"Got away," said another. "He fell right on top of poor Eli. Just about killed him. He's still lying there trying to remember how to breathe."

Another of the thieves laughed. "That priest is probably swimming back to Bondswick fast as he can."

"Just as well," said Caleb. "Them holy men make me nervous."

All at once, something landed in the center of the bonfire. Sparks flew in every direction. The thieves scrambled to their feet.

"Sinners!" came a voice, thundering out of the darkness. "Repent! The Lord says repent, ye sinners!"

Chapter 44

"Wha— Who is it?" wailed Caleb.

"Behold! The Lord hath seen your transgressions. 'You shall *burn*, BUUUURRRRN', saith the Lord, in ever*laaaa*sting fire!'"

Caleb dropped to his knees. The others did the same. "P... please!" Caleb pleaded. "Have mercy!"

Pieter twisted, trying to see what was happening.

"This is holy ground!" came the voice. "You have defiled the Shrine of Saint Theodus. You have turned a holy place into a *nest* of *scorpions*!"

"We's sorry," gasped Caleb. The other thieves dashed away into the darkness, but Caleb couldn't seem to move. "I don't wanna burn! Please!"

"Go, then. Leave this island. Present yourselves at the altar of the cathedral in Verden. Give to the Lord all your money. *ALL...of...it!*"

"Yes, yes."

"'Repeeeeent! Reeeeepent!' saith the Lord. 'Flee, lest you be cast into the eternal FIIIIIIRES!'"

Before the last word died away, Caleb too had vanished into the night.

For a moment, silence filled the camp. Then from the shadows came a chuckle. Brother Rufus emerged into the circle of firelight.

From the river they heard the splashing of oars. Rufus laughed out loud. "There they go. Nothing like a little fire and brimstone to move a sinner's heart."

He knelt down, and with his knife sliced the ropes from Gretchen's wrists and torso, then freed Pieter.

Pieter's wrists were welted, but the ropes had not rubbed deep. He clambered to his feet, feeling light-headed for a moment.

"Simon, my friend. Are you injured?" the monk said as he cut the ropes binding the old man.

Simon sat up, rubbing at his wrists. "Not seriously. Just a bit humiliated." He flexed his arms. "There was a time I could have broken their filthy necks."

"Rufus," said Gretchen. "You were magnificent. You had me worrying about my *own* immortal soul."

"Oh, my. I forgot to tell them that God loves them. Oh, well."

Simon snorted. "They weren't in any mood to hear that part of the sermon."

Pieter looked around. The first light of morning glowed between the trees. "Looks like we have the Shrine of Saint Theodus to ourselves."

"For a while," said Simon. "Sooner or later, greed will bring them back."

When they had enough light, they began exploring, moving outward from the thieves' campsite.

A decrepit shed housed a couple of empty wooden crates and a scattering of burlap bags, also empty. If the thieves had any loot, it was hidden elsewhere.

Off to the west of the fire pit, Pieter found some crumbling blocks of stone that looked to have been part of a foundation. "Over here!" he called. "I think this was the cooper's workshop."

If it was, little remained. Not a barrel or the remnants of a barrel could be found.

"Something 'rose,'" said Pieter, going over the rhyme in his mind. "What rises? Smoke from a forge?"

No one had any ideas to offer. As the morning passed, they explored the area over and over, turning up nothing.

At last, Pieter sat in disgust on a foundation stone. These ruins seemed like the end of the road. They held no clues, no destination, no direction, nothing. And the Piper's Song? There were no more clues, just a repeat of the refrain. If they didn't solve this clue, it was the end of the quest.

"Get up," Simon growled at him. "Keep looking."

Pieter glared the old man. "Why? There's nothing here."

"We just haven't found it yet."

"What if the song has stranded us on this foul island?" Pieter asked.

"So far," said Simon, "it has never abandoned us. We just have to figure out the riddle."

"You know what I think?" Pieter knew he was trembling, but he couldn't make himself stop. "I think this is the Pied Piper's last joke. Quite funny, eh? Lead the fools to some stinking place crawling with thieves."

Brother Rufus approached, his face as hard as Pieter had ever seen it. He sat on a stone opposite Pieter and leaned toward him. "How long, lad, do you plan to evade the truth?"

He glared at the monk. "I'm evading *nothing*."

Somewhere nearby, a wolf howled. Silverfoot had traveled far since Pieter had called her, but she had not yet reached Bondswick. Her voice, ringing in his mind, was wild, fierce even, but somehow echoed his frustration.

"This...is...the *end*," Pieter cried.

"It's the end only if your fear makes it so," said the monk, his voice firm.

Pieter crossed his arms tight across his chest. He glanced at Gretchen, hoping for an ally, but her green eyes blazed at him.

He stood and straightened his back. "I will not be another Pied Piper."

"Your path is not fated by what the Pied Piper did or did not do," said the monk.

"Nor is my path fated now," snapped Pieter.

"Aye, that is true," said the monk. "But choose your path out of wisdom, not out of fear."

Fear. That's what nestled in Pieter's breast, bristling like a hedgehog. And it had been there for a very long time. Each time he found a refuge, the Piper's Song wrenched it away from him. As soon as he had some notion of what lay before him, that vile song thrust him in a new direction.

Simon cleared his throat. "The monk is correct."

"Is he?" cried Pieter. "Well, you know all about fear, don't you?"

He tensed for the lash of Simon's tongue. Instead, the old man's eyes softened. "Aye, lad. That I do. Fear has haunted me every moment of my life."

"Maybe this is *your* quest, Simon. Maybe it has always been yours, never mine."

"Then why did you come?"

Pieter rubbed a trembling hand through his hair. "To be with you."

"Partly. But there's more. Truth, lad." He leaned closer. "I want to hear the *truth*."

Pieter held his head between his hands. "You want the truth? The truth is echoing in my head. It's in my dreams. It's the piping that pulls at me and haunts me and will not leave me in peace." He shook his head back and forth, gripping it with white-knuckled fingers. "And I do not know what to do!"

"The only thing you can, lad," said Simon. "Face it. Don't wait until you're an old man like me, wasting your life in unfulfilled yearning. You *face* it!" He took a long breath. "When you know what it's about, then you can choose."

Pieter surged to his feet. "I have already chosen. You can continue this journey if you wish. I am finished."

He whirled and kicked the foundation stone next to the one he'd sat on. He expected pain to explode in his toes, but to his shock, the large rock tipped back, landing on its side.

Pieter bent closer, his anger draining away. How could a rock be so light? The surface that had been against the ground was crusted with dirt. But he saw a faint pattern. He grabbed a stick and scraped at the soil. Even before he brushed it clean with his hand, he knew what was carved into the stone.

A rose.

Chapter 45

Gretchen knelt beside Pieter, tracing the rose etched into the stone.

Behind them, Simon sighed. "'That *rose* on ancient stone,'" he quoted from the Piper's Song.

Brother Rufus laughed softly. "Mind the Piper's puns, eh?"

"That stone is too light," said Pieter. "My kick should have broken my toe, not tipped the stone over."

Gretchen rocked it. "Could it be hollow?"

"Look," said Pieter, rubbing the surface. "This oval carved around the rose..." He explored the curve with a finger. "No, not carved. It's a crack."

Simon bent over, knife in hand. He inserted the point and pried. The oval moved. He did it again on the opposite side, then in between. This time the oval lifted just enough that Gretchen could insert a finger. As she levered, Pieter found purchase, and the entire oval popped out to reveal a carved-out hollow. Musty air wafted out, smelling of dust and oil.

"What do you see?" asked Rufus, trying to peer over them.

Pieter reached in and pulled out a packet of oilskin cloth, surprisingly supple in his fingers. Little by little, he unwrapped it, until it revealed a folded parchment sealed in red wax.

He looked up at Simon, then glanced quickly at Gretchen and Rufus.

"You found it," said Simon. "Open it."

But Pieter could not make his fingers move. If he broke the seal, he could never turn back. He would have to see this quest through to the end—whatever that end might be.

He examined each face once more. He saw silent agreement in every pair of eyes. They knew what he should do. But not one of them seemed sure if he would do it.

Neither was he, until he watched his fingers move, pulling at the red wax. The seal broke with a dry snap.

He unfolded the parchment and spread it out on the ground. It was cracked at some of the folds and the parchment had browned and smelled of age, but the ink remained amazingly bright and clear.

It was a drawing of a tower rendered in black ink. But someone had painted narrow rings of green between the large bands of grey.

Though he had never seen it, Pieter thought he knew what the tower was. When they had been at Keeper's, he had learned a ballad called "The Sage of Scopford." He meant to run through the lyrics silently in his mind, but instead he found himself singing.

"The heart of music dwells,
Within yon tower of stone.
The heart of magic grows,
Held by the ancient crone.

So seek yon tower of rings,
With bands of green and gray.
And once you've heard the songs,
You'll return another day.

"We learned that song at Keeper's. 'The Sage of Scopford.' I could never decide if it was a song of hope or a song of despair," Gretchen said.

"Aye," said Pieter. "One time the words fill you with dreams. The next, the tune is laden with sorrow."

"It is both, I think," said Rufus. "As in life. Hard times like the rough and pitted bands of granite, but also times when the days glow with a light of their own, emerald and shining."

"Like the green bands," said Simon thoughtfully.

"And I," said Brother Rufus, "have been to Scopford and have gazed upon that tower, called the Tower of the Lays. And listened to the songs sung by her—the Lady of the Lays."

"The Lady of the Lays," mused Pieter. "A lay is a ballad, isn't it?"

"Aye, lad."

"So she must be a singer."

"Oh, my, yes," said the monk. "Although 'singer' seems much too slight a word for her. You will understand when you hear."

"Where is Scopford?" asked Pieter.

"A mere thirty miles from here," said the monk."

Simon's face hardened. "If I recall correctly, it is thirty miles *south* of here."

"Aye," said Rufus. "South. As you no doubt feared."

"Back toward bloody Hamelin," said Simon in a tight voice.

The monk nodded. "But we are still far away. Our path may turn again."

No one spoke. Pieter stared at the drawing of the tower, as though it would somehow change if he peered at it long enough. At last he let out a pent-up breath. "Then that's where we go."

"Aye," said Simon. But Pieter read in his face that the old man would have preferred to go almost anywhere else.

In the morning light they trudged up a low hill south of Bondswick, sure of their destination, but with little joy to be going there, except for Brother Rufus. Rosie seemed glad to be on the move again as well.

At the top of the hill, Simon looked back and gasped.

They all turned. There lay the sad little town they had left, its brown dirt street running to the Weser. And the little road that crossed it as it approached the shore.

Crossed it?

All at once, Pieter saw what had caused Simon to gasp.

"Well, now," said Simon. "We missed a clue and still found the drawing."

"What is it?" asked Gretchen.

Brother Rufus said, "Look at the two roads. They intersect and form a cross. It points right at Cooper's Island."

Something about that cross gladdened Pieter's heart. He turned his back on Bondswick, but the image the two dusty roads created stayed in his heart, and his step was lighter because of it.

The road out of Bondswick followed the course of the Weser River, now on a hill above the blue waters, now at the very edge of the flow. The pungent smell of river grass, fish, and dank pools drifted in the air.

South. Back toward Hamelin.

A part of Pieter had known that someday his path would return him to Hamelin, but he didn't think it would be so soon. He still was not sure what lay at the end. Whatever waited there, he was not yet ready to face it. But a part of him wanted to return to Hamelin, needed to see his mother and Agnes.

It helped that Silverfoot remained vivid in his mind. When they reached Scopford, she would have to stay away, as she had before. He longed to have her closer. She returned the thought, and Pieter could all but feel the leaves brushing her coat, could smell the scent of soil and trees and terrified rabbits. Even the dampness in her paws had become a part of him.

I am becoming better at knowing how close you are, Great Hunter.

As he plodded along, the image of the tower replaced the cross of Bondswick in his mind. There were no more verses in the song. All they had was a drawing of a tower. The Tower of the Lays.

He slowed his pace until he was walking next to the monk. "This tower—tell me more."

Rufus cast a sidelong glance. "I think it would be better if you experienced it for yourself."

Pieter frowned at him. "So it is all a great mystery, then?"

Rufus grinned. "Rather a miracle than a mystery."

Pieter scowled at him, but the monk did not seem ready to tell him anything more.

Silverfoot remained nearby. Not close enough to frighten anyone, but near enough to sense clearly. She sent an impression of a den with roots protruding from the soil, snug and warm. *Safety*, she was telling him.

They camped within sight of the river. It had been some time since Pieter had wanted to sing, but this night he did. He and Gretchen made music until the fire died away. He fell asleep with images of Silverfoot flitting through his mind. How he wished she were next to him in the dark.

The next day, they reached Scopford just before noon. Unlike Bondswick, this town looked prosperous. Houses were painted in bright yellow, orange, or pink. Shops lined the street offering bread and rolls, fish, and fresh fruit. Craftsmen worked with their goods piled in front of their workshops—shoes, pots and pans, fabrics, and other crafted items.

A busy ford crossed the Weser River. Wagons loaded with goods traveled both directions from the crossing. It looked to Pieter as though the road across the ford ran north toward Hoya. Most of Scopford's buildings were but two or three stories. Not even a church spire broke the low profile of the town.

Just east of town, the tower rose above the other buildings. As in the drawing, it had been built with wide bands of grey that appeared rough and craggy, as though the stonemason had neglected to smooth the surface. Between the rough bands were narrow green rings, smooth and even, that glowed with a deep inner light.

"Ah," said Brother Rufus. "Do you see it?"

"It would be rather hard to miss," said Pieter, gazing upward.

The monk shook his head. "Oddly, many never seem to mark it at all."

"That's strange," Gretchen said.

Pieter tilted his head. "I hear something."

Gretchen and Simon exchanged puzzled glances.

"And what do you hear, friend Pieter?" asked Rufus.

Simon frowned. "A pipe, is it?"

"Nay," said Pieter. "Not this time. Someone is singing. A woman."

"'Tis the Lady of the Lays," said the monk.

Pieter smiled. "Is she in the tower?"

"Aye." Rufus looked toward Gretchen and Simon. "Fear not. Soon, you too will hear it."

By the time they reached the next corner, Pieter realized the woman's song was in another language. Every note floated in the air, intense and vibrant, then melted into the next, forming a rich melody. The range of her singing was incredible—now a high, sweet trill, now a deep, resonant alto. The foreign language freed him to concentrate on the notes.

And such notes they were.

Never off-pitch, each one clear and whole and perfect.

Pieter stopped, the better to listen. He glanced at the others. Ah, they heard the singing now. He saw the wonder in their faces. The song was far away, yet as close as his skin. From every direction at once, yet...

Then the music changed. No less beautiful, but the timbre was different—more like...like an echo.

He turned the corner and gazed down the street. At the end, just outside Scopford, awaited the tower, taller and more beautiful than it had seemed from afar.

The Tower of the Lays. Where the singer dwelt.

Chapter 46

"**O**h, my," whispered Simon.

Without waiting for the others, Pieter set out for the tower, striding over the cobblestones with new energy.

In a few blocks, the street left Scopford and changed into a narrow lane barren of weeds or grass. He found himself hesitant to step onto that path, his feet rooted to the cobblestone. With a pang of regret, Pieter realized the song was fading. But slowly, as though each note was reluctant to wane. The final shimmering notes blew away on the breeze, leaving Pieter still unable to move.

The others caught up. A tall, thin woman strode toward them from a side street, a cloth bundle on her hip. She must have seen the disappointment on their faces. She grinned. "Never fear. She'll sing again at twilight."

Brother Rufus said, "Thank you. We will look forward to that."

With a nod and a soft smile, she continued on her way.

A castle had once dominated the hill, but it had fallen into ruin long ago. Remains of a wall stood in some places and had crumbled in others. Within, only the Tower of the Lays remained, intact and strong amidst the ruins of the other buildings.

As they walked closer to the tower, Pieter realized the song was not over. Hushed, perhaps, but not over. The echo of an echo. It almost seemed as though the birds had taken up the melody.

Twisted trees grew, taking back the hilltop. The path wound among the ruins, with scarcely enough room for Rosie. The way led directly to the tower, but there was no door. Only the solid wall of stones hewn for the structure.

Pieter stood at the base, taking in the song. It had regained some of its strength, for now a chorus of birds trilled it, some inside the tower, others in nearby trees and bushes. They flew in and out of a series of narrow lancet windows, each one placed a few feet higher as far as he could see.

Without waiting for the others, Pieter began a circuit. But there was no door anywhere at the base of the tower. He returned and shrugged. "This is quite strange. I see no way in."

"And that means no way out," said Brother Rufus.

Simon gazed up, one hand shielding his eyes. Pieter followed his gaze and noted a series of narrow windows, about thirty feet above the ground.

"Do you suppose they lower a rope?" asked Gretchen.

Brother Rufus grimaced. "Hmm. Not likely that I shall enter that way."

"Nor I," added Simon.

Pieter stared at the closest window. "This doesn't feel right. There must be another way."

Simon pulled out the drawing they had found in Bondswick. "This is certainly the correct tower. There is no other like it."

"They say," said Rufus, "that the green bands are fashioned with pure jade."

Indeed, Pieter had never seen stone of such a green hue. It seemed as though you could push your hand into its depths. And it shone with a green that seemed to make its own light. "I...we were meant to come here," said Pieter. "So there has to be a way in." Meant to come here? How he had fought against that notion when Simon said it. Now he had stated the same thing. That they were meant to be here.

"Perhaps the door is concealed, hidden in the pattern of the stones," suggested Gretchen.

They circled it again, hoping to discover the outline of a door in the masonry. There was no hint of an opening.

For just a moment, Pieter thought he saw movement in one of the high windows. A flash of white. But when he looked closer, the window was empty.

"Let us rest and think this over," said Simon. He dropped into the shade of an oak tree. "Those birds never stop, do they?"

The others joined him. Rosie clearly liked the rich grass around the tower. Pieter stood, unmoving, listening so intently that everything else faded away. The birds chirped out a different song now. More and more it took form, a lay woven by the tiny throats of hundreds of birds. This was no clamor of unrelated sounds. The birds created melody, rhythm, even harmony. It was...music. True music.

With a shake of his head, he joined the others under the tree. He sat beside Brother Rufus, but he could not keep his eyes off the tower. The grass felt cool on his hands, and a part of him wanted to stretch out on it.

"Any thoughts?" asked Simon as he passed the water skin.

Gretchen looked from face to face. "Are we agreed that this tower is the right place?"

"Aye," said Brother Rufus.

"Without a doubt," said Pieter. "I can...sense it." All at once, Silverfoot entered his mind. He took a deep breath, comforted by the animal's proximity. A picture of this very tower radiated from her mind, shaded with a warm, safe yellow glow. "And I need to tell you, Silverfoot agrees."

Simon gave him a hard look, then nodded.

From Pieter's position on the ground, he could view the spot where the path met the tower. He squinted, looking closer, raising his gaze up the wall band by band. Then he scrambled to his feet and pointed to the window. "The sill of that window, the one above the path. I think there's writing on it."

They all joined him, craning their necks.

"Mayhap that's writing," said Simon, rubbing his head as he peered up. "But these old eyes can't make it out."

"Nor mine," said Brother Rufus, "although, of course, my eyes are far from *old*."

Pieter moved closer. He peered at the writing. Yes, he could make out the letters, but it meant nothing to him. "I can see the letters, but they make no sense. They aren't words I know. Almost like another language. Unless someone doesn't know how to spell."

Rufus stood at his side. He lowered himself onto one knee and picked up a stick. "Read the letters out loud and I'll write them."

Pieter studied the sill for a moment. One by one, he recited the letters.

Brother Rufus grinned. "It's Latin. It says, *Music is magic; magic is music. You are the key.*"

"I know those words," exclaimed Gretchen. "There's a line like that in the riddle song."

Pieter stepped closer to the Tower of the Lays, until he was scarcely two feet from the stones. *I am the key? Could it be a song?* But which one? None of the songs he knew seemed right.

Birds! Birds! Birds! came Silverfoot's voice in his mind. A vision of a flurry of birds came to Pieter. Then an image of Silverfoot herself, head cocked, one ear up.

Yes! Silverfoot was right. It had been there all along. He had been listening to the melody and hadn't recognized it. With his eyes closed, he let the birdsong flow over and through him. It streamed from the tiny singers in the tree. It grew in his mind, took form and structure, until he understood the lay.

He sensed the right moment and opened his mouth in song. *Music is magic; magic is music.*

There were no other words. Just the one line, over and over. The stones in the tower began to distort, as if they were melting. The surface shimmered a liquid silver, darkened, then resolved into a massive oak door.

Chapter 47

A head appeared in the window above the door. A woman with stark white hair and a rather misshapen face peered down. In spite of the hair, Pieter could not guess her age. Fifty? Sixty? Older?

She caught Pieter's eye and said, "Well, that certainly took a while. I thought you'd find the door much sooner. Now I'm late for my midday meal." She shook her head. "Ah, well. Come on in."

She disappeared inside the tower. Was she the singer? It was not a pleasant face, with that wide mouth, jutting chin and ridged forehead. But that didn't mean she couldn't sing.

Pieter grasped the smooth brass handle and pulled. The door swung out silently on its iron hinges. A wash of cool air caressed his face. A flight of stairs wound against the inside of the tower, lit by lancet windows. The space smelled of dampness and ancient stone. He began to climb. Birds flitted around him, flying up and down the inside of the tower, still singing the song that had revealed the door.

He glanced back, surprised that no one was following him, but then he realized that it was for him to climb the tower first.

The stair reached a landing with a doorway. Pieter knocked on the polished wood. No answer. He opened the door and peered in. Nothing but a couple of benches, an old bed, and a window. He was sure the woman had spoken from this window, but she was no longer there.

He left the room and continued his climb. He found two more landings with doors, but he ignored them. He sensed he needed to go to the very top. He hesitated, his pulse quickening. He swallowed hard. Her abrupt manner disconcerted him.

What will this woman want of me? Have I reached the end of the quest? And if it is, what will that end be?

The higher he climbed, the more birds darted through the air, slipping in and out of the lancets, their song more joyous the higher he climbed. He climbed on.

At last, the stairway rose through a wooden ceiling and directly into a large room the full width of the tower. The birds darted around him. More flocked through five large windows spaced evenly around the room. They perched on chair backs, nested on shelves, and clung to the chandelier with strong little talons.

The room smelled of old wood and, yes, bird droppings, but it wasn't as foul as he expected. Also, like at Keeper's cabin, he caught the pleasant odor of parchment and books. Indeed, rolls of parchment and books filled the shelves and littered a low table in the center of the round room. A tiny bed sat against the wall. But even with the small furniture, it felt nothing like a child's room.

Between the cupboards and shelves, on every inch of wall hung musical instruments. He recognized the lutes and some variations of the viol. And harps of many sizes, some plain and others decorated with jewels and gold. Many instruments he had never seen before.

He turned toward the huge fireplace on the wall opposite the stairway. More birds perched on the mantel, including a large grey owl.

Then he spotted the woman. In spite of her homely features, he immediately felt drawn to her. What eyes—a piercing grey with flecks of gold, eyes that held him and seemed to look right into his heart. A nimbus of white hair encircled her head.

She sat in a child-sized rocker, but she was no child. An aura of great age surrounded her. Stubby fingers were interlaced in her lap. She wore a plain black dress that reached to her ankles.

She leaned forward, her gaze hard. "So, you have come at last, my young piper."

Pieter was startled by the words, so close to what Keeper had said back in Harmony Vale.

The woman shook her head. "I am rather surprised. You had more trouble gaining entrance than I expected."

"Yes," said Pieter. "But I am not—"

"—not a piper. Hmmm. We shall see, won't we? Aye, we shall see."

Pieter stood taller. "I tell you—"

"I know, I know," said the woman with a wave of her hand. "Not a piper. Very well. Young *singer*. Is that acceptable?" Her face seemed to say that she knew very well he was a piper.

"I...I am indeed a singer."

"Very well. Pieter the singer it is. Have a seat."

How had this woman learned so much about him? She knew his name, knew he was a singer. What else did she know?

Pieter perched on a low bench across from the woman, not sure what to do next.

"I am Merle," she said. "And yes, I am a dwarf, which is the least important thing about me, save my unruly white hair. I am the Lady of the Lays. I am Merle the Music Master. I am friend and mentor to all with true music in their hearts. How did you come to find me, lad?"

Should he tell her? He hesitated only a moment. There was honesty in her eyes and true music in her singing. "We found a drawing of your tower. At Bondswick."

"Did you, now?" She sat back as though relieved. "Exactly where was it?"

"On an island, where a cooper's workshop used to be. Hidden in a hollowed-out rock."

She nodded. "With a garland of leaves etched in the stone?"

"Nay. With a rose."

"Is that right? How interesting. Then what?"

"We came here to find your tower." Pieter shifted uncomfortably on the bench.

Merle crossed her arms tight. "And just who is included in this 'we?'"

"Simon of Hamelin—"

"The Last Child."

Pieter gave her a sharp look. She even knew who *Simon* was. This woman appeared to be much more than just a singer.

"And who else?" she asked.

"Brother Rufus of Saint Ignatius, and my friend Gretchen from near Hova."

Merle frowned. "Gretchen? A woman?"

"Nay. A girl about my age."

"Odd," she said, as though to herself. "I did not foresee a girl."

Neither did I, thought Pieter. *She seems to be a surprise to everyone.*

Merle stared out the window for a moment. "Could it be? Could she be the one?" She looked up and said, "Is that all in your company?"

"There is Rosie," said Pieter, with a grin. "Our steadfast—"

"Donkey, yes. And there's someone else."

"No one." He ran a hand through his hair. *Should I tell her about Silverfoot? I scarcely know her.*

Safe! called Silverfoot, the closest to an actual word he had ever heard from her. A warm yellow shaded her message—comforting, secure, yet eager.

Very well, Pieter thought, *I shall tell her.* "No one save Silverfoot. A wolf who has followed us and helped us more than once."

"A wolf? My, my. How interesting. And why, pray tell, would a wolf follow you?"

"I have asked myself that question many times. But I still do not know."

Merle smiled. "It just happens that I do."

Pieter sat taller.

Merle folded her hands in her lap. "It is a type of wolf called an *agitato*. They are extremely rare. I have only met one other in my lifetime."

Pieter frowned. *How could she know anything about Silverfoot?* And yet, he found himself believing her. "Is it her coloring or size?"

"Nay. An *agitato* looks like any other wolf. The difference is they are bound by music."

"Bound?"

She waved a hand. "No, no. That is not the right word, for this is something they do willingly. Mayhap 'connected' is a better word."

"Aye," said Pieter. "Connected we are." He regarded her steel-grey eyes for a moment. "Her name is Silverfoot."

"And she is mentioned in the Piper's Song."

Pieter stiffened. "You know about that song?"

"Did I not tell you I am the Music Master? Think on this verse:

Seek fauna on your journey,
Fierce ally clad in grey.
Lest you miss the very being,
Who will aid you in the fray."

"Simon didn't read that verse to me. I found it once, but I'm sure we've met no one who wears grey."

Merle nodded. "What if I told you that 'fauna' means animals?"

He scratched his forehead. "Well, Rosie is grey. She's faithfully carried our gear."

"Nay. She is a fine donkey, I'm sure, but this is—"

"Silverfoot!" said Pieter. "Of course. She was meant to be a part of our quest from the beginning."

"Aye. The Pied Piper was never bonded with an *agitato* wolf, but he knew of them. And somehow he knew you would find one. Has Silverfoot aided you?"

"Oh, yes," said Pieter. "She saved my life."

Merle smiled. "A fine company that has gathered around you, young man. Here you are in my tower. The song has brought you here. So, tell me, what are you searching for?"

Pieter squirmed, the bench suddenly too hard. "We are... I am searching for..."

"For *what*?"

He shrugged hopelessly.

"'I search for what I fear to find,'" she said.

Pieter looked at her wide-eyed. It was a line he had created for a song back in Verden. Did she have the same gift as Keeper? "Aye. And I...I wrestle with that each day. Still—"

"Still you followed the Pied Piper's song."

Pieter nodded.

Merle spread her arms wide. "And lo, it has brought you to this very tower."

Pieter nodded again. "Aye. Though I know not why."

Chapter 48

$\mathcal{P}$ieter waited, watching Merle without breathing. The birds had gone still, except for the owl, which fluttered to her shoulder. Its huge orange eyes stared right through him.

At last she smiled, stroking the owl. "I shall help you discover why, young singer. Then you may venture on."

"Venture on?"

"Oh, I am merely another stop on your journey, as was Keeper, as was Verden, as was Bondswick."

She scooted herself to the edge of the rocking chair. "Now, enough of all that for the moment. As I said, I have missed my midday meal, as have your friends." She reached back and pulled a blue velvet cord. "You will all join me in the dining room below."

Merle stood up, and Pieter realized she was even shorter than he had thought. Not nearly as tall as he was at only twelve.

She ambled along with an awkward stride that lurched her body back and forth, as though something was amiss where her legs joined her hips. Pieter had once seen a dwarf passing through Hamelin, but he had never known one. However, he sensed the truth in her statement that that was the least important thing about her.

She worked her way down the stairs, one tread at a time, clutching the banister. They arrived at an unadorned door that Pieter had passed on the way up.

The dining room encompassed about half the tower, large enough to hold a sizeable table with room to spare.

The birds had not followed, although Pieter could hear them singing outside the windows.

Tapestries covered the stone walls, most with musical themes. One showed a nighttime forest scene. Deer, foxes, rabbits, and other creatures had gathered around an old man with flowing grey hair and beard. He played a musical instrument rather like Brother Henry's viol.

Another showed a giant of a man, striding through a garden of flowers and fruit trees. "Keeper!" said Pieter under his breath.

"Aye," said Merle. "My newest tapestry. Keeper has not yet seen it."

"Keeper has been here?"

Merle nodded. "Of course. Didn't I say I was the Music Master? How could I not know him?"

Perhaps that was how she knew so much about him. Was it possible that Keeper had been here since their visit to Harmony Vale?

Merle looked toward the door. "Ah, here are the others."

Simon peered in.

"Yes, yes," said Merle. "This is the right place. Enter and eat. I'm weary of waiting."

Simon limped in, followed by Brother Rufus and Gretchen. Gretchen seemed less awed by the tower and this strange woman. She glared at Merle, who glared right back.

"So," the old woman said, hiking herself onto a full-sized chair. "Find a seat and we shall begin."

Merle hadn't introduced herself or asked for names. Both Simon and Rufus looked rather intimidated, but Gretchen dropped onto a chair and crossed her arms.

Two women appeared through a far door, carrying large trays. After two trips, the table was covered with platters piled high with cheese, fruit of all kinds, and dried venison.

Brother Rufus cleared his throat. "My friends and I—"

"Eat," Merle ordered, waving a spoon in the air. "We will talk later." She filled her own plate and fell to her meal with great delight.

Pieter shrugged and served himself, and the others followed suit.

Gretchen picked at her food. She stared at the tapestries, with many a sidelong glance at Merle.

The old woman, however, did not deign to even look in Gretchen's direction.

What was causing Gretchen's strange attitude? It couldn't be because Merle was a dwarf; Pieter knew Gretchen better than that. But something odd was passing between them.

Everyone seemed to finish at once. Merle took a last hearty drink of cider, plunked the tankard on the table, and wiped her mouth on her sleeve. "That's better. *Now* we talk." She gestured at the ceiling. "Upstairs."

She scooted herself off the chair and waddled toward the door.

As they started up the stairs, Pieter turned and scowled at Gretchen. He started to speak, but one look at her tight face held him.

A few minutes later, they had settled around the fireplace. The birds had stopped singing. They perched silently throughout the room, their small eyes peering at the visitors. With a rush of wings, the grey owl plunged off the mantle and settled on Merle's shoulder once again. He continued to stare at Pieter. Those orange eyes seemed to pierce him. He wanted to shoo it away, although he suspected that would prove futile.

Someone had started a fire. Merle leaned back in her rocker and eyed them one by one. Pieter began to fidget. Gretchen sat straight against the back of her chair.

The woman's grey eyes locked on Simon. "So, the boy tells me you are Simon of Hamelin. Who do you think I am?"

"The Lady of the Lays," said Simon, his voice soft. "Your singing was quite—"

"And you, friend monk? What say you?"

Rufus smiled. "I have often come to Scopford. I have seated myself on the grass during many a warm evening and let your singing fill my heart."

"My, my, how very eloquent." She waved a hand. "But I asked *who* you think I am."

"Simon has the right of it. Without question."

Merle turned toward the wall. Gretchen had slipped from her chair and stood gazing at the musical instruments on display.

"What about our young girl, I wonder? She *senses* things, more than the rest of you. She perceives that I will send you from riddles into quandary. She is correct. Hard choices await. You shall not find another Harmony Vale."

Gretchen did not turn, but her hands fisted at her side and her shoulders tightened.

Merle stared at Gretchen's back for a moment, then shook her head. "Quite disappointing. Quite. Well, then, I shall have to tell you, although you will understand little more, I fear. I am indeed the Lady of the Lays. And Keeper is—"

Gretchen whirled. "What about Keeper?"

Merle glared at her. "So many questions. So little listening."

Pieter leaned forward, eager for Merle's words. Gretchen turned back and examined a tapestry. Merle crossed her arms tight over her chest. "As I was saying, Keeper gathers the music. I gather the magic. For music is magic and magic is music."

Chapter 49

Brother Rufus shook his head. "I hear your words, Merle. But I am not certain I understand."

"Aye. As I predicted."

The monk leaned forward. "Music has been a part of my life from the beginning. At Saint Ignatius, we sing and chant five times a day. It is beautiful and uplifting, but there is no magic to it."

Merle gave him a hard look. "Are you certain? Then don't call it magic. Just say it is sacred."

"Sacred," he murmured. "Aye. Music is sacred, indeed."

Simon shook his head. "But surely not all music is sacred."

"No, not all music," agreed Merle. "Like any gift, it can be corrupted. It is then no longer music—no longer true music. It becomes a bastard cousin, meant to manipulate, to compel, to unleash the darkness in our natures. In the same way, art, story, even poetry can become profane."

Pieter's spine went cold as his thoughts turned to the Pied Piper. He suspected every person in the room was thinking of that day sixty years ago.

Simon sat forward. "Such is the nature of the piping I hear on Koppelberg. I must listen. But it brings me no joy."

"Nor should it," said Merle. "But do not despair. You have been faithful. That melody shall be banished by a new song." Her grey eyes fastened on Pieter.

Before he could respond, Gretchen whirled, her arms crossed. "Explain Keeper," she demanded, as though she had heard none of the dwarf's words.

Merle threw back her head and laughed, a high sweet sound more like her singing than her barbed words. "Explain Keeper? Shall I also explain the stars, explain a butterfly's wings, explain the heart of man?"

Gretchen scowled at her. "What I meant was—"

"I know what you meant. If not for Keeper, I could not fulfill my calling. Without me, Keeper's calling would come to naught."

"You talk in circles," snapped Gretchen.

"Only when I have something important to say, shepherd girl."

Gretchen started to respond in anger, but Merle went on. "No more talk for now. It is time for us to make music." She stood and walked to a ladder built into the wall. "Come, Piper. Shepherd girl, choose one of the lutes."

Before Pieter could tell her again he was no piper, she pulled herself up the ladder. He and Gretchen stared at each other for a moment. Pieter shrugged and followed the old woman.

The ladder opened through a hole in the roof of the tower, where a hatch had been thrown back. A crenellated wall of deep green jade circled the top. The floor consisted of black marble streaked with swirls of emerald.

A low stool, plain and worn, sat in the very center. Merle stood beside it, her arms crossed. "Where is the girl?"

Pieter looked back down and saw Gretchen partway up, struggling to climb and hold onto the lute. He dropped to his knees and took the instrument so she could scramble up.

Gretchen strode directly to the wall and gazed into the distance. The sun was just touching the hills in the west. But Pieter was drawn to the south side of the tower. Toward Hamelin.

Hamelin. A pang of worry shot through Pieter as he thought of his mother and Agnes.

At that moment, Merle began to sing. Birds flocked from everywhere to join her, and they soon perched along the entire circle of the wall. To Pieter's amazement, her song perfectly touched his feelings about Mother and his sister. He knew it was not by chance. She had sensed his mood and expressed it in her song.

Pieter let Merle's singing wash over him. It didn't seem all that loud, and yet he knew it filled the entire town of Scopford. He glanced at Gretchen, who still stared toward the setting sun. Did he detect a softening in her face?

Merle moved into her next song, and Pieter's heart soared. It was one of *his* songs, a number he had last sung at The Square Pig.

And then, Pieter was singing, too. Mingled with their voices was a chorus of birds, hundreds of birds. And another singer—the almost-melodic cry of a wolf. *Yes, sing with me, Great Hunter. Sing for the joy of singing.*

Merle motioned to Gretchen with her arm and pointed to the stool. Gretchen left the wall and began to play her borrowed lute.

When the number was over, Merle looked hard at Gretchen. "This time, young lady, you shall sing."

"What?" exclaimed Gretchen, almost dropping the lute. "I do not sing."

"Perhaps," said Merle. "But more likely you have yet to try."

"Nay. I have never been a singer."

"Gretchen," said Pieter. "You sang at the abbey."

"Ah, well," said the old woman. "She'll sing when she is ready."

She began the next song, one that Pieter had learned at Keeper's. Gretchen joined her with the lute, and Pieter sang the harmony, which braided itself around Merle's voice.

Somewhere in the song, Pieter became aware of a new sound. Not Merle. Not the birds. A delicate, graceful voice. He turned.

Gretchen was singing.

Chapter 50

The next afternoon, they all sat together in Merle's room. She had given them each a separate room for the night. Pieter had slept soundly in a cozy chamber on the second floor of the tower. Later, Pieter and Gretchen had joined Merle in her midday music. Gretchen's singing had grown more confident, though still too soft to stand out.

"Well, my friends," said Merle, "it has been quite lovely making music with you. But the time has almost come for you to travel on."

"I agree," said Simon. "But where, pray tell, are we to go?"

"Aye," said Pieter. "The Riddle Song has no more clues. I was hoping...thinking that this was where our quest ended."

"Nay, Pieter," said Merle. "You know in your heart that is not so. You even understand, if you are honest, where this quest ends." She leaned forward. "And you are mistaken about another thing. There is another clue."

Pieter frowned. He glanced over at Simon and Brother Rufus, who looked as puzzled as he did.

"Nay," said Simon. "I checked the song against Keeper's copy. The song ends with—"

"It ends when you have finished. Gretchen, would you care to enlighten these mystified men?"

For a moment, Pieter thought Gretchen was as bewildered as he was. To his surprise, she nodded. Her face still solemn, she said, "Come with me."

Gretchen led them down the stairs and into the dining room. She stopped at the first tapestry, and Pieter saw that it depicted a mountain. Koppelberg? Perhaps, but shown from a different angle, mayhap from the south.

Gretchen led them on, past a picture of a valley that could be nothing but Harmony Vale. The next tapestry, two rivers meeting in a town—Verden.

None of the tapestries depicted Bondswick, but the Tower of the Lays, in which they stood, had been represented clearly, much like the drawing they had found on Cooper Island.

Pieter walked back and gazed at each one again. Needle and thread depicted almost every stop on their journey.

Gretchen moved along the curving wall, then stopped in front of the smallest one in the room.

It was a scene of a wide river valley that rose into foothills. Across the horizon stood a range of mountains.

Simon cocked his head. "It is as though we are looking east from this very tower."

"Aye, that is exactly right," said Merle. "Now look deeper."

Pieter's breath caught. Without touching the fabric, his finger traced a broken red line stitched into the scene. It ran from the bottom edge through the valley and up into the depiction of the foothills. There it ended with three white boxes, the second lower than the first, the third higher.

"It's a kind of map," said Pieter, his voice hushed.

Brother Rufus peered closer. "Is this where we must go?"

"Aye," said Gretchen. "But who knows what we will find there."

Once again, Pieter found himself traveling away from a place he had grown to love. Harmony Vale, Verden, the monastery, and now Scopford. But it wasn't the places so much as the people he had left behind—Keeper, Big Baldric, Mary Helen, and now Merle.

After another comfortable night in the tower, they were once again leaving. Always leaving, never arriving. He had let himself hope Merle would travel with them, but that was not to be. But she had given them the next step of their journey—the map on the tapestry. A map that led them away from Hamelin, but into the mountains.

And what would they find there? The Piper's Song provided not the slightest hint, nor did Merle. And the map showed nothing but the three small squares. Not knowing only fueled his fears.

As they traveled, Pieter sighted a flash of white or grey from time to time. Silverfoot had never before traveled so near to the party. He glanced at the faces of his companions, but no one seemed to be aware of her.

A rush of odd images swept through his mind. An oddly hazy picture of a hillside of rocks tinted in yellows and blues. *It's the trail we're on, and yet it is so different.* It was partly the touch of Silverfoot's mind, but another creature as well. He scowled. Certainly not another wolf. These perceptions were quite different from Silverfoot.

Then it came to him. It was Rosie. The impressions from Rosie's mind were dim and halting, nothing like the sharp intelligence of Silverfoot. Only a few colors glimmered through the awkward sendings, yet they were real enough for all that.

In a way, the two animals were not talking to him. They were communicating with *each other*. Through him, it seemed. Silverfoot's message to Rosie was clear—*you are not prey...this wolf is no danger to you.*

Most amazing of all, the donkey accepted it. She plodded along, her mind now quiet, her eyes calm.

He found himself alongside Brother Rufus, who walked with his head high. Pieter gave him a sidelong glance. "What did you think of the Lady of the Lays?"

The monk grunted. "I love her singing, but to tell the truth, she made me rather uncomfortable."

"Aye," said Pieter. "She does seem to have that effect."

"But she also made me think. Which is part of why I am uncomfortable."

"Think? About what?" asked Pieter.

"About music. About how Merle's magic and the power of God meld. Or do not."

They walked in silence for a while. Finally, Pieter said, "And where have your thoughts led you?"

Brother Rufus chuckled, deep in his chest. "In circles, as always."

"Perhaps it is like the stairs in her tower," said Pieter.

The man glanced over. "How is that?"

"You travel in circles, but you also draw closer to the top."

"You may have something there, young man," he said thoughtfully. "You just may."

On the second day out of Scopford, dark clouds rolled in and covered the peaks ahead of them in grey. The damp air sent cold spiking through Pieter's skin, in spite of his cloak. It dampened his spirits as well.

Brother Rufus took the lead, and Simon seemed content to hobble along next to Rosie.

Silverfoot had vanished during the night, but now she had returned. Gretchen seemed to have sunk into a foul mood, and no one had tried to talk to her. Simon as well had been most quiet, even around the campfire the night before.

The trail began to rise, winding through foothills of thick grass. Pines remained, though widely scattered and stunted—the remnants of the thick forest they had encountered outside Scopford. As the way grew steeper, Simon began to lag behind. Pieter slowed his pace until they traveled side by side. He tried to think of a way to begin a conversation, but nothing came to mind. Except Scopford.

To his surprise, it was Simon who broached the subject. "That woman," he said. "She is important."

"Aye."

"I believe she knew the Pied Piper."

That surprised Pieter, but when he thought about it, it was the only thing that made sense. Keeper collected the music and she was the Music Master—how could she and the Piper not have met? "It seems as though the Piper's Song should have just brought us directly to Scopford."

Simon nodded. "I have thought the same thing. Nevertheless, it appears we have traveled where we were meant to travel."

The road they were meant to travel? As though they had no choice in the matter. For the first time since Bondswick, his misgivings about this journey came near to quashing him. Yet, since that miserable moment on Cooper's Island, had he not been to the Tower of the Lays? Had he not talked to the Music Master herself? *Sung* with her? How could he harbor any doubt?

He noticed Gretchen striding just ahead, her tread hard. Since Scopford, she had retreated into a stony silence. He was eager to discuss her singing, but unwilling to try to break through her icy shield.

Pieter welcomed the evening fire, which Brother Rufus built up until it roared into the night. Simon dropped beside it, his face etched with exhaustion. Rosie seemed well-content with the grass on the hillsides. The cold never seemed to bother her. Nor was she concerned about the howling of a nearby wolf.

Brother Rufus's head came up. "That wolf is back. If it was ever gone."

Simon nodded. "Is this creature to follow us forever?"

"Aye," said Pieter.

The next howl echoed in a piercing, penetrating blade of sound that raised the hair on even Pieter's arms.

Chapter 51

"That wolf makes a most terrifying sound," exclaimed Brother Rufus.

Pieter reached over and grasped the monk's arm. "She wants you to know she is not to be feared."

"With a cry like that?" said Simon.

"She did aid us at the abbey," said Gretchen. Pieter gave her a quick smile, relieved she had spoken at last.

Brother Rufus shivered. "I know you consider her a companion of some sort, but she gives me the chills, I must admit."

Simon grunted. "I wish you would tell us more about this creature and your...uh, link to her."

Pieter let out a sigh. "Her name is Silverfoot. She is a friend."

Simon shook his head. "You keep saying that, but you cannot know she is safe. She is a wild animal."

"I agree," said Rufus. "Naming it doesn't make it a pet."

"She is not a pet," snapped Pieter. "Never. And I didn't name her."

All three gave him a quizzical look.

Pieter hesitated. "She...she told me her name."

Silence, save for the crackling of the fire. A log broke in two, sending sparks into the night air. At last Simon said, "She told you?"

Pieter held his head in his hands. "I can't explain it, but somehow I know her mind. Not words, really. More like...

pictures, images. I can see, hear, sometimes even smell what she does. And I know what her emotions are."

No one responded until Gretchen said, "I believe you."

Simon shrugged. "I don't pretend to understand how it works, but it does explain your closeness to Rosie."

"And it explains the sheep," added Gretchen.

Brother Rufus nodded. "And the birds at Scopford, as well."

"Yes," said Pieter. "It's rather like the..." His voice trailed off. A chill swept down his spine. He cringed under the stares of his companions.

"Like the Pied Piper. Like the rats of Hamelin," Gretchen said.

Pieter stiffened. But she was correct, he knew well.

"Still, I must tell you, Pieter," said the monk, "I am more than a little frightened by this wolf."

Simon leaned forward. "Can you control her?"

"Yes," he said. "At least...I believe so."

"You *believe* so?" said Simon. "See that she stays away from Rosie."

"She will."

Through Pieter, Silverfoot must have understood something of the conversation. The howling died away and he had a sense of her curling up in a swale of grass.

As the fire faded, Pieter rolled up in his blankets. He had tried to make them understand about Silverfoot, but they remained frightened. Except for Gretchen. He smiled into the dark. The person he had fought with the most had been his only support.

His mind drifted to the map that showed their journey into the mountains. Where were they going? And worse, what would they find there?

Only the warm sense of Silverfoot in his mind gave him comfort.

Sometime in the darkest hour of the night, soft fur rubbed against his arm. He raised his head and looked into the glowing blue eyes of Silverfoot, only inches from his face. Joy flooded his heart. *You came!* He reached out and stroked her head. She curled at his side. With a soft sigh, he wrapped an arm around her neck and fell into a deep and peaceful slumber.

When Pieter awoke, Silverfoot had departed. It appeared no one else had been aware of her presence. She had not left so much as a tuft of her fur. Loneliness crept through him, even though he was surrounded by friends. Already he longed for the wolf's return. The journey would be tolerable with her at his side.

And yet a small smile surfaced. *No one knows she was here. It was our time, shared with no one else.*

About midday, when they had scarcely entered the foothills, a heavy fog rolled in, laying a sheen of moisture on the trees and grass. They could see only a few yards into the grey mass that enveloped them. Pieter could not tell if they were even on the trail anymore. Simon slowed the pace, swinging his head back and forth as he peered through fog.

Still, by late afternoon, Simon brought them to a dell where they could camp. The old man's skill with fire failed him, and they sat around a pile of wet logs that gave off a lot of choking black smoke but little warmth.

Simon hunched over his copy of the map, squinting to see it by the meager firelight. "The scale is off," he grumbled. "We should be there by now."

"Aye," said Brother Rufus. "Whoever created the tapestry was an artist, not a mapmaker, it seems."

"Could we have passed the place?" asked Gretchen, tucking her hands in her armpits.

"Nay, we're not high enough yet," said Simon.

Pieter sighed. "The problem is we don't know what we're looking for."

Simon shrugged. "I'm not sure even Merle knew. A house or cabin, most likely."

"Maybe," said Pieter. "But it could be anywhere. How would we even know in this fog? It could be right over in those trees."

"Aye," agreed Brother Rufus. "But I agree with Simon. I doubt we have passed it yet."

Gretchen added, "Those strange squares on the map. What were those?"

Simon blew out a fume of breath, irritation in his face. "So many riddles. So many mysteries. It gives me a raging headache. If we missed, we missed it."

Pieter wanted to argue, just to release a bit of frustration, but he was too weary.

That night, he thought about singing. But, somehow, the fact that Gretchen was now also a singer held him back. He hadn't wanted to admit it, but it bothered him that Merle had insisted she sing. To what purpose was her insistence?

He sat by Gretchen as they ate. In spite of being upset with her, he wanted to know more about her ire. After a long silence, he decided to broach the subject. "Merle was—"

Gretchen whirled on him. She glared him down, her green eyes flashing. "I do not wish to speak of her."

Pieter shrugged. "Perhaps it would help."

She huffed out a long sigh. "And perhaps not."

"You didn't like her?"

Gretchen shrugged. "True. She would compel me to...to be something I am not."

"I know well what that is like."

She regarded him for a long time. "It's not the same."

"So what does she—"

"She would have me return to Scopford. When this quest is completed."

"For what purpose?" he asked.

"Enough," she snapped. "No more about that woman."

The next day, the trail began a steep climb that challenged everyone but Rosie. The fog had lifted, but a light rain fell. Silverfoot hadn't come to him during the night, and loneliness shrouded him, in spite of his traveling companions.

What could be in these barren mountains that they were supposed to find? There was nothing up here but frigid winds, scraggly pines, and stark rocks.

"Will this never end?" grumbled Pieter. With every step he grew more miserable.

Gretchen grunted, stomping along beside. "Is the way too hard for you?"

"Of course not," snapped Pieter.

"Then just keep walking."

"I *am* walking," he said. "That doesn't mean I like it."

Gretchen glowered. "Aye. No more strolls through the flowers, it seems."

He turned on her, grabbing her arm. "I am weary of your ridicule."

She yanked her arm away. "And I grow weary of your whining. Surely you can make your way up a bit of a hill."

They stood glaring at each other. Gretchen's green eyes blazed like the jade of the tower. He gave her one more hard look, then plunged up the trail after the others, who had gone on without them.

By midday, the rain fell in fat drops that soaked right through his woolen cloak. Pieter found himself thinking of their room back at The Square Pig. The soft blue carpet, the fireplace built into the wall, the— No, that wasn't helping. It was making this slog even worse. He squinted ahead, hoping to see a snug cottage awaiting them.

What he *did* see took his breath away.

On a rocky cleft next to the trail, he saw three squares scratched into the rock. Exactly as on the map—the second lower, the third higher.

"Look!" he cried, grabbing Gretchen's sleeve.

They all stared at the rock face. Heads turned one way and then the other; eyes studied the scraggly trees, the boulders, the brush.

Without a word they fanned out, moving out from the symbols, searching for some sort of structure or sign of habitation. Except Pieter. He stood in front of the boxes, his body rigid, his head cocked. Cold rain ran down his face, but it didn't matter. All he could do was listen. Clearly, no one else heard it. But to him it was unmistakable: the stark, clear notes of a pipe, drifting on the mountain air.

"Oh, my," he said in a hushed voice. The boxes—they were *notes*, like Keeper put on his parchments. Notes that matched the sound of the pipe he was hearing.

He stepped back and looked up toward the top of the hillside, and there it was, the black opening of a cave just below the top of the slope.

Brother Rufus came up beside him and followed his gaze. "Give me strength," he muttered, eyeing the steep climb.

Simon and Gretchen joined them. The old man said, "We will wait here." He placed a hand on the monk's shoulder. "This climb is for the boy alone."

Indeed, Pieter had already taken the first step. He picked his way up the rough slope, not looking back to see if anyone else was coming or if they heard the music of the pipe.

With his jaw tight, he simply climbed.

Chapter 52

When Pieter had clambered even with the cave opening, he found himself on a narrow ledge, part of a trail that ran off in each direction. To his left, the trail wound down the ledge. If he had known about it, he could have avoided the hard climb, as well as a skinned knee and stinging hands. But it didn't matter. The exertion had scoured out his fear; the struggle had muted the immensity of what lay before him.

How he wished Silverfoot stood at his side. A sense of mountains and wide valleys came to him. The wolf was far away. Pieter would have to do this alone.

He took the last steps and stood motionless just inside the dark opening of the cave.

Even before his eyes adjusted, he saw the fire, far back in what had to be a large cavern. Where the smoke went, or who had built the fire, he couldn't imagine.

He took another step in. The air in the cave was foul, a mixture of smoke and things near rotten. And something else—was it dung? A sound came from a slight movement near the fire.

As his eyes adjusted, Pieter could make out three wooden boxes and a chest carved with animal figures. A roll of purple fabric lay on top of it. A small log was tossed on the fire. Sparks exploded upward. The yellow and orange flames rose brighter. And Pieter saw a face.

A man's face, peering out from a jumble of ragged blankets. A thin face, with a prominent nose and chin.

A sunken face, as though the skin was collapsing inward. The face spoke of great age and of great sorrow. But most startling of all were his eyes. They gleamed a pale, icy blue from deep in the hollows of his sockets.

As Pieter regarded him, the man smiled; nay, it wasn't a smile, but a ghastly, spectral imitation.

"So, here you are," said the man, his voice ragged and cracking. "You've come at last."

Pieter fought to control his shaking hands. He clenched them together in front of him. Who was this man? He took in the ragged clothes, including a tattered cloak—wrought with yellow and red squares. Pieter could not return the stare of those piercing blue eyes. Then a line in Theodus's song came back to him. *Eyes pale and hard as shards of ice.* The minstrel's spiteful song about Hamelin.

His heart went cold. He shivered as awareness crept inward. He knew who this man was.

"I'm Pieter of Hamelin. And you are the one they call the Pied Piper," said Pieter, his voice quaking.

Chapter 53

he man huddled in the ragged blankets threw back his head and laughed, a horrible mixture of cackling and coughing. When he could speak again, he said, "I knew you would come. After talking with the dwarf, how could you resist?"

"I chose to come."

Again the manic laughter.

Pieter waited for him to stop. "You play the pipe beautifully."

The Piper's smile vanished. "Oh, no, young fool. I no longer play the pipe at all. Nor the harp, nor anything else. Look for yourself." He pulled his arms out from under the blanket and held up his hands.

At first Pieter thought his fingers had been broken, but at second look it was obvious they had been twisted by disease. His knuckles were huge, and each finger segment seemed to skew in a new direction. Pieter doubted the Piper could even move most of them.

"But just now...I heard the pipe."

"It was not me. 'Tis the ghost of a melody, and it has kept me alive." He shook his gaunt head. "So here I lie, in filth and rancor. Alive, yet not. I should have perished long ago. Do you know how old I am?"

"Nay," said Pieter.

"Well, neither do I. Over ninety, mayhap? Can you imagine living that long? So many years, in complete despair. It is my penance, I suppose."

They stared at each other in silence, the Piper regarding him with a small smile. The stillness was broken by a log shifting in the flames.

"Why? Why did you do it?" asked Pieter

His gaunt face hardened. "The people of Hamelin cheated me. Don't you know?"

"So I've heard. But where are the children? Where did you take them?"

Using both hands, the Piper managed to lift another log and drop it on the fire. The scent of burning oak wafted from the flames. For a moment, it covered some of the odors that fouled the air. The man's face flickered an unearthly yellow, revealing a mass of wrinkles and creases. "You will know the answer to that when you master the pipe. Only then."

"I am not a piper," said Pieter. "I sing."

"What? All this way, following my song—and you stand there and tell me you don't pipe?"

"Aye. That is indeed what I am telling you."

Abruptly, the Pied Piper lurched forward, thrusting his head toward Pieter. "Don't you lie to me," he said. "I haven't waited in this God-forsaken cave all this time only to have you turn out to be a coward."

Heat rose in Pieter's face. Sweat broke out on his back. "I have enough courage to refuse the pipe."

The Piper stared at him. Did something soften in those cold blue eyes? Not likely, but his head withdrew, the blankets shifted until all Pieter could see was the azure chill staring at him. "Does the Last Child wish to come in and gaze upon his Piper once more?"

"I think not."

The Piper shrugged. "He will. At some point he will."

Pieter did not answer, he only stared. He absently rubbed a thumb over the soft leather of his belt.

"You want to see the pipe. You long to hold it, to put it to your lips. Your fingers already know the fingering, don't they?" The Piper's voice crackled.

"Yes." Indeed, Pieter already felt the holes with the tips of his fingers, even though he did not hold the instrument.

"Then go look. It's wrapped in the velvet. Unroll it and look. Touch it. Taste of it."

"The pipe does not matter. What ma—"

With a scream, the Piper rose from his blankets, casting them off. He reeled, fighting to balance his emaciated body. His tattered red-and yellow cloak hung loose. "Of *course* it matters, you pimple-brained peasant. Only a very few are chosen to receive such a gift."

"I see what it has given you," said Pieter. "I see this palace of treasure in which you reside."

"Yes! Yes! That's it!" cried the Piper, raising his arms into the air. "Treasure. I have found...*treasure!*"

The man tottered for a moment with both hands raised. His eyes rolled back in his head. His mouth went slack and his knees began to buckle. Before Pieter could react, the Piper stumbled and collapsed into the eager yellow flames.

Chapter 54

For three days, Brother Rufus cared for the Pied Piper's burns as best he could, but it seemed unlikely the minstrel would survive. His ragged clothes had blazed eagerly and now clung to his skin in charred bits. The man's gnarled hands were a mottled red, his face blistered and raw. Pieter had dragged him out and smothered the flames with the blankets, but his injuries were grave. At least the Piper had been asleep since then. *No,* thought Pieter, *not asleep.* More like a child lost in a high fever.

"It's for the best," said the monk. "When he awakens, he will know nothing but pain."

Still, Pieter and Rufus took turns ministering to the Piper, cleaning his burns, rubbing on a pungent salve the monk had pulled from one of the saddlebags. But neither Gretchen nor Simon would go near the Piper. Gretchen helped with meals, did some clearing-out of the foul cave, but that was all. Simon roamed the nearby trails or sat staring out over the valley. He spent much of his time with Rosie, and the faithful donkey had never been so well-groomed.

On the fourth day after reaching the cave, Pieter and Rufus were sitting on each side of the Piper to salve the burns once again when Gretchen and Simon returned.

She stared for a moment, then snapped, "Why are you doing this? Don't you see what he is?"

"Unlike you, I begin to see what he once was. And what he could have been," said Pieter.

"What kind of reason is that?" demanded Gretchen. "It's time to leave him to his fate."

"Is it?" said Brother Rufus, holding a wet cloth to the burned man's blotchy forehead. "Is that for us to decide?"

"Someone else had to be caring for him before we came along," said Gretchen, her voice tight. "*Someone* brings him food and supplies. And cuts his firewood."

"You're right. Someone is watching over him. But we have to wait," said Pieter.

She stepped closer, her eyes flashing. "Wait? For what?"

"I'm not sure," said Pieter.

Simon put a hand between them. "We are waiting for his story."

It wasn't until the morning of the sixth day that the Pied Piper opened his eyes. "It would appear"—he coughed violently—"that I am not yet...quite dead." The crusted eyes shut again.

Pieter was watching over him alone at the time. He stared at the Piper, wishing his friends were with him. He moved closer. They had washed him as best they could, but the Piper reeked still from too long in his soiled clothes and the lack of a privy.

The man's eyes fluttered opened again. He groaned. "Why...do I hurt so?"

"You don't remember?"

"Nay."

"You fell into the fire. Collapsed. You have burns on your face and neck. Your hands and arms, too."

He scowled, raising a hand and examining it. "What a very...foolish thing to do." He flopped back. "Burns, eh? Then I ought to hurt more."

"It's the monk's salve," Pieter said, holding up the brown clay jar. "I'm sure you can smell it." The scent of oil and crushed leaves mingled with the sharp odor of mint.

"A monk is with you? Is he the one I knew in Verden?"

"Aye. Brother Rufus."

The Piper smiled grimly. "Excellent. It appears he has done...his part well. And do I recall a girl? Or was it a dream?"

"A girl, yes. Her name is Gretchen."

To Pieter's relief, the Piper said no more about her.

"And the Lady of the Lays?" the man asked. "How does she fare?"

"Well," said Pieter. "She still sings from her tower. It is heavenly."

"And she told you all about the poor wretched Piper, didn't she?"

"Aye. But she did not tell me I would meet you."

The Piper nodded. "No, I suppose not. You likely...would not have come."

"That is probably true.."

Silence filled the cave. The Piper fell into another fit of coughing. After taking a long breath, he lifted his head and peered toward the boxes. "And the pipe?"

"Right where you left it."

He scowled. "But—"

"I haven't touched it."

The man's eyelids fluttered. "You...have to...take it. *Have* to..."

His breathing evened and his eyes closed. It seemed to be a more restful sleep, different from his fevered state of the last few days. Pieter watched him for a long time. The devastated body, the burned face, those clawed fingers. He wanted to hate the Piper. But to his dismay, he could not, and he didn't understand why.

He leaned his head back and tried to calm the storm of feelings in his mind. There was no sound in the cave except the echo of the Piper's Song, which would not stop.

When Pieter woke the next morning, he was amazed to see the Piper sitting cross-legged before the fire. The mottled red of his bare arms glistened with salve. He had wrapped a scorched remnant of his cloak around his neck. His hands lay in his lap, gnarled fingers twisted upward in gruesome claws.

After breaking their fast, they all eyed the Piper, waiting. Waiting for the Pied Piper's story.

Brother Rufus looked almost prayerful. Simon's eyes smoldered. Gretchen merely scowled from the cave entrance. And the Pied Piper? He sat in his rags, oddly calm amidst the tempest of emotions.

Finally he spoke. "Pieter, can you imagine what it would be like...to lose your music?"

A shudder iced down Pieter's spine. Already, his life and his music had become one. "No. No, I can't."

"Still," rasped the Piper, "still...'tis better to have received the gift and lost it than..." His words trailed off. He smiled, his eyes fixed on something at the mouth of the cave.

Gretchen gasped and Pieter's head whirled. In the opening to the cave stood the silhouette of a man.

The Piper sniggered as he regarded the figure. "Unlike you, my poor miserable minstrel, who never had the gift at all."

"Theodus!" hissed Pieter.

Chapter 55

The minstrel, Theodus of Portishead, stepped in, pulling off a white glove one finger at a time.

"How easy you have made it." He leisurely peeled off his second glove. "You all but planted milestones for me to follow." He wore a thick green tunic, with a deep red cloak hanging from his thin shoulders.

The Piper cackled, rolling from side to side. "I cannot tell you, old friend, how delighted I am to see you. Just *delighted*." His laughter rattled through the cave, then changed to hacking coughs.

Pieter leaped to his feet. "Why are *you* here?"

Gretchen snorted. "You can't guess, Pieter? Clearly, the great Theodus of *Wart*ishead fancies himself the next piper."

By this time, both Simon and Rufus had risen. They stepped to either side of Pieter.

Theodus smiled at Gretchen. "No, my snotty peasant. I *am* the next piper." He raised one hand and snapped his fingers.

Three men rushed in, two with swords drawn and one with a bow, arrow nocked.

Pieter almost cried out at the sight of them. Big, angry-looking men, like the one who had guarded The Square Pig. Each wore chainmail and a battered helmet.

Theodus gazed about the cave. "What an appalling place. It smells like...well, like death, I do believe." His eyes stopped at the trunk. "Well now, what could that be, wrapped in that lovely purple velvet? How kind of you to have the pipe ready for me."

The Piper's eerie laughter continued. He fought for control. "Wartishead! Oh, lass, that is perfect. Absolutely perfect." His mirth died and he leaned forward, his gaze hard on the minstrel. "Beware, Theodus. Do...*not* touch the pipe. It is not for you."

The minstrel's lips curled into a sneer. "Besides you, my dear Piper, I see a fat monk, a decrepit old man, and two churlish brats." He turned to the swordsman beside him. "Eli, do you see anyone who can stop me?"

"Nay," growled the man, waving the tip of his sword.

"Nor do I." Theodus sprang forward, driving his shoulder into the monk's side as he pushed past. Rufus whirled to grab him, but Eli stuck the point of his sword against the monk's chest.

"Don't do it, Wartishead," said the Pied Piper in a mocking voice. "I say again, you are in grave danger."

Theodus snatched the bundle of velvet. He lovingly stroked the cloth.

The Piper cackled. "I hoped I would see the next Piper," he said. "But I did not *dream* I would see this as well. It makes it so worthwhile, waiting all this time in this miserable cave." The man's laughter rose to a manic pitch.

"Silence that fool," barked Theodus.

With a twang, an arrow sprouted from the Pied Piper's chest.

He cried out and sprawled backward onto his blankets.

Brother Rufus rushed to his side. Blood gushed around the arrow. The monk grabbed the edge of a blanket and stuffed it near the wound, holding it tight against the Piper's chest.

"You coward!" cried Pieter.

"Help me up," gasped the Piper.

Rufus dropped beside him and propped the Piper up. Stark red blood soaked the blanket and ran down his emaciated chest. Nevertheless, the Piper grinned at the minstrel.

Theodus, a smile of triumph on his face, began unrolling the velvet. He pulled the last fold away, and Pieter gasped. He had expected an instrument like the minstrel's harp—fine wood and elegant decorations, inlaid with precious stones and jewels, perhaps. Instead, before them lay a crudely carved instrument of mundane, unpolished wood. It looked as though it had been fashioned by a farm boy using a dull knife.

Theodus stormed to his feet. "Don't try to trick me. Where is the pipe?" he screamed.

"You have the swords...fair minstrel. And I have...an arrow...in my chest. Would I deign...to utter an untrue word?" the Piper choked out.

"Don't you die on me!" cried Theodus. "Tell me where you have put it."

"It is right before you, my tone-deaf fool. But I beseech you not to take it."

Theodus stood wavering, looking from the Piper to the rustic pipe. "We'll soon know."

"Yes, oh yes... We will, won't we?"

Pieter stared at the minstrel, unable to utter a word. Would Theodus obtain the pipe so easily? The minstrel picked up the instrument. For a moment he turned it, examining it from all sides. Gingerly, he set his fingers on the holes. With a scowl at the grinning Pied Piper, he put it to his mouth and blew.

A single pure note flowed from the pipe. Theodus paused to take a breath, but the note did not cease—in fact, it grew louder.

Pieter watched the minstrel's face. It flashed between pain and glee. Gretchen and the monk's eyes filled with wonder. Simon gazed in horror.

The sound throbbed even louder in Pieter's ears, resounding in his mind until he thought his head would split. Sweat poured down his face.

The soldiers' swords clattered to the floor as they slapped their hands over their ears. The archer lost his grip on the bow, and the arrow tumbled to the floor.

Theodus screamed and threw down the pipe. His eyes bulged. Blood erupted from his nose and flowed from his ears. Shrieking, the soldiers staggered out of the cave. Theodus dropped to his knees, his screams unheard over the rising tone of the pipe. The stench of blood, pungent, salty, and metallic, overwhelmed Pieter's senses. Theodus crept out of the cave, leaving a trail of red. Wailing, he disappeared through the entrance. And still the crude pipe sang.

Although they weren't bleeding, Simon and Rufus held their heads in pain. Gretchen groaned and curled in a ball on the floor. Pieter turned toward the Pied Piper. The man's mirth had vanished and he gestured toward the pipe with a gnarled hand, a questioning look on his face. Swearing under his breath, Pieter snatched up the pipe. The wood, crudely rendered, felt rough to his fingers, as though it needed to be smoothed and polished. He put it to his mouth. His breath hissed into it.

And the note stopped.

The others dropped as though cut loose from strings and there was but one sound in the cave—the shrieking laughter of the Pied Piper.

Chapter 56

When the piercing tone of the pipe ceased, Pieter peered with aching eyes at his friends. Relief showed in each face. Simon rushed out of the cave, only to quickly return. "A trail of blood goes to the edge of the cliff and into the fog. That's all I could see."

Pieter dropped the pipe as though it were a serpent. He ran to the Piper, who lay flopped back against Brother Rufus, his eyes squeezed tight against the pain.

"Is he...?" said Pieter, his voice trembling.

"N-not..." gasped the Piper, "yet."

Brother Rufus pulled off the blanket and cut away the blood-stained tunic. The bleeding had slowed, but the arrow was embedded deep in his flesh.

Simon looked Pieter in the eye and shook his head.

Pieter knelt next to the Piper. "That's the real pipe, isn't it?"

"Aye." He swallowed, then coughed up blood. With a shaking hand, he wiped at his chin. "The magic is not in the beauty of the instrument... It is in...the music. Pieter, take it."

"I don't need it."

"I know," said the Piper. "But it...needs you."

"I don't understand."

The Pied Piper spasmed, his back arching. Fresh blood oozed from the wound. He calmed, and for a moment, Pieter thought he was gone. Then the Piper gasped. "It's not so much a gift. Rather, it must be played by one...who is gifted."

"I told you—"

The Piper waved a hand. "If not you, it will be someone like Theodus. Or worse...someone like me."

Simon and Gretchen stood against the far wall. Brother Rufus still held the Piper, but he gazed off. For now, this concerned only Pieter and the Piper.

"I must know," said Pieter. "What happened that day."

"The Last Child and Merle can tell you most of it. What I think...you really want to know is...is *why* I did it."

"Very well. Tell me that."

"So simple. I was...angry. In a blind rage, I wanted to... to frighten the fools of Hamelin. But I lost control. Strange. Once you take the pipe and use it as a weapon..." His eyes closed. His lungs shuddered as he pulled in a breath. "It is most difficult...to change your path."

Brother Rufus put his free hand over his eyes.

"Where are they?" asked Pieter, his voice hard.

"The pipe...will show you."

"Are they able to return?"

The Piper laughed, a voiceless, wheezing sound. "Would they want to?"

"But—"

"Think on it, lad. Those children are better off where they are. Their parents are dead. Hamelin itself...is dead."

Pieter fell silent. The Piper's words had taught him little. They only served to create more confusion in his mind.

"Lad," said the Piper. "I...should never have had the pipe. I was...the wrong one."

"What do you mean?"

"The Piper before me...was dying. He knew it well, so he called three of us to his side. All of us...gifted musicians... Of course, I thought I was the best... Nay, I *knew* I was the best." A bout of coughing racked him. Bloody spittle ran from the corners of his mouth. An odd odor came off the man in waves. Pieter could all but taste the scent of death.

It was a long time before his breathing quieted and he spoke again. "The old Piper...had each of us sing for him... and of course, play the pipe. I was certain I would be the one...but I...was not.

"He chose Stefan... The correct choice, of course. He was a masterful musician. And he had an *agitato*. But Stefan would not take the pipe. Do you know why?"

He had a wolf? Stefan had bonded with an agitato, *just like I did with Silverfoot?* His thought returned to the piper's question. "Does it matter why this man didn't want the pipe?"

"Oh, it does." He lifted his head. "Stefan said he wasn't worthy...but the real reason was...he was afraid."

Pieter's jaw tightened.

The Piper said, "I did not know it then...but he was right. Right to fear the pipe."

A deep silence filled the cave. Pieter held one hand against his mouth, as if to hold in his own growing fear.

The Piper coughed, then said, "So...in my arrogance...I took it." He clutched himself, shivering from head to foot.

"Another log, please," Pieter said to Simon.

The old man did as he was asked, but it did little to warm the cave. It wasn't the lack of fire that chilled the Piper, nor Pieter.

Simon offered the Piper a drink from a waterskin. He took a meager sip before continuing. "Stefan would have been the perfect piper. My skill...was equal to his. What he had that I lacked...was heart."

"Heart?" said Pieter, glancing over at Simon.

The Piper swallowed. "I could entrance a crowd, compel them even, as I was to discover. But Stefan... They loved his music, truly loved it...and they loved *him*."

With great effort he raised his head again. Brother Rufus held it up in the crook of his arm. "You..." he gasped, "...you have that gift, Pieter of Hamelin."

"How do you know?"

"Because...you are here... You have followed my song, heard the notes on the wind, and you found me."

Pieter glared at the Piper. "Like Stefan, I shall refuse the gift."

"Will you? You will fail...to free the children? You have played your first note...have you not? You must take it. Absolve my transgression... Free them... The children await you—"

Chapter 57

Sometime during the night, the Piper died.

The sound of a mournful cry from Silverfoot awakened Pieter. He saw the man's clawed fingers resting on his chest. His icy blue eyes stared toward the rock ceiling, but there was no peace in his face, even now.

When the others arose, they gathered round. No one wept, but a deep sorrow filled Pieter's heart. Sorrow for a wasted gift. Grief over the Piper's weakness. Pity for the price he had paid. And at the same time, anger for what it had cost the people of Hamelin

Pieter could not deal with the confusion in his heart, except in one way. He began to sing, music that had been working in his mind since they had come to the cave.

Gretchen did not take out her lute. She sat on a box, glaring at the Piper's body, no forgiveness in her eyes. Simon's appeared baffled, as though the Piper's death had somehow robbed him, left him with his quest unfulfilled. Brother Rufus stood with hands folded across his stomach, eyes down, deep in his own thoughts or in prayer. Pieter gleaned all this in quick glances as his song came forth.

Such a gift was given,
Such a gift was lost.
Riches that were squandered,
You reckoned not the cost.

You did not heed your calling,
You bound the listening crowd,
And chose to sow despair,
Your music now your shroud.

So sorrow tells your story,
A legacy of pain,
Your fear begat your fall,
And all your gifts be slain.

Brother Rufus stirred first. "So apt that it falls on us to bury him. Perhaps in the valley below."

"No!" came a high voice from the entrance to the cave. A huge man stood there, his hands waving in the air, his fingers fluttered. "Stays here... Must...must stay here."

Chapter 58

Keeper lumbered toward them, face twisted in grief. He stood staring down at the Piper's body for a very long time. "Dead...dead for so long... Now body...dead, too."

Pieter ran to Keeper, hugging his waist. He took in the smell of the huge man—flowers and spring leaves and ink, all at once. The coarse weave of the man's tunic felt durable and solid against his cheek. Keeper thumped Pieter's back. "The song... Pieter, it is right...best yet. Full of heart, yes, much heart. I shall write it soon. I shall keep it."

Pieter looked up into the giant's round face. His slanted eyes flowed with tears; his chin trembled. "You were the one," said Pieter. "You took care of the Piper, didn't you?"

"Aye...cabin nearby... Cozy...lonely. Brought him food, scrolls... Cut firewood."

"Then why was he here?" asked Gretchen. "Why was he living in this appalling cave when he could have spent his days in a cozy cabin?" asked Gretchen.

"To wait...wait for the next Piper. Hoping you followed the clues. And because...this was meant to be...to be his tomb," said Keeper. "I knew... I knew, I *knew* you would find him."

Gretchen gripped one of Keeper's arms. "You let us traipse off to Verden when you knew where the Piper was? You could have simply told us."

"Oh, no. No, no...you must do it yourself. Not Keeper... You were not ready then. Not Merle, either. Help a chick out of its egg? No, no...weak, then. Weak, weak."

Simon clapped him on the arm. "I am glad you are here, my friend."

Pieter turned and gestured toward the monk. "This is Brother Rufus, who's been a friend and companion since Verden."

Rufus held out a hand that Keeper grasped and pumped up and down.

Extracting his hand from Keeper's grip, Rufus said, "Are you the giant who lives near Verden?"

"Yes...yes...Giant...giant of Harmony Vale... Yes, I suppose I am."

The monk smiled. "You have no idea the stories they tell about you."

"Stories? Don't know... *Songs*, oh yes. I hear them, many songs." He shook his head sadly. "Most...little truth, much fancy."

"Keeper," said Pieter, "what did you mean about not burying the Piper?"

"This—" He waved a huge hand around the cave. "His last home. Here he came to wait...here he stays. Rocks...need rocks."

He spun and hurried from the cave. In a short time, he returned rolling a large rock. Nay, a boulder. It was half as high as Pieter was tall, round and craggy. Keeper's arms bulged with great muscles. His face was bright red, his jaw clenched. He rolled the boulder forward, until it rested at the entrance to the cave, flush against one side.

Like the rest of them, Pieter began gathering his bags, even as Keeper returned, pushing an even larger stone.

"Take own things... Nothing else..." said Keeper, breathing hard. He peered inside at them. "Useless...all useless. Take nothing of Piper's...except...except one thing." He looked pointedly at Pieter.

Pieter knew exactly what Keeper was saying. But did this man grasp what it meant? If Pieter took the pipe, everything changed. How fitting to leave it buried in the cave.

Simon and Brother Rufus stood unmoving, their faces purposefully blank, making an effort to give Pieter no clue of their own feelings. Gretchen, on the other hand, scowled at him, her eyes flashing. There was no question what she thought he should do. But she wasn't the one who would have to live with the choice. *She* wasn't the one who would have to master the pipe's power or be destroyed by it.

Keeper left one last space for them to enter the cave. He began piling smaller rocks into the crevices between the large ones. He soon had the entrance blocked from top to bottom, except for the narrow access. And still Pieter stood, unmoving, shivering inside the cold mountain cavern.

Soon, much too soon, Keeper returned with the stone which would fill the last gap. He stopped a few feet from the entrance and sat on it, arms folded.

Pieter's head swam. The air grew darker and seemed to suffocate him. He ran trembling fingers through his hair. *Was* this the only way to save the children? *"Free them... The children await you,"* the Piper had said. But was the pipe the only way? He could not take the chance. He cried out, "Forgive me!"

He scrambled over the rocks Keeper had placed in the entrance.

Chapter 59

Pieter watched Keeper lift the final stone and place it high on the wall he had built. It fit into the opening perfectly, and with that the cave was sealed.

A chill rain had begun. While the others pulled out capes and hats, Pieter stood rigid, gripping the roll of velvet so tightly his fingers hurt. He turned and gazed blankly over the edge of the cliff into a grey nothingness where the valley had been. The sudden shower seemed part of the Pied Piper's burial, as though the moisture fell to grieve the man's death. Or more likely his wasted life.

Behind him, Keeper announced, "Finished...cave is closed. Done, done... Pied Piper...is done." He wiped his hands on his ink-stained tunic. Then he leaned his head against the grey rock wall he had built and wept.

Brother Rufus knelt beside him and chanted a prayer in Latin. Pieter broke away and bolted down the trail. He did not weep, but he understood. He had woven it into his song. For even though the Piper had destroyed himself, he had also destroyed countless lives in Hamelin.

The children! All those merry, dancing girls and boys. It would be easier to mourn the Piper if he knew what had become of them. How many green-eyed girls like Gretchen had been lost? How many toddlers like Agnes, with pink cheeks and high, happy laughs had the Pied Piper taken that day? Pieter wandered farther down the trail, his hands tucked under his arms. There was no forgiveness in him. Not until he knew the ending of this agonizing tale.

Keeper could do it, but he was a soul without bitterness. But Pieter was not.

His arms ached as he clenched the velvet against his chest. *I should toss the pipe over the cliff. Smash it against a rock so it can never cause harm again.* But he could not. If nothing else, the Pied Piper had said it was the key to what had happened to the children of Hamelin. And he had called them *children.*

Pieter would not ever be the Piper. But he would find out about the boys and girls of Hamelin. He would help heal this wound if he possibly could. He would give the townsfolk, if not peace, then at least a grasp of what had befallen the children.

He stopped about thirty yards along the path, aware that Brother Rufus was no longer chanting. He perched on a shelf of rock and leaned his head against the cliff. The Piper was gone, but his words lived—yea, they burned in Pieter's heart. All he wanted was to be back in Verden, or back in Harmony Vale, or back with the Lady of the Lays. Instead, he was on the road back to Hamelin. *That* was where the quest was taking them. All this time the answers had been in Hamelin.

Something brushed his arm. He jerked upright. With a cry, he dropped the roll of velvet and threw his arms around Silverfoot's massive neck. No words flowed, just a wave of affection and trust and support. He buried his hands in the soft, damp fur.

Stay with me. Don't leave me again.

But after a while, the wolf pulled away and licked Pieter's cheek. *Close. Always close.* She trotted away up the trail.

Pieter watched Silverfoot until she was out of sight. In spite of his sorrow, his heart beat with joy. Once again, he had touched his wolf.

How often he had he wanted to stroke that thick fur? But even better, the touch of that wild mind had washed away some of the despair that had edged into Pieter's thoughts.

Keeper rounded the curve of the path, his face still glistening. The others followed silently, trailed by the donkey. They stopped and gathered around, waiting, it seemed, for Pieter to decide something. The grey rain plastered his hair to his scalp. Rivulets of water streamed over his face.

Pieter picked up the dampened velvet. He brushed off some of the mud. He rose and stuffed it into a saddlebag. He looked at each face. A shuddering breath broke from deep within him. "I believe we are bound for Hamelin."

"Keeper," said Simon. "Do you know the trail from here to Koppelberg Mountain?"

"Keeper knows... Go home later." His voice ached with yearning, with the need to be back in Harmony Vale.

"If you'd rather, you could simply tell us how to get there," said Simon.

Pieter turned and saw the pain in Keeper's face.

"No, no..." Keeper began to rock on his heels, fluttering his fingers. "Knew you'd ask... I will lead... Ready to go."

The huge man stared up at the sky, oblivious to the rain that ran off his chin. "Many storms...rain, mud... Time to go. I will lead to Koppelberg." He glanced up at the slate sky. "Travel now."

Pieter walked to him, reached up and touched his hand. "Thank you, Keeper."

The giant nodded. "Go to grief? Go to joy? Cannot tell... Must go, that's all."

A wind rose, whipping the rain into Pieter's face like tiny needles. Simon tied the last bag on Rosie. Pieter walked back to the grey donkey and laid a hand on the smooth, oily leather of the saddlebag. He would do what he could for the children of Hamelin, and then the pipe would be out of his life.

They set off, following Keeper as he trudged away into the gloom. For the first hour, the trail followed the ledge. Deep green moss clung to the rocks, the only color in a grey world. The rain whipped about them, until Pieter could see almost nothing. He kept his eyes fastened on Keeper's grey tunic.

How he wished Silverfoot padded next to him. He glanced up, wondering if she made her way along the top. An image came into his mind of the wolf padding along past rocks they had already passed. She was *behind* them, following the same path, but out of sight.

Towards noon, the path dropped into a narrow gorge, which at least protected them from some of the worst wind gusts. Though Keeper wore only a tunic, his thick arms and huge legs bare, he seemed unaware of the torrent around them. Nor did his fingers flutter. His set face spoke of someone determined to complete a loathsome, but necessary, task.

Sometime past noon, they stopped briefly and huddled against a rock wall. Simon passed around some salted beef and dried yellow fruit. Keeper took his share and marched off down the trail. The others hurried after him, eating as they went. Pieter stuffed some meat into his mouth and led Rosie down the path.

The storm had penetrated all of Pieter's clothes. He could not control his shivering. He wrapped his cloak tighter and pulled the hood close. The clouds and mist had turned the world to a relentless swirling grey. Yet Keeper never hesitated, never stopped to get his bearings. Perhaps he knew the way as he knew the songs—some inner sense. Was it the same gift, the same magic?

Magic!

Pieter gasped. He stopped so fast, Rosie's head bumped him from behind. It was not a new thought—Keeper, of course, had magic. How else did he hear and record the songs? And yet there wasn't a breath of evil in him. He was the most upright man Pieter had ever met.

Pieter began walking again, thinking of Keeper's magic. And the magic of the pipe. How could they both be enchanted, when one was good and the other something evil? Was it all in the intention? Could something of light be used as a thing of darkness?

Darkness. It came early in the gorge, but Keeper showed no inclination to find a place to sleep. Pieter feared they were in for a long, cold night.

Soon Pieter could see only the shadowy bulk of Keeper ahead. Darkness closed around them. But at last the giant turned from the trail.

A cave lay level with the path. The yawning opening was high enough for Keeper to enter without bending over. They waited just inside the mouth, in complete darkness but out of the rain.

Click. Click.

A yellow spark flickered and died.

Click.

This time, a small flame caught. Keeper tucked the fire-starting stones back into his belt pouch. One at a time, he added twigs, then small branches to the growing fire. They soon gathered around the dancing orange flames, eager to dry off and warm up.

In the firelight, Pieter could see that this cave had been stocked with firewood. A large wooden chest sat nearby.

"Who does this?" asked Gretchen, looking around. "Who keeps this cave ready?"

"Friends," grunted Keeper, laying a log across the flames. "Friends...of the mountains. I shall return later... Cut more wood... Replace what used."

Pieter squinted up. Ribbons of glittering white laced the dark walls. Like the Piper's cave, a cleft ran along the apex of the cavern, and the dark smoke coiled up into it and disappeared.

They hung their soaked cloaks over nearby rocks. Koppelberg loomed in Pieter's mind, shadowing everything else. What was going to happen when he reached that cliff face once again? He did not know. He had learned little from the Pied Piper's cryptic story, it seemed.

A growl at the mouth of the cave brought Gretchen and Simon to their feet. Brother Rufus scooted backwards, bumping the wall. But there was no fear in Pieter's heart, for he knew who stood sentinel. He glanced at Keeper, surprised to see the giant sitting calmly, with a small smile on his face. And Rosie, in the rear of the cavern, seemed to be paying no attention to the wolf either.

Gretchen snatched Simon's walking stick and held it in front of her. Simon's knife appeared in his hand. Pieter sprang to his feet. "Silverfoot has been our companion and our guardian throughout this journey. Do not be afraid."

Without waiting for a reaction, he walked to the entrance. In a moment, he returned with Silverfoot at his side. Brother Rufus clutched himself. Gretchen and Simon seemed torn between fleeing and attacking. But Keeper merely grinned. "Nice wolfie," he said, with not a trace of fear in his voice. "Pretty...pretty wolfie."

Simon waved his knife. "Get that creature out of here."

"Look at Rosie," said Pieter. "She is not afraid." Indeed, the donkey chewed calmly on the grass thrown at her feet. She looked up, regarding them with large, brown eyes, as though wondering what the fuss was about.

Keeper bent over Silverfoot, ruffling the fur on the top of her head. He raised her snout and looked her in the eye. "Songs... Wolf songs... I understand. I know what they mean... I know."

Little by little, Gretchen lowered the staff. "She doesn't seem aggressive. Right now, anyhow."

"And she won't be," said Pieter. "Simon, put away your knife."

"Very well." He slipped it into its sheath. "It appears this creature means us no harm." Nevertheless, his hands shook.

"Brother Rufus?" called Pieter. "Come back to the fire. Silverfoot is part of our quest."

The monk's high voice squeaked from the shadows. "My mind agrees. But I...I can't seem to persuade my hammering heart, which is like to burst at any moment."

Pieter returned to the fire and sat cross-legged. Silverfoot stretched out at his side, leaning into him. One by one the others joined him. All but Brother Rufus.

Content with Silverfoot at his side, Pieter began humming a tune that had been forming for some time—wistful, fearful, but laced with hope. Gretchen made no move to join him, but that did not surprise him. She understood it was his song, his dilemma. For it spoke of what awaited him at Koppelberg. As usual, the lyrics formed in his mind, and the words poured out to meld with the tune.

A cliff looms high near Hamelin,
Smooth and stark and grey,
Its air infused with sorrow,
And the ghost of music fey.

I arise in awe before it,
With its sorrow and its hope.
My tortured heart near riven,
I tremble as I grope.

Will my meager song be true,
And free the children lost?
Can magic notes bring blessing,
Without a baleful cost?

I rejoice in my gift
But lament that it was given.
I'm burdened as I grope,
My tortured heart near riven.

Keeper closed his eyes as he swayed to the music. His hands lay quiet in his lap. When the song ended, he said, "So sad... Lovely, though, oh, yes, so pretty. But my heart... It hurts...hurts so bad."

"Oh, Keeper," said Pieter. "I'm so sorry. I should have kept it to myself."

"No...no. You share... We are blessed... Share...families share."

Gretchen cleared her throat. "I'm the one who's sorry."

"Why?" asked Pieter, scratching between Silverfoot's ears.

"Because I've pushed you so hard. As though all this was easy. As if the way was clear. That song—it helps me understand."

Pieter smiled at her. "Don't be sorry. I needed someone to push me a bit."

"Write it down," said Keeper softly. "I will, I will...soon. Soon." His fingers fluttered at the thought.

"Soon," muttered Pieter, his heart turning cold. He buried his face in Silverfoot's neck. So much was going to happen. *I must open the mountain. I must enter the Pied Piper's land and face the unknown.*

Soon.

Chapter 60

On the second night in the mountains, Keeper led them to a small wooden shack. The cabin smelled of dampness and decaying wood, but it proved comfortable. It had a small stack of wood and a few meager supplies. Keeper built a fire in the rustic fire pit.

Silverfoot had padded at Pieter's side throughout the day, but when they had arrived at the cabin, she had disappeared, no doubt to hunt.

The room was full of nervous chatter—idle talk about sheep and carving and life at the monastery. Pieter paid little attention to it, although the murmur of their voices comforted him. He spread his parchment on his lap and tried to practice his reading. He ended up staring at the letter T until it blurred in his sight. He scarcely noticed when the talk ceased.

"Pieter?" said Simon quietly.

Pieter started, pulled out of his thoughts. He realized Simon had repeated his name. He looked up.

Simon gazed into the fire. "Before tomorrow, there are two things I must tell you."

Pieter drew a deep breath and waited, rubbing his hands through his hair, the cabin starkly quiet around him. Even the fire had ceased crackling and had slumped into bright orange coals. He pulled his cape tighter around his shoulders.

"Son," said Simon.

The word sent a wave of warmth through Pieter. He turned his full attention to the old man.

"First," said Simon, clasping his hands in his lap. "I would remind you that this path you travel—you do not tread it alone."

Pieter nodded. That was true in one way, of course. But in spite of the man's kind words, Pieter knew that when he faced the cliff on Koppelberg, whatever the outcome, it would be on his shoulders alone. What's more, he was sure he would have to enter the mountain to find the children, and he was the only one who could do that.

"And second," said Simon, looking hard into Pieter's eyes. "Trust your heart. We all believe in you. Trust your heart and trust the music, and you will do the right thing."

"Will I?" said Pieter. "I have no idea what the right thing *is*."

"You will," said Brother Rufus softly.

"Aye, Pieter," added Gretchen. "I believe it also."

Pieter gave her a sharp look. *She* believed? She had faith in him? That bolstered him more than any other words. No one knew for sure that he would make the right choices. And yet...and yet, their confidence strengthened him.

Pieter's sleep that night was punctuated with wild dreams and a sudden cold piercing through his blanket. Deep in the night, Silverfoot returned and settled next to him, and Pieter fell into a serene sleep at last.

They awoke to a bitter chill. The rain had returned. The day warmed as they traveled, and at last the rain ceased. Clouds still hugged the valleys below, but the air around them began to clear. Silverfoot took her place next to Pieter. Brother Rufus trudged along in the rear, fear of the wolf still writ in his face.

When the clouds above them finally broke and drifted apart, the high craggy peak of Koppelberg was at last revealed, purple in the late-afternoon light. From this angle, it looked different than it did from Hamelin, but Pieter knew it nevertheless.

At first, Pieter thought they might reach the cliff before the day was over. But as the afternoon passed, he realized they would have to camp one more night.

As the mountain grew closer, Pieter's stomach tightened and his throat burned. Something would soon be expected of him. By the Piper, dead as he was. By his companions. And soon by the people of Hamelin.

But what? Why couldn't it all be clear and exact? Why must he grope his way along? The Piper had said that the answer would come from the pipe itself. But for that, he would have to bring it to his lips and play it. Was that the only way?

Could he help the children, the town of Hamelin, without becoming the Piper? Could he play it even once and not lose himself?

Chapter 61

It was with great relief that Pieter saw the faint pink light of dawn coloring the mouth of the cave Keeper had found for them.

During the night, Silverfoot had slipped away. Pieter hoped she would return soon. He did not wish to face this day without her.

The others soon roused. Silently, they gathered their things and broke their fast. In a short time, they were on their way. High clouds had rolled in, hovering over the peak of Koppelberg. The valleys and hills below remained blanketed in thick fog.

But in between, the mountain stood, stark and grey and huge in the sky.

Waiting for Pieter's arrival.

As the day went on, the trail dropped and wound back and forth. For a time Koppelberg was blocked by the surrounding hills. But by midmorning, they crested a rise, and there it was—so close, Pieter gasped. He couldn't make out the cliff face itself, but the clouds seemed to be opening the way before him.

Soon after that, Pieter began to hear the pipe.

Far away, but clear, oh so clear. The very melody he had heard here before, the music that had haunted Simon all these years. He halted in the trail, his legs unwilling to take another step, and cocked his head. How could it be? The Pied Piper was dead. The pipe itself was tucked into a bag on Rosie's back. And yet the song shimmered in the air, just at the edge of his hearing. What had the Pied Piper called it? The ghost of a melody.

He glanced at Simon. The old man stood rigid, staring straight ahead. The cords in his neck stood out. Aye, he heard it also.

Keeper turned and regarded them for a moment. Pieter nodded, and they trudged on.

The pale sun struggled to shine through the cloud cover, a perfect white orb hanging in the sky. It was scarcely noon. The moisture had dried from the lush spring grass and barren grey rocks. With the Piper's Song relentless in his ears and his friends surrounding him, there was no reason to delay. Pieter made his way toward Koppelberg.

Before long, Pieter heard something besides the Piper's Song. He moved next to Simon and whispered, "Are there wild animals around here?"

Simon nodded. "We're in the mountains, aren't we?"

"I hear something. Behind us," said Pieter. "I thought it was Silverfoot, but it isn't."

The old man turned, listening intently. "Aye. I hear it. Behind us and on the ridge above us as well."

"What are they?"

Keeper looked back, fingers flicking in the air. "Wolves."

Pieter immediately reached out for Silverfoot, but he caught only a dim impression of stealth and blood. Nevertheless, she touched his mind. Even where she hunted, she seemed to know where they were.

"Rest easy, lad," said Simon. "Except for our good Silverfoot, wolves normally avoid people."

"I wish I had my staff," muttered Gretchen.

Pieter did, too. He had seen her lay low that wild dog. Silently, Simon handed her his walking stick.

An eerie howling raised the hair on Pieter's arms. The howling was different from Silverfoot's song—it was mournful and wretched. Keeper halted, his hand up for silence. "So strange... Song not right... Wolves, but...but...something's wrong."

Chapter 62

The howls echoed off the cliffs and closed in around them.

The company huddled on the trail, the grey donkey stamping her front hooves and skittering from side to side.

Simon scowled. "I've known starving wolves to attack a lone traveler. But not a group."

"Pain," said Keeper. "Nearly mad...howls of despair." He rocked and held his ears. "Sorrow, despair... Song of... of doath."

A low growl came from above. On an outcropping of black rock, a grey and white wolf skulked toward the edge and crouched, staring at them with watery yellow eyes.

Simon pulled Rosie's halter tight, his other arm around her neck. "Easy, girl," he crooned. "Easy." The donkey blew and skittered sideways. Her eyes rolled back until only the whites showed. She knew this wolf was *not* Silverfoot.

The wolf's coloring was similar to Silverfoot, yet this animal's demeanor was quite different. His patchy fur hung on an emaciated body. Its eyes, full of threat and anger, glittered and watered. When he snarled, white froth dripped from his snout and ran from his mouth.

"He's diseased," said Simon. "He has the foaming sickness."

Another wolf crept beside the first, all black and in even worse shape. Then, on the trail close behind them, a third appeared.

Pieter no longer doubted they would attack. And none of his companions carried a weapon, save a couple of knives and Simon's walking stick.

"Slowly," said Simon, struggling to restrain Rosie's thrashing head. "Move away. Up the trail."

But that proved impossible, for another wolf crept toward them, blocking the trail in front of them.

Rosie would not take a step. Her wide brown eyes rolled in panic.

The two wolves above lowered their heads. Muscles bunched in their hindquarters, tensed to leap.

One behind, one ahead, two above. Pieter saw no way out of the trap. His fingers went cold; his breath came in painful gasps. At the same time, a flurry of dark, desperate images flooded his mind, overwhelming him. He slapped his hands to his throbbing head, unable to decipher the meaning.

Then out of the chaos, one voice became clear. Silverfoot. *Save them. Let them go.*

Pieter knew at once what Silverfoot wanted him to do. It streaked from his mind to his muscles, and without any more thought, his hands moved. Toward the bag on Rosie's back. He withdrew the roll of velvet, taking the edge in one hand. In a single motion, he snapped the cloth and snatched the pipe out of the air. He dropped the cloth and brought the wooden instrument to his lips.

A note sounded, urgent and low. His fingers moved on their own, and a melody came forth, sorrowful and despairing, echoing the cries of the wolves.

All four of the creatures froze, suddenly silent. Their muscles trembled. Pieter lowered the pipe and glanced at his friends, who stared gape-jawed at him.

"Go!" cried Pieter to the others, waving a hand up the trail. "Flee while I play." In that brief moment without the music, the wolf behind them advanced, growling low and deep. The pipe's music fluted again. In spite of the danger, Pieter's fingers loved the feel of the wood and the openings.

Once more the wolves stopped, their eyes fastened on Pieter.

Brother Rufus broke out of his trance first. He hurried up the trail, right past the wolf, which stood still as stone. Gretchen rushed after him, and Simon dragged Rosie. The wolf paid them no heed.

Pieter backed the opposite way up the trail, still playing. He knew the wolves would not attack as long as the song continued. As he approached, the wolf behind him sat on its haunches, its tongue lolling out of the side of its mouth.

Its eyes had changed. The anger had vanished, although madness glittered still in its deep amber orbs.

Behind him, he heard his friends rushing away. Rosie's hooves clopped on the path, but not a wolf turned toward the sound.

Yes, yes, sent Silverfoot. *Mercy. Give them mercy. Coming...coming!*

Pieter changed the tune into a more urgent melody. The wolf from up the trail joined them. The two above picked their way down and joined the others.

Pieter walked backwards, step by careful step. The closer they came, the worse they looked. Large patches of fur had fallen from their coats, leaving raw red skin full of running sores. These animals were not evil, just sick and desperate. But could he do what Silverfoot had asked?

As he played, Pieter continued to share the wolves' emotions, touching their canine minds through the song. The wolves were dying and they knew it. The disease was eating away at their organs and their minds, beautiful animals transformed into crazed creatures.

They wanted it to end.

Knowing that, Pieter could do what had to be done. Silverfoot sprinted closer and closer, sending strength with every stride.

Pieter led the wolves along the trail until they reached a high point where the cliff dropped to ragged rocks far below.

There, the tone of his song changed once more. The first wolf approached him, then lowered his head and shoulders in submission. Pieter played a song of sorrow. A song of farewell.

Farewell. The pack grieves...grieves, howled Silverfoot.

The first wolf bunched his muscles and sprang over the edge. He fell without a sound. A wretched thump signaled that the wolf's life was gone.

The second approached, crouched, then followed the first.

In turn, the last two plunged to their deaths. And their release.

The pipe left Pieter's lips. He began to sing.

Mighty creatures of the pack,
Noble hunters, grey and black,
Eyes once glowed with power bright,
Now be filled with death's grim light.
Life's rhythms, strong, I cannot bestow,
So in grief, I let you go.

Only when he had finished was he overcome. He collapsed to his knees, clutching the pipe to his chest. All the grief of the last few days poured out in salty tears that coursed in rivulets down Pieter's face.

He wept still when warm fur brushed against his face and a long tongue laved the tears. At the same moment, an arm encircled his shoulders, and he knew Silverfoot and Simon were both there.

Chapter 63

When they resumed their journey, Pieter led the way, setting the pace, his strides long and purposeful. Silverfoot padded next to him, her head swinging from side to side, her blue eyes taking in everything. Pieter sensed the wolf's growing discomfort as they neared more populated lands. But urgency drove him. He was desperate to reach the cliff on Koppelberg, to stand at that wretched place. It wasn't like the urging that had sent the wolves off the cliff. Nor, he knew, was it like the magic that led the rats into the Weser River. It was the knowledge that things—at least some things—could be made right. And if that meant using the pipe, then that was what he would do.

The Pied Piper had told him that the pipe would show him what to do. Using it to lead the wolves had made it so. With crystal certainty he knew exactly what had to happen in Hamelin.

The path intersected with another running west to east. Pieter halted in the middle of the crossroads, turning and studying each direction. Yes. They had reached the very trail he and Simon had used on their past treks to the cliff on Koppelberg.

How many times had he passed this crossroads without ever wondering where the path that intersected it might have led?

Silverfoot gave a deep growl and swung away, loping to the north and soon disappearing in the brush. *Nearby. Staying nearby,* the wolf sent.

Thinking of Simon, he looked back. The old man was far behind, lurching along with halting steps. Pieter ran back. "Forgive me. I have set too fast a pace."

Simon grunted. "My bloody leg isn't your fault, lad."

Pieter threw an arm around the old man's waist. Simon draped one arm over Pieter's shoulder, and together they made their way to the crossroads.

They turned toward Koppelberg Mountain. How long had it been since he had been here? It seemed ages, although it was only a matter of weeks. Pieter and his friends had traveled a long road since then. He had left Hamelin a blacksmith's son. Now he was, well, *not* the Piper, but certainly a musician.

Soon he helped Simon lower himself onto the same rock where he had sat so often, facing the sheer cliff on Koppelberg. Pieter walked to the base of the cliff, just off the scree that had gathered over the years. He pulled out the pipe, then stood staring at the rocks for long minutes.

As always, the song of the Piper drifted on the breeze, but Pieter realized the Pied Piper had been right—it was but the voice of the past, a ghost of that historical day. And that song, the one that had echoed in his mind for so long, would not stay. With the pipe, Pieter would blow away the old tune, scatter those haunting notes throughout the hills, and it would be gone forever.

He would create a new song. A song that had never been played—one that Keeper had not yet inscribed onto parchment. Pieter and the pipe would form it together.

At the same time, he sensed the danger, the risk of using such magic. That was why the Pied Piper had blundered into doing such harm. The man had never truly understood the magic of the pipe, even though he had no doubt played it perfectly.

But something held Pieter. The stories of the mountain opening. A gateway of sorts—perhaps a portal. He didn't know exactly how it would happen. But he had to open the mountain. He had to try.

Then a different song blossomed in his head. It swept away the haunting melody he had heard so often. This new tune filled his mind, and at the same time touched his heart. So full of sorrow, and yet infused with hope.

This is the one. This is the music that will open the mountain. Almost he pulled out the pipe, eager to play it. He shook his head. Nay. Not yet. The melody was still forming in his mind. Clear, but not yet complete.

Besides, there was something else that needed doing first.

He returned to his friends, who stood clustered together around the rock where Simon sat. They looked worried, as if they were afraid he had lost his resolve.

He tucked the pipe into his belt. "I know the song I must play. But first, I need to go to Hamelin."

Chapter 64

They paused beside the remnants of Simon's burned-out cottage. Ramblers and weeds already grew over the site. The rose that had once vined around the front door was now a twisted bramble, but alive and blooming. Fresh canes poked up between scorched beams and had begun to wind up the chimney stones.

Simon stood at the edge of the ruin, body rigid, arms tight across his chest, staring at what had once been his home. No one moved until Keeper stepped forward. He cupped a rosebud with his huge hands. In a soft but clear voice he said, "Behold, from the ashes a rose shall grow." He said it without a pause or a stammer.

Brother Rufus lifted his eyebrows. "Is that from the Bible?"

"No...a song... A new song, but I hear it. Oh yes, I hear it."

Pieter looked at him in astonishment. "But, Keeper. I haven't sung it yet."

"You will... Oh, yes...you will."

Pieter looked back at Simon, and it seemed the man stood a bit less rigid.

"Shall we move on to Hamelin?" Pieter said. "When we arrive, there is something I must do alone."

Simon scowled. "Is that safe? Last time he—"

"I remember well. Still, this is for me to do alone."

Simon nodded. "When you need us, we will be there. Until then, we will await you at The Tong and Anvil."

"No, no," said Keeper. "Not Keeper... Perhaps slip in... after dark, yes, yes. Cause a ruckus...scare people... Come later." He turned and disappeared over the hill.

Pieter stared at the place where he had vanished, relieved that Keeper would return. He wondered where Silverfoot was. He would feel so much stronger if she were with him. He could imagine, however, the panic that would ensue if he strolled into Hamelin with a wolf at his side. It would be worse than strolling in with a giant.

He pulled his cloak tighter and strode toward Hamelin without looking back. His steps soon took him onto the crumbling cobblestones of the town. The houses and shops he had known so well had not changed. And yet everything seemed different, as though each stone and brick had aged and blackened with soot.

The street was soiled with mud and trash and manure. He had never noticed the stench. Before, it had simply been ordinary, a part of every day. Now he saw it for what it was. Simon had said it best—Hamelin was a dying town. Its past had strangled its future. He hoped he could change that. But that was for later. First he needed to go home.

He turned a corner and stood staring at the oak door of the house where he had grown up. The scar on his shoulder twitched.

He began to hum the lullaby he had sung to Agnes so many times. With that tune on his tongue, he approached the house. Was his father home? No, he should still be at the blacksmith's shop.

How odd it was to knock on his own front door, but for some reason he couldn't just walk in. Cautious footsteps approached the door, and it opened a crack. His mother's brown eye stared at him. Pieter took a step back, but his mother's face softened. "I knew. I knew you would return."

The door opened wide. She was still, except for her trembling chin and the moisture that ran down her cheeks.

As always, she wore her plain tan dress. "I knew you were coming back."

The next instant, Pieter was in his mother's arms. "My son, my son," she sobbed, stroking his back. "I heard your singing. In my dreams, in my thoughts, in the hours of work, I heard your lovely songs."

It was an embrace such as he had never received before, and Pieter knew that his mother had changed, too.

A small voice piped from behind her. "Mama?" A tiny face, fearful and shy, peeked around her mother's skirt.

Pieter wanted to scoop her up, but he felt the same shyness she did. He dropped to one knee. "Agnes," he said, his voice soft and breaking with the tears he held back. "It's Pieter, your big brother."

The little girl pulled back and hid once again.

"That's amazing!" he said. "She's standing by herself! And she said 'Mama!'"

The baby peered out again. He held out his arms, frightened that she might not come. "Agnes? It's me, Pay-pay." Had she forgotten him? It hadn't been that long.

She would not come, and fear filled his heart. Then it came to him, as it had so many times before. He dropped his hands on his knee and began to sing, the very tune he had sung to her on those many nights in the loft.

Agnes leaned closer, a small fist held tight on her mother's skirt, a small smile forming on her tiny lips.

Oh, sweet little bairn,
Tucked safe in my arms,
With eyes of deep wonder,
And laughter that charms.

Oh, come, my sweet Agnes,
The sun's going down,
Soft shadows your bunting,
Warm darkness your gown.

Now sleep, little Agnes,
Just close your wee eyes.
Soft slumber enfold you,
'Til soon the sun rise.

So sleep—

With that, Agnes tottered forward, her steps wobbling, her hands splayed for balance, and she tumbled into Pieter's waiting arms.

Pieter sat on the dirt floor, playing with Agnes. Mother cut a head of cabbage with swift swipes of the knife. They were both avoiding talking about Father, who might come storming in at any moment. At last, Pieter could bear it no longer. "Mother," he said. "What about...?" His voice trailed off.

"What about your father?"

There. It was in the open. He brushed back a lock of hair from his sister's soft forehead. He didn't want to be afraid, but he couldn't pretend otherwise. "Mother. I cannot run again."

"I know, son."

"I want to, the saints know. But I must face him before I can answer the call of Koppelberg."

Tears pooled in his mother's eyes. "Perhaps...another day?"

"Nay, Mother." It would be so easy to avoid it, to slip away and hide until...until when? Until what? Would it be any easier tomorrow? Or the next day? "I'm not trying to be brave."

"But you *are* brave, my son."

"Nay," said Pieter, holding his head. "I am so frightened my stomach is all a-churning."

"Then perhaps you should flee," she said.

"No. Not again."

Mother covered her eyes. "I also am full of fear, but you are right. This thing must be done."

Pieter nodded. "My heart tells me my quest is not finished. After following the Piper's Song all this way, after returning to Hamelin, I do not believe it will all end at the point of my father's knife."

Mother glanced at the window. "The blacksmith shop is closed." Her knife hovered over the cabbage. "As usual, it is anyone's guess where he is. He might be on his way home; he might at The Tong and Anvil. Or passed out somewhere with his face in his own vomit. It matters little to me." The knife came down with a whack.

Pieter sat up straighter. "The Tong and Anvil?" That was where his friends were waiting. "Mother," he said, trying to sound undaunted. "I must find him tonight."

"Pieter, he will want to hurt you."

"I know, though I do not understand why."

"Just return to me when things are settled with him. Mayhap I can explain it. There is much to be said between us."

Chapter 65

Even as Pieter slipped into the darkened street, he had no plan, no real notion of what might happen when he found his father. His own body was somewhat stronger than when he had left, but Father had a blacksmith's muscles. And he carried a knife.

A man went by, leading an old mare that pulled a dray loaded with firewood. A goodwife hurried the other way, her jaw set, her steps hard. Pieter headed for the blacksmith's shop, keeping to the shadows. He listened intently, alert to any sound. His father always strode with a heavy tread. If he came this way, Pieter would hear him.

But something told him his father would not be found heading for home this night. Not yet. Surely he was heading for The Tong and Anvil. Nevertheless, Pieter worked his way along the street warily. The shadows lengthened. He patted his belt, comforted to have the pipe there. His heart hammered at an unbelievable rate, but the pipe calmed his nerves. The street smelled of stew and smoke and droppings from horses and mules. He heard the sounds of muffled voices behind shutters, of dogs barking in the alleys, of horses trudging along on nearby streets.

But he heard no music. No whistled tunes, no goodwife singing as she prepared a meal, no old uncle playing the fiddle.

He reached the blacksmith shop and found it shuttered for the night as he'd expected. He turned toward the inn, feeling relief that his father was not headed toward Mother and Agnes. But he *was* headed toward Simon and the others. Sweat collected in beads on his forehead. His shirt clung to his back.

He reached the inn and slipped inside. The lamps had been lit. Simon and Brother Rufus sat near the fire with Gretchen. He did not notice his father until Sam, behind the counter, caught his eye. The innkeeper's face was tight with worry. He nodded toward the far corner.

Pieter's father sat hunched over a tankard, eyes down. Somehow he seemed bigger than Pieter remembered. Ash and dirt caked his face. The hands that clutched the tankard were black with the grime of the smithy.

Pieter didn't look to see what his friends were doing. He headed for his father's table before he lost the meager measure of courage he had been able to muster.

He stopped directly across from him. His father's eyes lifted. He stared for a long moment through bleary, bloodshot eyes. "*You.*"

"Aye. I have returned."

"And here I thought I was rid of you," he said, his words slurred.

"It was my fate to come back to Hamelin."

"Was it, now?" He glowered at Pieter. "Don't you expect nothing from me. When you ran off, you stopped being my son."

"Perhaps," said Pieter. His hands were shaking, but to his surprise his voice remained steady. "But nothing has changed with my mother and my sister."

His father snorted and took a long quaff of his ale. He sat the tankard down and said, "Nay. On that you are quite mistaken. You have no family. You have no *house.* You have *nothing!*"

Chapter 66

"**F**ather—"

"*Nothing!*" the blacksmith roared as he lurched to his feet. He grabbed the edge of the table and heaved it up. Pieter leapt back. The tankard smashed to the floor. The table landed on its edge with a deep thud, just inches from Pieter's feet.

Simon appeared on one side of him, Brother Rufus on the other, his hands on his hips. Gretchen waited just behind them, Simon's walking stick held at the ready.

His father wavered, his breath rasping. "You scrawny brat. Think your new friends are gonna save you?" He lurched against a chair that spun into the wall with a crash.

Pieter's entire body trembled, but he stood as tall as he could. "You will not lay a hand on my mother or my sister ever again."

His father wobbled, steadying himself with a hand against the wall. "Who's gonna stop me? An old man? A fat monk? A girl?" He laughed. "*You?*" With a grunt, he staggered away. "Stay away from my house, you bastard!" he called over his shoulder and slammed the door behind him.

Pieter slumped against Simon. The old man eased him into a chair. Sobs broke from deep in Pieter's gut. "What have I done? He's going to hurt my mother. Or Agnes!"

"He's a coward," said Gretchen.

"But...but I've made him angry... My sister, she's too little to defend herself!"

"Come," said Brother Rufus. "We may be old, fat, female, and scrawny, but I think he's in for a bit of a surprise."

Pieter rubbed his fists in his eyes. "He's probably headed for my house right now."

Simon nodded. "Then we'll go by way of Crescent Alley. We can get there before him."

They dashed from the inn and hurried into the dark streets. With a new surge of strength, Pieter broke into a run, Gretchen beside him. They left the two men behind as they raced for his home.

He burst through the door. His mother, sitting in a chair near the fire, gave a little squeal and dropped the shirt she had been mending. "Pieter! You frightened me to death!"

"Has Father come home?"

"Nay. All is quiet here."

Pieter sagged in relief. "You were right. I have made him very angry."

Simon and Rufus appeared in the doorway behind Pieter. The monk stood with his hands on his knees, sucking in air. The old man leaned against the casing and rubbed at his crippled leg.

Pieter saw the fear in his mother's face, but there was a certain resolve in her eyes. As though she knew this confrontation had to happen.

"This is Simon, of course, and Brother Rufus, who befriended me on the journey. And Gretchen, who has traveled with us." He ran a hand through his hair. "I must find Father," he said. "Rufus, Simon, will you stay here?"

"Of course," said Simon. "But one of us should go with you."

"Nay. I—"

Brother Rufus broke in. "I think we should all stay here. Sooner or later, he will appear. Where else would he go?"

"There is wisdom in that," said Simon. "You could stumble around Hamelin for the rest of the night and never lay eyes on him."

"I will go with you," said Gretchen.

"Please, children, it is too dangerous," said Brother Rufus.

In the end, Pieter agreed. Sitting and waiting was much harder than taking action, even if it *was* stumbling in the dark. But, yes, at some point Father would come home, if for no other reason than to show Pieter that he could do as he pleased.

Pieter wished Keeper were with them. But as big and strong as the man was, he was not at all sure he would resort to violence.

Rufus took a chair and dragged it after him. "I'll sit outside the door." He grabbed the fire poker from the hearth and took it with him.

Simon made sure the backdoor was barred, then sat facing the front, holding his knife. Gretchen waited near the table, holding Simon's walking stick.

Somehow, the commotion hadn't awakened Agnes. Pieter walked over to her cradle and watched her sleep. It wasn't going to be long before she outgrew this bed.

His mother touched his shoulder, and they watched the baby together for a time. Then Pieter settled into a chair. His mother busied herself with various little tasks. Every faint noise startled him, even though he suspected his father would come raging home like a bull.

Pieter's mind turned to the song he needed to write. He had to explain the pipe to the people of Hamelin. They had to understand what he was doing.

They were *children*. Thrice the Pied Piper had spoken of those in Koppelberg as such. The man had urged him to take the pipe, asking him how else he would free the *children*. Had he simply meant that they were children when he led them into the mountain? Perhaps, but it seemed to Pieter that they were children still. Pieter would not know until he opened the mountain. But the more he pondered the Piper's words and the tone of his voice, the more confident Pieter was. The children of Hamelin were children still.

Hamelin needed to be a part of this. If the townsfolk were willing. If they would prepare. He shivered and glanced at the fire. Only hot orange coals remained. The firebox lay empty.

Glad to have a task, he headed for the back door. He reached for the crossbar, then stopped. Could his father be out there?

"Wait," said Simon.

"We just need a little wood."

Simon stood and walked toward him, knife in hand. "Then I'll come with you."

Pieter nodded and lifted off the crossbar. He pushed open the door, and a huge hand thrust through the opening and seized Pieter's shoulder. In a heartbeat, he was jerked out of the room and tossed into the dark night.

Chapter 67

Pieter slammed into the ground. His breath burst from his lungs. The door slammed shut, then opened partway as someone hit it from the inside. The huge figure pushed it closed with one hand, then dragged something large in front of it. Pieter heard a whoosh of water even as he was grabbed again and lifted off the ground. Blow after blow rattled the door from within.

Again he was thrown, this time over the stone fence. He managed to twist and land on his hands and knees. His father clambered over the wall and dropped beside him.

Pieter had known who it was the moment the hand grasped him. "Father!" he cried. "What—"

His father jerked him off his feet by the front of his tunic. He lifted him until they were face to face. He smelled of ale and coal and raging anger.

"Father!" Pieter cried again.

His father shook him. "Thought you'd keep me out of my own house, did you? That house is *mine*."

"I don't care about the house," cried Pieter. "Just don't hurt—"

A beefy hand hit Pieter in the ear, whipping his head back. A canvas sack came down over his head. He sensed a rope being wound around his body. Pieter twisted and jerked, but to no avail. His father strode off down the alley, with Pieter bouncing on his shoulder. The rough bag scratched at his skin.

Each time he struggled, his father's first pounded the side of his head. Dizziness swept him and he lay still. His head throbbed from the repeated blows. The pipe, still thrust in his belt, dug into his hip. His heart beat hard. His old shoulder wound throbbed as though it had never healed. For a time, his father's boots resounded off the cobblestones. But soon he realized they were on dirt. The smell of fir and pine and damp earth flowed through the fabric of the sack.

All of sudden, the scent of smoke joined the smell of pine. Through the coarse weave of the sack, Pieter glimpsed flickering yellow light. A fire. He was tossed to the ground.

The rope was pulled off of him and the hood snatched away. With quick hands, his father tied his hands in back of him and bound his ankles. He dropped him and trudged to the far side of the fire, where he sat on a log. "You shoulda stayed away. You never shoulda come back."

"Father, I—"

"*Never* call me that again. *Never!*" The man's face quivered with anger, the firelight burning harsh shadows into his features. "I may be a bit drunk, but it looks like I can still outsmart you and your flabby friends."

"Why are you so angry?"

"Don't be a fool. Don't pretend you don't know how you've treated me."

"I don't know what you are talking about, Father."

The man erupted off the log. He circled the fire in two steps and kicked Pieter in the side. "I *told* you. *Never* call me that again."

Pieter's father wobbled, then he stumbled backward and toppled into a small pine tree. "I'm gonna take care of you. For *good.*" He rolled out, the branches snapping under his weight.

For a long moment, he remained motionless. His ragged breath settled into a rasping roar. Pieter waited, trying to decide how deep his father's stupor might be. He turned his bound body just a little. A stick cracked under him, loud enough to rouse any sleeper, but Father did not move.

What was his father going to do when he woke up? Pieter could think of only one thing. Gingerly, Pieter twisted a little farther. He spotted his pipe on the ground, a couple of yards away. Somehow it had slipped out of his belt.

He began to roll toward it, as quietly as he could, eyeing his father the whole time. One more squirm, and he maneuvered his head next to the pipe. He had no idea how the pipe would help, but it lay there, so close, and it seemed his only hope.

He stretched his head as far as he could, until he was able to grasp the end of the pipe with his teeth. He closed his lips and blew. To his shock, no sound came. Nothing. He blew again. This time, far off at the very edge of his hearing, he caught a faint tone.

It didn't seem to accomplish anything, but he continued blowing, stopping only to gasp in air. But the distant, whispered note never stopped, a rich tone murmuring in the night.

His head felt light. He stopped and sucked in a lungful of air. Again, the faint sound continued.

He was about to blow again when his teeth lost their grip; the pipe dropped to the ground. He swallowed hard. In the darkness, two large eyes, glowing an intense blue, stared at him. Silverfoot!

She stepped closer on silent paws. Pieter could not even hear the animal breathing. How stupid of him. He should have called to her immediately.

Help me. So angry...

Silverfoot leaned over him. The wolf's warm breath laved his face. Her snout thrust toward him. She nuzzled his wrists; her teeth nipped at the rope. Strands snapped as the creature delicately severed them without catching his skin. With a soft snap, the rope parted.

Again he glanced at his father, who remained motionless except for the rising of his chest.

Pieter worked at the knots on the ropes tied around his ankles, while Silverfoot licked his face. When he was free, he pulled away the cords and snatched up his pipe. "I am so grateful, my friend," he whispered, pulling her close. He clung to the wolf, reluctant to let go.

He heard a sound behind him. His father had clambered to his feet, and staggered into the firelight. "What the hell?"

Silverfoot pulled away from Pieter's embrace and snarled.

His father's jaw dropped. His reddened eyes grew wide.

Even without looking, Pieter knew the wolf was gathering herself for a leap at his father. *Wait! Don't attack!* cried Pieter. Silverfoot did not respond. He felt her muscles tighten for a spring.

Silverfoot's mind surged with a mishmash of images—a roaring bear, an armored man waving a sword, a snarling wolverine. To her, his father was a mortal threat, and she was reacting as a wolf.

In despair, he brought the pipe to his lips and played an urgent three-note strain. *No, no!* he sent as he played. Silverfoot stopped.

"That critter's gonna—" cried Father.

"No!" Pieter cried. "As long as I play, you're safe." He resumed the song as quickly as he could. Even in the seconds he had spoken, Silverfoot had tensed once more for attack. *Please. No!* he sent, but the wolf sent only flashes of rage and aggression. Usually a message was enough, but this time only the music held her.

Father pulled out his knife and took a step backwards. Pieter, still playing, circled the fire toward the man. He lowered the pipe just an inch. "Run," he cried. He played. Again, "Run while you can!"

His father crouched. "You'd like that, wouldn't you? You play your damn flute while she kills me."

"No!" cried Pieter. He played, moving closer. "I can hold her. Go! Go!"

His father reached out and yanked the pipe from Pieter's grasp.

"Nooo!" cried Pieter.

Father threw the pipe into the fire. And the wolf sprang.

Chapter 68

Pieter screamed. He stumbled back, tripped, and sprawled on the ground.

Another scream broke through the growling of the wolf. A man's scream, terror in his cry.

"No, no!" Pieter shrieked. "Silverfoot! Don't!"

The wolf stopped and raised her head. Pieter gaped at her bloody muzzle, shining wetly in the firelight.

Evil, came Silverfoot's whispery voice, as close to a clear word as she had ever sent. *Gone.*

With that, the wolf turned and slipped into the darkness, her paws making no sound in the night.

Pieter held his head, turned his back to his father, and wept.

How long he sat, he would never know. The logs on the fire settled, sending a cloud of sparks into the darkness, a darkness that pressed on Pieter's heart until it ached. The moments slipped by, the black night the only thing left in the world.

When he thought the darkness would never end, he heard heavy, running footsteps pounding in the forest. Strong arms lifted him and carried him away.

Pieter opened his eyes and wished he hadn't. His head throbbed. A pulsing pain crouched behind his eyes.

He looked about. He was home, but in his mother's bed. Sunlight flowed in from the single window.

His hands explored his face. Both sides were swollen. One ear had puffed up and crusted with blood. But his mouth had fared better. His lips were not split and no teeth were loose. *I should be able to play the pipe. Father didn't hit me in the mouth.*

Father! What had happened to him? Pieter again saw the fire, his father's face, the pipe in the flames, the wolf...

His pipe!

He sat up and swung his legs over the edge. Dizziness swept him. He steadied himself and then started for the door. Cool air over his bare legs sent shivers throughout his body. He wore nothing but a linen shift. His clothes hung on a chair in the corner. He turned and staggered across the room. He swept up his clothes and tossed them on the bed.

It took a while, but he managed to get dressed without falling on the floor. He pushed himself up and stood swaying.

The door swung open and Gretchen peered in. "What are you doing?" she demanded. "You can't get out of bed yet."

"Pipe...have to find it."

"Brother Rufus says—"

"My pipe..." gasped Pieter. "He took my pipe...threw it in the fire."

Gretchen shook her head. "Come on, then. We'll go together."

They left the house and headed through the streets of Hamelin. They passed through the walls and headed for a small wood north of town. Generations of local children, including Pieter, had played among the trees here. They called it the Spirit Wood and told frightening tales to each other about what dwelt in its depths and shadows.

It did not take long to find the ashes. In daylight, it was clear this was a gathering place of some sort. Logs had been arranged for benches. Empty ale bottles lay scattered on the ground. A well-worn path ran toward town. Was this where his father drank when he failed to return home at night? Father and a number of friends, by the look of it.

Pieter tried to ignore the patches of black on the ground where his father had bled. Instead, he stared at the fire ring. He shook his head. "I don't know why I came. He threw it right in the flames. It's gone." A great sorrow settled on his shoulders. "It's all lost. How do I open the mountain now?"

Gretchen stood helpless at his side. "I do not know."

Pieter kicked a half-burned log. Ashes fell away, and Pieter gasped. A bit of brown wood poked from the ashes. Pieter pulled it out and held it high. "Gretchen! Look! The pipe! It didn't burn!"

And yet...somehow it had changed. The wood looked darker, richer—a deep burnished hue, as though lovingly fashioned from the finest rosewood or ebony. He ran a finger over the smooth wood.

"It's been transformed. Renewed, somehow," Gretchen said, her voice soft.

Pieter's entire body sagged, his weakened legs scarcely able to hold him up. She was right. It was no longer the same pipe. It was *his* pipe now. He put the instrument to his lips and began to play. It produced the same rich sound as always, yet in a subtle way, the tone was even more beautiful.

Simon and Brother Rufus burst through the foliage.

"*There* you are," snapped Simon.

Rufus shook his head. "You are a very hard lad to keep track of."

Pieter held up the pipe. "Look! He threw it in the fire. But it didn't burn. It *didn't*. But my father. He's...he's..." He teetered as the weight of what Silverfoot had done last night settled on his shoulders.

The monk slipped a hand under Pieter's arm. "Come, lad. We can talk later."

Pieter pulled away. "No. Tell me now." He could no longer control the trembling of his hands.

Rufus lowered him on a log. The monk looked at Simon.

Simon sat next to Pieter and said, "Yes, son, your father is dead."

"I thought so."

"I'm afraid the wolf tore out his throat."

"Silverfoot. And I...I called her. She came because of the pipe. But I didn't want her to *kill* my father!" His body shook uncontrollably. "I tried to hold her back. I *tried*."

"Calm yourself," said Rufus, gripping his shoulder. "Now tell us everything."

With a deep sigh, Pieter related how his father had caught him at the back door.

"I couldn't get out," said Simon. "He had rolled the rain barrel across the doorway. By the time we forced the door open, you were gone."

Rufus shook his head. "And I charged out the front door like some idiot sheep. I fear I was lost within ten steps."

Pieter told them of the sack yanked over his head, of being carried to the fire and bound. "I saw the pipe on the ground and managed to wiggle over to it. I had no idea what the pipe would bring, but I was desperate."

Rufus nodded. "You were trying to survive. It only makes sense that your wolf would attack."

"Yes," said Pieter. "But after she came, I held her off with music from the pipe. When my father grabbed it and threw it into the fire, I had no way to control her." He broke into sobs. "I didn't want him *killed*. Oh, Silverfoot. What...what have we done?"

"Nothing," said Simon, "save defend yourself. The wolf saved your life. Now come. Your mother needs to talk to you."

Pieter nodded and looked up. Out of the gloom of the night, a huge figure appeared. "Keeper!" he cried.

Keeper lifted Pieter as though he was a toddler and carried him against his massive chest with Pieter's head against his shoulder. By the time they reached his home, Keeper's tunic was damp with tears.

Chapter 69

The next morning, Pieter sat with his mother near the fire. He had slept at home in the loft, while the others had returned to The Tong and Anvil.

Agnes, always an early riser, sat tethered in the depression around the center post. With great seriousness, she dropped rocks one at a time into a metal pail, then dumped them out with a clatter, only to repeat the task.

Pieter leaned back against the chair. The slightest movement made his head throb. "Mother," he said, his voice close to a sob. "I didn't mean to. I just wanted—"

"Pieter!" snapped his mother. "I will have no more tears. You have expressed your regret and guilt over and over. No more, do you hear?"

"But he's dead and—"

"What happened to Karl he brought upon himself. You were trying to protect yourself. And the wolf was being a wolf."

"What...what happens now?"

"Well, for one thing, he won't beat you anymore. Nor will he hurt Agnes or me."

"But you're alone now," said Pieter. "I'm so sorry."

She sat taller and glared at him so hard, Pieter shrank back. "Sorry for me? Your sorrow is wasted. I should have fled from him long ago."

"After all these years?"

His mother's face quivered. "All these years of letting him beat you?"

"No, I didn't mean that."

"But it's true," she said. "I was so afraid, such a coward. I could not imagine how I would make my way in the world with a baby."

"But something changed?"

"Aye. First he stabbed you, and I feared you were dead. Even alive, I thought I'd never see you again. And then..." Her eyes filled with tears. "He struck Agnes."

Pieter stiffened. "Oh, Mother."

His mother scrubbed her cheeks. "I had never defied him before. But that night, Agnes had another fever. You weren't here to comfort her. When she would not cease crying, he slapped her. I flew into a rage. I attacked him. I clawed and bit until his face ran red."

"What did he do?"

"He threw me to the floor. I had never stood up to him before. He didn't know *what* to do. Finally, he stormed off to find comfort in a mug of ale. His anger boiled hotter and hotter after that, but he never struck me or Agnes again."

A long silence. Pieter heard only the gentle rhythm of his sister's breathing; she had fallen asleep with her rump in the air. Was this the change he had sensed in his mother? It seemed she had found a new strength since confronting Father.

"There's something else," his mother said. "I should have told you long ago, but my fear held me."

"What could be that terrible?"

"It's not terrible. Not really." She gazed directly into his eyes. "This man who beat you and cut you and never loved you... He was not your father."

Chapter 70

"Not my father?" Shock stabbed through Pieter's chest. "Then who is?"

"A fine man. A man I loved dearly. I was born here in Hamelin, but we lived in Nienburg then. The fever got him before you were born. His name was Aaron. Aaron, son of Dierk."

Questions and emotions raged in Pieter's head. He took a long breath. A turmoil of anger and relief filled his heart. "He was...only my stepfather?"

"Aye."

They talked for a very long time. About how his father, Aaron, had loved music. About Pieter's great-grandfather, Stefan, who had been a minstrel.

Mother said, "Of course, I never met Aaron's grandfather, but they say he was a musician without peer. Aaron had hoped to follow in his footsteps." She studied her hands. "But he died too soon.

"How overjoyed your father was when he knew I was with child. He cherished you even as I carried you in my womb. And though he never held you in his arms, I know he loved you more than life."

"And my...and Karl?"

"Fear again. I fled back to Hamelin. I clutched to him because he could keep me safe. I thought I needed a husband, and I took the first one who seemed willing. I am so sorry."

The baby stirred, and Pieter said, "But he gave us Agnes."

"Aye. Even from such a man, joy has come."

Knowing something about his father, his *real* father, was startling. Frightening, even. Yet it moved him closer to being ready to face Koppelberg.

Perhaps Pieter wasn't yet sure who he was, but he was *not* the son of Karl the blacksmith. He was the son of a man who'd loved music, even as he himself did.

"Mother, I would know more. I would hear everything I can about my real father. But—"

"I know. You have returned for a reason."

"Aye. I must climb once more to Koppelberg Mountain, to the very cliff where the children disappeared with the Piper."

Mother put her hands over her face. "That's what you said in the song I heard. But what do you expect to find? Perhaps only more sorrow."

"Perhaps. But perhaps also redemption." Pieter leaned closer. "I need you to let everyone in the town know," said Pieter. "The people of Hamelin must gather on the green. Tomorrow. Just after noon."

"So soon? Karl hurt you. You must heal first."

"Nay, Mother." He pushed himself up from the chair. The room whirled around him. He reached out for the chair, but he and the chair fell over. Pieter pushed it away and shook his head. "I feel so weak."

Mother put an arm under him and helped him sit once more. "Tomorrow is too soon. Don't you see that?"

"But I will have a song they must hear, and it cannot wait. Poor Hamelin, without music for so long, must listen to what I sing."

"The day after tomorrow is soon enough. So rest while you can. Use my bed. Meanwhile, I shall spread the word. The villagers will come, I promise."

Pieter lifted Agnes off the floor and stood, holding her on his shoulder. Her gentle breath wafted against his cheek. He placed a kiss on her damp forehead and laid her gently into her cradle, fearful of letting her go. He embraced his mother and crawled into her bed. His head ached, the scar on his back tingled, his muscles complained. Yet he dropped into a deep, dreamless sleep.

*P*ieter lay half-asleep, letting the sunshine that flowed through the window warm his shoulders and head. He had multiple bruises on his face and one large bump on the side of his head, but he would have no trouble playing the pipe on the morrow, no matter how much his head hurt. No trouble singing. But first, he needed the song.

It was difficult to create a song when his mind boiled with thoughts about pipers and lost children. And fathers.

In his mind he saw Silverfoot springing at his father. He heard the horrible sound of tearing flesh, smelled the stench of blood.

I called her. But I didn't kill him. Through the pipe, he'd had the wolf under control. The animal never would have attacked if Father hadn't thrown the pipe into the fire.

Father. *But not* my *father...only a stepfather.* Was that what had angered the man? That his only son was not his son at all?

Aaron the son of Dierk...a *man who loved music.* His thoughts wandered, and Pieter dozed off.

Movement at the foot of the bed brought him awake. A tiny arm reached up and grabbed the blanket. A head followed, then another hand. Little by little, Agnes scrambled and struggled, until at last she pulled herself up onto the bed.

"You did it!" said Pieter. "All by yourself."

"Self!" Agnes crowed as she crawled toward Pieter. She nestled herself next to him, resting her head on his shoulder.

"Well, small one," he said. "What do you think of all this?"

Agnes only snuggled deeper.

"My song, sweet Agnes. I need some ideas for the song I must sing tomorrow. What shall I say? How do I tell them that the children piped away so long ago are still alive?"

Chapter 71

When next Pieter awakened, sunshine no longer filled the window, and Agnes was gone. Long afternoon shadows were gathering.

He sat up slowly, then swung his feet to the floor. He took his time standing. Pieter's head still swam, but it was better than this morning.

Mother appeared in the doorway. "How do you fare, son? Are you dizzy?"

"A little. But I'm better."

"Come and have a bit of supper. Then we shall see."

It was good to be sitting at the table, with a meal prepared by his mother. It was her usual soup with onions and cabbage, and Pieter loved it.

"Pieter," said his mother, sitting back in her chair. "While you were sleeping, Gretchen came by."

"Aye?"

"She didn't want to wake you. But she said to come to The Tong and Anvil as soon as you can."

"How late is it?"

"The sun has just set. There is much evening left."

Pieter pushed himself out of the chair, then stood, wobbling.

"Slowly," said Mother. "If you fall, you'll make things worse."

"I have no time to take things slowly. I need to get to the inn."

When he started for the door, Mother squeezed his arm. "Take your time. No sudden movements."

"Aye. I'll be fine."

And he was, for the most part. He plodded along, sometimes wobbling, sometimes steady for a bit. Nevertheless, he arrived at The Tong and Anvil sooner than he expected. A number of patrons were scattered about the room. Simon and Brother Rufus sat together near the fireplace. Gretchen perched on a stool, fingering a delicate melody on her lute.

Pieter stood near the door for a moment, listening to her song. To his astonishment, it brought tears to his eyes. Even without words, it spoke of deep loss. It captured some of the very emotions that had swirled in his heart since returning to Hamelin.

She had given him a gift with that song. In that melody lay the reflection of the turmoil in his heart. A gift only a friend could give. In light of all the fighting between them, it was odd to think of her as a friend. But it was so.

When she finished, Gretchen looked up at him and nodded before beginning a new tune.

Pieter joined the two men, pulling up a low stool. Only then did he notice a thick white candle burning on a table in the corner. Keeper. The giant had acquired pen, ink, and parchment. His thick hand flew as he wrote. Was he inscribing one of Pieter's songs?

Pieter leaned back against the wall, content with the lack of talking, entranced by Gretchen's playing. He stared into the leaping yellow flames that filled the fireplace. In a few moments, his thoughts turned to the song he would need to sing for Hamelin on the morrow. He had not yet found the lyrics. His mind was empty of ideas. A log broke apart into glowing orange coals. Startled, Pieter looked up.

Gretchen had stopped playing. Keeper had laid down his pen and regarded Pieter with his strange slanted eyes, his ink-stained fingers fluttering above the table.

Pieter cleared his throat. "My father is dead."

Simon nodded. "Aye. So we have heard."

"No, you do not understand. The man Silverfoot killed—Karl the blacksmith... He was not my real father."

Simon rocked back, nodding his head. "Now, that makes sense. I often thought I'd never seen a father and son so little alike."

Rufus laid a hand on his shoulder. "Do you know of your birth father?"

"Aye. Aaron, son of Dierk. He died before I was born." He took a deep breath. "Mother says they both loved music. In fact, my great-grandfather was a minstrel."

"So," said Gretchen, "a musician from a line of musicians."

"So it would appear," said Pieter. "My great-grandfather's name was Stefan, and he was—"

Simon stiffened. "Did you say 'Stefan?'"

"Aye. That's all my mother knew about him."

The old man scowled for a moment. Then a smile broke on his aged face. "I believe I know something more."

Pieter frowned. "How could that be?"

"Remember the Pied Piper's story in the cave—about choosing the heir to the pipe?" Simon laid a hand on Pieter's. "Who was chosen first?"

Gretchen gasped. "Could it be?"

"What are you saying?" asked Pieter.

"Oh, my," said Brother Rufus, a hand to his mouth. "Pieter, Simon is right. Who was the one who refused the pipe?"

A cold shudder ran up his spine. "His name...was Stefan." The shudder melted instantly into a warmth that infused his heart. And spilled freely from his eyes. *A line of musicians. A great-grandfather with a heart for music. And he, too, bonded with an agitato wolf.*

A deep silence settled over the room. Pieter stared into the fire, watching the flames dance and flutter. Stefan—the one who should have been the piper. A minstrel with a wolf. But he had refused the pipe.

The ice in his spine returned. *Because he was afraid. As am I.* He watched Sam appear and lay a new log on the fire. For a moment, the fire did not change, but abruptly the log surrendered to the heat. The flames leaped high. *I shall rectify this. I can put things aright.*

He looked up. Keeper remained at his table, but Pieter had no doubt he had heard and understood all that had been said.

The others sat waiting for him, as though they knew he had much to ponder, much to resolve in his heart.

Pieter looked long at each of them in turn. "So many things are now clear to me. It makes tomorrow even more important. Tomorrow I must reveal a new message for the people of this town. Through music."

Brother Rufus leaned forward. "Are you sure? Lad, your face does not look good."

"It is time."

The monk nodded. "Aye. But if you need to take a few days before—"

"Nay," snapped Pieter. "I have wasted a day already. I will sing for Hamelin tomorrow."

Everyone nodded. Keeper walked over from his table dragging a large chair.

"I have the song I need to open the mountainside," said Pieter. "Every note." One by one, he looked each of them in the eye. "It is not the one the Piper played. The music that opened the mountain before holds only anger and bitterness. Keeper?"

"Aye?"

"Did you copy the song the Piper played at Koppelberg that day?"

"Aye."

"You must destroy it."

Panic showed in Keeper's face. "I...I cannot... I am Keeper. I keep the songs...*all* songs."

"But Keeper, no one must ever sing that song again."

Keeper nodded, his head bobbing. "Keep it... Aye, that I will do... Keep it and not share it. No one...no one shall see it."

Pieter sagged with relief. "Thank you. Tomorrow I sing for Hamelin. On the next day I will climb to Koppelberg to the very cliff where the Pied Piper took the children. There I shall sing a new song, a song that has been growing in my mind and heart for some time."

"And then?" asked Gretchen, speaking for the first time.

"I cannot be sure. I know I must enter the mountain. My heart tells me they are children still. I shall find them."

Gretchen nodded, apparently satisfied.

"But first, Hamelin must be prepared," said Pieter. "Tomorrow the people of Hamelin will gather. My mother is spreading the word." His face tightened. "But the song for the folk of the town—I need something that will prepare them for the return of the children. But this song, the lyrics that I must share tomorrow, I... I have no notion what they will be. "

Chapter 72

Later that night, long after The Tong and Anvil had emptied of customers, in the darkest hour between midnight and morning, Pieter sat alone at a table. Sam had long since closed up, though he appeared every so often to throw another log on the fire or replenish the thin white candles that illuminated Pieter's work.

Pieter leaned his forehead onto one hand, staring at the scratchings scattered over the parchment. The pen in his hand hovered in the air until the ink on the tip had dried.

And still no words or melody came.

Always before, the music had flowed. From the time he had left Hamelin, songs had sprung into his mind. Whether it was the silly ditty about the donkey or the song of grief for Gretchen's mother, it had always come together unhindered.

But not tonight.

The song he had to sing tomorrow. The song that must persuade the folk of Hamelin to come and be a part of a miracle.

And he had nothing.

He glared at the mocking white parchment, strewn with a scattering of phrases, words, scraps of melody—and none of them worked. What's more, he was wasting an entire side of Keeper's precious parchment. He should never have begun writing until he had the song in his mind.

A candle sputtered. Sam, still wearing his soiled white apron, appeared out of the gloom, lit a new candle, and placed it in the holder. He slipped away without a word.

Pieter must persuade Hamelin. Persuade them that he was indeed a piper, but not the *Pied* Piper. Convince them that the music that had wrought such grief could also heal.

Where were the words?

Despair rushed through him. He threw down the quill and bolted from the inn. He dashed through the dark streets until he stumbled outside the walls of Hamelin. He found himself heading east—towards Koppelberg.

He halted, bent over to catch his breath. The night closed around him, pressing him relentlessly. He hunched on a large rock at the side of the road. Why had he run?

Out of the darkness Silverfoot appeared, first her blue eyes, then a white foot, followed by her grey muzzle. Pieter wrapped his arms around the thick fur of her neck. *What am I to do?*

He sensed something deep in the wolf's mind. She had more than once endured terrible hardship. Where had Silverfoot been before they met that day in the dell? What had happened to her when she was younger?

A jumble of images flowed from the wolf's mind. A huge grey male, dying in the snow. Two pups, torn apart by a great brown bear. Her pups. Silverfoot, traveling alone, without purpose, full of despair. Silverfoot had experienced much sorrow.

Sorrow. Perhaps that is it. I dwell in sorrow, for my father is dead. Mother and Agnes have endured such pain. Deep sorrow has carried Simon close to despair. And the Pied Piper, with his twisted hands and wasted gifts—and, of course, Hamelin itself. Pieter had left it and he had returned, but the deep sorrow of its lost children bit deeper than he could imagine.

Aye, that was the place to begin—with sorrow.

He stroked the wolf's chest, taking in her wild smell, feeling the power of her muscles. *Thank you, Great Hunter. You have given me the place to begin my song.*

The wolf licked his cheek, whirled, and disappeared into the night.

Pieter watched the shadows where she had disappeared. He pushed to his feet and headed back to The Tong and Anvil.

At the table once more, he took the guttering candle and lit a new one. He found an empty corner of the parchment and began to scribble some new words. Yes, this was right, for they all knew sorrow. Every person had endured the sting of loss, whether at the hand of the Pied Piper or not.

He bent over the parchment, dipping the quill, writing, dipping, writing again. Time ceased to exist.

He had no idea how much later it was when he looked up. Gretchen stood on the other side of the table, still clad in her brown traveling clothes. She held her lute in her hands, a small smile on her face.

"What do you want?" asked Pieter.

She laid the lute on the table and crossed her arms. "Shall we fight, or do you wish to have my help?"

He glared at her for a long while. Candlelight flickered in her green eyes. The muscles of her jaw clenched and unclenched.

What was she asking? She seemed to be waiting for something. Perhaps she needed to know if Pieter could set aside his jealousy long enough for them to work together.

It was as if there were two Gretchens—the one he argued with constantly and the one he sang with. The one who seemed so much stronger than he was, and the one who had played the song on her lute that had left him in tears. And yet, she had believed in him. She had created a melody at The Tong and Anvil that captured his feelings and acknowledged them.

At last he spoke. "Why don't you sit down?"

She nodded and perched on a chair.

He cleared his throat. "Everywhere we've gone, you have been a surprise. To everyone. No one seemed to expect you in this tale."

"So I've noticed."

"But Simon told me something soon after we met. In truth, he and I were arguing."

She nodded again. "About whether I should travel with you?"

He felt his face warm. "Aye. He called me an ass. And he was quite right about that."

"What else did he say?" she asked.

"That his heart told him you had a part to play in our story."

"And?"

"And he was right. Gretchen, I can't tell you that we won't argue anymore. We probably will." He took a deep breath. "But I wouldn't be here if it wasn't for you. I cannot do this without you."

She smiled. "I am delighted that you have realized this. I knew the moment you led my sheep with your singing."

"So long ago? It seems I was a bit late in understanding."

"Aye. Quite late." She sat forward, elbows on the table. "So, what shall we fight about?"

Pieter grinned at her. "How about the song I must sing to the people of Hamelin?"

"Very well."

He sat back, flexing his fingers. "I have the words. At last." He sighed deeply. "But nary a note of music."

"I see," said Gretchen, bringing her lute into her lap. "Well, I've been up all night as well. How would this work as a melody?"

She fingered a bit, struck a chord, and began to pick out a melody. To Pieter's joy, it fit his lyrics line for line, word for word. It was so full of mourning and loss that he could not breathe. "Gretchen! You found it! That is the very melody my words needed."

"It's not finished, but we can complete it before the sun is up."

"Aye," said Pieter, sitting forward. He dipped his pen and began inking square notes under the words.

He no longer noticed whether Sam came or not. He and Gretchen dwelt together in a different place, where the music ran free at last.

Chapter 73

Pieter sat on a rough log bench outside The Tong and Anvil, leaning against the whitewashed wall. The noonday sun warmed his face. He listened to the sounds of the people in the streets.

Thanks to his mother, the folk of Hamelin were gathering. Everyone in Hamelin knew by now that Pieter was back. No doubt many already knew of his father's—of his *step*father's death.

Would they blame Pieter? Would that ruin what he had come to do? Would anyone listen to a boy who had caused his father's death? Some concern about the wolf had been bandied about, but on the whole the town had accepted the story.

But they also knew that Pieter had the pipe, the very one that had once belonged to the Pied Piper. As they gathered in the square, what were they feeling? Were they angry? Bewildered? Curious?

He and Gretchen had worked well into the morning, and the song was ready. It had not come as a gift this time, but as the fruit of hard effort. Despite his injuries and lack of sleep, he was full of energy. The thrill of creation, the joy in seeing his words and Gretchen's melody come together had given him renewed strength. *I believe I could sing forever.*

Sam came out, carrying a bundle of white cloth. "Your mother came by earlier, Agnes on her hip, and dropped this off. You and Gretchen were working. She didn't want to disturb you, so she left it with me."

"I'm sorry I missed them." Pieter unrolled the outer linen and found something made of a deep green brocade. He shook it out and stared—it was a cape. Not pied with bold colors, but the cape of a musician nonetheless.

It tied at the neck with a silken cord of gold, which also ran around the edges and hem. It was rich with embroidery in gold and black thread.

Gretchen appeared beside him. "Oh, Pieter! A cloak fit for a minstrel, without a doubt!"

"My mother made it."

"Oh, my," she said, fingering the cloth. "We weren't the only ones working all night."

"Aye. But she must have begun this long ago." He looked up at Gretchen with moist eyes. "She knew before I did that I was meant to make music. I think she started this before I even left Hamelin."

"It will be perfect."

"Have the townsfolk seen Keeper yet?"

"Aye," said Gretchen. "This morning, I had him carry me on his shoulders. We strolled all through town. We garnered many stares. But they have decided, it seems, that if I am safe with him, they are, too. He took me through the green. People are starting to gather."

Pieter ran a hand through his hair. "Do they seem ready for our song?"

"Some are simply curious, most are excited, but many are uneasy about the rumors sweeping Hamelin."

Pieter nodded. "I wonder what they're anxious about. Do you think it is about the wolf and all that happened in the woods?"

"I didn't sense that," said Gretchen. "Mostly anticipation."

"Good. I would expect them to be anxious to some degree."

She smiled at him. "Come inside. Sam has prepared a light meal for us."

That afternoon, as they approached the green, Pieter sensed a tumult of emotions throbbing in the air. Fear, curiosity, excitement. Aye, some anger. But it didn't seem to be directed at him. It was a potent mix.

He paused, viewing the crowd from the back. They were dressed mostly in humble garb of green and brown and grey. He wondered where the mayor and councilors were; he needed them here as well. His hand went to the pipe, tucked in his belt and hidden by his new cloak.

A low dais stood at the edge of the gathering space. From there Pieter had heard town criers shouting the news and had listened to storytellers.

But never musicians, never a minstrel. Not in Hamelin.

Would they allow it now? A boy who called a wolf? The son of a blacksmith? A deep breath escaped. *But I am not the son of a blacksmith. I am a minstrel and the son of Aaron, who also loved music. A man who would have celebrated my gifts.* He stood taller.

Gretchen's hand touched his elbow. "I believe it is time."

Arm in arm they threaded through the crowd toward the dais.

The people stilled, moving aside to give them a path. Children crept close to their parents. Something in that quiet gave Pieter hope that they would listen. He and Gretchen climbed the few stairs. She took her place on a small stool, still wearing her worn traveling clothes. Pieter gazed out at the folk of Hamelin.

Since the first night at The Square Pig, he had seldom been nervous before a crowd. But this one was so important. The fear of failure made his knees weak and sent sweat rolling down his forehead.

So many faces. Many a goodwife with children in tow. Worn faces of laborers and farm folk. Craggy faces half-hidden by hoods. Young people, their faces twisted in worry. And in the back, a few dressed in quilted tunics and rich wool robes. Pieter hoped one of them was the mayor.

He sensed Silverfoot, somewhere in the hills above Hamelin. How he wished she were by his side, wished he could stroke her thick fur. *Stay nearby, Silverfoot. I shall need your strength.*

Simon and Brother Rufus waited on stools off to the side. Keeper sat cross-legged on the grass; even sitting, he was the tallest person in the square. To Pieter's delight, he even saw Tracker, his hair and beard as bushy as ever.

Best of all, Pieter spotted his mother, holding Agnes. The baby peered about with wide eyes. He bowed his head toward them, and lifted up one corner of the cloak, a silent thank-you for the gift.

Agnes. That was the focus he needed. This was for her, for all the children—those who dwelt in Hamelin now, who had grown up without music, and most of all, those who had been lost on Koppelberg.

He could sing for Agnes, sing without a hint of unease. "People of Hamelin. I am Pieter, son of..." Cold washed down his back, but he recovered quickly. "Son of *Aaron*. I left Hamelin a frightened boy. A boy I remain, but I have become something more." His voice was soft but clear. To his amazement, it held something of the power of his singing voice, for the crowd immediately listened.

Smoothly, almost without thought, he slipped into song. At the perfect moment, Gretchen joined him with her lute.

I dwelt in warmth deep in the woods,
I slept beneath the sky,
I traveled toward where rivers join,
I heard the sheep's tense cry

I met a giant past a cleft,
I sang the days away,

Then traveled on to Verden,
And did not go astray.

I strode through poor sad Bondswick,
Pressed toward the mountains chill,
I found the fey Pied Piper,
At his death, my heart stood still.

Along the paths my journey took,
Many friends I made anew,
A mountain man, a shepherd lass,
A giant where green grass grew.

A monk of courage and passion,
A guide into the wild,
And like a rose from ashes grows,
The steadfast, strong Last Child.

Lo, in a tower built of stone,
There dwelt a woman wise,
Whose heart holds music's spirit,
And all souls' anthems rise.

I journeyed and I found these friends,
And found my calling true.
I found my song; I found the pipe.
I bring these gifts to you.

It wasn't until he finished that the faces again became clear in his sight. The first music in Hamelin in sixty years, except for the whispered lullabies for Agnes—and the crowd looked stunned, as though they had had no idea what was missing from their lives. Oh, there were a few hard faces out there—some of the older folk, and a scattered few like his old enemy, Hans. But for the most part, the web of his music had held them in its silver strands.

Pieter knew in his heart he must not let the trance be broken, lest old fears resurface. He spoke into the silence. "Before I could come home, I came to the hardest moment of all. I had to face the Pied Piper himself."

The intake of breath startled him. It had been in the song, but now he had *spoken* the dreaded name. A moment of panic seized Pieter, and sweat broke out on his forehead.

Just then he heard a small voice crying, "Pay-pay! Pay-pay!" Agnes squirmed in her mother's arms, thrusting her little hands in Pieter's direction.

He smiled and waved at her.

"Pay-pay!" she called again.

The crowd murmured, this time with the amusement and affection only a child could bring.

At that moment, Gretchen launched into a tune they had sung in Saint Ignatius. Frolicking and lively, it spoke of the joy of children. It caught the spirit Agnes had shown and brought a grin to many a face. He sang it out with delight.

Then came the number that he had wrestled with throughout the night. He needed to convince them that he could be a piper without being another Pied Piper. Would the folk of Hamelin embrace his message? Or was it too late?

He glanced at Gretchen, who nodded. The sound of her lute filled the air as she fingered a prelude. As Pieter waited for his entry, he thought, *Listen, poor silent Hamelin. Listen and heed my song.* And his voice rang out, strong and clear. A song etched in sorrow, but also full of hope.

I sing for you, fair Hamelin,
I sing your sorrow and grief,
The Piper stole your children,
And your joy, like a thief.

This town hath dwelt in sorrow,
For, lo, these sixty years.
No joy in the morrow,

Grief watered by your tears.

But behold, the dawn now cometh,
Soon ends our bitter night.
The fair sweet lute now trumpet,
To herald the sun's new light.

For joy comes soon upon you,
In the laughter of a child,
As water beads as morning dew,
Their beauty hath beguiled.

Unlatch long-closed windows,
Fling open wide your door,
Prepare your hearts and homes,
For the children lost in lore.

We travel to the mountain,
Where once your elders wept,
For the lost remain as children,
In a place where time's not kept.

When wee ones come returning,
Sad and frightened they may be,
Their families torn asunder,
By the Piper's enmity.

Will you walk with me in sunshine?
Will you open warm arms wide?
Will you care for long-lost children,
That in love they may abide?

A new song comes with morning,
To restore and bless and heal,
To light this town's dank corners,
And all your hopes reveal.

Chapter 74

The next morning, Pieter sat once more on the log bench outside The Tong and Anvil. Up and down the street, shutters were opened and doors flung wide. People bustled through the village. Clouds of dust puffed before busy brooms. Blankets and bedding were shaken out, mattresses emptied and stuffed with fresh green reeds.

According to Gretchen, this scene was being repeated throughout Hamelin. Pieter wondered if he'd waited too long. The townsfolk had seemed receptive and, for the most part, eager. But that was yesterday. Now they had had time to think, to worry, to see the difficulties that lay ahead.

Perhaps he should have led them to Koppelberg as soon the song had ended. He rubbed his forehead. No, they had needed time to prepare rooms and beds, to clean and repair and build, so the children would have something to come home to, even though these homes would be different than the ones they remembered. The bustle throughout Hamelin assured him that he had done the right thing.

Pieter studied the sky. Nearly noon. He opened the bag of bread and white cheese Sam had given him. He worked to calm his ragged breathing. His hands trembled as he thought about this enormous day. His gut had tightened so much that eating was impossible. The innkeeper had offered another elaborate lunch, but Pieter had refused. Mayhap when this day had passed. If the town kept faith.

Beside him lay his cloak, carefully folded. The pipe was tucked in his belt, heavy despite its meager weight. The song he must soon play pulsed through his mind.

The time seemed right. He stood and shook out his green cloak. He fastened it around his neck and strode down the road, out of Hamelin, and on towards Koppelberg.

Gretchen appeared, holding her lute with both hands. She walked just a step behind him, as though she knew that this, for good or ill, was Pieter's task alone. But her presence eased the tightness in Pieter's chest.

He glanced over his shoulder. Rufus, Simon, and Keeper had appeared behind Gretchen, with Tracker following. Then came his mother and Agnes.

Pieter smiled. Perhaps these wonderful friends could not help, not today, but their very presence bolstered his resolve.

Behind them, many of Hamelin's folk followed, more than he had dared to hope for. By the time they reached the charred rubble of Simon's house, the crowd had grown.

He paused to regard the roses. Soft pink blossoms reached toward the sun, twining up the chimney. He glanced at Simon, but the old man stared toward the mountains. To be returning to that dreaded cliff, even with hope, caused pain and fear in many a heart. But they followed nonetheless.

He sensed that Silverfoot had joined the crowd. Pieter wondered if anyone would notice her. He wanted no one frightened at this critical moment. *Play!* she sent. *Play the pipe...enter the mountain... find the pups.* An image of a grey boulder appeared, telling Pieter that no one would see her.

Pieter slipped the pipe from his belt. *This is what I was meant to do. This is why I have followed the Pied Piper's song.* He brought the instrument to his lips, and without hesitation he began to play.

After a few bars, Pieter whirled and walked backward. So startled was he by the size of the crowd, his playing faltered for a moment. Like sixty years earlier, the villagers followed the song of the pipe. Not just children, but adults, the elderly—the whole town, it seemed. Was the song compelling them? Were they following because of the spell of the pipe and the song, just as the children had so long ago?

He hoped not. He wanted them to come because they believed in the song he had shared the day before. Because despite their fears, hope was stronger. He whirled again, sending his cloak flying in a great circle of green, and continued up the trail. The song of the pipe echoed off the rocks and trees, louder and stronger than Pieter's small lungs could have made it.

He turned again and caught sight of his mother carrying Agnes. She had dressed the baby in a little green dress that matched his cape. Agnes cried out in joy, bouncing in her mother's arms, flapping her hands as though she wanted to fly to him. He held the note with one hand on the pipe and gave Agnes a quick wave. He spun back, swirling the cloak again. The song of the pipe filled the air with a joy that swept through Pieter's chest.

When they reached the cliff face, Pieter turned to the crowd, still playing. They fanned out around him, some arm in arm, others clasping hands, all expectant and a little fearful. No one spoke.

He ended the song, then turned back and faced the stark grey cliff of Koppelberg. He stood silent for a long moment, a soft breeze ruffling his hair. The edges of his cloak fluttered, but nothing else moved. A torrent of memories and disquiet ran through him, but he was no longer haunted by them. It was time for him to step into the mountain and face whatever awaited him. Pieter again put the wooden pipe to his lips.

The first vibrant note swelled and filled the dell. The next note, a third higher, all but lifted Pieter off his feet.

It was exactly the melody he had heard in his mind, except it was more powerful, more haunting, now that it echoed through the mountains. The melody built and built, the notes leaping brightly, bursting with energy, full of hope.

As he played, a gap appeared in the cliff face. The rock vanished, and before them was a high, wide opening. Beyond it lay a different world. A land of spring and summer. Fruit trees, heavy with peaches, apples, and cherries—and yet at the same time brilliant with blossoms. Among the trees, grass and flowers grew in abundance. Pieter had not known that reds and yellows and oranges could be so vivid, that grass could be such a rich shade of green.

At the same time, the scene struck Pieter as curious. He peered closer, struggling to understand. His gaze moved from the grass to the trees to—

Then he saw it.

A stream split two boulders, then wound across the meadow, a lucent flow of blue-green water.

But it wasn't a flow at all. The water wasn't moving.

Not frozen, like the Weser in the winter. Not still like a pond in summer. It seemed to have stopped in its rush, held in its movement. It was more like a tapestry created with the brightest colors of thread possible.

Pieter noticed a greenfinch. It looked to have soared from an oak tree, but like the stream, it was utterly still. It hung in the air like a child's toy suspended on a wire. Its emerald wings were spread. Sunlight glistened off its brilliant green and yellow feathers.

Other birds dangled in the air—sparrows, starlings, a scattering of nuthatches, all with plumage that would shame a peacock.

All held in midflight.

Was this all that was left of the wondrous land the Pied Piper had promised? Nothing but a landscape painted with the most lurid colors in an artist's palette?

Pieter's heart tightened in his chest. This garish image was useless. It had no power to reverse the Pied Piper's evil.

The land inside Koppelberg was a gaudy tableau and nothing more.

He glanced at the faces behind him. Gretchen scowled, her green eyes flashing. Simon's face sagged, as if he watched a dream being shattered. Brother Rufus's eyes were closed, his head in an attitude of deep prayer. Keeper simply smiled.

Pieter hoped his own face didn't reveal his despair. He had given Hamelin false hope. How would he explain that the Pied Piper had wounded them once again?

Unexpectedly, an urgent voice broke into his dejection. *Play... enter... find the pups.*

Enter? This was naught but a mystical vision of a land that no longer existed, if it ever had.

Looking... not seeing, insisted Silverfoot's voice.

Not seeing what? The trees remained still, the water held in its rush, the greenfinch remained pinned against the sky.

Wait! He *did* see it.

The greenfinch's wings had changed. They were lifted higher by no more than the width of a twig, but lifted all the same. The bird flew, but as if through air as thick as sugar syrup.

Yes, Great Hunter. I see it, but what does it mean? His heart lurched. *Oh, my.*

Time.

This astonishing scene was about *time.* Time held in the grip of some enchantment. Inside the mountain, *time moved slower.* That was why nothing seemed to move. That was why the children remained children. And Silverfoot had sensed it first.

So what would happen if he stepped in? What would happen to time then?

He did not know, but his task had not changed. The quest had returned him to Koppelberg, and now he would somehow have to enter.

The pipe. Silverfoot's voice snapped in his mind. *Play... do not forsake the pups.* It was the clearest, sharpest message the wolf had ever sent him.

Glancing once more at the crowd, he turned and faced the mountain. After a long breath, he brought the pipe to his lips. At first nothing came to him. What should he play? Nothing seemed right.

Anguish filled his chest. A pain worse than he had ever known lanced through every nerve of his body. Pieter had failed them all. The people of Hamelin, Silverfoot, the children.

Toddlers as small as Agnes were trapped in there. His quest was to free them. Little by little his thoughts turned to the children and away from his disappointment.

Yes... the pups. Yes. Enter the den. They are pack.

Silverfoot's words burst from Pieter's heart to his mind to his fingers.

He never knew where the notes came from. Only seven tones, but they seared through his pipe, stronger than anything he had ever played.

A sound echoed all around him, a sound like iron striking iron. The reverberations enveloped Pieter, resounded throughout the dell, crashed off the cliffs and crags.

The scene inside the mountain rippled, like a pond's surface when ruffled by a sudden wind. The noise ended and a heavy silence filled the dell.

Out of the stillness, new sounds touched his hearing. The gurgling of a stream. The murmur of vivid green leaves in the breeze. The songs of a hundred birds. All from *inside* Koppelberg.

Pieter did not know how or why, but some enchantment had been broken. Captive time had been released. Because of Silverfoot the Pied Piper's curse had been shattered.

From far over the flower-clad hills came a different sound, the one he had hoped for—the noise of children. It was subdued, yet it filled Pieter with joy.

Someone touched his elbow. Simon, gazing at the land beyond the portal. "I've waited a very long time for this. I'm entering with you, son."

What might the magic of this place do for Simon? Or *to* him? Still, after this long, he could not deny the Last Child of Hamelin. Pieter nodded. "What will you find, I wonder?"

"I know not. An ending, perhaps," said Simon, his voice hushed. "And mayhap a beginning."

"Then come, Simon," he said. "We will walk together."

Side by side, they stepped as one into the land beyond the mountain. A howl of support, joy even, came from Silverfoot's mind.

Wait for me, sent Pieter. *Great Hunter. I shall return soon.*

Silverfoot sent a picture of a group of wolves running through a meadow. They charged through the grass almost as one organism, separate creatures, yet one. One pack.

Aye, my friend. We are pack.

Find the pups, said Silverfoot. *Find them.*

Chapter 75

Over the fair grass, a girl approached, about Pieter's age, radiantly dressed in a pink and yellow dress. She strolled lightly on the turf, holding a bouquet of flowers that matched the blossoms entwined in her hair. She smiled at Pieter. "Is it time? At last?"

"Aye. It is time," he said.

"But you are not the Pied Piper."

"No."

"He promised to return and take us home. He is late. We have been here six days."

Six days? She thinks they've been in the mountain for only six days? Oh, what a cruel trick the Piper played. "He meant to, but in the end he did not know how."

"So he sent you?"

"Yes."

Simon spoke. "You...you are Mary, are you not?"

She nodded. "I am. But I don't remember you. Either of you."

"I am Pieter. A minstrel."

"And I," said Simon, "am his friend."

"You are of Hamelin?" she asked Pieter. "Why do I not know you, then?"

"It is...a hard story to tell."

"Ah. Then a hard one to hear, I warrant."

"Aye," said Pieter. "The most difficult you have ever heard, I'm afraid."

Her brows creased in deep thought. "So I have feared. Even as we entered, I sensed it was for ill."

"And yet you followed."

Her deep blue eyes darkened. "If you are now the piper, you know why we followed."

Pieter nodded. "Aye. I do know. But Mary, I play a different song."

"Different?"

"I hope you and the other children will want to follow, but I will not compel you. You must choose."

"And the story?"

"I would like to tell you all together."

She nodded, gazing at him with worry in her eyes. "I will gather them. They will want to go home, I believe. We must leave this place. It is not what the Piper's music said it would be, not what it seems." A shadow passed over Mary's face. She pointed to a nearby hollow. "We will gather over there."

She turned and walked away. Her steps were soft upon the earth, full of grace but also sorrow.

Simon shook his head. "Oddly subdued for a child in paradise."

"Aye," said Pieter. At first, he had worried the children would not *want* to leave such an enchanted place. If the others were like Mary, they would be eager to go home. But would they still be eager when they understood the trick that time and the Pied Piper had played on them? "I must talk once more to the people of Hamelin."

Simon said, "I believe I shall wait here." He lowered himself on a large stone surrounded by morning glory and purple wild iris.

Grief clogged Pieter's throat. Simon meant to stay in this place, he was sure. He wanted to dissuade the old man, but how could he? Simon had waited sixty years for this moment. Would he still sit on the stone when Pieter returned?

He gripped the old man's shoulder. "Simon, the children are indeed yet children. For them, a mere six days has passed. I will be back shortly."

Simon did not respond, so Pieter left him and walked out of the portal.

"I have found the children," he announced to the waiting townspeople. "And, yes, children they remain."

The people cried out and wept for joy. A murmur swept the folk of Hamelin.

"I must prepare them, even as you have been prepared. I believe they are anxious to come home, but they do not yet understand that the homes and families they remember no longer exist. Prepare yourselves for their joy as well as their sorrow."

To Gretchen, he said, "Come, my friend. I need you."

She nodded. With her lute in her hand, she followed him through the gap.

Simon sat as Pieter had left him, his position on the rock unchanged. He did not so much as glance at them.

Pieter turned to Gretchen. "Mary says they've only been here for six days."

"And for Hamelin, six decades," said Gretchen.

Pieter rubbed his brow. "We must help them understand. We'd best wait and give Mary time."

He and Gretchen sat, one on each side of Simon, silently gazing out over the verdant hills. Again, Pieter took in the beauty of the land, but as before, something seemed a bit askew, as though the green of the grass was too lurid, as though the hue of the flowers leaned too much toward the gaudy.

Pieter formed the song within his mind. And his heart. No hesitation this time—the song rang clear. The lyrics tumbled into place as quickly as he created them.

At the very moment Pieter's song was complete, Gretchen said, "There they are."

Children of all ages had gathered in the nearby dell. Pieter said, "Simon, will you come?"

"Nay. I believe I will remain here for a bit." He shifted on the rock and clutched his walking stick. "I shall just drink in the beauty for a few moments."

When Pieter and Gretchen arrived at the dell, the children sat and stared at them. Eyes of deep brown, vivid green, intense blue...but all dark with fear.

"We are all here," said Mary.

Pieter nodded toward Gretchen. "This is my friend Gretchen."

A girl of five or six peered around Mary. "Are you going to take us home?"

Pieter dropped to one knee beside her. "Yes. But first we would like to tell you a story."

The little girl nodded. How somber her huge brown eyes were.

Pieter's gaze swept the rest of the children. A strange gathering, indeed. Not one of them wiggled or cried out or laughed. They did not romp or wrestle. Even the toddlers sat silently, with no spark of life in their faces.

Pieter began to sing, knowing that Gretchen would join him with the lute once she sensed the melody.

Scant time has passed in paradise,
Midst blooming flower and tree.
But time inside this mountain,
Has been your enemy.

For, lo, the Piper led you,
With the promise of delight,
But through your days of joy,
Hamelin's time has taken flight.

One day may pass in this fair land,
For Hamelin, alas, ten years.

For Hamelin's heart is shattered,
A long, bleak time of tears.

Farewell to tender mothers,
To fathers and to kin.
They're in the arms of angels,
Where comfort they shall win.

So what of you, dear children,
Cursed by the music mad?
Hamelin now stands ready,
To embrace each lass and lad.

So weep for anger's wounding,
And cry for what you've lost,
Rage at the Piper's evil,
And rage at its great cost.

Then follow me to Hamelin,
Where arms will open wide.
For the pipe that did you evil,
Will see love glorified.

Chapter 76

$\mathcal{P}$ieter hoped the song would be enough, but he wasn't sure.

Mary said, "The song has frightened them, although some do not know why." Her chin trembled. "But I understand. Most of we older ones do. We shall tell them in simpler words."

Each of the children who had grasped the meaning of the song gathered a group and sat with them. They talked earnestly, directly. Some children cried. Wee ones crawled into laps or clutched nearby arms. Weeping filled the dell.

"Who will take care of me?" wailed a small boy.

Gretchen knelt next to him and held his hands. "We all will."

Pieter stood before the flock gathered on the garish green grass. "Children of Hamelin, I cannot give back your mothers and fathers. But we will give you homes. Hamelin will take you into its heart."

"What does this mean?" cried a girl. "Where is my mother? Where *is* she?"

Pieter knew nothing to tell them but the truth. "While you were in the mountain, she grew old and...she died." Tears came anew from many an eye.

"But know this," said Pieter, lifting his voice. "For every day that you were gone, for every hour and minute of every day, they missed you and wept for you and never stopped loving you."

Mary said, "Come. It is time to leave this place." The children rose and gathered themselves together. Every child touched another, with clasped hands, with arms around shoulders.

Taller ones picked up toddlers. Mary lifted a small boy into her arms. He buried his head in her shoulder. "We are ready," she said.

How could they be? How could the children imagine what lay ahead? Hamelin had changed so much. Yes, they would have each other. But what would life be like without their parents, their families, all the people they had known before?

But the song Pieter and Gretchen had written that night at Sam's, that they had performed in the town square— Hamelin had embraced it, he was sure. That song was a promise, and the folk of the town would honor it. Hamelin would be their family. The townsfolk would rise to enfold these children in their time of need. Hamelin had begun to heal. The lost children would hasten that. After all the hollow years that had passed, they would heal each other.

Pieter turned to Gretchen. She smiled at him, her eyes moist, her lute hanging on her back. Playing a familiar tune on the pipe, Pieter led them back to Simon, where they stopped, the children fanning out behind.

"Simon?" said Pieter. "My friend?"

Simon leaned forward and covered his face with his hands.

Mary walked up to him. "You are Simon? The one who did not come with us, the street boy with the withered leg?"

He looked up, staring at her with reddened eyes. "Aye," he choked out.

"Do you not yet understand?" Mary asked.

"Nay, I do not. Not as I wish to."

Mary laid a hand on his shoulder. "This land is a lie. It seems beautiful, but it is empty. It has no heart. Its colors are vivid, but there is no love here, except what we children found with each other."

"How can that be?"

Mary said, "For the first few hours, we romped and laughed and played, and it seemed a paradise. Never cold, ripe fruit to eat, sweet grass to roll on." She took a shuddering breath. "It seemed like heaven itself." She turned and looked back at the somber faces around her.

"But soon, oh so soon," she said, "we grew weary of our games. The Pied Piper's land provides a brief time of shallow joy. But it is not paradise. And we knew it could never be home."

Simon waved a gnarled hand. "I waited so long to glimpse paradise. No, no. Say nothing more. I believe I know the truth, have always known it."

Simon stared off into the meadow. He was so still, Pieter feared he no longer breathed. At last, a sigh shuddered from deep in the old man's chest. He looked at Pieter, his brown eyes misty. He stood from the rock and turned toward the portal. "Piper, will you take us home?"

Pieter embraced Simon. How he loved this dear man. How grateful he was that, after so long, the Last Child was coming home. He began to play his pipe and walk backward toward the portal.

Gretchen shifted the little boy on her hip. Pieter's eyes moistened as he watched the old man hoist a small girl up onto his shoulders.

He whirled and played on. Once they had all passed through the opening in the mountain, Pieter looked back once more. The children clustered around.

"Wait a moment," he said.

Pieter stepped back into the land inside the mountain. He raised his chin. "No child shall ever enter here again," he called out. "I am the last child who will ever set foot in this vile land."

He stepped out and played a quick, fierce cadence on the pipe. The portal flickered and vanished, leaving only the sheer grey cliff of Koppelberg.

Then Pieter, Aaron's son, the Piper of Hamelin, turned and led the children home.

The End

Acknowledgements

Having a book published has been a vast learning experience. The biggest lesson I learned is that many talented people are a part of it, not just the author.

First of all, special thanks to my agent, Karen Grencik, who believed in me and made it all happen.

For many years, I have had the support, encouragement and feedback of an unbelievable critique group, all writers *par excellence* themselves—Debbie Zigenist-Lowry, Pat Knight, Angie Greenwood, and Gayle Lockwood. Two members who we lost were huge influences on my writing—Penny Cooper and Diane Hamm.

Also my gratitude to SCBWI-Oregon. Children's writers in Oregon are an incredibly supportive community.

I was fortunate to find a wonderful editor at Spencer Hill Press, Jennifer Carson, without whom *The Last Child of Hamelin* would never have happened.

My family—children and grandchildren—have been a constant source of encouragement and support. Thank you so much.

I am also grateful for all the children I was fortunate enough to teach and tell stories to over the years. They helped me understand what children seek in a tale. They taught me the meaning and power of story. When I write, I see these children in my mind's eye.

Special thanks to the woman who has believed in me all these years, my gracious wife, Louise. She gave me the courage to persevere in this frightening, rewarding work called writing. With all my heart, I love you and thank you.